THE UNDEFENDED LAND

Timothy Pilgrim

authors online

An Authors OnLine Book

Text Copyright © Timothy Pilgrim 2012

Cover design by James Fitt ©

British Library Cataloguing Publication Data.
A catalogue record for this book is available from the British Library

ISBN 978-0-7552-0696-4

Authors OnLine Ltd
19 The Cinques
Gamlingay, Sandy
Bedfordshire SG19 3NU
England

This book is also available in e-book format, details of which are available at www.authorsonline.co.uk

It was nearly tea time by the time Paul arrived back at the base of the All Arms Unit, having been recalled.

'This is getting bloody daft,' he commented to the duty receptionist as he signed in and collected the keys for his office, 'I didn't even have time to unpack this time!'

'I'll let Taff know you're back boss,' replied the soldier.

He just had time to say hello to Claire, the loyal secretary he shared with Taff, and make a coffee, before Taff, the base commander walked in.

'So where did these biological attacks take place?' Paul asked.

'Now we've had chance to have a closer look, I'm not sure it is a biological attack Paul,' replied Taff. 'Whitehall paniced, even the new Prime minister seemed caught up in the frenzy.'

'Are you telling me this is all a panic over nothing?' Paul didn't sound too pleased.

'I wouldn't go quite that far, yet,' replied Taff. 'We have established that the plague victim has indeed got bubonic plague. The authorities couldn't work out how he could possibly have caught it, niether he or any of his family had been overseas for years.'

'But our team has found a link?' asked Paul.

'It would seem so, we put Helga's team on it, it took them all of an hour to find a flea which proved to be a carrier. One of his nieces' puppies had been to the vets, a nurse at the vets had just returned from a visit to her family in Taiwan. Trying to be kind, she used one of her jumpers for bedding for the puppy. It seems as though it had been soiled by some pet out there and she hadn't noticed until she returned. It is all highly improbable but checks out.'

'And the others, what was it, Anthrax and what else?' asked Paul.

'Well the hemorrhagic fever wasn't, if you see what I mean. It was something else, I can't remember what now, only something to worry about if you had it. Put simply it was a mis-diagnosis.'

'And the Anthrax?' asked Paul.

'Ah! That is looking a bit sensitive,' replied Taff. 'Initial enquiries suggest a leak of contaminated water from a research facility.'

'Sounds careless,' was Paul's observation, 'your tone suggests there's a bit more to it?'

'It's all a bit vague, but it seems as though a lot of money was allocated to the site, to ensure it was safe. The money has gone but the work was never done to make the site secure.'

'Another M.O.D. cock up?' Paul asked.

'Actually it seems it was the Ministry of Agriculture this time,' replied Taff. 'It is all very odd, there are 'Min of Ag.' notices up, but they say the site has nothing to do with them.'

'Who's on it?'

Taff replied, 'I put Kenny and his lot on it as soon as things started to look iffy.'

'Good call Taff. So why am I here?'

'The new minister for defence wants a meeting with you, he wouldn't say why.'

'I've met the Secretary of State, seemed alright, if out of his depth, I wonder what his number two wants,' said Paul. 'When and where?'

'The cabinet office at 0900 hrs. sharp!' replied Taff.

'I've just realised,' Paul began, 'I don't even know his name! Better do a bit of research me thinks!, and no indication what it is all about?'

'No idea mate'.

For once Paul was on time, it was the minister who was over half an hour late, almost predictably Paul had got fed up and gone outside for a cigarette.

The minister was not impressed and said so, Paul, for once resisted the temptation to retaliate, confining himself to, 'Why am I here Minister?'

'As you must be aware we have inherited serious problems, not the least of which is a massive black hole in the finances of the Ministry of Defence. The supply of equipment needed by frontline troops is beset by delays, which always results in rocketing costs. The lack of vital supplies, many items of which seem to me to be basic needs for armed forces, suddenly become urgent and again costs spiral. At first glance this appears to be total incompetence, the senior military commanders seem to be aware of all of the problems but powerless to sort it out.'

'And you think I can?' Paul interjected.

'I am convinced your infamous direct approach, for which you are renowned, will prevent anyone pulling the wool over your eyes, and therefore you are more likely than anyone to get to the source of the problem. There is also the question of 'overstretch', I am led to believe your unit has technologies available which could make the job of troops on the ground safer and less stressful. I want to know why these systems seem to have been replaced by more expensive, yet less effective American systems.'

'I can answer that now Sir,' replied Paul, 'the fuel for our high altitude planes has quadrupled in price, that is if it was available. Fuel ordered six months ago still hasn't been delivered, every quote is higher than the last, the oldest outstanding order was priced at 28p per litre now, the quote is over a pound, a year ago it was 12p and as much as we wanted.'

'You have my word Colonel, this will be sorted out,' replied the shaken Minister. 'I'll expect your report in six weeks Colonel, we will base the extensive economies in the defence review on your report. As you are outside the normal command structures I can be sure of an accurate, unbiased report.'

'I'm not sure you've got the right person for this task Sir,' replied Paul. 'But I'll do my best, you might not like it Sir, but it will be my honest opinion.'

'I realise I know little more than the reputation of your unit Colonel, but in a way is symptomatic of the problems we face. I have to trust your judgement on such matters, I wish you well, and at the same time I apologise for dumping such an arduous task on you.' The Minister glanced at the clock, 'I must be getting back Colonel, have a good, and safe trip.'

'Thank you Sir,' Paul replied.

'I just hope your report will throw some light on what has happened to such a vast sum of money, which has produced so little in the way of the new equipment it was supposed to have purchased.'

That night Paul left on an R.A.F. C17 bound for Kandahar, noting it was barely half it's capacity. He also noted much of what was on board was fairly basic day to day stuff, the need for which would have been predictable weeks, or even months before.

CHAPTER ONE

The irritating buzzing of his mobile phone forced the exhausted commander of 'The All Arms Unit' back to a state resembling semi consciousness. Fumbling around in the dark he managed to not only find the mobile phone but press the correct button.

'Yes', he snapped. 'What the hell has gone wrong now?'

The duty telephonist at the base was well aware of the violent temper of the operational commander.

'I'm sorry to disturb you Sir,' he began, 'but I was told to get everybody in as quickly as possible Sir'.

'Might I ask why and who by?' replied Paul, 'and stop calling me Sir! I bloody hate it!'.

'Sorry Sir, I mean Boss,' the young man quickly correcting himself, 'It was General Leach issued the call out.'

'I don't suppose he said why by any chance?' Paul enquired.

'Sorry S.., I mean Boss, he didn't, but I do know there is a security alert and the base is on lock down, there has been some sort of incident involving an aeroplane, it hasn't crashed or anything like that, but there is a general 'flap' on the base'.

'All right,' Paul replied, 'I'll be there in about half an hour'.

As with most of the senior officers of 'The All Arms Unit' Paul lived in a secure compound hidden deep in the Breckland forests near the units original base, known as 'The Farm'.

Jet lagged and totally worn out, he half dressed and stumbled towards the kitchen, trying not to wake his wife. Times were when he could have got away with only four hours sleep in three days, those days were long gone, a cigarette and a cup of coffee might help restore him.

'OW SHIT!' he exclaimed as his bare toe came into rapid contact with the corner of a solid Welsh dresser, which his wife loved. At least it woke him up!

He might have been more awake by the time he arrived at the security barrier for the main base nearly forty minutes later, but his temper hadn't improved much. He did notice that the staff on the gate seemed distinctly edgy, spotting the sergeant in charge, he called him over, 'What's up Ronny?' he asked.

'No idea Boss,' was the unhelpful reply, 'All I know is we're on lock down, something to do with a plane which made an emergency landing about an hour ago, beyond the fact it was a big'un, I can't help much. Sorry Boss, but being a mere snowdrop sergeant, no one tells me why'.

'Oh well, I dare say I'll find out soon enough,' replied Paul, 'Thanks Ronny, you have a good night.'

As he drove off towards the head quarters block Paul noticed blue flashing lights in his mirror, lots of them! 'What the hell is all that about,' he wondered. His attention was then drawn to the car park, all the parking places were full, including his 'reserved' space, noting it was General Leach who had nicked his spot. He ended up parked nearly a hundred yards from the main entrance. As he made his slow painful progress towards the entrance, the source of all the blue lights was resolved. A convoy of about a dozen 'Humvees' swept past, no less than six parked in a semi circle, effectively blocking the main entrance to the head quarters building to any thing other than a single pedestrian access. With amazing speed roof hatches were flung open and machine guns mounted, M60s by the looks of them, he noted.

His progress was slow, uncertain which leg to limp on, his back, injured many years ago was 'playing up', affecting one leg and his stubbed toe on the other foot was still throbbing.

As he was by now quite close to what were obviously American air force police he gave a sartorial clap, 'Very impressive gentlemen.'

A young captain, who seemed to be in charge, barred his way.

'I need to see some identification please Sir.'

'As unlikely as it may appear son, I am the operational commander of the unit which lives on this base, I am not accustomed to having guns pointed at me, not here anyway. Would you care to explain your presence on my base?'

'You mean you don't know Sir?' asked the young officer.

'If I knew, I wouldn't bloody well ask would I?' Paul snapped back as he reached for his I.D. card.

There was a shout from one of the newly arrived military police 'GUN!' and the previously lowered weapons promptly came up again. Paul was certain he heard the distinctive click of a hammer coming down on an empty chamber of a junior officer's .45 automatic pistol.

'This appears to be in order Sir,' replied the captain, 'it's just that you are not displaying any badges of rank Sir.'

'We rarely do captain,' replied Paul, 'if you see anyone around here showing their rank, then odds are they are on attachment from the more conventional armed forces.'

'That's as maybe Sir, but I'm afraid I can't allow you to enter this building.'

Paul was about to explode when his communicator started bleeping; he pulled it from his belt, 'Yes'.

It turned out to be Taff, the base commander, nominally Paul's superior officer, although operational matters where left entirely to Paul.

'Where the hell are you Paul?'

'Just outside the main entrance, about to shoot some of our American friends.'

'Don't do that, calm down. I'll come and get you,' replied the unflappable Welshman.

'You didn't mean that did you Sir?' asked the Captain.

'You'll never know son,' Paul replied. 'I'm not known for my patience or diplomacy at the best of times, I am desperately short of sleep, jet lagged and have a sore toe after struggling out of bed half asleep, which resulted in me kicking a large solid piece of furniture, so how do you think I feel?'

Taff appeared in the doorway, noticing Paul limping more than usual, he couldn't resist taking a dig at his old friend.

'What did you do, kick a cat and it retaliated?' he chuckled.

'Very droll Taff. If you must know I stubbed my toe going to the kitchen to make a cuppa, the idea was to wake me up enough to drive here without dozing off on the way.'

'It's not bust is it?' Taff actually sounded concerned.

Paul was making his way towards the entrance, when to everyone's surprise he snatched the heavy colt automatic from a young American officers hand. It was the manner which shocked the Americans, no apparent effort, he hadn't even checked his stride. As casual as could be he worked the slide, to put a round into the chamber, checked the safety catch was on and handed the weapon back, butt first to it's owner.

'A word of advice son,' he began, 'next time you point a gun at an armed man, and pull the trigger, you had better be sure there is a round in the chamber! Make the same mistake again and it is likely to be your last!'

The military police captain was about to say something, but Paul stopped him. 'Two things Captain, first get your lot of cowboys to put their guns away, this has to be the most secure base anywhere. The greatest danger is from you lot playing with your noisy toys, what ever brought you here has obviously made you nervous, now get a grip! The other thing is, get these bloody hummers off the pedestrian area. Now!'

'I'm sorry Sir, my orders are quite clear,' Paul cut him off.

'Understand this, on this base, I or that man there,' pointing at Taff, 'give orders. Now I don't know what crisis brought you here, and me dragged out of the first bed I've seen for a week, and at the moment I don't care. But those guns go away NOW, before your jumpy troops, some still wet behind the ears, panic and shoot someone. Also, this hatched area is to be kept clear at all times, it is a drop off and pick up point, NOT a bloody park. Now move it! or are you in the habit of arguing with full Colonels!'

'Sir, with respect, my orders were clear. No-one is to enter this building.'

Paul turned to Taff, 'Did you issue that order?'

'Don't look at me Paul, this is the first I've heard of it.'

By now the rest of the convoy of Humvee's had reached the aircraft stopped on the runway, with a cluster of fire trucks gathered around the tail. With the extra lights he could now see the plane was 'Air Force One' and the tail assembly was a mess. Not only was the rear of the plane covered in foam, the great rudder was clearly bent and several chunks were missing.

'Now I understand your over enthusiasm Captain,' Paul turned to the young officer. 'I presume your Commander in Chief is inside our head quarters block.?

That being the case, I will overlook your over zealousness. However, my orders stand, guns away, and these things off the hatchings, NOW!'

'I agree, with the Colonel,' added Taff, 'you can take up positions on either side and still more than adequately cover this entrance, I do not recommend disobeying his direct orders. By the way, who gave you your orders Captain?'

'They came from the secret service Sir over our radios, I haven't got a name,' replied the American Captain.

Paul looked at Taff and shook his head, 'Just get those things off this forecourt Captain, nothing bad will happen to your President on this base, I promise.'

As the big four X fours began to move, the two long time friends walked into the entrance hall of the old red brick building, where they were confronted by two very large men with shaven heads, both dressed in sharp suits.

'He's with me' Taff explained, 'he is the operational commander of the unit based here'.

'You will have to be searched Sir, before you can go any further,' said the slightly larger of the two men.

'I've had enough of this crap,' snapped Paul. 'I can save you the trouble, I am carrying a Smith and Weston three- fifty -seven magnum under my left arm, three full speed loaders in my web belt and another twenty four loose rounds in a pouch, also on my web belt, right next to my communicator. My office is the second on the right, and that is were I am going. Get one thing straight, the only people on this base who give orders are the two senior officers standing in front of you right now. I know who is here, I have no idea why, yet.' Paul added.

'However I will no doubt be told what happened when I get to my office, now, get out of my bloody way!'

Just after Paul reached the sanctuary of his office one of the secret service men turned to his colleague and asked, 'Do you think this lot are as good as their reputation?'

Paul stuck his head back around the door, 'Oy, I'm old, not bloody deaf! and trying to find out is not a good idea!' He closed the door.

'My-My, we are tetchy tonight aren't we?'

'So? what's new about that?' asked Paul as he headed for the kettle, 'want one?'

'Daft question,' replied Taff.

While Paul sorted out a couple of more or less clean mugs and made the coffees Taff brought up the information screens.

Flopping into his comfortable chair Paul opened a draw in his desk and removed a couple of pills from a pack, quickly swilling them down with the coffee.

'You must be hurting to take those things,' observed Taff. 'In all the years I've known you, that is only about the third time I've known you take two, an odd one now and again, but two?'

'I'll be alright, stop fussing.' replied Paul. 'It's my back playing up, not my brain.'

Taff pulled his chair closer to Paul's desk, 'And while I remember, what kind of crazy stunt was that outside, disarming that sproggy American military cop, are you wanting to get shot?' Taff looked concerned, 'they were as jumpy as hell. Another thing, how the hell did you know there wasn't a round 'up the spout'?'

'Easy,' replied Paul, 'I heard the click of a hammer coming down on an empty chamber when I reached for my I.D. and someone shouted 'gun' when they spotted my side arm.'

'You mean he actually intended to shoot you?' exclaimed Taff , 'You really are mad! not a flicker of emotion over something which could have been fatal. You are going to see the shrinks mate whether you like it or not!'

CHAPTER TWO

'We'll worry about that when this is sorted out, bring me up to speed Taff.'

'You worry me sometimes,' Taff shook his head.

Paul cut him off. 'Why is Air force One sitting on our runway, and why is it looking so second hand?' Paul asked, then drained his mug of coffee. 'Want a refill?' he asked as he headed towards the kettle again.

'You must have an asbestos lining to your throat, I've hardly touched mine yet!' replied Taff. 'As far as Air Force One is concerned, someone took a pop at it with what we think was a shoulder launched S.A.M., probably a stinger.'

'Where did this happen?' Paul asked sounding surprised.

'It was on approach to Mildenhall, about an hour ago. The missile was fired from somewhere between Brandon and Thetford, we think from a point on east side of Wangford warren.'

'Hang on Taff, that plane is fitted with every anti aircraft missile defence system there is, so how the hell did it get hit by a stinger?' His coffee mug refilled Paul returned to his seat.

'Oh, you don't know the best bit, the thing actually dodged an F15 which tried to block it.'

'You what!?' exclaimed Paul, 'how the hell did it do that, come to that, what missile can dodge one plane to hit another?'

'The sequence of events was something like this,' Taff paused to have a sip of his coffee. 'The launch was detected, almost immediately, the systems on Air Force One kicked in with no measurable delay. This should have deflected any known guidance system, radar, infra red, sonic whatever, but the thing kept coming. By this time the electronic 'cloak' had hidden Air Force One from all radars, even the sets on the escorting eagles couldn't detect the President's plane, and they could still see it!. The flight leader positioned his fighter between the missile and Air Force One, lit his afterburners and pulled his nose up, with all his flaps and air brakes out, presenting a plan view of his plane to the missile, which promptly swerved round him and exploded right beside the tail of the 747.'

'Apart from recommending the F15 pilot for the highest award possible, or a trip to the shrink, I really don't know what to say. The stinger, if that is what it was couldn't have been radio guided, the system on the President's plane would have jammed it, infra red, or radar, all would have been decoyed, I don't understand'. Paul looked puzzled, 'it doesn't add up Taff.'

'To make matters worse, we can't find the precise launch site, a Canberra should be taking off soon to try and pinpoint the spot, as well as check for anything else out there. We've got enough fuel for a two hour sortie'.

'You mean the fuel still hasn't arrived, Oh for fucks sake! how the hell are we supposed to operate, I thought all this had been sorted out!' Paul headed for the kettle once more.

'You haven't drunk that as well!' asked Taff.

Paul ignored his friend other than to respond with a shrug of his shoulders, leaning back on the work surface while the kettle heated up again, he asked Taff, 'So how did the 747 end up on our runway?, we're fairly close, but well off course for anything going into Mildenhall.'

'I presume you saw the bent tail, well although he could stay in the air, he hadn't got too much control on direction. The bent tail sort of forced him round in great circles, someone in our tower was on the ball, put our lights on and invited him down, as it seemed he would at least be pointing the right way. The pilot used flaps and the throttles to guide the broken bird down in a curving approach. He actually made a good landing, how the hell he kept the thing straight after he touched down until the speed dropped off I have no idea. There was a small fire in the tail, our fire crews were chasing the plane after it touched down, they had the fire out before the thing stopped rolling! And we are where we are.

Playing host to the President and his entourage, a gaggle of mainly American media hounds and a posse of very nervous assorted American security operatives. Most of the latter don't trust each other never mind us!'

'Well, thanks for the briefing Taff,' replied Paul. 'Have our techs had a look at the damage yet?'

'A couple had a quick look before the secret service shooed them away.'

'Did they find any clues?' Paul asked more in hope than expectation.

'Maybe', Taff replied cautiously, 'a bit of luck really, it was Terry and his team. As they were the ones who designed and built the system, then if there are anomalies they have the best chance of spotting them.'

'Knowing them they'll have nothing to say until they are certain of what, if anything they've got,' muttered Paul.

'I know him well enough to know he's got something he doesn't understand,' was Taffs reply, 'but like you said, it's a waste of time asking'.

'So, what are we supposed to be doing about 'El Presidente', are they taking him on to Mildenhall by road or chopper. Or is another plane coming in to pick them all up?' Paul asked.

'I've no idea Paul, General Leach is looking after big wigs, showing them a few bits of what we do, just to keep them entertained until our P.M arrives and the American Ambassador. We are waiting for calls from the officers mess to let us know they are ready, and from Northholt for an E.T.A. for the Prime Minister and party.'

'Every thing is under control then,' observed Paul, 'I was going to suggest I could go back to bed! but the caffeine has kicked in now.'

An 'Alert' began to flash on his computer terminal. For once Paul found the right button first time. As he scanned the message, Taff headed for the kettle, at last ready for a refill.

'Forget that Taff, get the head of the secret service detail in here, he has got to see this.'

'Yes Sir! right away Sir!' replied Taff with a grin. 'For C.O. read G.F.'

Paul looked up, 'Hey, you what?' he asked.

'For C.O., commanding officer, read G.F.,go for'.

'Twit!' replied Paul.

'What's up, someone found something interesting?' asked Taff.

Paul turned the monitor so his friend could see it, 'Aah, I see what you mean,' Taff replied, 'I'll go and get him, please be diplomatic, the guy is a bit paranoid right now, and understandably so.'

'Yes mother!'

Taff left on his errand, Paul went for a breath of fresh air and a smoke, it was the walk he needed really as his back was beginning to stiffen up again.

He returned to his office and was making yet another coffee when Taff returned with an obviously agitated secret service chief.

Before Paul had chance to even say hello and offer the man a drink and a seat the director of the secret service went for Paul. 'This had better be good Colonel, if you have got me away from the President on some cockamaynie story I will not be happy.'

Having taken a deep breath Paul calmly replied, 'Good to meet you Sir, please take a seat,' and gestured to a chair opposite to his own.

'Cut the crap Colonel,' the man snapped back, 'I've got the President to get home safely, haven't you got an Al Qaeda cell to find?'

'Oh there are plenty of those Director, but they didn't have anything to do with this, of that I am very sure.'

'If it wasn't them, then who was it?' replied the harassed secret service chief. 'What makes you so sure?' he added.

'This' replied Paul, turning the monitor towards the man.

'What is it?'

'I'd say it was the serial number of the missile fired at Air Force One. One of our techs picked it up off the runway, just behind the plane, best guess is one of the foam cannons dislodged it.'

'And you have traced it already?' asked the shocked American.

'Someone has, it is from the very latest mark of stinger, it hasn't even begun proper testing yet. The only place it could have come from is the manufacturer, this is a proto type! My lot are checking to see if they have had any security breaches lately.'

'You can do that?'

'You would be surprised what we can do Director. Now, I need my men back on Air Force One to find out why the defences didn't work. I would greatly appreciate if you would help in this.'

'Out of the question Colonel,' the American replied, 'much of the equipment is beyond top secret in the defence pod.'

'I know, we designed and built most of it, as the officer leading the team is the same man who designed the system, I'd say he was the perfect man for the job, wouldn't you agree Director?'

The American was lost for words for a second or so. 'Let me get this straight, the defensive pod on Air Force One was built here?'

'Oh yes, and a lot more besides,' replied Paul. 'What we can't understand is how the missile seems to have defeated the system. We think there must have been a homing device of some kind on the plane, in or near the tail. There simply isn't another possibility that we can see.'

'Could the system have failed?'

'There is always a first time for anything, but we monitor everything around this area, and it all seems to have worked fine. Show the director the imagery Taff.'

The big plasma screen came to life. 'There is Air Force One, on approach to Mildenhall, with it's escort of four F15 Eagles, I'll turn the sound up a bit so you can hear the radio transmissions'. Taff adjusted the controls. 'There's the missile, it was about 100feet up when our radar picked it up. Within two seconds of launch the automatic defences on the President's plane activated, you see, it's gone. No radar, or infra red, no sonic signature, nothing it has vanished from our screens. If you listen you can hear the Eagle crews answering their control who have also lost contact .'

'How do you do all this stuff?' asked the now confused Director.

'I only know what it does Sir,' replied Paul, 'It is all alchemy as far as I am concerned.'

'Watch the trace of the lead eagle Sir,' said Taff. 'He is one of the bravest men around. You see, he has put his fighter between the missile and Air Force One. You can even see all his flaps, dive brakes, even his under carriage going down, after burners lit, and exposing as much of his aircraft to the missile as possible. Anything to get it to hit him rather than his President .' Taff had been using the pause button, now he restarted the recording. 'There see that?' he asked.

'Damn it,' exclaimed the secret service chief, 'the thing swerved round the Eagle.'

'Now you see why we think there must have been something on Air Force One for the stinger to have locked onto.'

'I do indeed Colonel.' replied the American.

'Would you like the coffee I was going to offer you when you came in, had I had the chance?' Paul asked.

'Yes, that would be good, I can sure use one. Would you be offended if I made my own, It's just that I like it 'just so', and no-one ever gets it quite right.'

'I know exactly what you mean Sir, Taff and I have known each other for years and he's never made a good cup yet'.

'I am finding it difficult understanding how this unit works Colonel,' the man accepted the offered clean mug. 'Rank seems to be largely ignored hereabouts, and yet it seems to work smoothly. The C.I.A. know about you guys, and the F.E.D.s , both said we'd be fine here once we had landed safely. The exact words were, well if it had to happen, this was the best place, and we would all be safe. That is one hell of a compliment for them to agree on anything, never mind on something as important as this.'

The man returned to his seat, complete with his 'just so' cup of black coffee, 'Not bad, Colonel, not bad at all. In fact this is one of the best instant coffees I've ever had, might I ask what brand it is, or is that a secret too?'

It was Taff who answered, 'Actually, I think it is the local super markets own brand. He', indicating Paul, 'virtually mainlines the stuff, so we get the cheap economy brand, otherwise we'd blow our budget keeping him in coffee.'

'Oh, cheers Pal.' responded Paul. 'Any way, back to the matter in hand, getting your President home. I assume the back up plane is at Mildenhall, is it coming here, or are we going to take the President and his party there?'

'That's the other problem I have Colonel, the back up plane was being checked over at Mildenhall when a fire broke out near the tail. As yet we have been unable to locate a suitable aircraft to get the President home.'

'We can solve that problem for you Sir, I'll show you in a bit. But first, can we speak to the technician who was doing the checking when the fire started on the back up plane?'

'Might I ask why Colonel,' the now relaxing American asked. 'You think there might have been a homing device on there as well?'

'It's possible Sir, your tech. noticed an anomaly, checked it out, and triggered an anti tamper device,' Paul suggested.

'I take it you would like your team to have access to that plane as well?'

'It couldn't hurt could it Sir, Terry, the young officer who designed it would certainly spot anything which shouldn't be there.'

'Very well Colonel, so what now?' asked the secret service chief.

'I would suggest getting the President over to the officers mess with the V.I.P.s of the party, for a light meal and a bit of a relax. Our Prime Minister is en-route as is your Ambassador. The officers mess is much more suitable than the common room and canteen in here. I'll get the cars sorted out to transfer thirty five of you over to the mess. The rest can stay here until we arrange a charter plane or a RAF VC 10 to take the hangers on home.'

'The media circus won't like that Colonel, they are contracted to fly with the President.'

'Not on this flight they're not.' was Paul's reply, 'I've had a memo from the bar steward in the common room bar, that shower have drunk more in an hour or so than my lot consume in a week. I'll be damned if I'm financing their jollies. An odd drink, especially after what happened, fine, but the amount they're going through!'

The Big American actually allowed himself a little laugh. 'Fair enough Colonel, here's my card,' he passed a laminated business card to Paul, 'send their tab to me, we'll sort it out.'

'Thank you Sir,' Paul slipped it into his top pocket on his faded shirt. 'Right, transport for thirty five to the officers mess please, mostly VIPs .' He spoke into the intercom, having pushed the 'MT' button.

'We'll be there in five minutes Boss.'

'Thanks Brian', replied Paul, 'drive the limo yourself.'

'Do you know all your men by their first names Colonel?' asked the American.

'Pretty much Sir.' He stabbed another button marked reception, 'Mark, get the duty section to organise the evacuation of the common room, liase with General Leach and the secret service to select the thirty five to go to the mess.'

'Will do boss'.

'Right, that's taken care of that,' just as Paul moved to get up, the alert on his computer screen began to flash. 'Oh shit, now what's happened,' he muttered.

Stabbing a button on the console, 'Yes Terry?' .

'You were right Boss, we've got it.'

'Got what?' Paul asked.

'The homing beacon. I'll get it back to the lab, we'll have the frequency in half an hour.'

'Well done that man!, call in to reception and pick up a pass for Mildenhall. See if you can find one on the back up plane, it seems as though there has been a problem with that as well. It could be related.'

'Will do boss,' came the reply.

'Bye the way Terry, how did you get on board?' asked Paul. 'The head of the secret service has only just agreed to your crew boarding Air Force One.'

'We didn't have to Boss, it was on the runway, attached to what was left of one of the emitters, sneaky really, as it took it's power from the emitter, it would only activate when the jamming was turned on to confuse a missile.'

'Give it to one of your tech's and get over to Mildenhall and check the other plane, A.S.A.P.'

'On my way Boss'.

Paul turned to the American, 'this could get interesting.'

'How the Sam Hill could something like this happen?' asked the American, 'those planes are guarded tighter than Fort Knox!'

'Let our boys do their job Sir, I'm sure they'll come up with an answer, although it does seem as though some sneaky sod has wriggled through security. If you'd like to write a note to get Terry onto the back up aircraft please, with any luck we'll have some answers before our plane is ready to leave.'

'Yes, yes of course Colonel, I'll also call them and warn them he's on his way.'

Paul passed the American the telephone on his desk. 'It's a secure line Sir'.

When he had completed his call he turned to Paul, 'Could I have your man's service number please Colonel, and his name and rank. I'll put it on the back of one of my cards and sign it. With all that has happened, the guards will understandably be a bit jumpy.'

Paul typed something on his key board, and turned the screen towards the man once more, then pushed print. He handed the high definition print out, complete with the units logo, to the American for him to add his signature to Paul's.

'Let's go and check your transport out, I think you will find it satisfactory.'

'What about a fighter escort, Colonel, in the current circumstances I think it is essential.'

'Come on, we'll see what we can do, we'll leave Terry's paper work at the front desk. Oh shit!' Paul suddenly exclaimed.

'Now what's gone wrong?' asked Taff.

'My bloody car is on the road, at the other end of the car park, vehicles were abandoned all over the bloody place, it was the nearest place I could find.'

'Getting lazy in your old age, walking a hundred yards isn't going to kill you Paul,' then noticing the worse than usual limp, 'but then again?' chuckled Taff.

Paul spotted a passing trooper, not obviously occupied, 'Here, Bob!,' he called, 'do me a favour please.'

'Sure Boss, what's up?'

Paul tossed the trooper the keys to his old Jaguar, 'Could you bring my car to the front entrance for me, it's on the road, about fifty yards beyond the car park.'

'What's it doing right up there Boss, the brakes haven't packed up have they?'

'Just get the car, leave the jokes to me!,' replied Paul.

The young soldier set off on his task, chuckling to himself.

'I must say you run an extraordinary unit Colonel. I'm intrigued, waiting to find out what you have to get the President home, I've sort of worked out it isn't a 747. If it's one of those small H.S type jets, it might prove to be a bit of a bumpy ride. I'm telling you this as there are more than one or two in the party who get air sick real easy, and it's a long old haul to Andrews Air Force base.'

'I don't think you need worry about air sickness Sir, I've never known anyone be air sick on this aeroplane.'

'All right, you're keeping it as a surprise, my money is on a hotted up V.C.10, beautiful old planes, I have travelled on them in the past.'

'You'll see,' replied Paul.

The President's chief of staff approached, 'Where have you been Frank? We need to know what happened, and then find a safe way to get the President out of this God forsaken place'.

'Calm down Gerry, you'll have a heart attack. Meet 'Taff' the base commander, and the Colonel here is the operational commander of the unit which lives here. I assure you we are in very safe hands.'

Conversation suddenly became impossible as the thunderous roar of a heavy jet taking off drowned out all other sounds.

Once the sound had subsided sufficiently, the chief of the Presidents staff asked, 'What on earth was that?'

'I would have thought you would have recognised one of your own air craft sir,' replied Paul, 'that was a K.C 135 tanker'.

'What was that doing here, and where is Air Force One?' the official demanded.

'The tanker lives here and your bent bird has been towed into a hangar, out of sight from prying eyes.'.

'Who authorised moving Air Force One, I demand to know!'

'I did,' it was Taff who answered, 'We had to clear the runway, as we have flights due in, and now some more due out. You really should learn to park better, then we wouldn't be having this trouble.'

'You had no authority to move it until it has been examined by experts, I'll see to it that..'.

Paul cut him off. 'Oy! motor mouth! shut your flapping lips before I shut them for you. He has the authority, he is the base commander, and for the record, our experts have already identified the missile which did the damage and know how it evaded the counter measures. Now some advice, keep this up and you'll return to the common room and go home on the same plane as all the extras.'

'You can't do that, colonel what ever you are.' the man shouted back .

'Watch me.' Paul snapped back. 'You might be good at what ever it is you do, clearly you can't handle stress. For the last time, if you want to travel back with your President, then stop flapping like a bloody old hen and let us get on with our jobs. One more outburst at me or Taff and you'll be back in there so fast your feet won't touch the ground, and home will be a very long flight away on the draughtiest, slowest old crate I can find to charter at this time of night. Do you understand?'

It was Frank, the head of the secret service who backed Paul up. 'Take his advice Jerry, these guys are good, I've just spent the last forty minutes in the office with these gentlemen. They really do know what they are doing, we are just going to check out the alternative for getting the President home. You run along, or you'll miss your lift to the officers mess and a free buffet they've laid on, and go easy on the booze!'.

The last car for the officers mess pulled up, the orderly sergeant was checking off the names on his list, when he noticed young Bob approaching having parked Paul's car in it's now vacant reserved space.

'Where the hell have you been?' shouted the immaculately turned out sergeant.

'The Boss asked me to fetch his car for him sarge,' came the casual reply.

'Oh, that's alright then, you haven't dented it I hope.'

'As if I dare do that!' exclaimed the young man. 'Your keys boss, the brakes pull to the left a bit if you brake hard, I'd get the M.T. boys to check it if I were you Boss.'

'Thanks Bob,' replied Paul. 'Might I enquire as to how you found out about the grabbing brake?'

'One of our American friends in a damned great Hummer forgot which side of the road to drive on over here, no problem, I missed him Boss. I'd better get on otherwise Sergeant Foster will find me something else to do'.

'Get out of here, and thanks Bob.' replied Paul suppressing a grin.

'Let's go and check out your emergency taxi Frank. Are you coming over to the mess Taff , B.J. can handle things here for a bit.'

'I suppose I'd better come, someone has got to keep you out of trouble, and General Leach must have his hands full playing host to our guests.'

'I'm not being funny Frank, but I think you'd better ride in the front, Taffs little legs will fit in the back easier.'

'You guys don't take anything seriously do you?' asked the big American.

'Oh, you are so wrong Frank,' replied Paul. 'There isn't a unit on earth more serious about it's work than us, although generally we don't care about rank and the day to day formalities of conventional units. You know the sort of thing.'

He fired up the powerful old Jaguar and headed towards what appeared to be a couple of low hills which concealed the giant hangars.

'Why waste time,' he continued, 'passing a request up the chain of command, then waiting for an order to come back down, when the guy on the spot knows perfectly well what needs doing. Surely it is better for him to just do it'

'And if he doesn't know, what then?' asked Frank.

'He asks, either me or B.J, or if neither of us are around then Taff. We usually just let him get on with the job of running the base. All I can say is it works for us, but then the only people who join our happy crowd have usually had a fair bit of time in the armed forces, and often a six month attachment here from their parent unit. Most are specialists, some decide it's not for them, some aren't for us, in a small unit like this the face has to fit, it is as simple as that.'

Paul pulled up near the open doors of the first hangar, 'Your ride home Frank'.

'Good god! exclaimed the American, 'It's a Concord, I thought they had all been scrapped! Is it safe?'

'Safest thing in the air,' replied Paul.

'Surely they are getting old?' asked Frank.

'In terms of years you have a point, but an air frame's age is measured in flying hours and take off and landing cycles, this one is barely a teenager. She'll get your Boss home in style.'

'Now I know why you were so casual about fighter escorts, there aren't many which could catch one of those things, never mind stay with it.'

'You'll have your escorts Frank, get ready for another surprise,' chuckled Paul as he moved off towards the next hangar.

'What the hell are they doing here?' gasped the American.

There, on the hard standing where two sinister big black darts. The ground crews were hoisting a rotating magazine into the belly of the nearest plane.

'What?' was all Frank seemed able to say, pointing at the group of men in overalls.

'Anti missile missiles, they'll take out any thing I know of, from a sidewinder to a stinger even an amram, they have also knocked down a four point five inch shell in tests. These two have reached the end of their flying hours, even with the upgrades, they were due to fly to Andrews Air Force base later today anyway, so we brought things forward a bit. We have already got a crew out there with a Hercules to take our gear out before these two are put on display.'

'That is going to be one hell of a sight, a Concord escorted by two Blackbirds. You guys certainly know how to turn on the style,' observed Frank.

'I don't know about style,' replied Paul, 'but while we're here we might as well take a quick look at Air Force One.'

The three men got out of the old Jag and walked into the brightly lit giant cavern which was hangar two.

Two security guards appeared out of no where, 'Hello Boss, we don't see you very often, could you sign in please, and your lighter please boss. You know what our skipper is like, he'll check to make certain you left it once he sees your name on the charts.'

Paul laughed, 'I do indeed Des. This is Frank, the Director of the American Secret Service, we're just going to have a quick look at the damage and a chat with Terry's crew.'

'Don't forget to collect your lighter on the way out Boss.'

'As if,' replied Paul. 'Come on, lets see what our lot have found.'

Now the foam had been washed off the true extent of the damage could be seen.

'Says a lot about the strength of the plane and the skill of the crew to get that down in one piece,' observed Paul.

'I'm glad I didn't know how much damage there was,' replied Frank. 'Will it fly again?'

'I've no idea, aah, there's the guys I want a word with.' Paul headed towards two of the unit's techs, one was scribbling furiously on a clip board.

'Morning lads, what can you tell me about that homing device?' Paul asked, not really expecting much.

'It's down in the lab at the moment, being tested, Terry has gone to Mildenhall to check the other plane.'

'What did it look like?' asked the American.

'That was the clever bit Sir.' replied the technician, 'It looked like a metal label, like a vin plate on a car'.

'What got Terry's attention then?' asked Paul, 'There must be hundreds of them on a plane like this.'

'Our logo boss.' was the unexpected reply.

'You what?' exclaimed Paul and Taff in unison.

'The plastic box with all of our gismos in is sealed here, just the external fixings and sockets for power cables are the only things on the outside apart from a stamp 'made in the U.K', and each one is also stamped with a unique number, no plate'.

'Sneaky bastards', muttered Paul.

'It gets worse boss. The plate seems to have been stuck to our box of tricks with a thin sheet of explosive. There was a detonating circuit, and a timer. We haven't finished analysing it all yet but it looks as though the thing would explode a few minutes after the system was activated. We think it was supposed to destroy the box, but those thermal plastics are a lot tougher than they seem, all this one did was blow the plate off.'

'Thanks Jack, I'll be over in the mess, then flying out on the speed bird. Keep me informed please.'

'Will do boss, have a nice flight.' replied the tech.

'Just a thought,' Paul turned towards the techs again, 'Can you check our planes, just in case'.

'All ready done Boss, clean as a whistle'.

'Good lad', there was a degree of satisfaction in his voice, not so much as to the fact their planes were clean, but his team had already thought of the potential problem and checked.

After collecting his lighter and signing out at the security desk, the little party headed towards the mess. Paul stopped at the edge of the runway and asked control if it was safe to cross. 'Go ahead boss, there is a C17 inbound, due in twenty minutes.'

'Thanks, out.' replied Paul.

Half way across the wide concrete strip there was a noise, it sounded like running over a tin can. 'What the hell was that?' he muttered and backed up. There lay a piece of torn aluminium, about the size of a saucer. He called the control again.

'Get that C17 to circle, I've just run over a chunk of Air Force One! Get the F.O.D. team out here and sweep the entire runway again. And kick some ones arse for missing it!'

'You are on the northern crossing point aren't you boss.'

'Yes. Why.' snapped Paul.

'Well, Air Force One came in on a curve and was a couple of hundred yards past were you are before it was even over the runway, so the northern bit didn't get swept.'

'Well get the whole thing swept, now!, and woe betide you if they miss anything else. Get it done!'

'Yes Sir' came the sheepish reply.

'And don't call me Sir! I bloody hate it !'

'Sorry Boss'.

'That was a bit harsh Paul,' observed Taff from the back seat.

'May be, but if speed bird had run over it, or the tanker which left a while ago, we'd have had a right mess on our hands. They know better than to assume, sure we cut corners, but some can't be cut. They know that.'

'I've just realised something,' said Frank, 'the tanker, it's for the black birds isn't it. They would need a top up to make it to Andrews at speed.'

'He's quick, give him a jelly baby Taff.' chuckled Paul, 'and before you ask, there are one of your lads and a couple of aides sorting the baggage out, so only the bags for those on the list go on the speed bird. Fast she might be, but it's no load lugger, some of your lot take more bags than my missus does when we go on holiday!'

'I'm surprised you can remember mate,' replied Taff, 'it is so long since you've had a holiday.'

'Yeah, well someone has to watch out for you!'

Frank decided things were back to normal with these two odd ball commanders.

Finally they reached the officers mess, 'Let's just hope our guests haven't eaten everything before we get to the buffet,' said Paul, 'I'm bloody starving!'

'Does anything phase you guys?' asked Frank.

'Oh yes,' replied Taff, 'it is not a pretty sight seeing him being phased. If you ever see Paul getting really upset, then it's time to take cover'.

'Cheers Taff!' retorted Paul, 'how often do I really let go?' asked Paul, sounding hurt.

'The civil servant messing us about with the fuel supplies, for a moment I thought you were going to kill him.' said Taff.

'As long as he thought the same thing, then our fuel should get sorted'. Paul remained unbowed.

'You didn't lock your car Colonel'.

'Every one on camp knows it's my car Frank, I would like to think it is safe.'

'What about outsiders? surely there's a risk of someone sneaking into a base this size? You seem very trusting Paul.'

'I think confident is a better description Frank. The S.A.S. regularly try to break in. they haven't managed to, yet.' said Taff. 'They will manage it one day no doubt, it's a matter of pride, as most of our combat strength have served with them at sometime, and the current crop at Hereford would love to get one over on the old hands.'

Having satisfied security they were who they claimed to be, the three men joined the main party. The President himself approached, hand extended in greeting. Frank introduced Taff and Paul.

'You are welcome Mr. President, it's just a pity about the circumstances, but we are making progress in identifying the problem, we will keep you fully informed.'

The President turned to his security chief, 'Any luck finding an alternative aircraft Frank. Time is getting short, it would not look good if I'm late for the speech on the 'Hill', my detractors will have a field day if I don't make it.'

'We have indeed solved the problem Mr President, right here, it is being fuelled as we speak, and the luggage of all those in the mess here is being sorted and loaded. The remainder are to follow on a charter plane later.'

'I don't want to sound ungrateful,' the President addressed Taff, 'but time is getting short if I am to make that speech on time, you know what the media can be like.'

'I'm sure you'll be on time Mr President,' replied Frank, 'I've had a look at the replacement plane, she's a beauty. You have my word you'll be in plenty of time.'

'I know you won't let me down Frank, how long before take off?'

Frank looked enquiringly at Paul.

'About an hour Mr. President.' replied Paul.

'Very well, but that will be cutting it very, very tight on time.'

What sounded like a volley of gunshots echoed across the airfield, guns appeared in the hands of most of the American security men. Before Paul could calm things down a second 'volley' rang out, causing something near to panic.

Confusion replaced concern, none of the British had reacted.

'It is a reconnaissance plane starting up, the jets use a ring of blanks to start. I presume that allays your fears gentlemen', Paul announced, 'Cannons away!'

CHAPTER THREE

The White House chief of staff rushed up as the President returned to his seat and accosted Paul and Frank. Taff had gone in search of General Leach to bring him up to speed on events.

'I heard you say it will be at least an hour before our flight is ready to leave. This is not satisfactory, I demand you get things moving Colonel.'

'Oh give it a rest will you', snapped Paul, 'things are under control and running remarkably smoothly. Stay out of it and they will continue to run smoothly. Our Prime Minister and your Ambassador will be here shortly and joining the President on the plane for some urgent talks on topics higher than our pay grades. So don't you dare rock the boat, stay out of things and calm down.'

The next few minutes got a bit hectic, what with the arrival of two helicopters ferrying the Prime Minister and a concerned Ambassador. The other thing was a stream of protests from those who had been left behind for now. To say they were unhappy would be to understate the situation.

Taff bravely volunteered to go and calm things down. 'Their choice is simple, a comfortable bed and a breakfast, compliments of The All Arms Unit, or a night in the guard room.' Noticing Paul's raised eyebrow, 'Well, I can get tired and 'crabby' too, you haven't got a monopoly you know.'

The sound of powerful jets being run up made the windows rattle in the old red brick building, as they powered down, the sound of different jets took over, this plane obviously took off.

When the sound died away Frank asked Paul what was happening.

'The first one was your taxi, just running final checks, the other was the recon taking off, just to make sure there are no more surprises lurking in the forests. With any luck they will also pin point the launch site and find the launcher.'

'They can do that? after all this time?' asked Frank.

'They'd better, or I will not be pleased.'

Yet more jets started to run up to high power across the airfield, by far the loudest yet, as the noise subsided it became obvious the ones which were still running were much closer than the hangars, then these too shut down.

Paul left his half finished pork pie on his plate and made his way to the small stage at the end of the large function room. 'Your attention please!' he shouted above the babble of voices. 'Ladies and gentlemen, if you would like to finish your drinks please, you may board your 'taxi' home in ten minutes. Thank you for your patience.'

'You are one for the dramatic Colonel,' said Frank, 'using the engine tests on the Black Birds to hide the noise of Concord taxiing over here. I'm not too certain how some of the passengers will react, I really should have told the President.'

'Frank, for the most part the next four hours are likely to be the most boring flight most of them will ever have been on. I'll grant you take off is a bit of an adrenalin rush, but those 'old planes' as you called them are so smooth you have no idea you are travelling faster than a rifle bullet. There is no turbulence at the altitude it flies at, it is twenty thousand feet higher than other passenger jets, once it is cruising there is nothing to even indicate you're moving, as it's dark!'

'I'm sure hoping you're right, for me this is a career maker if the President approves, or a breaker if he doesn't!' Frank sounded worried.

Paul quickly finished his pork pie and inevitable coffee, then headed for the exit, to make sure everything was ready.

On his return he announced loudly, 'Your taxi home is ready, if you would like to follow me please.' Then he stepped aside, not only to watch the reactions but to have a quick cigarette before boarding himself.

The President emerged from the mess with the British Prime Minister, both stopped dead in their tracks on spotting the unmistakeable shape of Concord. It was parked about a hundred yards away, the path to the steps lit by the headlights of several 'hummers' all pointing towards the planes steps.

'I always dreamed of flying on one of those,' remarked the President, 'I thought they were all scrapped a few years ago.'

'I'd heard rumours this unit had acquired some, quite how no-one knows.

Frankly Mr. President, I'm as surprised as you are, although even with my short time in office I have learned this unit are a law unto themselves. You never quite know what they will do next, but they are very good at what they do and are definitely on 'our' side.'

'They have certainly looked after us well tonight, in spite of the circumstances, but this is almost too good to be true, fulfilling a dream of my youth, arriving at Andrews on a concord, unbelievable!'

The chief of staff spotted Paul and Frank in the shadows, 'What sort of stunt do you think you are pulling Colonel, I demand we use an American aircraft.' Then he rounded on Frank, 'How can fighters hope to keep up with that thing! I demand we have fighter protection for the entire trip!'

It was Paul who responded, 'Oiy! I've told you several times to button it, you'll have your fighter escort, all the way to Andrews, the tanker left ages ago to refuel them off the west coast of Ireland.'

'What fighters would they be Colonel, the British haven't got any thing to do the job!'

'Will you calm down Jerry!' said Frank, 'the Presidents security and safety is my job, trust me, these guys have it covered.'

'What with? a couple of spitfires?'

'Is he always such a pain in the arse Frank, or is it just for my benefit?' asked Paul. 'If you must know there will be two Black birds with us, each with a belly full of missiles which can knock down any anti aircraft missile I know of, they can even destroy a four inch shell, not that they can reach sixty thousand plus feet. We'll be travelling faster than a rifle bullet most of the time, I'd love to know what could hit us up there at that speed. Now sod off and shuffle some papers, your boss will be home with time for a snooze before he has to leave for the 'hill' and give his speech'.

At the top of the steps two immaculate officers in W.R.A.F. uniform, welcomed the passengers on board and directed them to their seats. Paul, the last to board stuck his head into the V.I.P. suite, just behind the cock pit bulkhead. He addressed General Leach, 'I'll be on the aft communications terminal if you need me Boss. Keeping up to date on the search and any developments on those homing devices.'

'Very well, Paul , don't forget to keep us up to date.'

'I will Boss,' then addressing their principle guest, 'Enjoy the experience Mr. President.'

'I'm looking forward to it Colonel,' was the reply.

'If you'll excuse me, I have things to do.'

As Paul walked through the main cabin, still limping a bit, he was stopped by several 'officials', with all manner of queries, mostly about luggage.

He held up his hands, 'A moment please ladies and gentlemen.' He greeted the relative hush with, 'thank you. Just to put your minds at rest, all of your luggage is in the luggage bay, every bag for everyone on this flight is on board. The cargo hold is pressurised and heated so all of your illicit cigarettes, bottles of Brandy, Scotch and perfumes are perfectly safe! Everything was scanned before it was loaded, a reasonable precaution under the circumstances, I am sure you will agree. Enjoy your flight. Thank you,' and he headed once more for what was in effect a communications centre at the rear of the aircraft.

A slight tremor ran through the plane as the engines started up, then another as it taxied slowly towards the end of the runway. Stopping a little way before the end of the taxi way to allow one of the Blackbirds to take off, bouncing slightly as the brakes came on. Those watching were left with spots in front of their eyes, so bright were the afterburners as the old super jet shot into the still dark sky.

The concord moved easily out onto the runway, it rocked gently as the brakes were locked on. All those on board could feel the trembling as the engines ran up to take off power, then it was moving, ever faster as it followed the blackbird.

The under carriage and the nose came up, the afterburners went out and the great dart climbed effortlessly into the lightening sky. Had those on board been able to see behind them they would have seen the other escort climbing behind them, taking up it's protective position above and a little behind them.

The formation headed westward, ever higher, but still sub sonic, just. The higher they climbed, the lighter it became, until they were in bright sunlight.

The refuelling of the Blackbirds went like clockwork soon after crossing the west coast. One of the escort pilots came on the radio to the Concord, a message patched through on the intercom for the passengers to hear.

'Can't you take your brakes off ?'

The concord captain replied, 'commencing climb to cruising altitude.'

Those who could see the rear edges of the wings saw the long blue flames of the after burners as they powered the great plane through the sound barrier and up to sixty four thousand feet.

The President was watching the display on the bulk head as the altitude and mach meters clicked ever higher.

He turned to General Leach, 'Is that correct General? mach two point five? it all seemed so effortless.'

'I should think so Mr. President.' replied the elderly officer, 'You'll be home in plenty of time for breakfast'.

'I really would like to have a talk with your Colonel.' addressing the Prime Minister, 'He seems to run a remarkable unit.'

The Prime Minister looked at General Leach, 'I'll call him Sir'.

The President turned to his head of security, 'You've spent a bit of time with him, what's he like Frank, as a man?'

'I've no idea Mr President,' was the initial reply, 'As a commander, certainly respected, trusts his men to do their job. I'd say he is not a man to cross. He is aware of the immense power he has, but is careful not to abuse it and soaks up pressure like a sponge. I suspect deep down he would rather not be in his position, he is certainly carrying some scars from the past, emotional as well as physical.'

'Do you trust him Frank?'

'Totally, Mr President.'

'That is good to know, you have always been a good judge of character.'

'Thank you Mr. President.' Frank turned to General Leach. 'You must know him fairly well Sir, would I be correct in thinking there is a darker side to your Colonel, like a ruthless streak?'

The General wasn't quite sure what Frank was looking for, but answered anyway. 'He can be totally ruthless if the need arises, he can also be difficult on occasions, such as now! I called him five minutes ago to join us.'

The General pushed a button on the consol beside him, 'Paul, your presence is required, now please.'

'I'll be about five minutes Sir, things are developing quite quickly, I'll be with you as soon as I can Boss.'

'Sooner rather than later Paul.' The general released the 'transmit' button, 'You see what I mean.'

The American secretary of state thought it was out of order and said so, 'I cannot see any of our Generals, especially the senior ones allowing a colonel to get away with telling them to wait. A strange way to command if I might say so General.'

'With respect Madam Secretary, in my long association with the Colonel, if there is one thing I have learned, it is if Paul says wait, then there is usually a very good reason for it,' replied the General.

The Prime minister supported the General by adding, 'The other thing to consider is the All Arms Unit is also outside the normal chain of command. This gives them a great deal of autonomy, allowing speed of action, impossible if everything has to be cleared at several levels before any action can be taken. Operating conventionally they would need many more personnel to achieve their objectives.'

'That surely removes political control,' observed the President, 'which requires a great deal of trust, I would have thought it was dangerous too.'

'Is that all bad, you must also take into consideration the unit, although basically a British unit, it is in fact multinational. I must confess I haven't had time to really get to know much about the unit as a whole since taking office, but their reputation speaks for it's self.'

'Indeed it does Prime Minister,' replied the President, 'as is clearly illustrated by our present situation.'

The conversation in the V.I.P. lounge turned to the rapidly deteriorating situation in many African and Mediterranean countries.

The President asked what the British Premier thought was behind it all.

'I don't think there is a truly common cause Mr. President, much is without doubt a genuine desire for change, but to what? They want an end to corruption, whether perceived or real, but most of the demonstrators have no idea what to put in place of what they already have.'

'What do we do about it?'

'What can we do, Mr. President. It is true, wealth in the worst affected countries is spread very unevenly, but it seems as though it is the so called middle classes, who by local standards are quite well off, who are behind much of the trouble.'

'So you don't think it is militant Islamist's behind it,' the President asked.

'In some cases they are the targets rather than the agitators, although I have no doubt they will take advantage of a situation if they can. Many of the seats of unrest are in basically Christian countries, even in Africa.'

There was a knock on the door, as Frank, the American security chief, was closest it was he who rose to answer it.

'Ah Paul, we've been waiting for you, I was beginning to think you'd got lost.'

'So good of you to join us at last,' added the Secretary of State.

'Prime Minister, Mr. President, Madam Secretary. You might not be so pleased to see me when you read this report'. He handed each of the leaders a copy of a thin folder.

'This is what?' asked the President.

'A preliminary report on what we know about Air Force One being attacked, and the disabling of the back up plane,' replied Paul.

'You've got them already Colonel!' exclaimed the secret service chief, 'well done, and the proof is there,' he added.

Paul was leaning against the door, as he knew the Chief of the White house staff had followed him through the plane. Now Paul opened the door, 'will you kindly return to your seat.' The man showed no sign of complying, the large trooper in the seat nearest the door began to get up. 'Rick, kindly escort Jerry back to his seat.'

'Sure Boss', replied the soldier.

'Get your hands off me you ape!' the senior official shouted.

'Allow me', an even larger American security man stood up, this induced one of those brief , 'oh shit' moments until the American guard turned to the aide and said calmly, 'If the Colonel said sit down, then it is only polite to do as he requested, it is after all his plane. He, and his unit have been very hospitable to all of us, the least we can do is behave as grateful guests'. The guard used his bulk to more or less bulldoze the man back to his seat.

Paul confined himself to 'nicely done' and closed the door again.

'I find all this hard to believe Colonel,' said the President. 'I don't understand how you got all this information so quickly. If this is true then it is as serious as things can get. The two men you picked up were American civilian contractors and their assignment was to check the electronics on Air Force One and the back up?'

'That seems to be the case Mr. President, their accreditation documents to work on Air Force One were signed by your Chief of Staff. They were employees of a company who tendered for the electronic counter measures equipment on the Presidential aircraft. The tender was rejected and given to us. Our stuff was less than one tenth of the size, could defeat any known system and was a tiny fraction of the cost. It may be coincidence but a subsidiary of the same company made the homing beacons, and the tracker on the missile. Clever really, one of our techs explained it to me, I think. Frankly I didn't understand a word he said, other than it wouldn't ever defeat our system again. Apparently they have upgraded the systems on here and the two escorts while we have been in flight. Don't ask me how they do such things because I have no idea.'

'So it won't work again?' asked Frank.

'Not against our systems.' replied Paul.

'That at least is something Colonel.' replied the President. 'Might I ask what has happened to the men?'

'We have handed them over to the F.B.I. unit based at Mildenhall, it's their problem now, and they are welcome to it. There is worse,' Paul continued.

'What can be worse Colonel?' asked the President.

'My lot are following the money trail, we lack absolute proof right now but it traces back to this man,' he handed Frank a picture, 'It seems as though he is an aide to a leading opposition senator, a very senior one. The money passed through accounts all over the place, Caymen islands and the likes, several holding companies, but his sticky fingers are all over it. It might take an hour or two but we will know for certain one way or another before you get back to the White house Mr President.'

'How sure are you about this Colonel?' asked a clearly worried President, 'this man is very powerful and has very influential friends.'

'Oh, I'm bloody certain it was him, or his boss, it's just that I can't give you evidence you could use in a court of law,' then after a pause he added 'yet'.

'This puts a whole new perspective on the matter, I'll admit, now I am worried Frank,' was the Presidents reply.

'I don't know if this will help, but he has made one mistake, a small but stupid one, brought about, I suspect by over confidence,' said Paul.

'Like what?' asked the head of the secret service.

'You remember those plates, like Vin numbers?' Paul suppressed a satisfied grin. 'Well, the company which pressed the actual plates had nothing to do with the beacons or anything else, they merely made the little metal plates. The bill came to forty eight dollars and twenty cents, including tax. Normally a couple of such plates would be a few cents each, but because they were a special order they were dearer.'

'How does that help us?' asked Frank.

'Matey,' waving the aides picture, 'didn't have enough cash in his pocket, he paid for them with his platinum Amex card.'

'You are kidding,' remarked Frank. 'He couldn't be so stupid!'

'Arrogant more likely,' Paul noticed the 'incoming' light flashing on the terminal. 'May I?' he asked General Leach, who was effectively in the way.

'Of course, my boy', as he levered himself out of the comfortable seat.

Paul tapped a couple of buttons and a hidden printer began to whirr, a couple of seconds later a sheet of paper with the copy of the Amex receipt fell into the collecting tray under the desk.

'I'm not even going to ask how you find out these things so quickly Colonel' the Presidents shock was turning rapidly to anger, 'I assume there was a degree of compliance from those holding the information you have acquired?'

'A degree, yes Sir'. Paul replied.

'And by definition a degree of none compliance, which means hacking!'

'I prefer to call it being nosey, Mr President. If it is important, and I'd say this is pretty important, then I couldn't care less. I'll do what ever it takes to get to the bottom of something like this. I'll confide in you all, with the technology we have there isn't an electronic file on earth we can't copy, and no one will know we've done it. It's no use asking me how it works, because as with most things like it I have no idea, I only know what it can do. It probably isn't a good idea to repeat any of this. Give us a few hours and you'll have all the evidence you need for any court, and gained legitimately, it's not too hard once you know what you're looking for. Now, if you will excuse me, I should be able to get an hours sleep before we land, it is something I am desperately short of.'

General Leach nodded his approval, and Paul heaved an inward sigh of relief and left in search of sleep.

He made it back to the sanctuary of the rear compartment, giving the chief of staff an icy glare on the way.

CHAPTER FOUR

For once Paul managed to get his hours sleep, one of the stewardesses woke him as requested with a cup of coffee.

'Time to wake up Sir.'

It took a couple of seconds for him to get his bearings, 'What? Oh yes thank you, we're not there already are we?'

'It won't be long Sir, we have just begun to descend and slow down.'

He took a drink of the coffee, 'Not bad. It could do with a little more sugar.'

'I'm sorry Sir, I'll get some more.' replied the stewardess.

'It's alright, honestly, thank you,' Paul replied, 'One thing though, please stop calling me Sir, you know I hate it. Go on, look after our V.I.Ps. and thanks for the coffee.'

He checked any messages which had come in during his short sleep, there was nothing of consequence, and they had all been relayed to General Leach. He idly flicked a switch so he could listen in on the conversations between the crew and the control tower at Andrews Air Force base. He knew Taff had been in touch with their control informing them of their impending arrival and the fact their radars would not detect the incoming formation. The first sign of trouble came when the assigned controller refused them clearance to land.

Paul heard his pilot repeat his request and give his position.

The controller came back, 'Speed bird one, your stated position is incorrect, there are no aircraft within forty miles of your stated position.'

Paul listened as the pilot of the Concord relayed his new position and repeated his request for approach instructions.

'Speed bird one, I have no contacts any were near your reported position, please check and advise.'

'This is speed bird one, this aircraft cannot be detected on radar, you will have visual contact before radar can see us. We will remain invisible to radar until we lower our undercarriage, the same applies to our two escorts. Also, our transponders will remain switched off, terrorists can track them as well as you can.'

'This is Andrews Tower, do not enter American airspace, you will be treated as hostile. I repeat do not enter American..'

Paul flicked another switch. 'Just give our pilot the instructions he requested, I know for an absolute fact you were advised of our arrival. I also know you were advised your radars would not pick us up. Now just do your job and clear the air corridor into your base as requested.'

'I repeat,' came the controllers voice, 'if you enter American air space you will be treated as hostile.'

'Get your Boss,' snapped Paul, 'hopefully he will have a measurable I.Q.!'

In the back ground Paul heard someone give an order to scramble a flight of F15 Eagles to intercept the source of the signals.

'Listen to me, I am the operational commander of the unit which operates this aircraft. It is a passenger transport, we have a total of sixty six people on board, including the British Prime minister and your Supreme commander, your secretary of state, your ambassador to the U.K the head of your secret service and a host more of American V.I.Ps. Now get your shit together and clear that flight path.'

'I don't know who you are, but our President was stranded in the U.K and is not expected until mid day eastern standard time at the earliest. Now, identify yourself or you will be treated as hostile.'

Paul flicked another button on the control panel in front of him. 'Taff, get hold of the base commander at Andrews and point out to him we have his President on board. The duty controller is being a royal pain in the arse and has flagged us as hostile. He has scrambled a flight of F15s after us, they are airborne.'

'I'll sort it,' came the reply.

Paul heard the leader of the fighters call the tower, 'Please confirm the position of the hostile flight, we have nothing on our radars which could be him.'

The pilot of the concord heard it too and promptly corrected the duty controller as to his position, and added, 'we are just dropping to sub sonic speed.'

'This is your final warning to turn back, you are in American airspace and flagged as hostile.'

There was suddenly a 'holy shit!', from one of the eagle pilots as he almost hit a blackbird. The pilot of big old plane had hit his afterburners to full power to climb out of the way of the approaching fighter, the huge turbulence tossed the eagle around like a leaf in the breeze.

In answer to his flight leaders worried call, the junior pilot of the flight replied.

'I guess we have found what we were looking for Sir, I nearly hit another aircraft, it's slipstream flipped me over.'

'Did you get a look at it ?'

'Yes Sir, it was an SR71 Black bird, I am absolutely certain.'

'I've got nothing on radar or infra red, but I saw the afterburners light up'.

Paul called the flight commander, 'This is speed bird one, please tell your lads to look where they are going, one of them nearly hit one of our escorts. We have, among others, your President on board, I am certain he has had enough excitement for one day. As you may, or may not know Air force One was damaged by a missile late last night, it made an emergency landing on our base and we have brought him and some of his party home. This plane is, and will remain totally invisible to your radars and infra red detectors until the landing gear is lowered. The reason for this is to protect this plane, and those on board from any similar threat when we come into land at Andrews.'

'And you are Sir?'

'I am the operational commander of the All Arms Unit, I am sure you have heard of us Major as I know you where at Lakenheath with the 48th tactical fighter wing until last year. At least if this computer in front of me has identified you correctly you were there.'

'You say you have our president on board?'

'And the British Prime minister'.

'We can't see you Sir.'

'If I get our pilots to put their landing and navigation lights on for a minute can you get in formation with us, and hold position if our crew gives you height and speed read outs. There is not much point in being invisible if you then fly with lights on, is there?'

'No Sir,' replied the fighter leader. 'Hang on Sir. I think I can see you, a big delta winged plane, It looks like a concord!!'

'That's correct Major, one of our escorts is about half a mile off your port wing and at the same altitude. The other is the same distance to starboard and dropping down to our height. If you would like to organise your flight accordingly, I am sure your commander in chief will be very grateful.'

'This is Andrews tower to eagle flight leader, we have you on radar. You were ordered to intercept the hostile aircraft using the call sign 'speed bird'. Why are you on approach?'

'We are escorting them in control.'

'Eagle leader, this is Andrews control. What do you mean escorting them in, we have your four eagles on radar, but nothing else near by.

'I'm looking at them Andrews control. One Concord and a pair of S.R 71 Black Birds. I have nothing on radar, or infra red but I can see them clearly now we are over land. It seems as though they have our President on board. Which accounts for the marine helo's being readied.'

As soon as the nose drooped down and the under carriage doors opened then the concord showed up on the radars. It was a spectacular sight, even in the near darkness, as the graceful transport touched down the two black birds thundered past, one either side of the runway. Their job done, the afterburners lit for the last time, both executed a spectacular climbing turn to port before coming into land, a great deal closer together than regulations allowed. The two retiring cold war warriors were then parked up one either side of the Hercules from the all arms unit in a secluded corner of the airfield, their mighty jets running down for the last time. The team from the all arms unit then descended on the planes to ensure all the 'secret' bits and pieces were removed before they were handed back to the Americans to be put on static display .

The concord taxied to it's allotted position and the steps rolled out to allow the passengers to disembark.

Perhaps surprisingly the President seemed in no hurry to leave, and after making a point of thanking all the crew personally he returned to the forward cabin, he spent another half an hour talking in private to the British Prime Minister.

Frank, the head of the American secret service approach Paul and General Leach.

'Excuse me gentlemen,' he began, 'I don't suppose you have any idea how long our respective leaders are going to be talking?'

'No idea at all Sir, I for one don't feel inclined to disturb them, but feel free,' Paul gestured towards the concord.

'I think I have taken enough potentially career ending risks for one night Colonel, what's the expression, quit while you're ahead?'

Paul's reply was almost drowned out as the flight of eagles sent to intercept them came into land in tight pairs.

'Now I've topped up my nicotine levels why don't you and I go and see a certain controller Frank. He was ordering those F15s to shoot us down, and I know for a fact our arrival was arranged with the base commander. Something went tits up, the General here is waiting for transport to take him to the Commanders office, we've both got communicators so we can stay in touch.'

Franks I.D quickly got them past security, it didn't take long to discover who had caused the problem. Some how a senior controller had slipped through the constant tight vetting procedures over the years, he was, in fact, next in line to be in command of air control at Andrews.

Frank wasted no time in calling the feds resident detachment on the huge base, to take the man away. The man was a U.S.A.F. major, and due for promotion, he actually went for his gun, it wasn't even clear of the holster when he realised he was staring down the barrel of a three fifty seven Smith and Weston.

'I am sorely tempted to say make my day,' Paul said calmly. 'A typical bully Frank, too much of a coward to do his own dirty work. May I give him a slapping while we wait for the Feds?'

'As tempting as it is, I think we'd better hand him over intact,' replied the big American.

'You think you're good enough,' was the challenging response from the extremist.

'I've seen these guys in action, unless you like pain I suggest you sit down and wait quietly for the feds.' replied Frank.

The FBI arrived a few moments later, 'Watch yourself with him,' advised Frank, 'charge him with conspiracy to assassinate.' Then as an after thought, 'No Lawyers, for now.'

'Very well Sir,' replied the feds.

'It will be interesting to find out how he passed the positive vetting, he's so right wing he makes Hitler look communist!' observed Paul, 'Something went wrong, when you find out, let me know please Frank, just to make sure we haven't got a similar problem.'

'I certainly will Colonel,' replied the big security chief, 'Lets go and hear what the duty controller has to say?'

As things turned out the man was only on his second solo shift and lived in mortal fear of his now ex boss. 'I think I'll leave this one to you Frank, my instincts are to recheck his vetting, a bit of retraining and see how it goes.'

'Sounds like a solution to me Paul, the less fuss about all this the better.'

'Why don't we nip back on board, I want to have a chat with Taff, I think you might be interested.'

'Okay?' Frank sounded intrigued, 'I know your reputation, what have you spotted everyone else has missed?'

'I'm not sure I've spotted anything, to be honest. Knowing me I've made two and two equal seven or something daft, it's just something I want to check. As usual it's none of my business but it could be yours.'

The two men went straight to the rear communications terminal, within five minutes the information Paul requested was in the hands of the secret service chief straight off the printer.

'Looking at that Frank, I'd say you have one hell of a problem mate. I'm just glad it's not mine.'

'The boss of one of our biggest defence contractors is behind all this!' exclaimed Frank. 'Trying to orchestrate a major war simply to make money?'

'It looks that way,' replied Paul, 'Look at the list of people he pays, the money all tracks back to the same slush fund, channelled through the same senators aide who bought those little plates on the ECM boxes on the Presidents planes. Before you start worrying one of my techs has just checked Marine one and both escorts, they are clear and the systems updated. Marine security turned two men away who were supposed to check the systems. The problem there is we don't know who they were, their I.Ds have come back as fakes.

I wish you well in sorting that list out Frank, I'd say you have one hell of a home grown problem there. Come on, lets go and find the rest of the party, I could do with a fag and a coffee.'

As they came down the steps they walked straight into a heated argument.

'Hold on,' Paul almost shouted, 'what seems to be the problem?'

The flight engineer from the crew of the concord turned to Paul, 'It's this dip stick Boss, he say's he is from the FAA and has ordered the ground crew not to refuel the speed bird. He says there is no certificate of air worthiness and he is impounding the plane.'

'Oiy! Come here you!' Paul shouted at the official, 'You lads. carry on fuelling, don't take any notice of this pratt, he's talking out of his backside.'

'It is a federal offence to threaten me, I'll have you arrested, who ever you are. These antiquated wrecks were grounded years ago for safety reasons.'

'I would simply shoot the idiot Frank, but with all this fuel around and your President and my Prime Minister still on board it might not be such a good idea.'

'That's it, I'm having you arrested,' replied the official. 'There is no air worthiness certificate for this type.'

'And there is for Aroura?' Paul interrupted.

'It doesn't exist,' was the official's answer.

'Interesting,' replied Paul, 'I've actually touched the thing and seen it several times, so sod off and hassle the CIA.'

To everyone's amazement the official was unbowed and produced a 'seizure notice' and was about to stick it to concords landing gear when Paul physically stopped him.

'Listen to me you useless bastard, I am only going to say this once, this is a military aircraft, it is none of your business and if you don't shut up and bugger off immediately you will be going to the dentist when you wake up. Do I make myself clear?'

'You have just threatened a federal official and interfered in the carrying out of his duty, I am going to fetch a federal officer and have you arrested!'

'There is no need to fetch an officer, you've got two here already, me and one of my best men on the steps.'

'And you are?' asked the official. Frank produced his secret service badge.

'Then arrest him!' the man demanded.

'I think he should hit you.' replied Frank. 'For what it is worth that old wreck as you call it has just flown us across the Atlantic so fast a couple of Black Birds were the only possible escorts.

If it is good enough for our President and the British Prime Minister then I think it is safe to say it should be good enough for you.'

That was when they became aware of the President half way down the steps. He actually came over to the group of men, sensing the atmosphere he asked if there was a problem.

Frank explained.

'Carry on fuelling gentlemen, put it on the Whitehouse tab.' He turned to Paul, 'Thank you Colonel for the hospitality and the lift home, you have made a boyhood dream come true. It was a great experience, one I would love to repeat, just under different circumstances. Thank you again Colonel.'

'Glad we could help out Mr. President.'

As Frank left to escort the President to the waiting helicopters he turned to Paul, 'I'll be in touch, and thanks again, and if he gets in the way again, just hit him.'

'You take care now.' replied Paul.

'I do hope you won't make so much noise taking off as you did landing.' said the official.

'I should think there will be a lot more, as we will be climbing as fast as possible, and for a very good reason, which incidentally has nothing to do with you. Get in the way again and I just might take Franks advice!'

Half an hour later the concord took off, as soon as the wheels and nose were up it climbed so fast the two eagles detailed by the base commander as escorts, just in case, were left behind. The thunderous sonic booms caused a good deal of consternation on the ground, quietened by the base commanders assurance that the pilot responsible would be dealt with.

The President, who had delayed his departure to watch, simply said, 'Wow'.

Paul would liked to have slept, but he had to brief the Prime Minister and General Leach on what they had discovered. He also raised the thorny question of fuel again.

'I really don't understand Colonel, my information is the problem has been resolved.'

'All I can say to that Sir is someone has been telling lies. The only things we have fuel for are our transports, and that is getting seriously low, and the remaining Black Birds and their tankers, but that is supplied by the Yanks.'

'You have my word I will look into it when I get back Colonel,' replied the Prime minister.

'I can tell you exactly where it is Sir,' said Paul, 'one train load is stuck in a siding west of Oxford, the locomotive pulling it allegedly broken down. The other hasn't left the refinery yet, the excuse being no suitable engine is available.'

'Is there any indication how long before the fuel will be delivered?'

'The last I heard was it might take 'some time'. Now you can call me a cynic if you like Sir, but the freight company contracted to deliver the fuel is part of a multi national group, the same group we have traced links to over this business with the stinger missile fired at the Presidents plane. With your permission Sir I will contact another company with suitable engines and get them to deliver the fuel and tell the other lot just where they can shove their contract.'

'They will then sue H.M.G. Colonel.' replied the startled Prime Minister.

'Let them, they are in breach of that contract by failing to deliver on time without reasonable excuse. I know for a fact they have almost a third of their engines standing idle, if they claim they are waiting for servicing or repair then they are guilty of promising something the knew they couldn't deliver.'

'It sounds a dangerous strategy Colonel,' was the Prime Ministers reply.

'No where near as dangerous as having our recons grounded Sir, it is costing lives already. Incidentally, the same multinational company has a stake in the UAVs our forces are buying to help cover some of the gaps left by our recons being grounded.'

'Are you suggesting an international corporation is deliberately manipulating events to sell us their products?' asked the Prime Minister, 'surely not?'

'It is beginning to look that way Sir,' Paul replied, 'I've had some more information from our tech's about the missile fired at Air Force One. Among other things it would seem as though the lads have found the fuse. I don't think it was supposed to have shot the plane down. It was a proximity fuse, designed to explode just near enough to do a little damage. The eagle which tried to block it meant the missile ended up closer than it was supposed to have been to Air Force One. It was all about getting our kit taken out and their over priced crap put in. While we are on the topic, I can safely say our new modifications work. I am informed by our systems operator something tried to get a lock on us when we took off from Andrews. He thinks it was another stinger, the upgrades prevented it getting a lock and sent a signal back to source which I am assured fried it's electronics. The feds were given the location but found nothing, although the perimeter cctv may have got the culprit on film.'

'You mean to tell me someone tried to shoot us down Paul?' asked General Leach.

'Seems so Sir.' was Paul's casual reply. 'It will be interesting if the Feds can catch the culprit and get the missile, any bets it has the same distance setting on the proximity fuse as the one fired at the Presidents aircraft?'

'Good Lord,' exclaimed the Prime minister, 'What on earth do we do about this?'

Timothy Pilgrim

'Easy Sir,' replied Paul, 'stand up in 'The House' when you get back and publicly rip up every contract issued to the corporation in question, tell them to take a hike. Then go to the MOD and find out which 'officials' are in their pockets and fire them on the spot, no pensions, only the basic state pension. If they kick off, say the alternative is court on corruption and treason charges. There is always a trail of money and that is easy to track.'

'It all sounds rather dangerous Colonel,' said the Prime Minister.

'I suppose there is always a risk they might try to retaliate, they are every bit as dangerous as any terrorist, the big difference is these are high tech, which makes them vulnerable.'

'I'm a bit concerned about your lack of emotion about all this Paul,' said General Leach. 'Had the attempt succeeded then you, along with everyone else on board could well be dead by now, there was also this incident on your arrival back at base. Taff told me all about it, we are worried Paul. I'm not going to order you to take a psyche-eval, but I am asking you to get checked!'

'I'm alright Sir, honestly, I'm just extra tired and hurting more than usual, I'll be fine when I catch up on my sleep. I've been there before Boss, and I have no wish to go there again thank you. It is no fun being scared of your own shadow following you on a sunny day.'

'Well just take it easy for a bit, you've got a brilliant team, let them take up the slack. You can keep a fatherly eye on your flock by all means, but try letting them just get on with their jobs. I know it's hard, Peter, my deputy is always telling me the same thing!'

'You pretty well leave us to get on with it, Boss,' replied Paul.

'Exactly!', was the ageing Generals heart felt reply.

'Fair enough Sir, is it alright if I try and snatch an hours catnap?' was Paul's response, 'I need it'.

'Go ahead M'boy.'

'Thank you Sir,' then an acknowledgement, 'Prime minister.'

After Paul had left, the Prime minister asked General Leach why he seemed so concerned about Paul.

'He's good at his job Sir, catching terrorists, he has is no equal. However, he has been in the job a long time, possibly too long, he is as tough as they come, but the pressures in his job are immense. Ordering men into harms way is something every C.O. has to cope with, inevitably sometimes there are casualties, it is all part of the job. What makes the all arms unit special is it's size, in terms of actual combat troops it is not much bigger

44

than a squadron at Hereford, you have to remember all of those troops are seasoned veterans. Paul has known most of them for years, in a nut shell they are all friends, so any loss is felt even more keenly than normal units.'

'I assume from that they have lost men recently, although I cannot recall any mention of casualties in the reports,' replied the P.M.

'All I know is they have a missing patrol, normally when something goes wrong, it is a simple matter to send one of the units old Canberra aircraft to locate them, but at the moment all are grounded as they have no fuel. Even if the fuel has arrived in our absence it will be several days before any of them fly again, it is more than simply filling them up. The problem is the fuel they use, it reacts with the seals in the fuel systems, no problem as long as there is fuel in the pipes, it is if they dry out, then the seals crack and leak. Of course the same applies to the high altitude tankers.'

'You have my personal assurance I will get to the bottom of this General, the Colonel seemed to think it has something to do with this mysterious multi national consortium, could he be right?' the Prime Minister asked.

'That is the real worry Sir', the General sighed, 'his 'feelings' usually are right. On this occasion however, it would be better if he were wrong, but I fear he isn't wrong this time.'

An hour or so later the head flight attendant carefully woke Paul from his deep sleep, 'We'll be landing in twenty minutes Sir.'

'What? already.' muttered Paul as he tried to move, 'Oh, bloody hell my back hurts, serves me right, I know it's going to happen if I sleep sitting up. Any chance of a coffee please.'

The attendant reached round the door frame and retrieved the mug she had placed on the handy shelf before trying to wake Paul.

'Your Coffee Sir!' she smiled.

'Very good, but I wish you lot wouldn't call me Sir.'

CHAPTER FIVE

Paul limped back into the head quarters building, having left General Leach to see off the V.I.P. helicopters. He was surprised to see Taff signing in at reception.

'What might I ask are you doing in? I thought B.J. was on duty?'

'He was, or rather is, he has taken a team to investigate why our marooned train load of fuel has blown up!'

'You what?' exclaimed Paul. 'When did this happen?'

'A couple of hours ago apparently, we only found out just before you landed. I'm surprised you didn't hear the chopper leaving.'

'I heard a chopper about somewhere, nothing unusual in that.' replied Paul, 'how did we find out?'

'It seems as though fire trucks from as far away as Brize Norton and Lyneham have been called out, but it was Abingdon who called us, there is it seems, a news black out on the incident.'

'Do you ever get the feeling some one, some where really wants to put us out of business?' asked Paul.

'Like who, terrorists apart?'

'I don't know, Taff. Come on, my office, lets see if we can figure out who could have done it?' replied Paul, stifling a yawn.

Before he could sit down Taff had to move a stack of files out of his usual chair, he noticed Paul sorting through the mugs to find a couple which didn't need too much washing up. He carefully made enough room in the rubbish bin for the contents of the over full ash tray and swept a hand full of empty sweet wrappers off the end of Paul's desk and added them to the already full bin's contents, pressing the lid down to prevent them escaping onto the floor.

'You really have got to get a grip of this tip Paul, how on earth did it get into this state?''

'The same as always, for one thing, while I've been here I've been too busy to notice and these new locks on the doors.'

'What about them?' asked Taff. 'The cleaners get the key cards from reception, no problem there.'

'There is when I clear off half way round the world and forget to leave my card!' replied Paul. 'Remember that door locks automatically, sure, you don't need a key card from the inside, if we are already in here then the sensors leave it unlocked. Thirty seconds after the last person leaves, the system locks it, and the door from Claire's office needs her code as well as her card to open it.'

'I worry about you some times' muttered Taff shaking his head. 'Right, who blew up our fuel Sherlock? I presume you have an idea?'

Paul placed the steaming mugs of coffee on a couple of more or less clear places on his cluttered desk.

'Give me a chance Taff!' replied Paul as he tapped some keys. An aerial shot of the site came up on the screen, he zoomed the picture out a bit. 'It's a long way off a road Taff' he observed, 'By the looks of things that siding used to be a branch line, see where it ends a couple of hundred yards on from the supposedly broken down engine. There used to be a bridge over the river there, see the supports either side.'

'Your point?' asked Taff.

Paul reached round behind him and pulled an atlas off the shelf. He quickly found the page he sought.

'What are you looking for Paul?'

'Here, look, see these contour lines, there is no way anyone could have seen that train from either of the nearest roads, assuming this ordnance survey map is accurate, it would be completely hidden from view.'

'So you are saying is it rules out a random opportunist terrorist attack?' said Taff, trying to follow Paul's train of thought.

'The other thing is it was full of jet fuel, which isn't the easiest stuff to set on fire. From the initial reports coming through it would seem as though the entire train was on fire in a matter of moments. The crew of a passing mail train reported several large explosions, the main line is over a mile away from the site. That's another thing, why take it so far down the siding if you intended to move it quickly, the engine was uncoupled in that picture and some way away from the first fuel tanker.'

'All of which helps us how?' asked Taff.

'Get onto rail track, see if there have been any maintenance crews in the area the past couple of days.'

'Fair enough, they might have seen something I suppose.'

' Taff!' exclaimed Paul, suddenly having a eureka moment, 'how much explosive would it take to blow up all of those tanks, even if you had opened most of the valves first?'

'I've no idea, more than I would want to carry though.'

'Quite!' replied Paul, 'Mind you,' he continued, 'If you had opened some valves first so there was vapour in the tanks, then it is easy to get them to blow up, but you do need that vapour'.

'That is why it blew up tonight,' said Taff. 'It has been windy for the past week, tonight has been flat calm. The vapour would have to be outside Paul, those tanks have a haylon system, or something like it, to prevent the vapour building up in the tanks, other wise they would be like bombs just waiting to explode.'

'Okay, so we can guess the how, now the who?' said Paul. 'It can't be seen from a road, and it is well away from the main line, on a siding which hasn't been used for ages by the looks of the tracks in front of the engine. Ergo, it must have been someone who knew it was there!'

'Brilliant,' muttered Taff, 'So how do we find out who knew!'

'We can sit here and play guessing games all day, we'll wait and see what the team can find, if anything. My guess is the fire would have been so hot it would have destroyed any evidence.

We have got to find a way of getting our fuel up here from Southampton safely, get a team to work out how, what we need to guard it effectively from an attack. Once we can operate a Canberra then the job becomes easier, we'll be able to pick up any potential threat before it becomes a problem.'

'Where are you going?' asked Taff, sensing Paul was about to leave him to it, again.

'The back office, to have a kip! Wake me up if World War Three breaks out.'

'Will do Paul'.

The exhausted Colonel was asleep within minutes of his head hitting the pillow, he was vaguely aware of movement in his secure office, but passed it off as Taff using it rather than his own. In fact Taff had lifted the security key card from Paul's faded combat jacket pocket and left it for the cleaners, along with an instruction to be quiet doing their work, as Paul was asleep in the back room, and a reminder of the Colonels' short temper.

By the time he woke up it was dark out side, he took his time sorting himself out before heading for his office. In spite of having washed and shaved, and a change of clothes he still wasn't fully awake as he headed in search of a coffee in his office. To his surprise he didn't have to search for a clean mug, although it took a moment to notice they were all in the rack for the first time in months. He sank into his comfortable chair, ash trays, not only empty but clean, all the bins emptied, no sticky rings on the desk top! The down side was the stack of files in the 'IN' tray.

'Oh great!' he muttered. and began glancing through the loose pages of the first folder. To his utter amazement the team B.J had taken to the site of the sabotaged fuel train had found several interesting bits and pieces, the most surprising was an unexploded Thermite grenade, seemingly dropped in the haste to escape the inferno the saboteurs had unleashed, the serial number was still clearly visible according to the report.

He stabbed the duty officer button, B.J. casually sauntered in, 'You called Boss?'. Noting the confusion on Paul's face, he asked innocently, 'You weren't expecting Taff by any chance? You haven't looked at a clock since you woke up have you? It is four o'clock in the morning!'

'Aah, that would account for me being a bit hungry, I haven't eaten since, well for some time. Come on, the canteen is open, you can brief me over breakfast.'

'Fair enough, I was about to head that way myself,' replied the big powerful man who was Paul's deputy.

As they passed reception the soldier on duty called out, 'Boss, you might want this back.' waiving his key card.

'Taff I suppose?' commented Paul as he took the card back.

'Who else?' replied the trooper.

'Thanks.'

Paul quickly caught up with B.J. 'This bloody grenade, traced it yet?' he asked.

'Sort of, well we know where it was supposed to have been, but it seems as though it has never been there and was never ordered by the company it was supposed to have been ordered by.'

'Will you stop talking in riddles,' exclaimed Paul, 'I've got a head ache as it is! So who sent it to someone who didn't want it?'

'Well you know there is a U.S. army logistics company at Mildenhall?

Of course you do.' B.J. answered his own question. 'Well, the factory in the states which makes them sent us a copy of the order for six boxes of them for the logistics unit up the road. Our American friends at Mildenhall confirmed they had a special order in for five boxes of twenty four per box. They even listed the serial numbers of the grenades, as did the factory. Manifests have been checked and double checked, crews questioned, there seems little doubt only five boxes were dispatched to Mildenhall, box number three simply vanished. The loading crew even made a note of there being no box number three on the manifest. The people who unloaded it confirmed it, they checked as it was odd to have one box in a sequence missing. Also, it turns out those things need special handling and careful stowage, there seems to be no way one got over looked.'

'I wish I hadn't asked now! so what happened to box three?' Paul asked, more in hope than expectation.

'No idea.' replied B.J. as he held the canteen door open for Paul, 'You will how ever be relieved to know the grenade we found was out of box number three.'

'I will?' replied Paul. 'You obviously know when it should have arrived, I take it you have checked any other flights it could have arrived on?'

'Oh yes, all two hundred and sixty something which left the 'States since those boxes left the factory and arrived in the U.K. in time to have got them to Oxford.' was B.J.s reply. 'You're never going to eat all that! ' he commented as he saw Paul's plate as they helped themselves.

'Two eggs, three rashers of bacon and a fried slice of bread, topped of with a heap of mushrooms and two large spoonfull's of devilled kidneys. Have you got hollow legs Boss or picked up a worm in your travels!'

'I'm hungry, alright?' replied Paul, 'granted I'd have had less of the fried if I'd spotted the kidneys earlier, they are one of my favourites.'

As they tucked into their food Paul suddenly stopped, a fork full of kidney and mushrooms half way to his mouth. 'I've just had a thought, how were they picked up from the factory, military or civvie contractor, so bloody obvious we missed it!'

'No we didn't, the factories own armoured van delivered them to the air base they were flown out from.' replied B.J.

'Shit!' was Paul's response, 'I thought it was too easy. When we get back to the office we'll get them to check the paper work for that van, there must have been a switch somewhere.'

'Not at this time of day we won't, there will only be a security guard on, not every where is open around the clock!'

'Fair enough' replied Paul, 'I don't suppose there is another airfield on the route the van took?'

'We thought of that one as well Paul. You're thinking he had two invoices, one for five and another for a single box. The flaw in that is it would have still showed on the cargo manifest on any transport it was on.'

'I suppose it would B.J. we've missed something mate, that box number three didn't fly here by it's self!'

B.J. watched in amazement as Paul took a double size chunk of a chocolate gateaux the duty chef had been about to remove from the self service counter.

'Are you sure you haven't got a worm boss?' he asked.

'I thought it would go down well with the cup of coffee back in the office' replied Paul, 'We've got a stack of files to go through.'

'What's all this 'we' business, I've got enough on my desk to last a couple of shifts.' said B.J. as he headed for the door. 'Nice try though,' he added.

It must have been about four o'clock that afternoon when Taff walked into Claire's office. Claire acted as secretary for both of them in her office sandwiched between the two commanders. 'You haven't seen Paul around have you? asked Taff.

'No, not now you come to mention it, I presumed he was around as his combat smock is on his chair, I've been in twice with some files.'

'I wonder where he's gone?' asked Taff, 'He never goes anywhere without that old smock.' He turned to go back to his own office, 'I suppose he is alright, I know he was very tired, B.J. was saying as much when he handed over to me earlier, I'll bet he's asleep in the back room. Can you let me in please Claire, he must have his card on him, I've had several people in my office looking for him, saying the other door is locked.'

Sure enough when Taff checked there was Paul, curled up on his bunk in the back room.

'Sleeping like a baby' Taff reported to Claire as he crept back, 'Seems a shame to wake him up, I'll be back in an hour. If I forget pop into my office before you leave or I won't be able to get in to wake him up. These new locks are a bit of a mixed blessing.'

As the shift change approached Taff went to wake his old friend.

'OIY! sleeping beauty, rise and shine!!'

After a couple of grunts, Paul finally tried to stretch and open his eyes, 'Oh, bloody hell, that hurts,' he muttered as his back refused to straighten. 'Can't a bloke have forty winks around here any more?'

'I hate to be the bearer of bad news but it's your watch mate! you've been asleep for the past ten hours from what I can make out.'

'Good grief, is that the time! I know I was tired, but that is daft, sleeping so long.'

'Are you going to be alright for your shift?' asked Taff sounding concerned about his old friend.

'Nothing that a shit, shower and shave won't cure,' replied Paul, as he looked for his cigarettes. 'Did B.J. find out what happened to box number three of those grenades?' he asked as he lit the inevitable fag.

'Oh yes, well sort of.' said Taff

'Not more bloody riddles, please.'

'Not so much a riddle, you were right, the van's paper work was for six boxes loaded, the invoices were for five and one. Five for our American friends up the road via the USAF the other was sent on a commercial cargo flight from a regional air port which is home to a small cargo carrier with flights into Heathrow.'

'Obviously there's more.'

'When it arrived at Heathrow some hawk eyed type noticed the box number didn't tally, turns out the van driver left the wrong box with the carrier, but because the rest of the paperwork was in order about the contents etc, it was sent through any way. The carrier at Heathrow wasn't exactly helpful, but were persuaded to tell us where the box they got was shipped on to, it was a haulage and distribution company in Witney near Oxford.'

'And they delivered it where?' asked Paul.

'They didn't,' replied Taff, 'It was marked 'to be called for', we think the signature is Dan or Don Smith.'

'Oh great!' muttered Paul, 'another dead end?'

'Not quite, the haulage company has CCTV and we got a van number. We have traced the van, surprise, surprise it is a hire van. We have traced the licence holder who hired it, he has been on holiday for the past ten days, fishing in Thailand, as the local airports had been closed for three days because of a cyclone, it is safe to say it wasn't him. We got the local plod to check his house and they confirm it was broken into. We have also checked the industrial unit given as the address. No prizes for guessing it was empty, and of course the van and the unit were paid for in cash. Everything signed for with the same signature as the box.'

'Great!' exclaimed Paul, 'got any good news?'

'Oh yes,' chuckled Taff, 'we've got pictures of three of the four involved, they kept out of the way of the CCTV cameras on the estate where the unit is in Tame, what they didn't know was there is a camera opposite which logs all vehicles on and off the estate. All three of the cars they used were stolen shortly before, probably used before the owners noticed they were gone. All this is being checked as we speak.'

'No IDs on any of the pictures I suppose?' Paul asked hopefully.

'Not here, the feds are running them, to see if they have got anything.'

'Then answer me this Taff,' Paul began, 'If there is no photo of them, how the hell did they get into the country? For over a year now every pass port is supposed to have been scanned and the details stored. It therefore follows this lot have either been here for a long time, or are Brits, but then there should be one among them with a driving licence. Why the hell can't this job be easy, just for once!'

A light began to flash on one of the terminals on Paul's desk, as Paul was making the inevitable coffee Taff checked the incoming message.

'Ha! not often you're wrong mate, guess what, the Feds have got two of them already. You are going to love this, they are both employed by the same defence contractor as the one who planted the tracker on Air Force One and the pair who fired the missile.'

'You are joking! What the hell is going on Taff? Added to all this buggering about with our fuel deliveries, the contractor is owned, or is at least part of the same multi-national conglomerate. The same lot own the company which makes many of the UAVs the forces are buying to replace our Canberras.'

'We're being stitched up here Paul, but why?, damn it we have even sold technology to some of the companies involved, not our latest stuff, but better than anything they have got.'

'I'll get cleaned up and have a bit of grub, you get a couple of computer techs to see what they can find out about this group, who runs it, owns it, were does the money go. We need to know which companies belong to this group, there is something very bloody wrong about all of this Taff. I'll make an appointment for tomorrow to see the PM. In the mean time, lets find an alternative contractor to drag the other fuel train up here, I'm not being buggered about by any money grabbing yank anymore, as of now all links to anything connected to that corporation will be severed.'

'That should be interesting, they'll sue for sure,' replied Taff.

'Shouldn't it just, they were contracted to deliver the fuel, vital for the defence of the nation, they didn't do it. End of story.'

'You know as well as I do they will claim the engine broke down, and produce paper work to prove it.'

'I hope they do Taff, then I can prove they are liars as well as saboteurs. The thing was standing there for what, ten days, supposedly unable to move. This morning BJ sent two engineers, one from here and one from a company which services such things, guess what, it started up and ran like a clock. They drove it up and down the line as far as they could go. A single wire had been detached on the electrical system, it hadn't fallen off, it had been taken off, quite deliberately. Here's the killer, BJ got one of our sections to check calls to the crew of the loco, twenty minutes before it turned into the siding they got a call from their office. A couple of minutes later Rail track, or who ever runs these things also got a call to open the points so as this train would enter the dead end. Best bit, there is a recording of that call.'

Taff put his feet up on a corner of Paul's desk, 'So you are going to ask the Prime Minister to black list any deals, existing or pending with one of the most powerful corporations in the world?'

'Unless you know a good reason why not.' replied Paul.

'What do you know that I don't.' asked Taff, 'clearly there is more.'

'I'm certain there is a lot more. My theory is they are trying to engineer the situation where they have a virtual monopoly on electronic surveillance. With all that's going on in the middle east it will take one spark and there will be major conflict in the area. This in turn will lead to huge arms sales, much of the equipment these days depends on electronics and highly accurate intel. Put simply, the greedy bastard running things is looking to make a vast fortune, at the expense of soldiers lives by selling the military inferior kit at exorbitant prices. He will then claim to be the saviour of the free world.'

'You have got a burr up your backside about this,' commented Taff.

CHAPTER SIX

Just then an alarm began to flash on the terminal on Paul's desk. 'It's the Kelly on the panic line Paul.' called Taff, Paul was in the back office changing his shirt.

'Well answer it then!' Paul called back.

All he caught of Taffs reply was, 'Yes, of course. Keep us posted.'

'Now what's gone wrong?' Paul asked as he returned, still tucking in his shirt.

'It seems as though HMS Warwick has been hit by an anti ship missile fired from one of those blasted Iranian gunboats. Kelly was asking permission to go to her aid, the thing is she is supposed to join a mainly American task force which is headed into the gulf in a few hours time, supposedly to counter the threat to international shipping posed by these boats.'

'Can't they cope without Kelly, damn it all Taff, there will be two, maybe four cruisers with the carrier, not to mention a flock of destroyers and frigates, surely they can deal with a handful of bloody nutters in what are basically recreational speed boats!'

'You would have thought so, it seems as though they want her to prevent any of these gunboats sneaking round behind them,' replied Taff. 'The Admiral in command says there is a chance the radar returns from the wakes of so many ships close together going through the Straights of Hormuz could conceal these speed boats. He wants HMS Warwick and Kelly to ride shot gun about ten to fifteen miles behind the battle group.'

'Well, he will just have to want!' retorted Paul, 'Taking care of Warwick is the first priority'.

'I suppose you know we have a new skipper on the Kelly, he only joined

55

us a couple of months ago and took command over the week end,' said Taff. 'I was sort of hoping he'd have a quiet start to his detachment pottering about off Aden looking for these bloody pirates.'

'The only things which float I'm interested in are the things with an outboard motor on the back and I sit in when I'm fishing!' observed Paul, 'you know I can get sea sick in a garden pond!'

'Kelly on again Paul.'

Paul flicked a switch and introduced himself to one of the newest members of the All Arms Unit.

'What is going on Skipper?' he asked.

'I don't know the exact circumstances, yet Sir,' came the reply, 'but it seems as though HMS Warwick has been hit amidships by something similar to an exocet.

We have her in sight, and should be along side shortly.'

'All right Skipper, do what it takes, you are the man on the spot, and take care.

If any of those bloody nutters come your way, they get one warning shot, then blow them out of the water. You help the Warwick, getting her to safety is your ONLY task, until she and her crew are safe, understood?'

'Understood Sir,' came the clear reply.

'Good, carry on. Oh, and while I think of it, call me Paul on one to ones, or boss if others are around.'

'Fair enough,' then after a pause, 'boss' .

Taff turned to his old friend, 'You do know the American Admiral in command of the battle group is the same one who wanted you banged up over that F18 getting shot down off Somalia last year.'

'I do now,' replied Paul. 'Not that it makes a difference, Kelly gets the Warwick out of there, end of story.'

The next hour was spent going through the files which always seemed to appear by magic on Paul's desk, what with the boring nature of most of them and the tension of waiting for Kelly to call in on the condition of Warwick, the wait seemed much longer.

When it came the news was bad, eight dead, two of them from the small female contingent on board, twenty five wounded, at least a dozen seriously. Damage to the ship was bad, apart from two holes in the hull, a big one above the water and a smaller one below and the medical centre was destroyed. It was an exploding oxygen bottle which had killed the only female officer on board as she physically dragged one sick berth attendant and the ships doctor to safety. An amazing feat by a relatively petite woman, both the men had been knocked out by the blast of a missile but were otherwise uninjured. Even though there was a fierce fire she simply dived in and grabbed them by their collars and dragged them clear together. As she cleared the door and help arrived an oxygen bottle exploded and a large chunk hit her in the head killing her out right.

The control room in the heart of the ship was also destroyed along with those in it at the time, leaving them defenceless as far as the main weapon systems were concerned and more worryingly without effective communications.

The crew had got the fires either out or under control by the time Kelly came along side and transferred most of her medics and about twenty other personnel to help. Further checking revealed the Warwick must have been hit by three missiles, two appeared to have been little bigger than RPGS, it was one of these which had destroyed the lynx helicopter.

The good news was the ship still had power and now the two portable pumps, sent over from Kelly were working they were pumping faster than the leaks and the fire hoses combined were adding to the flooding.

Just as Paul was thanking the young skipper of The Kelly for the update, he had got as far as to ask for a list of the dead so families could be informed when he heard the action stations sound, then to his consternation the missile warnings blare out.

'I'll have to go Boss, we're a bit busy. I'll call you back'.

Before the link closed he could hear the manic clattering of the chain guns ending with bangs which were presumably missiles exploding. He also heard 'full speed ahead' followed by the banging of the main battery.

'I rather think young Sam is getting his baptism of fire,' Paul said to Taff. 'By the sounds of things something got close, too close! I heard him order full speed, if he hasn't ever been on Kelly at full lick he is going to get a bit of a shock.'

On board the Kelly the young Skipper was about to find out the affect of his order for full speed.

At first he was furious, the hum of the fans dragging in air for the running engines stopped and the ship slowed. 'I ordered full speed number one! Why are we slowing down?'

'We have to wait until the props stop so we can retract them skipper, if we don't retract them they'll act like anchors or rip off all together. Hang on skipper, here we go,' there was a loud hissing sound, the stern dropped and the bows began to rise as the destroyer headed at incredible speed towards the attacking gunboats.

As the startled Captain picked himself up, the gunnery officer asked him if they were to destroy the two larger ships supporting the dozen or so speed boats.

'Absolutely guns.'

Eight thousand tons of fire spitting fury appeared out of the darkening western horizon, tearing directly at the flotilla sent to finish the Warwick off. The two larger vessels were equipped with radar, the missiles fired by the elusive little boats needed radar to guide them to within a mile of their targets.

The air burst shells from Kelly's pair of four point five inch guns decimated the deadly but fragile speed boats. The other two larger ships were still about ten miles away when the last of the speed boats were shredded and sinking.

The crews on the fast missile patrol boats, recently bought from China were reloading the main launchers when they realised what ever was coming at them was likely to pose a problem. What ever it was had shot down the first salvo of the latest sea skimming missiles intended to finish the Warwick. They thought it was the Warwick on their radars until they had fired and this ship moved away from what they had thought was a single target and then casually destroyed their salvo of missiles. What ever this mystery ship was, it then obliterated the screen of speed boats, all with no apparent effort.

As they executed a hard turn to take them back to the safety of territorial waters one of them was hit full in the side by four shells and vanished beneath the foam. The last one straightened up and headed for home flat out. A rapid series of gun flashes seen dimly through the flying spray signalled another salvo of shells on the way, this time there were six shells against a fast but steady target, even at eight miles range none missed and two hundred tons of missile patrol boat headed straight for the bottom of the sea along with her crew.

'Might I respectfully suggest we slow down a bit skipper, much longer like this and we'll be several miles inland in Iran.'

'What? Oh yes, by all means number one, take us back to Warwick please.'

The young skipper looked at the smug grins on the faces of the long time crew of the Kelly. 'You bastards, you knew what would happen! I knew this ship was fast, very fast, but that was unbelievable. Alright gentlemen, you have put the new boy well and truly in his place. Yes 'Guns',' as the gunnery officer approached.

'All targets destroyed Sam. Welcome to the All Arms Unit. Ammunition expended; forty eight rounds of 4.5 fired, thirteen hundred of thirty millimetre from the 'goal keepers' and two thousand one hundred of twenty mil. from the 'darleks' plus three super sea wolf missiles. Two Huodong type guided missile patrol boats and fifteen small speed boats destroyed and sunk. In addition eight sea skimming type C802 missiles shot down. We have one casualty in sick bay, the chief navigating officer was caught by surprise by the sudden increase in speed and spilt his cup of tea in his lap, could have been a nasty scald Skipper'.

'Thanks guns, do you think they'll come back? ' asked the still shaken new commanding officer.

'I doubt it, the only thing they are capable of mounting out here for now might be a sneak attack with an odd speed boat, and they'll have to get in close, about a mile at most. Their main weapon is a sea skua type missile, but it needs radar to get it close for the on board guidance to lock on, as long as we stay alert we should be safe enough for a bit. Hadn't you better tell the boss what has happened, I'm sure he'd like to know Skipper.'

The young officer was still buzzing from his first taste of combat as he relayed his report to Paul.

'Well done,' was the simple reply.

'In all honesty Boss, I didn't have much to do with it! I spent most of the critical time sitting on my backside against the rear bulk head of the bridge. I wasn't ready for the terrific acceleration! About all I did was point at the threat and said full speed ahead, I think I gave the order to open fire when ready. Everything happened so quickly by the time I got my wits back it was over!'

'Mad bugger! I like it, charging the enemy!! You'll do.'

Paul might have been impressed, the same could not be said for the American Admiral in command of the battle group crawling over the southern horizon.

He was demanding Kelly join them as agreed.

'It's not going to happen Admiral,' it was Paul who had replied.

'I demand you comply, there are numerous threats in the area, your ship has already had one engagement, according to one of our scout planes.'

'Then speak to the 'hawk eye' crew and they will confirm the threat was destroyed. Next time it would be nice if they warned us we were being stalked.'

'That aircraft's mission is to protect this task force, now order your destroyer to take up it's agreed position ten miles astern of this carrier!'

'No,' was Paul's reply.

When the furious American paused for breath, Paul flicked the transmit switch. 'Just so as you know why Kelly will not be joining your regatta, it seems as though you are unaware that HMS Warwick has been attacked and is currently unable to defend herself. At least three missiles struck her a few hours ago. The mission of The Kelly is to get Warwick to a place of safety. For your information, Intrepid has been detached from the anti pirate patrols and is headed towards you at her best speed, when she arrives Intrepid will take over as escort for Warwick and then Kelly can join your fleet. Make no mistake Kelly stays with Warwick until relieved by Intrepid. Out!'. Paul flicked the communications switch to 'off'.

'How to win friends and influence people,' observed Taff.

'Well, what else do you expect. He knew full well what happened to Warwick, those recons aren't called 'hawkeyes' for nothing. If I remember correctly they were updated last year with some of our systems.'

A light flashed on the terminal Paul had only just left.

'It's Kelly again Taff', he told his friend as he picked up the hand set.

'Yes Sam?' he began, 'what's up now?'

'We have a bit of a problem Boss. It's the Warwick, we're not sure she'll make it to Aden without some emergency repairs. The trade winds began out here a couple of days ago and the sea is beginning to kick up. Her crew have had a chance to get a closer look at the damage below the waterline. We knew about the hole, the thing is there is a ruddy great crack running straight down from the hole.

Her crew plus a couple of our guys are trying to weld some braces across the crack, but it keeps opening up with every swell and splitting the weld before it is strong enough to hold. We need to get divers down on the outside as well, but it is far too rough out here for that.'

'You are the man on the spot Sam, any ideas?'

'Yes actually, and it might solve another problem at the same time Boss,' replied the young Skipper.

'Lets hear it then,' replied Paul.

'The task force has only just passed our position, for some reason they are only doing about twelve knots. What I am suggesting is we follow them through the straights as originally intended, with a following sea the Warwick will have an easier time of it. She can easily do fifteen knots if need be against about five headed into the sea. If we keep as close to the coast of the Oman as we can without risking running aground, we can guard old sour puss's arse then turn to port, that's left to you Boss, and anchor up in a place called Elphinstone inlet.

It is plenty deep enough, I was there a couple of years ago on an exercise putting marines ashore. It is protected from this wind by high ground and the swells sweeping into the gulf from the ocean go straight past, it should be flat calm in there Boss. It might take a day or two, between us we should be able to not only patch Warwick up to make her sea worthy again, but get most of her systems up and running again.'

'If you think that is your best option Sam, then go for it. Good luck .'

'Thanks Boss.' replied the captain of the Kelly.

Paul turned to Taff, 'what did you make of all that?'

'He's a smart young officer Paul, that's why he's on a years detachment. I think he'll do well. I loved the 'that's left to you, Boss' comment. He'll fit in well,' chuckled Taff.

'No you twit!' replied Paul, 'that wasn't what I meant at all!'

'Now what did I miss?' asked Taff, sounding a bit puzzled.

'The battle group, why are they only doing fifteen knots? those bloody great carriers are normally doing thirty! By all accounts they are difficult to steer at low speeds, especially in a wind, and we know it's getting up to a near gale out there. You must admit it's a bit odd.'

Taff got up and headed for the kettle. 'May be he's waiting for Kelly and Warwick?'

'That is about as likely as me letting you make the coffees!' replied Paul with a grin, 'Sit down I'll be Mum'.

Paul returned to his comfy chair, he had just picked up the next folder on the stack, beneath which lurked his 'in' tray when Kelly called again.

'Yes Sam?' he acknowledged the call.

'There is something very odd going on Boss, we have just moved away from the coast of the Musandam Peninsula to stay well clear of the reefs. It's really odd Boss, the battle group are dead ahead of us, about ten miles away, they are going so slowly we are catching them up.'

Paul flicked another switch on the panel on his desk, this opened the video link to the Kelly. 'What the hell are they doing Sam?' Paul asked,

'Surely they are in the middle of the outward bound lane for shipping, I hope there isn't one of those super tankers outward bound right now.'

'We are alright on that score Boss. With Iran acting up they come through in groups with a couple of warships in company, just in case,' replied the Kelly's new skipper. 'Our ops room report at least three side scan sonar's are being operated close to the carrier, it seems as though they are all connected to a small escort close to the port side of the carrier. Our operator says they seem to be examining a particular small contact on the sea bed, he doesn't think they are looking for mi......'

'What the hell!?' exclaimed Paul, as the screen went white and the links broke, all he could get was static. He stabbed another button on the consol in front of him, 'AL, my office please, asap!'

'Yes, oh mighty master!' came back the voice of his old friend from REME days. 'Pushed the wrong button again have we?' chuckled Al.

'I don't think so, not this time,' replied Paul.

'On my way.'

'Any ideas?' asked Taff, every bit as puzzled as Paul.

'Several and none of them good!'

The door opened to reveal the substantial frame of Al. the electronics boss for the unit. 'What have you done now, you silly old fart?' he asked somewhat irreverently, well used to Paul having 'finger trouble' with buttons.

'It weren't me, honest Guv.' was Paul's almost apologetic reply.

'Move over, let the dog see the rabbit,' as Al slid a spare chair to a position were he could get at the control panel from. A series of 'grunts' and 'umms' issued from the big man.

'For once I think you are right, the only link which is down is from Kelly, I assume you were on the coms. video link at the time?'

'Yes, so?' replied Paul, 'But I didn't do anything, Young Sam, the new Skipper was telling me something about a side scan sonar, on one of the task force ships, then .... nothing.'

'Don't quote me on this Paul,' said Al, sounding worried, 'but I am fairly sure that was an EMP which has taken out communications, in fact,' Al continued ,'I'm almost certain.'

'A Nuke?' Paul and Taff said in unison.

'Looks like it,' replied Al, 'The Kelly is well screened against such things, that was either very big or damned close to have taken out her communications gear. We should be able to contact her if she's still afloat in a minute or so. It will take the computers on board a couple of minutes to reroute things around the fried circuits.'

As usual Al was right, the first signal was very crackly. 'Boss, Boss! do you read me?'

'I can hear you now Sam,' Paul replied with a sense of some relief. 'What the hell was that all about?'

'I don't really know Boss,' came the shaky reply. 'The task force has gone, vanished. We are scanning the area but all except one ship, which was about half way between us and the carrier have vanished. Our main radars are out, and our mast is bent backwards about ten degrees, Warwick is the same, the blast has bent her mast and taken out her bridge windows. We think it must have been a nuclear device of some kind, yet the radiation monitors are barely registering any increase over normal back ground levels.

We are clear of the reefs now Boss. Do I head for the last position of the battle group or continue to Elfinestone Inlet with Warwick.?'

'Warwick is your priority, any signs of life on the surviving ship of the battle group? has it changed course?'

'You are saying check for survivors on that ship first Boss? she's only about five miles away, and changing course, more or less towards us. We can't see a thing in that direction, it's like an orange fog! It was a lot brighter, it's fading noticeably now.'

'Alright, check her out, but do not risk Warwick and watch those radiation monitors.' The tone Paul used was as near as he ever got to giving an order.

'Warwick should be safe enough on her own as far as the inlet Boss, she is already out of the heaviest swells and will be in the shelter of the high ground very shortly.'

'You are the man on the spot Sam, use your judgement, just as a precaution hose your ship and Warwick down to shift any lingering radio active particles. I hate dealing with dangers I cannot see.'

'Will do boss, I'll call you back in a few minutes, out'.

The crews of the two British ships didn't need a lot of encouragement and set about hosing their vessels down with some enthusiasm, consequently both had several fire crews on deck when a very battered ship emerged from the thinning mists created by the explosion.

Which ever ship it was, now it was hardly recognisable as a once proud Ticonderoga class missile cruiser. All paint on forward facing surfaces had gone, right back to the scorched bare metal. The flat front of the forward missile silo was stove in, everything above the main bridge was either flattened or missing altogether. Several fires were burning on her decks to make things look even worse.

Both Warwick and Kelly had almost finished hosing their decks down so they swung onto a parallel course either side of the badly damaged ship and turned their fire hoses onto her, full blast. All attempts to contact the crew by radio had failed, but the sound of the propellers of the two ships could be heard below the decks, as could the cascades of water being sprayed onto the decks by the high pressure fire hoses. It wasn't long before a head popped up through a hatch, clad in flash gear and with breathing apparatus, it was almost alien in appearance. The head quickly ducked down again, only to reappear with an aldiss lamp, and began to signal Warwick in morse code. The message was simple, 'Danger, Radiation'.

One of Warwick's signallers, sent back, 'No Danger once washed down, follow The Kelly'.

An hour later the two damaged ships dropped anchor in the flat calm waters of the inlet, to take stock of the damage and repair what could be repaired. The identity of the American cruiser had been established as 'The Lake Erie' more by the golden anchor on her bow, now brighter than it had been since she was built , than by communication.

Kelly remained in the entrance to the inlet, maintaining her position with her thrusters rather than anchors, just in case of another attack.

On board Warwick top priority was given to the welding, now divers could get into the water safely it was a remarkably quick job to stop the crack by welding braces across it and drilling a hole in the plates just beyond the point of the rupture. While one team worked on the crack another team tidied up the jagged hole and after welding a couple of small braces in place tacked on new plates. Within two hours Warwick was water tight again, it was another two hours before the welding was complete. By mid morning the pumping out was also completed and the mobile pumps and some personnel were returning to the Kelly their job done.

Almost as soon as the waves had closed over what remained of the ships of the battle group, the search for the cause began. Strident voices in the U.S.A. began to call for an all out nuclear strike on Iran, who, according to the 'hawks' were responsible. Mercifully wiser councils prevailed, 'We will wait until we know for certain the exact cause of the detonation,' was the Presidents response.

In his impromptu address to the nation, shown live, coast to coast, he made it clear that until he knew, for absolute certainty he would not unleash his nations firepower in revenge. 'His instincts were', he continued, 'that as much as he detested the current Iranian regime, they were not capable of producing such a weapon as appeared to have been used, based on available information.'

Paul sat in his office watching the live feed, 'You know what Taff?' he observed, 'he definitely has guts, with everything else which is going on the easy way would be to tell his military to get on with it.'

'Do you think it was the Iranians?' asked Taff.

'Initially, I suppose, they were the obvious culprits, but it doesn't add up if you stop and think about it. The sheer power of the device for one thing, and the lack of radio active residue suggests something very advanced to me. I don't know a lot about nukes, don't want to either, nasty things, but we must have someone who does. What about some of our gremlins?'

'Damned if I know,' was Taff's reply, 'I suppose I had better find out, hadn't I.' The tired camp commander eased himself out of his chair, 'I'll be back in a bit.'

'I'd better update the P.M. No doubt there'll be 'questions in the house'. Better he gets the information from us than the hounds of the press,' said Paul stifling a yawn.

In the event Taff was gone for nearly an hour, Paul had long since finished his call to an extremely worried Prime Minister and had, rather surprisingly dozed off in his chair. Not so surprising was the fact he woke with a start as Taff returned with one of the 'Gremlins' who not only thought up a lot of the units hi-tech gear, but often actually made it in their mysterious world deep beneath the head quarters building.

'OOOWWW, shit!' Paul exclaimed as he tried to move, 'I must have dozed off!'

'Nothing like stating the obvious I suppose,' was Taff's un-sympathetic reply . 'This is Archie,' Taff introduced the long haired young man trailing behind him, 'It would appear he knows about nukes.'

'Oh good, if he can tell me where it can from and who made it, then I can go home and sleep for the rest of the week.' replied Paul.

'Given the information I should think that will be possible Sir,' the reply left Paul gob-smacked for a moment.

'Like how?' was the best he could manage.

'Every device has a very specific set of characteristics Sir,' replied the young man, 'If I could see the explosion and the fall out figures, blast radius, propagation rates then it should be possible to be specific Sir.'

Paul punched a few buttons on the terminal and a screen lit up. A couple more clicks on the control panel, once he found the buttons he was looking for and the digital recording from Kelly's bridge camera came up, in the bottom corner of the screen was a log of the radiation levels.

It was the first time Paul had seen the 'cleaned up' recording himself, he was horrified at the force of the blast. The units technical department had managed to retrieve the images from the system right up to the point were the electro magnetic pulse temporally knocked out the system.

'Oh my god,' muttered Paul, 'the poor bastards never stood a chance.'

The video was greatly slowed down, in the last image the huge carrier seemed to have been blasted clean out of the water and was already in at least two pieces.

'Bloody hell, what ever did that? Paul asked.

'Is it possible to speak to 'The Kelly' Sir,' asked the Gremlin, 'I believe that video was shot from her?'

'By all means, if you think it will help,' Paul flicked open the link.

'Hello Boss,' said Sam, the skipper, 'if you are after an up date, I can tell you Warwick is now watertight and about half of her systems are back on line. The only thing of ours not yet back up and running is our long range radar. Well it is working but it won't depress enough to be of any use, because of the angle of the mast, about all it can do right now is detect satellites passing overhead. Oh, and sadly one of those injured on Warwick has died of his wounds.'

'Thanks Sam, but that wasn't why I called, one of our 'Gremlins' would like a word, here, all yours.' Paul moved aside to let Archie take his seat. 'Don't get too comfortable in that chair, it's mine!!' Paul hobbled off to make the inevitable coffee. 'Want one?' Paul asked, meaning Archie, inevitably it was Taff who said 'Yes'.

'I know that, twit!, I meant our guest from the underworld!'

'Sorry Sir, what was that?' replied Archie.

'Would you like a coffee? and stop calling me Sir, My name is Paul, call me Boss if you like, but drop the Sir. Please.'

'Actually, I won't thank you Sir, Boss, I only ever drink bottled water.' replied the young scientist.

'That's okay Son, what ever yanks your crank,' replied Paul.

'Pardon, I don't understand.'

'It's alright, don't take any notice of him Archie,' said Taff, 'You wanted to speak to Kelly'.

'Oh yes, yes of course. I need some readings from some of your monitors, I'll just hook this up to a computer here, hang on a tick.' The young man typed furiously on a thing which looked like a 'game boy'. 'Alright, I'm ready now. There is a small yellow and black box in the top right hand corner at the front of the bridge. It is clearly marked do not touch, could you push the red button down firmly and count to three before you release it.'

'Forgive me for asking, it's just I'm a bit reluctant to push red buttons on strange boxes clearly marked do not touch!' replied the skipper, 'what exactly does this box do?'

'It records all the data from all of the monitors throughout the ship, when you push the button on my mark it will transmit that data to my computer. Ready?'

'Boss?' called a very unsure Sam, 'Is this alright?'

'Probably, best just do it Sam,' Paul replied.

'Ready?' asked the scientist, still blissfully unaware he was talking to the Captain of one of the most formidable ships afloat.

'Ready', was the reluctant reply.

'Mark! one ,two, three, and release,' the young man then added 'thank you, that's all I needed'

'Well?' enquired Paul.

'Oh, it's just as I thought.'

'What is?' Paul asked.

'The detonation was a very powerful nuclear device, and of the very latest type.' the Gremlin replied, as he got out of Paul chair and headed towards the door.

'We had figured out that much ourselves. How long before we get the results?' asked Paul, 'Like who designed the thing and where'.

'Oh, I know that now.'

Paul shook his head and took a deep breath, 'any chance of sharing that rather important information?'

'I thought you knew Sir.'

Taff, sensing Paul was about to blow up at the scientist spoke up, 'we will when you tell us.'

'Actually, it was me, right here, well in my lab.'

'You What!' exclaimed Paul, looking visibly shocked by the Gremlin's reply.

'It was about six months ago Sir, don't you remember, you signed off on the work for an American corporation. They were trying to design a new nuclear device for the open cast mining industry and major engineering projects. The point being there would be little, if any radiation risk from the fall out. They knew it should work but it didn't. One of their scientists had read my masters thesis on the potential energy yields from liquid cored hydrogen devices using isotopes of hydrogen eighty five and how to extend the life of this short lived isotope.'

'Carry on, even if I haven't got a clue what you are babbling about.'

'Well Sir, they sent me a load of data to analyse, it was so obvious what they were doing wrong, the remuneration was quite embarrassing, it only took about an hour to prove the theorem. I also designed a new trigger for the device as the one they were proposing to use was quite unsuitable.'

'Of course it was, so what went wrong?' asked Paul, as mystified as ever.

'It would appear they used their own compression trigger design, this in spite of my warnings that the unstable hydrogen isotopes would destabilise the detonators in their trigger charge. I made it very clear what was required was an electromagnetic containment field, all it required was a few hundred turns of thin copper wire and a couple of torch batteries, if they used the new lithium based ones they would safely last a year. I sent them the exact designs, they couldn't possibly have made a mistake.'

'It would seem someone did.' remarked Paul.

'I am absolutely certain the device was detonated by a compression trigger, the data from Kelly proves it beyond any doubt Sir.'

'Well thank you for your insight professor, I don't suppose you have copies of all this stuff down in the 'underworld ' by any chance?' Paul asked.

'Oh yes, every detail Sir, we never throw any research results away, you never know when they might prove useful.'

'One other point, before you go. What do you need to carry a device such as the one which destroyed that task force, a B52?' Paul asked, imagining such a device must be quite large.

'Oh no Sir, you could easily carry it, even with your bad back,' was the unexpected reply.

'So how big is this thing?' he asked.

The 'Gremlin' pointed at the bright red fire extinguisher near the door.

'Nearly as big as that'.

'That will be all for now Archie,' said Paul still not really grasping the magnitude of what had happened. 'Stay available, we might need you again, and thank you.

Shut the door!' Paul called after him as the young man left.

Paul turned to his old friend, 'No prizes for guessing who filed the patent on that one.'

'Not even a jelly baby,' quipped Taff.

CHAPTER SEVEN

The biggest questions remained unanswered, how did the device get there in the first place, never mind the why it was there. Paul left for his meeting with the Prime Minister and the chief of the defence staff, for once very unsure of the out come.

The current chief of the defence staff was an Admiral, very much 'old school' in the way he dealt with matters, he was also wary of the All Arms Unit. In his eyes they lacked the discipline he expected to be shown in the armed forces, he was new in the post and rather surprisingly had never met Paul before.

His greeting had been somewhat frosty, eyeing Paul, as usual clad in his faded fatigues, his badges of rank barely visible on the epaulettes with a degree of distain, 'We meet at last Colonel', but no extended hand of welcome.

'Good to meet you as well Sir' was Paul's reply.

'I have to say I'm not too happy about some of the reports I have seen on the way your unit operates Colonel, there is a cowboy element in the way you run things.'

'OH,' Paul began, 'I thought we normally do an okay job, given the conditions at the moment.'

'I was going to add, the Admiralty send their thanks on the rescue of HMS Warwick. Please extend the gratitude of their Lordships to the Captain and crew of the Kelly. You can add my personal thanks to the message, my own son is an officer on board Warwick and was among the injured. He is recovering, due I'm informed, in no small part to the efforts of some of your medical team from Kelly. Please inform me when Kelly returns to home waters so I might thank them personally.'

'Thank you Sir,' replied Paul to the unexpected plaudits.

'The other thing Colonel was the way the Kelly recklessly attacked such a large number of missile armed speed boats. It seems to me that it increased an already significant threat to unacceptable levels, did you authorise that attack?'

'I told the Skipper he had freedom of action, he was the man on the spot, and to act as he saw fit. No doubt the crew had a say in things, but they undeniably got it right. I know Kelly had a longer reach, but if she had simply sat back and waited then she would have faced a co-ordinated attack which almost certainly have had nasty consequences. Even with her firepower I think it is unlikely she would have downed all the missiles, attacking as she did totally disrupted the attack. The results speak for themselves Sir.'

The Admiral looked at his watch, 'Not like the P.M to be late'.

'I think he is making a rather difficult call to the White house Sir,' replied Paul. 'Talking of phone calls, have you spoken to your son yet?'

'I understand he is in Kelly's sick bay at the moment, I did try his mobile phone after the incident but it seems to be dead.' replied the senior Naval officer. In spite of his 'stiff upper lip' reserve, the underlying worry was etched in his features.

Paul unclipped his communicator from his web belt, he pushed a couple of buttons, 'Kelly?' he enquired. The duty operator seeing the callers name flash up immediately responded, 'Hello Boss, is every thing alright?'

'Well, if you mean has any thing else gone wrong, the answer is not as far as I know, but that could change. Can you patch this through to sick bay for me please, I have the father of that injured officer from Warwick with me. If possible he would like a word with his son.'

'No problem Boss,' the operator replied.

A new voice came on the communicator, 'Hello Boss, checking up on us?'

'Someone has to,' replied Paul. 'Is that Dereck?, Paul asked.

'It was the last time I looked, what can I do for you Boss'.

'The officer you brought over from Warwick, is he up to taking a call from his Dad'

'I should think it is just what he needs, he's doing very well, better than we could ever have hoped physically. He's a bit down, missing his mates. You do know who his farther is?'

'Oh yes, I'm with him at the moment waiting for the P.M. here I'll pass you over, let them have a chat. I'm nipping outside for a fag.' Paul handed the communicator to the Admiral, 'Just push the red button when you've finished Sir, and it's a radio, not a 'phone, so there's no need to worry about the bill.'

'Why thank you Colonel'. replied the man, 'thank you very much'. as Paul left for his inevitable cigarette.

Having wandered along Downing Street to the security gates, had a brief chat to the guards he returned to 'number ten' on entering he found the senior Admiral close to tears, 'Sir? is everything alright?' he asked.

'In some ways, yes, as my son will certainly pull through, thanks in no small measure to the prompt actions of your medics. The sad part of it is he is almost certain to be discharged from the Navy on medical grounds, and with the cut backs it is unlikely he will be able to get a job with the MOD, had this happened a year later then he would have been senior enough to have stood a chance. It wasn't just because I have been in the navy so long which made him choose a career at sea, he simply loves the technology of a modern fighting ship. It could break him having to leave the navy, but it is a risk in such a career, at least I still have my son, others are less fortunate.'

'There is always the possibility of joining our mob, as I understand it it's his legs which don't work, his brain is still working, and as my techs don't advocate kicking the various humming boxes they deal with, then the inability to kick them isn't really a factor'.

'I really don't know what to say Colonel,' replied the elderly Admiral.

'It's not up to us is it Sir, it depends on your son, and if that's what he wants. Aah our turn, this could be difficult.' as they were summoned into the Prime Ministers office.

The Prime Minister clearly was worried following his conversation with the President, it seemed as though the general feeling throughout the 'states was to 'nuke the bastards' as one congressman had put it.

'We have something of a dilemma gentlemen,' the harassed Prime Minister began. 'As you must be aware the general feeling both here and America is this was an act of war by what most of the world sees as a terrorist state, an act they should pay for. Then you come along and assert it was definitely a device made in the USA, in effect a monumental own goal. Both the President and I have our doubts, yet you seem absolutely certain of this.'

'I am certain Sir,' replied Paul.

'Very well,' the Prime Minister paused. 'If you are correct then two questions need answering, the first how on earth did it get there and secondly why was it there.'

'Why not ask the Pentagon Sir, clearly whoever was in overall charge of that battle group knew about it, and more or less where it was. We now know why the group was travelling so slowly. There was another ship in the group, in addition to the units they admit were lost, it was the USS Grapple, a deep sea recovery ship.

As far as I can tell she was on her way back to the 'states, but had put into Pearl Harbour so the crew could have a run ashore before returning to Norfolk naval yard for an extensive refit. It seems her crew were recalled from shore leave and she was ordered back to the Indian ocean, initially to Diego Garcia. This was changed and she rendezvoused with the fleet north west of the Maldives. The relevance of this is The Grapple only does about fifteen knots flat out, hence the slow speed. This speed got even slower shortly before the detonation. I think they were looking for the device, our ship, the Kelly was monitoring the sonar activity. The Grapple had deployed a third side scan sonar shortly after the group virtually stopped, they barely had steerage way against a strong tide, but with a following sea. We know they were 'interrogating' the contact with all three sonar's when it exploded.'

'The official explanation for their caution in going slowly was they were searching for mines Colonel, at least, that is what the President was told,' said the Prime Minister. 'It sounds reasonable to me, given the circumstances, but I take it you do not agree.'

'No Sir, I do not agree. They had three ships at the head of the group with mine hunting capabilities, none of them had their sweeps out, or their mine hunting sonar's on. They were there for one reason, and one only, to locate and retrieve that device. It must have been lost weeks ago, some time shortly before the Grapple was sent out of Pearl in such a hurry. Some one very high up knew about it Sir. The other thing is there is a long standing convention, which even the Russians adhered to during the cold war, if either side lost a nuke they would inform the other side of a 'broken arrow' and give a rough area for the mishap. Granted both tended to wait until they at least had located it or could screen the site from the others, but they always reported it. I can state with absolute certainty no such alert was issued about this.'

'I can confirm that Prime Minister, we have always been the first to be informed in the past, by both sides. I also agree with the Colonels assessment on the presence of 'The Grapple,' the Admiral added, 'which incidentally, technically is no longer a naval vessel, it is part of sea lift command, classed as an auxiliary.'

'Do you also agree with the Colonel about the origin of the device, Admiral?' the Prime minister asked.

'It is the most likely explanation Sir, I am certain of one thing, it wasn't the Iranians,' replied the chief of the defence staff. 'It was far too powerful, and the radiation levels way too low for the type of relatively crude device they might be capable of producing.'

The Prime minister took a deep breath, 'very well, if it was, as you say an American device, how did it get there?'

'A question for our Colonel's redoubtable unit to answer, maybe?' suggested the senior naval officer.

'And there was I thinking we just might be friends!' replied Paul, then almost as an after thought he added, 'what was that you said about the 'Grapple' not being navy Sir?'

'Well she's quite old Colonel, but still very capable, she was transferred to sea lift command a good many years ago, more than ten, anyway most of her crew are civilians but is under permanent contract to the US government. I don't see the relevance Colonel,' said the Admiral.

'I'm not sure I do either', replied Paul, 'but when you add it to what one of my 'gremlins' said when he identified the device, it may hold a clue to the problem. We, and everyone else have been talking about the device as though it was a bomb, military in origin and intent. This is not the case, it was developed as a mining explosive, for large scale open cast projects, the very low and rapidly degrading radiation levels confirm this, there is nothing else remotely like it so I am told. I'll bet someone at Langley knows something, or in the inner ring at the Pentagon. I think we can discount the American military, but it could well be a certain 'civilian defence contractor' we know, if he is involved then so is a section of the CIA, it is how government funds are channelled to some of his projects.'

'Are you seriously suggesting some one in the American 'black ops' world deliberately destroyed those ships and killed some six thousand sailors?' asked an incredulous Prime minister.

'No Sir, but I do think they are behind it's presence in the area. I have no idea specifically what their plans were, but clearly something went wrong about eight weeks or so ago. Hence the Grapple's marathon return to the area. I will do some research when I get home, something happened there, a plane crashed, or a small ship sank, it must have been small from the sonar readings. Leave it with me Sir, I'll see what we can find out.'

'Very well Colonel, sooner rather than later,' the Prime Minister said with feeling. 'As I said at the outset, The President is under huge pressure to retaliate, if he is forced to yield and go to war on Iran, we are bound by various treaties to support the Americans. In this instance it is neither desirable or frankly affordable for us, as despicable as I find the regime, another war in the region is undesirable as it would destabilize the entire region, and beyond.'

'Isn't there a U.N. security council vote on the matter tonight Sir?' asked the Admiral.

'Your point being?' asked the Prime Minister.

'What would happen if our Ambassador stood up and said we had evidence this was nothing to do with Iran, as despicable, was the word I think you used to describe them. As despicable as the regime is, we cannot support measures against, in this instance, an innocent party.'

'The Americans will never go along with that, we will be a lone voice against any action,' replied the Prime Minister, 'the consensus has never been so strong in favour of retaliation. Given the political situation in the middle east and the current economic plight, personally I would be delighted if a way could be found to defuse things, it would look good for Britain if we can prove we are right.'

'Why don't you call the President Sir, and inform him of your proposal of wait and see, explain why it could not have been Iran who made the device, see what he has to say, you might get a surprise,' suggested Paul.

'What happens if they don't agree?' asked the less than convinced Prime Minister.

'Then we are between the proverbial rock and a hard place, and there is nothing new about that Sir,' was Paul's reply.

The Prime Minister phoned the White House, Paul phoned his base, the P.M. got the President, Paul got B.J.

'Hello mate,' Paul began, ' I've got a bit of an important job to organise. I'd like Kenny to pick the best team available and check absolutely every thing which happened within ten miles of that detonation in the ten days before The Grapple left Pearl Harbour. Radio signals intercepted, any brushes with gun boats, merchant ships in the area, absolutely anything in that time window. The sooner the better please B.J.'

'Will do Paul, any idea what we're looking for?' asked Paul's deputy.

'Any thing which could have put that blasted device on the sea bed, probably by accident.'

'He'll love you Boss,' chuckled B.J. 'see you later, have a safe trip home.'

Paul heard the Prime Minister say, 'excellent, I'll be in touch.'

Turning to Paul and the defence Chief, 'you were right Colonel, The President has withdrawn the motion to launch retaliatory strikes against Iran. Officially this is to allow time for the actual individuals responsible to be identified, and a plan formulated to remove just those culpable.'

'If I might say so Prime Minister,' the Admiral began, 'the statement the President and your good self have just agreed is one of the most masterful pieces of ambiguity I have ever heard. It neither satisfies the hawks or alienates the doves. The only ones to fear it will be those responsible, whether by accident or design, absolutely brilliant. All we need now is for our Colonel here to produce the proof and we will all be able to sleep that much easier.' The Admiral allowed himself a flicker of a smile.

'Well thank you both for attending,' said the Prime Minister. 'If there is nothing else, I must prepare as I am due 'in the house' there are questions about what happened to HMS Warwick, I am indebted to you for your clear and concise reports gentle men.'

'There is one other snippet of information Sir, unsubstantiated but worrying if true. It would appear from reports unrest may be brewing in Pakistan. Indications are there is liable to be substantial unrest, aimed at ousting the current leadership. I stress, this is little more than rumour, but if true it could be disastrous for our troops in the Afghan theatre, not to mention British nationals. I think it would be prudent to have in place some sort of plan to deal with the civilian problem, should evacuation become necessary, not simply the physical problem, but the inevitable influx of militants and potential terrorists. In my view there is a considerable risk in this situation, especially as those posing a serious threat to us are likely to leave before anything actually kicks off. I'm not saying I have got it right Sir, merely to have something which can be quickly implemented should things pan out this way.'

'Very well Colonel, keep me appraised of any changes please.'

'Certainly Prime Minister.' replied Paul, as he gathered his papers into the slim brief case, the double lid of which concealed his powerful lap top computer.

As soon as they were out of the door of 'Number Ten' Paul lit the inevitable cigarette.

The Admiral turned to Paul, 'Do you think you were right in suggesting it could have been an 'own goal' all be it a spectacular one by the Americans?'

'Frankly Sir, I'm bloody certain, it's the sort of proof we will need that is going to be hard to come by. At a guess, and this is only a guess, I'd say it was one of these NGOs allied to the big defence contractors, who are behind it. As to how? your guess is as good as mine. The why is much easier to answer, pure bloody greed, with the passing of the five grand for a spanner era they are looking to swell their already bloated coffers. My theory is something along the lines of, 'we have got a President who wants these wars over and our boys home. At the same time, he will spend what it takes to reduce casualties, so we need to engineer threats which could require military intervention further down the line in order to keep spending on our products as high as we possibly can.'

'Call me cynical if you like Sir, but that is the way I see it. My unit is seen as a threat to this strategy as we would certainly find out who is behind any given incident.'

'I am aware of the on going row over the non delivery of your fuel. Lawyers for the company contracted to deliver it are threatening to sue the MOD if you bring in an alternative contractor.'

'Let'em,' was Paul's reply. 'They don't know it yet, but there is a train every other evening into our base, and will be until our tanks are full.

I can prove there was nothing at all wrong with the engine which allegedly broke down, it was immobilised by the crew, on the orders of the company. We can prove the company were lying about not having any other locomotives available. We know who destroyed the fuel train, and how they got the grenades which destroyed the train.

I'm sure you are aware of the saga of 'Air Force One' and it's back up, well guess what all these things have in common, they are all linked to the same conglomerate, it is so huge it makes micro soft look like a cottage industry.

I know who calls the shots, the difficulty is proving it, made harder as he must know we're onto his game. The latest trick is an insurance company is refusing to pay out for the blown up train, as you know, such things are handled by brokers, any guesses who owns the company they work for? and the insurance company it's self?'

'Good Lord!' exclaimed the senior military man. 'What will you do if it goes to court over the breach of contract?'

'It depends on the nationality of the legal eagles bringing the case to court. I have the power of arrest, if they are Brits, then assisting in an act of treason endangering the citizens of this country. should do nicely. If they are Yanks, arrest them on terrorism charges, if we think we can make it stick, take them to court, otherwise on the next plane states-side as undesirable aliens.'

'You can't do that Colonel, they'll appeal , the judges won't allow it.'

'The easy way is how we've always done it, stick them on a plane and not tell anyone we've done it. It works just fine, if they try to get back into the country, then they find passport control have them flagged as a security risk and refuse entry, it really is that easy Sir. The trick is to make sure you're right.'

'It seems as though your reputation is justified Colonel, you really don't suffer fools, gladly or otherwise do you?' The Admiral was quite shocked by Paul's uncompromising attitude after he had been so diplomatic within Number Ten, or had it been the same 'no compromise' under a different guise? The senior military chief decided this was probably the most dangerous man he had ever met!

'If anyone puts the citizens of this, or any other friendly nation at risk over something as simple and detestable as greed then as far as I'm concerned they are fair game. We have more than enough problems without some greedy bastard making more, just to line his own pockets.'

Paul turned to head towards Cannon Row police station, where he had left his car and driver, the Chief of Staff was about to turn the other way towards his office in the Admiralty when he paused and extended his hand.

'Good to have met you at last, I understand the defence staff often meet at your base. I am looking forward to seeing it. Thank you again for enabling me to speak to my boy, I appreciate it.'

'Good to meet you too Sir, I'll see you next week at the monthly raid on our drinks cabinet.'

'Until then Colonel, have a safe trip home.'

CHAPTER EIGHT.

Not surprisingly Paul slept for much of the trip home, he woke with a start as his driver hit the brakes hard to avoid a van which jumped the traffic lights in the middle of the little town near the units base.

'Sorry about that Boss, the dozy bastard must be colour blind.'

'Don't worry about it Ray,' replied Paul, 'you missed him, it's all that matters.'

'Home sweet home,' muttered the driver as he swung the car into the access road to the units main base. 'Frankly Boss I'll be glad to get a bit of sleep, I don't know why but the M11 always leaves me knackered, I used to blame the long concrete section but it is all tarmac now so it wasn't that.'

'I know what you mean,' replied Paul, 'drop me off outside H.Q please.'

For once he remembered to sign in, then he headed for the intelligence section in search of the wheelchair bound Kenny, the section commander. Kenny was one of the 'originals' who had been badly wounded many years ago in a hostage rescue which got very noisy. Although in a wheelchair most of the time he could still walk a few steps, against all medical predictions, as long as he had something to hold on to.

'Hi Kenny, any luck yet?' Paul asked optimistically.

'You must be joking Paul,' replied the tough old soldier. 'Have you any idea how many ships a day usually pass through those shipping lanes?' Kenny asked.

'I don't know mate, there must be a few, what with tankers and supply ships for the allied forces still in Iraq,' replied Paul innocently.

'Very funny,' replied Kenny, 'some days it is like the M25, and at least three days in the period you want us to look at it's like a Friday afternoon rush hour!'

'So you've got a few possible suspects to check then!' replied Paul with a grin.

'I'm not sure we're going to find anything useful Paul. If we had a plane overhead at the time then may be. What we are trying to do is build up a picture of any skirmishes with those speed boats, there can be as many as twenty reported incidents a day. From what you said to look for I suppose it means we ought to be looking for an incident in which one was sunk.'

'That would have been my first option,' replied Paul.

'It was ours as well, and we came up blank, we think!'

'Oh?' Paul sounded interested, 'What do you mean by you think?'

'Well there was an incident, about five hours before the Grapple left Pearl Harbour in such indecent haste, it seems as though a chopper had to pick up fifteen of her crew who got left behind and take them out to her. So it is safe to say there was a bit of a panic. The entire deployment is full of questions I can't answer as yet Paul.'

'Like what Kenny?' Paul asked.

Kenny paused for a moment, obviously arranging his thoughts. 'For a start, the short time lag, between the incident we think could be related and Grapple sailing. It takes serious clout to get anything moving in such a short space of time. Another thing, why the Grapple, one of her sister ships was in Norfolk Naval yard at the time and could have got there five days sooner, both have identical capabilities, so the way I am thinking is it must be something to do with who was on board rather than what, if you see what I mean Paul.'

'So far I'm following you, go on there is clearly something else bothering that devious brain of yours,' replied Paul.

'The incident we are interested in, it's self only received a passing mention, no-one reported it as harassment, never mind an attack, which is a bit odd.'

'What happened to raise your suspicions then?' Paul asked his old friend.

'Odd really,' Kenny began. 'A small boat was seen buzzing about in the wake of a supply ship bound for Kuwait main harbour, it was full of gear for some American troops who had just rotated into Iraq. The supply ship didn't make a report but a gun boat belonging to the UAE navy spotted it and fired a warning shot from it's three inch bow gun, from pretty well maximum range. I've got a rough translation of the captains report here and it says an explosion was seen near the suspect craft which shortly disappeared from our radar. It goes on to say this could simply be explained by the freighter coming between us an the suspect craft.'

'If the suspected craft was behind the freighter then how did it 'hide' behind the big ship, which I presume was doing nearly twenty knots.' asked Paul, 'was it a speed boat after all?'

'As usual there is a simple explanation,' said Kenny, 'I had asked the same question as the gun boat was on a parallel course to the freighter. The gun boat was one of three the UAE bought from Vosper -Thorneycroft last year, and they are seriously quick. The other thing was, at the time there was some talk it might have been a fishing boat they fired at and, not surprisingly it was covered up.'

'So, what's the theory?' Paul asked, more in hope than expectation, ' you must have one?'

'Oh, I've got plenty of what ifs! what I haven't got are facts!' replied Kenny.

'Can I do anything to help?' Paul asked.

'Darned if I know, I've asked for a list of crewmen on the Grapple, to see if there are any dodgy characters on the list,' Kenny sounded frustrated when he replied to Paul's enquiry.

'I take it from your tone the request was not well received?' said Paul.

'I got a list back, in a matter of minutes,' said Kenny, 'every navy man on board, name, rank, serial number, date of birth and blood group! Twenty six seamen of various ranks and trades out of a complement of one hundred and twenty seven plus two.'

'What the hell does that mean?' asked Paul, 'The twenty six sailors means a hundred and one civvies, even I can work that much out, but the plus two? Plus two what? Martians, CIA?'

'I have no idea Paul, I can't find out anything about the list of civvies from sea lift command, their security is better than Langley's. It's the same thing with the freighter we think could have had something to do with it. There are eight naval personnel on board, even though the role of three of them is officially classified, we were given their names and bumph without a fight. As far as the civilian crew are concerned I can't even tell you how many there are.'

'Sea lift command again?' Paul ventured.

'Spot on Paul.' replied the annoyed intelligence chief , 'I do how ever have one little gem which might lift the gloom Paul.'

'Go on, I could do with something, seeing as your abode is both a smoke and coffee free zone.'

'We have got several varieties of tea Boss.' replied Kenny , 'most of the crew drink Earl Gray or Assam Premium, with a twist of lemon.'

'Surely that would curdle the milk,' replied Paul.

'No Paul, they drink it b.... Oh gawd!' muttered Kenny, 'I don't believe I walked into that old favourite, how do you do that! be so bloody convincing!'

'Quite Kenneth, you were about to lift the gloom, I believe?'

'We had a couple of lads in Kuwait, loading some gear on a Navy auxiliary for return to the U.K . As luck had it the ship on the next berth was the freighter we were interested in. At my suggestion they nipped on board and had a chat with the skipper.'

'Crew List?' asked Paul, hope rising once more.

'No chance, however, it seems they did have a passenger for the trip. Kept himself to himself the entire voyage, he was seen on deck, about the time the small boat turned up, and was observed throwing something overboard. As soon as the ship docked he almost ran down the gang way and jumped into a big four by four with blacked out windows.'

'Oh great!,' Paul muttered.

'There's more,' Kenny sounded cheerful again.

'Right,' said Paul, 'We finish this in my office, I'm getting withdrawal symptoms for both of my addictions.'

'I'll be there in five minutes Paul, I need the bog and the one with yours and Taffs offices aren't wheelchair friendly!'

'Want me to wait?' Paul asked.

'You go and get your fix of nicotine, and a cup of coffee, you can make me one as well while you are at it, strong, black and one sugar please.'

'Have I been promoted to office tea boy at last, and no one told me?' was Paul's reply. 'See you in five.' Paul left with a grin. Working, or at least spending time with old friends was all that kept him from walking out of his stressful job, he'd got most of them into this in the first place years ago at the inception of the original unit. He saw it as his personal duty to protect each and every member of the tight knit unit as far as it was possible for him to do so. On a personal level, he had long ago accepted, if a bullet didn't get him, the stress would.

He settled into his chair, coffee in easy reach, beside his ash tray and began checking the multitude of messages. The door opened to reveal Claire, his faithful secretary holding the door open for Kenny in his wheel chair, complete with an unwieldy bunch of files wedged down beside him.

Just as the disabled major turned to thank Claire a man in a grey suit pushed past the startled secretary and headed for Paul.

'And you are?' enquired Paul, having resisted the reflex to draw his gun.

'I am an officer of the courts Colonel, and you will come with me to give evidence tomorrow morning in a serious breach of contract case brought by my clients. It appears you have acted unlawfully in breaking a lawful contract to deliver fuel to your base, and for blocking payments for work already carried out on your behalf by my clients.'

Paul eased himself out of his chair and walked round the end of his desk towards the man in the suit, who held out several sheets of paper, obviously in the hope of Paul taking them to read.

'Boss!,' said Kenny, sounding very concerned, 'don't hit him!'

The man in the suit heard what Kenny said, but showed little concern, why should he worry, he was six foot two, and worked out regularly in the gym. The wiry man in front of him was barely five foot ten, slightly built, was old enough to be his farther, had an obvious limp and smoked! No threat there.

Paul calmly took the papers from the mans hand, without looking at them tore them into four pieces and stuffed them into the mans shirt front, during all of this there wasn't as much as a flicker in the icy cold stare from the soldier.

'Get out of my office, and off this base, I don't know how you got on here in the first place. Go back to the over paid bewigged fools who pay you and tell them from me to shove it up their arses. The only people who broke anything were the idiots the civil servants employed to deliver our fuel, tell them to go to hell. Any attempt to interfere with our fuel deliveries, by any means, will be regarded as an act of sabotage to interfere with the defence of the realm, that is also known as treason. Now get out while you still can! Go.'

The duty clerk from the front desk suddenly rushed in, gun in hand, just as Claire was apologising for him slipping past her.

The clerk also apologised, 'he must have slipped past when I was helping the Major, he had dropped some files getting out of the lift. I thought the outside doors opened, but when I turned round I didn't see anything, so I thought I must have imagined it Sir.'

'Put it down to experience, take this piece of detritus with you and get security to escort him of this base. If he attempts to resist or re-enter the base,' Paul paused, 'shoot him.'

'You can't do that!' exclaimed the man, still seeming confident.

'Yes I can, very easily. I recommend you go before I yield to the temptation, now to use a colloquial expression, if Claire would please cover her ears, Fuck Off!'

'Very well, Colonel , what ever you are, I'll go, but I will be back tomorrow with a warrant and you will appear in court as required.'

'Go!' Paul almost shouted the command, this time the man withdrew to the doorway, escorted by the duty clerk, who still had his automatic pistol in his hand.

'I will be back.' the man reiterated.

'Don't bother.' muttered Paul under his breath. 'Now Kenny, you had some more on the happenings in the Gulf I believe.'

'Right, now where were we,' Kenny thought for a moment, 'Oh yes, our strange passenger on the freighter, who couldn't wait to get ashore. We traced the four by four which picked him up. You will not be surprised to hear it belongs to one of the largest suppliers of private body guards in the area. Now it gets interesting,' Kenny paused for effect. 'We know our subject of interest left Kuwait airport on a private jet, less than an hour after coming ashore. He was one of four passengers on the flight bound for a private air field near Dallas via Morocco, the Azores, and Bermuda.'

'A bit of a convoluted route,' observed Paul, 'do we know why?'

'Well, we know the official reason,' replied Kenny. 'The stop over in Morocco was at a service air strip supposedly for a huge construction site for a new dam project.'

'The real purpose being?' Paul asked.

Kenny shrugged, 'who knows what goes on at a facility with several C.I.A guys running things from the shadows.'

'Who wants to know?'

'Quite. Anyway, the plane was only on the ground a few minutes, next stop the Azores for fuel, on to Bermuda, it then was diverted to a 'secret' military facility in Arizona about a hundred miles from Vegas, then finally on to Dallas.'

'Apart from clocking up the air miles and making more stops than a number nine bus, do we know any thing else about the flight, or any of it's stops?

'Not a lot, the Arizona facility is, among other things, a missile testing site, coincidentally it is where they test stingers.'

'And matey, let me guess, nowhere to be seen.' suggested Paul.

'Oh he disembarked in Dallas alright, it was two of the other original passengers who were missing, although there were still four passengers.'

'Alright, I'll bite, what have I missed,' said Paul. 'I know the signs, little green men abducted the two who vanished?'

'Nope, we did!' replied Kenny with a grin. Over the years it had almost become a cult to keep 'the Boss' in a state of suspense over such gems, and Kenny was one of the best at it.

'Don't tell me it was the pair we picked up who fired that bloody missile,' exclaimed Paul. 'Then how the hell did they get here?' having received a gleeful nod from his old friend.

'Pass' was the reply.

'So, what have we learnt we didn't already know?, asked Paul. 'Is there any indication how the device got onto the freighter in the first place, indeed is there anything to suggest, never mind prove it was there in the first place?'

'Nope,' was all he got in the way of a reply.

'You're a lot of bloody help!' chuckled Paul, 'clearly from the files you have with you, you've got something else you think it's worth keeping me awake for.'

'A couple of juicy little tip bits, again nothing to help us much, at least not on their own.' said Kenny.

'But?' Paul asked, 'I can play that game too.'

'Fair enough,' laughed Kenny, wincing as he shifted awkwardly in his chair. 'I think I know where the stinger fired at the Presidents plane was modified, and how it got there.'

'Great,' replied Paul, 'but shouldn't that have been here, not there?'

'Let me explain, knowing your suspicions I made a call to Langley. It turns out a fleet logistics ship docked in Kuwait a day or so before our freighter, among all the assorted containers for various units was a small container bound for a compound near the northern most part of the border with Iran. Off the record the Director admitted they were his men based there, co-operating with Kurdish rebels in Iran. They have been plagued with over flights of reconnaissance drones from Iran, their stingers couldn't reach these spies in the sky, so they requested something better. In response Langley acquired ten of the latest prototypes direct from the makers. The trouble was only nine arrived.' Kenny picked up his coffee mug, 'You still make a decent cuppa Paul.'

'A bit bloody careless, losing a new missile.'

'Oh, it wasn't lost, or nicked, it was damaged in transit, allegedly.' replied Kenny.

Paul looked interested at least, then said, 'Am I to play guessing games,?' he asked.

'Go on' chided Kenny, 'you know you love it.'

'Right,' Paul began, 'let's just check the time line on all of this. The logistics ship, with the CIA missiles on it, docked the day before the Grapple went scuttling out of Pear Harbour. Also, earlier on the same day the Grapple sailed, the freighter was buzzed by a small craft which could have picked up something which might have been thrown off the freighter. A U.A.E. gun boat fired a single warning shot and the small boat vanishes, the incident was hushed up through fear it may have sunk a fishing boat.

On docking, our nameless individual who is thought to have dumped something over the side of the freighter, runs off the ship, jumps into a four by four and is out of the country on a corporate jet, within an hour of the ship docking.

Clearly you have established a tenuous link between who ever was in the four by four, the missing missile, allegedly damaged, and the people on the corporate jet. I'll take a wild guess and say there were traces of dust on the adhesives on the back of the false identification plate, if it was from Kuwait it would prove nothing, I'll take a stab at the dust, sand what ever was Moroccan and it probably got delivered to Milldenhall on one of those 'flights which never happen' for the C.I.A.

All of this, what three, may be four weeks before Air Force One ended up here.'

'Nice summary Paul, and everything is linked to this sprawling net work of companies. And so are all of these files,' Kenny added, dumping a thick hand full on Paul's desk. I think we can establish links to almost every country were there is, or has recently been unrest.'

'Are you trying to tell me this lot, who ever they might be, are deliberately stirring up trouble across the Med and middle east! I'm curious to know how, but I think I can guess why. The price of crude oil goes through the roof and because most of their interests are in the 'States, they coin it in without the additional risks or expense of extra security. Of course they had already got their linked security companies in place to take advantage of the 'crisis' and by over charging make another fortune. Where I'm short of ideas is how they engineered such wide spread unrest without anyone noticing.'

'It is so simple you'll kick yourself Paul,' chuckled Kenny.

'Probably less painful than kicking that sodding great dresser in our kitchen bare foot!' retorted Paul.

'Like I said it was simple, this group have interests in all of the affected countries, over a period of time they have either employed government supporters and paid them huge wages, by local standards, driving up commodity prices out of reach of the rest of the population. The opposite strategy is also employed by paying such low wages to the locals they can barely survive. Clever really, as where they pay low wages, it is made to appear the company ripping off the locals, is owned by someone from the ruling clique.

In Egypt it was very blatant corruption, massive back handers to get the contract to replace the old turbines on the Aswan high dam, and then brought in cheap immigrant labour to do the donkey work. The locals got nothing at all, the same sort of thing is going on all over the place and people are getting pissed off. Of course, there is another spin off, in as much as increased tensions require increased security and surveillance, it really is one hell of a scam.'

'I agree Kenny, but can we prove anything substantial was illegal, apart from the attempt at shooting down Air Force One and buggering us about with fuel. The rest is mainly guess work and deduction on our part and unethical and immoral business practice on their part, it might be illegal somewhere I suppose. So what do we do about it, what can we do for that matter. Then there's this blasted nuke, apart from being certain we know it's origins, we're only guessing as to how it got there, and we have no idea why it was there, not even a guess.'

'All very true unfortunately,' replied Kenny, 'If I were you I'd take a couple of vallium before you read the thickest of those files. It's a brief look at what the same group are up to in Pakistan, and you are not going to like it one little bit. If we're right, I think we might have a week, two at the most before it all goes pear shaped.'

'You really know how to cheer me up,' said Paul, 'any good news?'

'For once, oh great leader, I regret I cannot oblige,' replied Kenny.

'Twit!'

CHAPTER NINE

Kenny was getting himself sorted out to return to his department when, following a brief tapping on the office door, Taff rushed in, obviously in a state of considerable excitement.

'Guess what?' he asked.

'Judging from your unbounded delight, I'd say,' Paul paused, 'you've won the lottery?'

'Better than that!' replied Taff, 'much better than that!'

'Our fuel is now flowing without hindrance.'

'Not even close Paul, we've located them, our missing team aren't missing anymore!'

'Thank heavens for that, I take it from your demeanour they are all safe?' replied Paul.

'That's really good news Taff,' added Kenny, 'Tom and I have known each other for the best part of thirty years.'

'Obviously something had gone tits up for them to have been off the grid for so long,' observed Paul. 'Do we know what happened yet?' he asked.

'I know what we are being told is a load of bull shit,' replied Taff. 'According to the Iranians they were captured by their border guards trying to cross into Iran. We now know they were captured when they were on their way to a prearranged extraction by a Pakistan border force helicopter.'

'Don't tell me they are guests of the blasted revolutionary guard,' Paul sounded really worried.

'Now it gets strange,' said Taff. 'Our patrol was released on the orders of the Iranian President, as, and I quote, 'a gesture of good faith, in return for the units intervention in recommending the U.S. A. not to retaliate for the destruction of it's aircraft carrier.'

'Which begs the question how the merry hell did they know it was us counselling caution?' asked Paul. 'They seem remarkably well informed, very odd.'

'Oh it gets a lot odder yet,' Taff clearly had more information to share. 'As you no doubt know Tom's team was about fifteen miles from the Iranian border, their O.P. had a clear view for miles along the valley in both directions. The objective was to ambush a notorious drugs and arms smuggler, well, three weeks ago said nasty walks straight into the trap. Things got a bit noisy as such operations tend to, but job done, one very nasty individual and his even more unpleasant body guards eliminated.

We are blissfully unaware of all this as the satellite link goes down, allegedly due to a solar flare. Turns out they can still raise the Pakistani border force on their radio, and an extraction is arranged, but they have to cross about twenty five miles of pretty inhospitable terrain to the extraction point. I don't know if you are familiar with that part of the world Paul, but it is very hard going, if, like the team you have to go across the grain.

Tom, quite sensibly chose to wait so they would be crossing the worst terrain in the cool of the early morning. Now it gets even stranger, a strong patrol of Iranian border guards turn up, the commander spoke darned nearly perfect English and called Tom, by name, to come down from their O.P. The long and the short of it was the team were surrounded and had no practical alternative but to do as they were told. It seems as though they were treated more like heroes than captives, asked only to surrender their weapons, no attempt was made to even search them or their kit. They were asked a few questions, like how long had they been there, how were they going to be picked up etc. He says they were really well looked after. When the order came through to hand them over at the border crossing into Pakistan they were given their weapons back, unloaded, and driven as close as possible. It seems as though the Pakistani border guards were more aggressive than the Iranians had ever been. It is all very odd, whereas they had been relatively free to wander around the Iranians camp, they were virtually held prisoner by the Pakistanis. It wasn't until some General turned up they were released, it seems as though the presence of our guys hadn't even been reported to their own head quarters.'

'So what now?' asked Paul.

'B.J. is organising the Lear jet to go to Muscat to meet the Pakistan air force transport and bring them home. If he goes tonight he'll have time to check on some of our lads who are out there, as it will be a couple of days before Tom and his team are released by the Pakistanis. It seems as though they are holding some sort of inquiry as to what went wrong.'

'I think I might tag along for the ride Taff, it will give me a chance to get to see Kelly, and meet Sam. At least I'll see first hand the damage that blast inflicted.'

'If you say so Paul,' replied Taff. 'Personally I think it's to dodge those legal eagles.'

'Damn it,' retorted Paul, 'was it really so obvious, any way, the government has a whole posse of over paid legal eagles of their own, let them sort it out, it is after all their job!'

'You're not getting away with it that easily old Son,' replied Taff. 'You have conveniently overlooked the fact it is our turn to host the next meeting of the chiefs of staff.'

'Oh, rats!' exclaimed Paul, 'you're right, I'd totally forgotten. I swear I'm beginning to lose my marbles!'

Kenny coughed then with a laugh said, 'what's with the beginning bit, we all reckon you'd lost them years ago.'

'Oh cheers pal,' Paul turned to Taff, 'What did I ever do to deserve you lot?'

'Or you could look at it from our point of view,' Taff replied, 'what did we do to deserve you?'

'Bugger off back to your own hutches and find something useful to do,' chuckled Paul. 'Before you vanish Taff, any ideas on when the recons will be operational again?

'The last I heard, late tomorrow, if all goes well, and the first of the tankers a couple of days after that. It has been a bit of a blessing in disguise really having them grounded, it means for the first time in over a year the ground crews have caught up with the maintenance schedules and up dates. So as soon as they have finished replacing seals on the fuel systems we will be in pretty good shape.'

'Makes a pleasant change I suppose, having a bit of good news for once.' replied Paul.

'I'll leave you to get prepared for your staff meeting, apparently the new head of the joint chiefs is a bit of a stickler for protocol, so you'll have to be on your best behaviour.' said Taff with a chuckle.

'He's alright, I met him when I went to see the P.M.' was Paul's reply. 'You know his son was badly hurt when Warwick got hit, the poor young sod is going to end up like Kenny. He's in Kelly's sick bay at the moment, by all accounts it was only prompt action by one of Kelly's medics which saved his life.'

'That should have given us a few brownie points with the new boss then.'

'I've just had another bright idea Taff.' Paul sounded enthusiastic. 'The R.A.F. have been asked to lay on a cazy-vac flight to get as many of the more serious cases home as they can. The situation in the gulf being what it is they can't work out where to land, Bahrain has been placed off limits for the time being. Kelly can't really leave the Warwick and the yank cruiser for another couple of days, by then Intrepid will be in the area. I thought if the cazy-vac flight landed at Abu- Dhabi, one of them, probably Kelly, could take the casualties to meet the flight and a long range sea king could pick up Tom's team from Muscat, so they come home on the same flight. We could take some of the injured into our medical centre which is mercifully pretty empty at the moment and the Vickey 10 could then go to Birmingham airport with the rest..'

'Sounds good to me Paul, as long as you don't try to sneak off.' replied Taff.

'I can't, can I, I've got this blasted meeting,' replied Paul, 'some times I hate this job!'

'What's bugging you?' asked Taff. 'There is something out there that you want to see for yourself. I've known you for more years than either of us are prepared to admit to and I know the signs'.

'I don't know Taff, there is just this 'feeling' I need to get my idle arse out there. I can't explain it, but it just will not go away.'

'Alright, what have I missed, something you have noticed but no one else has?'

'Like I said, I don't bloody well know. It is driving me mad trying to work out what it is we have missed. I just know we have overlooked something which really matters.'

'How sure are you?' asked Taff, 'I've lost count of the number of times your 'gut' has averted a major disaster.'

'I'm bloody certain, absolutely positive, we have missed something which really matters.' replied Paul with a level of conviction rarely seen by Taff.

'I'll tell you what Paul, why don't I ask General Leach to chair the meeting instead. I know from past, bitter experience ignoring one of your feelings is not a recipe for success.' suggested Taff.

'Fair enough, I don't suppose anyone will be too happy, but other than to report our recons are nearly ready to start operating again I'll have nothing much to offer. It certainly sounds like a solution to me Taff.'

The old V.C.10 began it's curving decent into Abu Dhabi airport, B.J gave Paul a cautious prod with his boot.

'Oi, sleeping beauty, time to put your seat belt on.'

'Good heavens, are we there already!' exclaimed Paul.

'When we get home, you have got to get yourself checked out Boss. I know you'll tell me to stop fussing but you're worn out and it is beginning to show. That is the third time you've simply crashed out in the last week or so. The moment your head hits a pillow, zonk! you are out of it and you are constantly twitching, I'm no medic, but I'm telling you, that ain't good'

'Who needs to be married with you and Taff around to nag me?' replied Paul. 'I'll concede, you've got a point, but it is because I'm tired, not cracking up, I've been there before, and have no desire to repeat it, but your point is taken.'

'Fair enough Paul, here take a dekko at this,' B.J. was watching something below as the plane banked gently round .

'What's that you're looking at?' Paul asked his old friend, indicating his fastened seat belt.

'There's a destroyer, travelling at speed, straight as an arrow, looks really smart.'

After the briefest of formalities both headed for the harbour, it turned out the destroyer B.J. had been so impressed with was the old Manchester, hastily diverted from other duties. Her first task was the transfer of the most seriously wounded sailors from the Warwick to the harbour in Abu Dhabi for their flight home.

Paul would hitch a lift back on the Manchester to the Elphinstone inlet were the damaged ships were doing such repairs as were possible to either get them home or back on task. A sea king from Intrepid, still speeding across the Arabian sea stopped off to pick up B.J to take him to meet his recently released team when they landed in Muscat

The sheltered, normally quiet inlet was a hive of activity when Manchester arrived off the entrance, Paul transferred to her cutter and was ferried to The Kelly.

'You're looking a bit green Boss,' was his welcome as he stepped on board.

'Thank you for those few kind words Chiefy,' Paul answered the veteran navy man. 'where is the skipper, I sort of expected him to be here.'

'He's ashore Boss,' replied the old hand , 'he's supervising anchoring the guy wires, we've come up with an idea to straighten our main mast up. They are making the brackets in the machine shop, it should work, then we can put our main radar scanner back and we should be able to see what is happening again, instead of tracking passing satellites.'

Paul sat on the helipad on the stern smoking the inevitable cigarette talking to the long serving chief, who had been one of the originals from the first naval contingent to join the all arms unit.

'This has been the most eventful trip in all my years at sea Boss, and I get the feeling it's not over yet. The fact you're out here means something is brewing, so when we heard you were on your way we thought we'd better get everything up and running again.'

Paul had looked at the bent main mast, 'that must have been one hell of a blast Chief, was that the only damage to the structure?'

'To us, yes, but it took out Warwick's bridge windows and lifted the roof along with everything on it, she's also got a few slightly buckled plates, but I've seen worse damage caused by an Atlantic storm.

The boys have done a hell of a job patching up her hull, she's sea worthy now, but there is still work to do so she can defend herself again. It will help a lot when Intrepid arrives tomorrow morning, we'll soon be back in business with her help.

The Americans will be here in force as well by then, they have sent three of those sea knight helicopters on ahead. They have been busy ferrying their injured to Abu Dhabi for a flight home. I'll tell you Boss when that yank cruiser, the Lake Erie, came out of the orange cloud the nuke created, it was one of the scariest things I have ever seen.'

'I can imagine it must have been a bit of a mess Chief,' observed Paul.

'I doubt it Boss, there were fires all over her decks, and what was left of her upper works was well alight. You know both Warwick and Kelly turned their fire hoses on her.'

'Yes, I was actually watching on your bridge cam, damned fine job your lads did too,' replied Paul.

'What you won't know, and we didn't know at the time was those little fires all over her decks were the incinerating remains of over fifty of her crew. They had been on deck at the time, no flash gear nothing and the blast and heat simply disintegrated them, then we washed them away.' The Chief sounded really upset by the experience.

'Are you saying their crews were on deck in their shirt sleeves while they were passing through the straights so soon after your brush with the Iranians. That's bloody daft Chief, I'd have thought they would have been at action stations.'

'I'd have thought the same boss, we were, the Skipper saw to that, everyone had their anti flash gear on, even below decks. It wasn't very pleasant, but no-one got burnt, and judging by some blistered paint, if anyone had been in the open and unprotected they would have been injured, even at the distance we were from the explosion. The 'Boy done well' Boss.'

'Get me ashore please Chief, it's time I met young Sam.'

Paul noted the blistered varnish and paint on the little whaler which took him ashore, it was possible to tell exactly which surfaces had been facing the blast. His arrival sparked more interest from the locals than from those in the working party. Every one seemed concentrating on their tasks. Sledge hammers were being wielded with considerable enthusiasm as the men, assisted by locals, where knocking in heavy iron spikes in a definite pattern, in effect guying the guy pegs which should pull the mast back straight. As every one was in shorts it took him a minute or two to work out which one was Sam, the Skipper.

It was one of the longer serving members of the crew who was first to spot it was Paul walking along the beach towards them.

'Come to give us a hand Boss?' asked the sailor with all of the innocence he could muster.

'Looks like you're doing a fine job without my help,' replied Paul.

The young Skipper hurried off the rock he had been bashing a spike into, wiping his hands on his shorts before extending his hand in greeting.

Paul's comment caught him totally off guard, 'What's the idea bending my bloody ship Captain?'

Just for a few moments the young officer thought he was going to be in serious trouble, then he noticed the grin spreading across the unit commanders face, and inwardly heaved a sigh of relief.

Paul perched on a comfortable rock, sitting in the sun, of course with the inevitable cigarette, he listened intently as the Captain told him what had happened. The Officer then went on to explain the purpose of the spikes and network of ropes, and how he wanted everything in place, ready for the attempt to straighten the mast as soon as Intrepid arrived. It seemed as though engineers on the big ship, due in the morning, were making a vital pin in their much larger workshop. This, he explained to Paul would stabilise and support the mast, rotating it on this pin, as it was pulled back to it's correct angle and allow plates to be welded in position. If all went well, Kelly should be fully operational two days later, including her main search radar.

A young sailor approached, 'Excuse me Boss, Skipper, one of the outer guy pegs has cracked the rock, I'm not too happy with it. If, for any reason extra strain goes on it, it might not hold. I'd like to double guy it, just in case.'

Sam simply said, 'Fine, do it.'

'I'm impressed,' was Paul's response, 'you trust the judgement of your men, you'll do well in your time with us.'

'They are damned good at their jobs, no skipper could ask for better. The biggest lesson I have learnt in my short time with your unit is, you put the best man for any particular job in charge of a given task and let him get on with it, rank doesn't come into it.'

'Well I suppose that is the units strength,' replied Paul. 'Our detractors say it shows weak command, I think it is exactly the opposite. It has been my experience it is confirmation of a strong commander, one who has faith in his men to do their job.'

'If you don't mind me asking Boss, why are you out here?, I can understand wanting to show support for a unit, and I could see the point if you had been there to greet the team who had been missing. I get the feeling there's more to it than this, is there something we should know about?' asked the Captain, sounding worried.

Paul lit another cigarette, 'Frankly Sam, I haven't got a clue. I just know we have overlooked something, probably to do with that blast. I've no idea how the device got there in the first place. Several theories but little evidence. I thought it might have had something to do with a minor incident a few weeks back, a fishing dingy messing about near a freighter, something being thrown overboard. A U.E.A. gun boat fired a warning shot, which the skipper assures us missed by quite a bit, this is backed up by the crew of the freighter. Yet the dingy vanished shortly after, very strange. As is the fact the individual thought to have thrown something over board ran off the ship when it docked, and was picked up by some very unsavoury types and was on a private jet out of Kuwait in less than an hour.'

Sam looked hard at Paul for a moment, then said, 'was this five or six weeks ago?'

'About that, why do you ask ?' replied Paul.

'This might not have anything to do with it, but the locals are holding a couple of individuals they fished out of the straights. According to rumour they are a couple of Iranian fishermen who had been fishing illegally in Oman waters. The locals are waiting for them to be picked up, they see them as poachers and want them tried.'

'If you are right Sam, and these two were out of the dingy which seems to have sunk, then I think we should have a word. We might get lucky.'

One of the young locals approached, he obviously wanted to talk to Paul, and his English was pretty good.

'My father sends his respects, and asks you join him for tea.'

'I would be honoured,' Paul gestured for the young man to lead. Turning to the Skipper, 'I'll see you later Sam.'

'My father says you were one of the men who dropped from the skies many years ago and rid us of the Adoo.'

'Your farther is wise and has a good memory, that was long ago,' replied Paul, suddenly feeling his age as he thought back to the first time he got injured.

Paul was surprised how quickly he remembered the little things, like removing his boots. The old man sitting before him was blind now but he held out his hand in greeting, the grip was still firm and he slid his free hand inside the loose sleeve of Paul's shirt , feeling the scar on the bicep he smiled.

'This is the man who saved your life when you were three years old Ali.' said the old man. 'When the Adoo attacked you were on the beach, everyone ran, but you stood and cried, he ran out and got you to safety.'

'I did have the help of my friends and some of the villagers who had guns, Sulliman. It is good to see you again after all these years, life has not been so kind to you though.'

The old man waved his hand, 'It is true I can no longer see the birds to guide us, but I have food and my family. We are comfortable, not rich it is true but I have the things in life which matter, not being able to see is not so terrible. I can still see a little, I can tell night from day. You did not come to see an old man, you must be a commander to still be a soldier. It is not because of the damaged ships anchored in our bay. I think you want to speak to our prisoners. One may be an Iranian poacher, the other is not

Iranian, even though he says he is. There is evil in his heart, you can hear it in his voice.'

'I think you are a very wise man Sulliman, and your English is so good, much better than when we last met.'

The two chatted for over an hour about the old times, the youngsters fascinated that their village elder could speak so well in a foreign language.

Paul was no medic, but to him it seemed as though his old friend had cataracts , which were often cured by surgery.

'Would you agree to one of our doctors having a look at your eyes, I am not promising anything you understand. There is a small chance he may be able to help.'

'What is the price of this medicine?' asked the old head man, 'there is always a price.'

'For you my old friend, there will be no price, indeed, it is I who am in your debt, always so hospitable to one such as I who offers so little in return.'

'Very well, get your doctor, let him look, our own doctors say they can do nothing.'

Paul pulled out his communicator and called the Kelly.

'Patch me through to the medical officer please.'

He explained the problem to the medic, could anything be done?

'If you are right Boss then the answer is yes.'

'What are the odds Doc?' Paul asked.

'You know darned well I trained as an ophthalmic specialist, I lost count of the number of cataracts I have removed in my years with the U.N.'

'Well I've got another one to add to your list Doc, and this one really matters.'

'Alright, bring him aboard and I'll take a look.'

'How long will it take, including keeping an eye on him afterwards?' Paul asked.

'If you're right, bring him out now, a couple of nights in the sick bay, give him some drops to last about a week and the job should be right.'

Paul re-entered the little house.

'How would you like a trip out to our big ship Sulliman?' he asked.

'Can Ali come too. I need his eyes, and he is strong, should I stumble. I am old and not strong. Do you really think your doctor can make me see again, Ali has a daughter, I have never seen her.'

'Of course Ali can come, and if I am right then our doctor can help, remember it depends on if I am right.' replied Paul. 'Would you like to go by boat, or helicopter, it is up to you Sulliman.'

'The sea has been my life, we'll go by boat.'

Two days later there was one of the most emotional scenes Paul could remember. The bandages were removed and the old mans eyes gently sponged with saline until they opened in the dimly lit medical centre. Gradually his eyes opened and things began to appear as light entered for the first time in years. The first thing he saw clearly enough to recognise was a little girl with her index finger to her lips, in the universal 'ssshh' sign. Tears of joy flowed down the old mans cheeks as he realised it was his grand daughter.

The Doctor heaved a sigh of relief and said, 'Now I am going to spoil the party, I insist my patient has an hours rest before he leaves.' and promptly herded every one out of the medical centre. Some how he overlooked a little girl snuggled up beside her beloved Grand-dad.

That evening as Kelly was preparing to put to sea, her repairs complete, Paul took a small squad ashore, he left them with the whaler on the beach. The old head man came to meet him, obediently wearing his dark glasses.

The head man was sad Paul was leaving but knew it must be so.

'You have given me a priceless gift, you must have something in return, name it and it is yours.'

'No, Sulliman, I have my reward, seeing you with your grand daughter is reward enough.'

'You know you must be repaid, or I will die in your debt and you know enough of our beliefs to know what it will mean for me.'

'Very well, Sulliman, but all the village must agree to this request, or I cannot accept.'

'Very well, honour will be satisfied what ever the request. Name it.'

'Your two prisoners, I would like them. You know it could be months before the authorities arrive to collect them, and it will cost more to feed them than you will be paid as a reward.'

'And this will make you happy, and clear my debt to you?'

'It will make me very happy Sulliman, and it will clear your debt and then some. To clear my debt to you, I have an extra gift for you. Two barrels of fuel for your outboard motors, so you can fish whatever the wind and two barrels of the very best cooking oil for your wives to cook all the fish you will catch using you motors.'

To Paul's surprise the old man beckoned to someone in the village, and four of the young men led the two captives towards the boat and the waiting marines.

Paul pulled out his communicator and called Kelly. A couple of minutes later the Lynx helicopter lifted off with a cargo net containing the four barrels.

'I can now see much clearer Paul, but I do not need my eyes to see what is in a mans heart.'

'I wish I had your wisdom Sulliman.' replied Paul.

'You already have that gift Paul, what else could have brought you to this place again after so many years.'

'I must go, my old friend, and I hope you live to see many more grand children.'

Kelly moved swiftly past the Intrepid which now stood guard in the entrance to the sheltered inlet. Most of her Engineers and electricians were on board the Warwick, tomorrow they would try to straighten her mast in the same way as Kelly's had been repaired. The Lake Erie was tied up to a big repair ship detached from the Indian Ocean fleet along with a destroyer for protection.

'You've done a damned fine job out here Sam, not many experienced officers could have pulled that off.' said Paul.

'It couldn't have been done without the crew Paul, every one of them did their job superbly.'

'Yes, but you made the vital decisions, now I've got to do my job and find out what that pair of rat bags were doing swimming around in the middle of one of the worlds busiest shipping lanes.'

'They were the real reason for your visit I suppose,' said Sam, 'the reason you couldn't explain?'

'To tell you the truth, I still don't know, but the knot in my gut has gone. Time will tell, the leading regulators and a medic are getting them cleaned up then I'll have a little chat and find out who they are. If they really are a couple of Iranian poachers, then you can hand them over to the Oman navy who won't treat them too well. From what I've seen and heard of them so far, I agree with Sulliman. The bigger one ain't Iranian,' Paul said with some feeling. 'I'll send a picture of him back to H.Q. as soon as he's cleaned up, see if we can get an I.D. '

'You've got a fair idea who he is, haven't you?' Sam asked.

'Not really,' replied Paul, 'Just a feeling we have met somewhere before.'

To his considerable annoyance Paul didn't get round to having a chat with the two 'guests' during the short trip along the coast to Abu Dhabi. Fearless was on her way through the Suez canal to relieve Intrepid which was due to return home. Some one had taken a pot shot at her with an R.P.G and blown a hole two feet across just above the water line near her bows.

The new Egyptian government actually apologised for the incident, and had then turned round and complained to the U.N because Fearless had returned fire. The burst of fire from her port 'darlek' straight back down the missile's smoke trail had killed three 'civilians', what was left of one of the 'victims' was still holding the launcher and the other two had A.K 47s and two spare missiles each.

Paul called the skipper, 'Are you taking water?' he asked.

'Not at this speed in the canal, I was planning on stopping in the Bitter Lake to weld a patch on Boss.'

'Can't you weld one on the inside while you are still under way?'

'Yes, but that would only be a temporary fix.'

'Then do it,' Paul replied, 'You can join the rest of them in 'cripples creek' to do a more permanent job. The last thing I need is you stuck in the canal if the Egyptians get funny over the incident.'

'Fair enough Boss,' replied the Skipper, 'As long as you realise it will slow us down until it is fixed properly.'

'I realise that Skipper,' Paul replied, 'normally I would have agreed with you, but with things as they are, better safe than stuck.'

The rest of the trip he spent reading the mass of messages from all manner of sources, not that many of them contained anything he didn't already know. One thing which emerged, was the rapidly deteriorating situation in Pakistan. The overland route for supplies to the forces in Afghanistan via the Khyber pass was in effect closed. Even the logistics area in the docks had been attacked twice in one night, this in spite of assurances given by the government the area would be protected.

Paul took Sam aside before he disembarked, 'our old freighter should arrive about the same time as Fearless. Use the opportunity to get all three of our ships fully stocked and as many systems as possible serviced, I have a nasty feeling things are about to go 'tits up' in Pakistan. If this does happen then there are likely to be major evacuations to contend with. Have a chat with the skipper of Manchester, offer him any assistance he needs with any repairs, she's getting old and if I'm right, losing a unit could be serious. I understand Warwick should be nearly as good as new by the weekend, as long as one of ours is keeping watch, use the time to get as much done as you can.'

'Will do boss, enjoy your flight home,' replied the young Captain.

As there were only ten injured sailors on the flight, for once there was plenty of room in the V.C10 on this second evacuation flight, plus B.J. and the squad who had been listed as missing.

'Okay, I'll play,' was the greeting he got from B.J. as he boarded the plane. 'What have you been up to Paul?' noting the two guests were being guarded by four of the marine detachment from Intrepid who were long over due for leave.

'A long and convoluted tale old friend, one which can wait for now.' He turned to the four men with B.J. 'I look forward to reading your report Tom, I trust you are all fit and well?'

'Yes thanks Boss,' they replied in unison. 'We were a bit concerned when we couldn't contact anyone apart from the Pakistan border guards, but we're alright now thanks,' Tom added.

'Alright, I'll let B.J. do the debrief, good to have you back, you had us worried for a bit. I'll see you later, B.J.'. With that Paul turned and walked to the other end of the plane where the extra passengers sat contemplating their uncertain future.

Paul sat down, facing the two prisoners, he dropped a thin folder onto the table between him and the two uneasy looking captives.

'Right you pair,' he began, 'I know who you are, so please do not embarrass us all by trying to make me speak Farsi. You,' he indicated the smaller of the two men, 'are indeed Iranian, exiled as a subversive years ago, many of your family were killed by the republican guard. I need to know what you were doing, all I know is you were being paid by the C.I.A.

And you,' he looked at the other man , 'are an American citizen, a former green beret and a member of a delta force team, current status uncertain, but connections with Langley and a 'private' supplier of so called security personnel. How am I doing so far? according to my information your name is James Bowie!'

'I don't know where you got that load of crap from Colonel,' was the Americans response before Paul cut him off.

'Don't insult me by lying Captain. I know it was an explosive device you were supposed to pick up after it was thrown over board from the freighter. I need to know the intended target, and purely for my own satisfaction what went wrong?'

'What's in it for us if we tell you what we know?'

'Not a lot, it means I am less likely to shoot you, or hand you over to someone even more unpleasant than I am, I suppose it depends on your answer.'

'Do you think you'll find out any way Colonel?' asked the Iranian.

'No. I'm bloody certain I'll find out, it's just that I would prefer to hear it from you.' replied Paul.

It was the American who answered. 'Well, you were correct about us picking up an explosive device, it was thrown off the freighter, as you said. It had a floatation device to aid us picking it up, it wasn't very big, in fact it was disguised as a fire extinguisher. Well, we picked up the buoy alright and we were hauling up the rope when a gun boat fired at us. We didn't realise it was just a warning shot, we thought it had aimed at us, so we turned as quickly as we could. The rope fouled the propeller just as we hit the wake of the freighter and the boat capsized and sank. A fragment from the shell must have hit the buoy as it burst and the whole lot sank, leaving us in the water. The current carried us towards the coast of the Oman and some fishermen picked us up and held us prisoner until you turned up. The old headman stopped some of the others using us as shark bait, by saying we were worth more alive, as the authorities rewarded them for catching poachers.'

'He is a clever old sod, he had you weighed up from the very beginning, or as you would say from the 'get go'. Old Sulliman might have been blind but he knew you were lying about why you were there and what you were doing'. was Paul's reply. 'So what was your target for this act of sabotage? It must have been important to have taken such a risk. You would have been publicly hung if you had been caught.'

'Our target was Bushehr, it is supposed to be a power station, but there are two pressurised water reactors there. The plan was to use the waterway from the gulf to get to the plant and place our small device in the pump house which is outside the security fence. If we could knock out the main pump then there would be a real chance of the facility going critical. This, it was said would tip the balance and Iran could be taken out.'

'Instead you took out a carrier task group Captain,' Paul said, with a note of sarcasm in his voice.

'Don't be daft Colonel, the thing couldn't have weighed much more than twenty pounds!' exclaimed the American. 'I almost had it in my hands when things went wrong, it wasn't more than about two feet long and about ten inches wide. It was supposed to destroy just the inlet pipes.'

'You expect me to believe you didn't know it was a nuclear device?' asked Paul.

'No way Colonel, No way on this earth was that a nuke!' the American replied. Both prisoners were clearly shocked. 'It was so small, I don't believe you Colonel. You mean to tell me that little thing destroyed all those ships and their crews, tell me that it isn't so, my brother was on the Lake Erie, a cruiser attached to the battle group.'

'Now how would you know that, I suppose you spotted her when we took you out to the Kelly.'

'No Sir, I thought the Lake Erie had gone as well. The locals told us all of the ships in the group were sunk, we were surprised the Iranians could produce something as powerful as that. We felt the blast and saw the fire ball in the village.'

'Well it was your fire extinguisher bomb which destroyed the battle group, you think of the consequences of it blowing up in a nuclear power station.'

'Oh shit , you're not joking are you Sir?' replied the American.

'No Captain, I am not. You are either very good or have been used, which is it?'

'I suspect you are well aware I am a trained saboteur Colonel, every one in the 'black' world of deniable operations knows the reputation of your unit. You seem to be able to get any information you want, so you probably already know Inter-corps Security International asked the 'Firm' for me for this job. They said if I was successful it would stop Iran stirring up all this trouble, destabilising friendly states and the likes. I was told the investigation into the explosion would prove they had been lying all along about their nuclear industry, if what you say about our fire extinguisher is true then it makes a lot of sense. There is no way we would have survived such a blast.'

'Well, I'd take a guess and say you got that much right,' replied Paul.

'What happens to us when we land in the U.K. Colonel ?' asked the Iranian.

'To be honest I haven't got a damned clue, I suppose we'll have to look after you until we get to the bottom of all this. Until I can establish if you have told the truth we'll hold you at our base, you won't exactly be free to roam at will, but you won't be in a cell, and you won't be able to call anyone. The longer I can keep you 'dead', the safer you will be and the more likely I'll be able to establish the truth behind all this crap. I'm sorry for your nearest and dearest,' sighed Paul, 'but it is all part of the price you 'black ops' bodies have to pay.'

By the time the old V.C. 10 touched down at the base of the All Arms Unit it was dark and the two 'guests' could see little other than the lights scattered around various installations. The soldiers guarding them escorted the two men to a waiting Lynx helicopter. To the mild annoyance of the American he couldn't see anything of consequence out side, as he had been seated as far back as was possible, he suspected this was not pure chance. The only clue had been a glow in the sky away to the left of the far end of the runway, may be a small town, may be the main base, this lot were being very careful until they were sure about him.

'Hello B.J, have a good trip?' asked Taff, as the big man walked into the H.Q foyer.

'About as good as it could be, thanks. Tom and his team have headed for their bunks, I've got the preliminary report here, makes interesting reading. Talk about role reversals, it's all a bit confusing.'

'Where is Paul?' asked Taff, 'I thought he was on the flight?

'He's gone to 'The Farm', that is why the lynx was standing by when we landed.'

'Not like him to make the effort to get to a meeting he'd got out of?' replied Taff. 'I'm expecting a call from the steward any moment telling me the joint chiefs have emptied the drinks cabinet in the main briefing room.'

'I don't think him going to 'The Farm' has anything to do with the meeting, Taff' replied B.J. 'The sod hasn't let you know has he?'

'Know what! dare I ask?'

'You remember the dingy which he thought might have been trying to retrieve something thrown off a freighter a few of weeks before the nuke went off?' said B.J.

'What about it?' asked Taff sounding intrigued.

'He's only found the two blokes who were in it hasn't he'. was B.J.'s reply.

'What? not the two who's pictures he sent for I.D.'s? asked Taff.

'The same.'

'Just how did he happen to find them? He is the jammiest bugger around when it comes to turning up unlikely leads like this.' muttered Taff, 'come on. I think we have work to do.'

CHAPTER TEN

Paul went with the two 'guests' and their escorts to the accommodation the unit provided for such occasions.

'I'm sorry,' he began, 'but I am sure you understand why you will not be allowed the free run of the place, feel free to use the common room at the end of the corridor and the facilities there. One of the lads here will show you how to operate the menu pads to order your food, drinks are available twenty four- seven in the common room. I'll get the Q.M. to call in tomorrow morning to sort you out some clothes and other bits and pieces you may need. Your rooms are air conditioned so just set the dial to the temperature you require. Have a good nights sleep gentlemen, there will be an awful lot of questions to be answered in the next few days.'

With that Paul spun on his heel and headed for the lift, 'Good night Colonel,' the American called after him. Paul merely raised his hand in acknowledgement, his thoughts already on what he was going to say to the senior military men meeting several floors above him.

In spite of, or may be because of, the fact both men on guard on the door of the large briefing room knew Paul well, they asked to check his case. Paul flicked it open to reveal several thin folders and the base of the lap top built into the lid.

'Did you have a good trip Boss?' one of them asked.

'Not really,' Paul replied, 'I didn't get chance to go fishing, apart from the sand flies and sea sickness, then yes, the rest went alright.'

Paul swiped his card through the electronic lock on the door to the briefing room.

'Aah! the wanderer returns,' said General Leach, who was chairing the meeting in Paul's absence.

'I got back as quickly as I could Sir,' replied Paul. 'Sorry to interrupt the meeting, please carry on, I'll just get myself a drink.' he noted the bottle of his favourite whiskey was nearer empty than full.

Sitting down near the back of the room, he put his feet up on a chair, easing his aching back a little, the disapproving glare from an immaculate staff officer being deliberately ignored.

'Before we carry on with the agenda, maybe Paul would like to give us a quick up date on the happenings in the gulf area,' suggested General Leach.

Lowering his feet, Paul painfully stood up, 'certainly Boss.' The informality of his reply provoking another glare from the 'staffer' .

'Intrepid has joined Kelly which is now fully operational again, Fearless will be joining them shortly but will take a day or so to complete repairs following the R.P.G. hit in the Suez canal, I am advised apart from the hole in her hull there is little damage, I am also advised our supply ship should arrive with Fearless.

I can also inform the chiefs of staff the first of our reconnaissance aircraft are undergoing proving flights and should be fully operational again as soon as the tankers dedicated to them are ready again, probably the day after tomorrow.' He paused and took a sip from his glass of malt.

'As for the detonation which destroyed the American task force, I can now say with absolute certainty it was not the Iranians, in fact they were to have been the target for the device. Specifically the Bushehr nuclear power station was the intended target.'

'You know this how Colonel?' asked the disdainful staff officer.

'Simple Brigadier,' replied Paul, 'I have the two men who were supposed to plant it in secure accommodation. I still need the names of the people who issued the order and it is still unclear precisely how it got there from America. The other thing we need to establish is who ordered the task force to retrieve the device, as this is precisely what they appeared to be attempting when it detonated.

Finally,' Paul paused and took another sip of his drink, 'some really good news, our missing squad are by now tucked up in their own beds, safe and sound.'

'Thank you for the up dates Paul,' replied General Leach, 'I look forward to your report on how you located the two would be bombers with some interest.'

Paul resumed his previous pose to the obvious disapproval of the immaculate brigadier.

'It is my bloody chair, and if I want to put my feet up then I will, O.K? I've just had a three thousand mile flight and my back is playing up, more than a little. So I think I am entitled to get as comfortable as possible Sir'. Paul almost snapped at the man.

'I think you could at least show a bit more courtesy Colonel,' replied the man, clearly annoyed. 'Combats and desert boots are hardly the correct attire for such an occasion.'

'Tough.'

'Gentlemen please,' commanded General Leach.

'Sorry Boss,' Paul responded, 'I know it's no excuse, but you know I get tetchy when my back is playing up.'

The elderly General grunted a non committal reply.

The Admiral who was currently the senior officer turned to Paul, 'Any update on the situation in Pakistan?, I recall you were quite concerned about it.'

'I am even more concerned now Sir.' replied Paul. 'To the extent I think we should put in place contingency plans on how to get all of our troops, and those of our allies out of the Afghan theatre, with as much of their equipment as is possible should Pakistan become closed to us. Also what if the Suez canal becomes blocked. it would only take a couple of ships to be sunk in the wrong place and our supply lines for heavy stuff would be shut.'

'That is ridiculous Colonel,' said the officer Paul had disagreed with earlier.

'Why is it ridiculous, Brigadier,' Paul asked. 'The Khyber pass has been shut to military traffic for several days, and don't think Fearless will be the only ship attacked in the canal, there will surely be others. As for Pakistan, I will be surprised if they still have the same government next week, also, there is no guarantee of continuing safe passage through the various unpronounceable 'stans to stage on Turkey. Turkey, at least Asiatic Turkey is becoming increasingly unstable. My personal opinion, for what it is worth is now would be a good time to haul arse out of there. Work out what heavy kit we really cannot leave behind and start getting it out asap. Every flight outward bound, as of now should carry only essential food and fuel, and every home ward bound flight should bring expensive hi-tech kit out.

All ground units should 'twin' with an Afghan army unit, where it hasn't already been set up. The idea being the twinned unit could then operate the kit left behind.'

'Not a pleasant scenario Colonel' observed the senior Army officer present. 'I've known you long enough now to take notice of such suggestions.'

The Admiral looked worried, 'Are you suggesting I should inform the Prime Minister there is the possibility our troops might become cut off in the near future?' he asked. 'We depend on the overland route through Pakistan for the bulk of our supplies, things could get rather difficult if this line was cut for any length of time.'

'You might want to add the fact that the Suez canal is likely to be blocked as well, Sir. As things stand, the Americans think the only viable route out is going to be to the north.' Paul added. 'The other thing which needs looking at is the entire supply chain Sir, there are so many screw ups with supplies for the conventional forces it is getting silly. Things are getting totally out of kilter, the overall plan is for no more than twenty per cent of non urgent supplies should go by air. Things are so bad I am informed this has risen to nearly eighty per cent because the M.o.D. procurement program is in such a mess they even have to wait for ammunition to be manufactured to fulfil orders for frontline units who are running low. Even basic supplies, such as filters for engines are left to the last minute and thus become urgent, the extra costs involved runs into millions, never mind wearing out aircraft!'

The immaculate staff officer rounded on Paul, 'Who do you think you are Colonel?' he snapped at Paul, 'You have no idea how hard the personnel in my department work to provide the supplies for our frontline troops. Our mission, in my department is to ensure the timely arrival of what ever our boys need to complete their dangerous mission.'

General Leach winced fearing one of Paul outbursts.

Paul looked at the General who was the current head of the army, 'I can think of two possible postings for our Brigadier Sir, one being the armies forward logistics compound in Sangin or the dole office.'

Before the furious officer could reply, the Admiral, who was the current chief of the defence staff intervened, 'The Colonel makes a valid point, the matter of procurement and delivery for all the armed forces is under review. There are likely to be wide ranging changes. It is a fact, as the armed forces have contracted the numbers of civil servants in the M. O. D. has increased substantially, as has the cost of equipment and the delays in supplying that equipment. Put simply the department is not fit for purpose.'

Paul's communicator began to bleep urgently, as he reached for it, the chastened Brigadier commented loudly, 'Mobile phones are not allowed in these meetings Colonel.'

Paul ignored the man to General Leaches relief, this relief quickly turned to concern when he saw the expression change on Paul's face.

'Gentlemen,' he began, 'I rather think the time for planning a contingency withdrawal strategy has passed.'

'Might I enquire what has happened?' asked General Leach.

'I was speculating about Suez,' replied Paul, 'it is no longer speculation. The canal is blocked, three ships have been sunk at various choke points. They certainly picked their targets, a gas tanker, a chemical tanker, both loaded, and worst of all an ammunition ship, chartered by the Americans, loaded with over eight thousand tonnes of assorted ordinance, and is slewed across the channel . Both tankers it seems are also cross ways on and resting on the bottom.'

'That's put a spanner in the works Paul,' observed General Leach.

'Oh, it gets better Boss, there has been a failed coup attempt in Egypt.'

'That is not good news, it is bound to create unrest,' said the Admiral.

'There also appears to be an ongoing attempt to overthrow the Government in Pakistan. Those involved, according to this message are a good deal more sympathetic to the Taliban than the current incumbents.'

'That could make life difficult Paul.' General Leach sighed.

'Personally Boss, I'd say we are screwed. Once we figure out how to do it, I suggest we call the operation to get our troops out 'Operation Haul Arse'!'

'Are you suggesting we begin withdrawing our troops without reference to our political masters, Colonel. We cannot do things like that, it is not allowed.'

Paul turned to the immaculate Brigadier who had just spoken.

'What I am saying we had better get our arses into gear and figure a way to extract not only our troops from the Afghan theatre but those of our smaller allies. If, as seems likely Pakistan goes tits up, or at least a large part of it goes 'off limits' then would you mind telling me exactly how we get all our service men and their equipment home?'

'Air lift of course Colonel,' replied the office waller.

'Who let this idiot in here?' asked Paul.

'For your information Colonel, I am also head of the army legal services. It is my brief to ensure all contracts with suppliers are legally binding and also all decisions reached at meetings such as this are legal. I am also used to being addressed as Sir buy lower ranks, I suggest you conform on all counts Colonel.'

'Have you finished, or just pausing for breath?' asked Paul. 'Now I have some advice for you, shut up! speak only when spoken to. Little boys should be seen and not heard.'

To the consternation of the 'new boy' no-one spoke in his defence.

'As you will discover Brigadier,' Paul continued, 'we deal with the brutal reality of warfare at these meetings, as opposed to the cosy world of theory and endless haverings on the technicalities of the English language to extract some perceived advantage. Our problem is to work out a practical way of extracting an army, our army! as well as other service personnel and a mass of civvies from a potential disaster.'

'I have already told you the solution Colonel, an airlift,' the man was unbowed.

'What with? and to where?' Paul asked.

'R.A.F. transport command of course, and into Lyneham.'

'And you think a half a dozen C17s and about twenty hercs can do it? Fully loaded the distance of the round trip is too great, where do you suggest they refuel? You do know the southern part of Turkey is now an Islamic republic? I'm not saying it was a popular uprising, but the nutters have control and will do what they can to disrupt things.

We can't go butting in there, the legal government, in the north, have enough on their hands without helping us. If we staged through Turkey it would only add fuel to the militants claims the old regime is anti Islam, which it patently isn't.'

Paul paused for a drink, before continuing.

'It would take months to get all our gear out, at least the stuff we can't afford to leave behind. There is also the question of fuel to consider, you are supposed to be logistics, explain to me how we can air lift our lot out. Out of effective range fully loaded, the need to service already overworked airframes and engines, never mind the fuel. Getting the men out is do-able, by simply chartering a fleet of jumbos, after a concerted effort to ferry in sufficient fuel. But that would leave all the vehicles and equipment behind, including most of the helicopters.'

'It is quite a problem Paul,' replied the Chief of Staff, 'any thoughts? You are the usual source of original ideas according to the 'old hands' around here.'

'If speed becomes an issue, maybe a relatively short air lift into Georgia, then by sea. But there are problems with that, in as much as it necessitates using the Bosforus, there are also hostile shores on the south of the Med.

All of our ships are stuck south of the canal, as I believe are over half of the navy's logistics fleet, as well as at least six major units. Which ever way we bring them out it is almost certain to get noisy.'

'Are you saying we will suffer casualties however we do it?' asked one officer.

'I can't see any totally secure route Sir.' replied Paul. 'At least two of our tankers were shot at when we pulled them out when the fuel supply became critical a while back. There wasn't any damage, but it was a wake up call.'

'See if you can come up with a plan Paul, one which gets all the stuff which matters out and poses the lowest risk to our troops.'

'Very well Sir,' Paul replied to the Admiral. 'Before I go Sir, have you seen your son yet?'

'I haven't had the opportunity yet Colonel, I understand he is still enroute to the U.K.. I presume he will be flown into Birmingham airport.' replied the Chief of the defence staff.

'Actually Sir, he is two floors below us, I'm told he is doing well, I'm sure a visit will do his moral no harm at all. You may stay as long as you like, a room will be made available if you would like one.'

'I really don't know what to say Colonel,' the senior officer paused. 'Thank you seems somewhat inadequate, when did my son arrive?'

'He was on the same flight I came back on Sir, the medics should have him settled by now. Now if you gentlemen will excuse me, I'm afraid I must have some sleep. I'll start work on a plan to get our troops out in the morning, for me to try to do anything in the state I'm in would be a recipe for disaster.'

'What time will you be in your office Colonel?' asked the Admiral. 'If it is possible, I'd like to drop in for a chat before I return to London.'

'Any time after nine will be fine Sir, we can provide transport if need be.'

'Nine it is then, and thank you again for bringing my son home.'

'You're welcome Sir, good night gentlemen.'

General Leach followed Paul out of the meeting, offering his apologies and saying he would be back shortly.

He called after Paul, just as the Colonel reached the lift, Paul leaned against the door, holding it for his Boss.

'Need some fresh air Boss?' he asked.

'That too,' replied the elderly General. 'What I really wanted was your opinion on the wider situation, just how bad is it, and how bad do you think it is likely to get?'

'Off the record Sir?'

'Off the record,' the man affirmed.

'Pretty dire, one mistake and it will become a total disaster. No matter what we do, even if everything goes perfectly oil prices will go through the roof, with all that implies. From the military stand point, if we get things wrong, we'll be lucky to get half of our troops out, never mind those of our lesser allies. I'll know more in the morning Boss, it might take a little while to get a handle on what is happening. The night shift are gathering as much information as they can. I'll see you in the morning Sir'.

'I know you're tired out Paul, but I really would like a little chat, just to get a feel for the potential problems we are likely to face.'

'Alright boss, the old common room is likely to be empty, and it has a kettle and coffee', replied Paul.

The two senior officers settled into the comfortable old arm chairs, 'What do we do now the Suez canal is blocked Paul?' asked the General. 'With all the upheavals in Pakistan, it is by no means certain we'll be able to get out overland to use their ports. As I see it our only options are an air lift and the heavy stuff overland through the former Soviet republics, with all the problems that would entail'.

'Other than for non combat troops, the airlift is a non starter boss, we simply haven't got the cargo carrying capacity.' replied Paul. 'The greatest single problem is fuel, we should know our requirements in the morning. Some how we are going to have to get enough in place, and secured, before we even start to withdraw.'

The elderly General looked worried. 'I saw some figures from the M.O.D. the other day and they were suggesting it would take up to four months just to get the fuel in place for an airlift to get just our service personel out. The suggestion was made that all advanced technology weapons would have to be destroyed and the remainder handed over to the Afghan government.'

'So we end up with an army equipped with rifles, hand guns and dependant on clapped out trucks for transport, sound familiar?' replied Paul. 'One thing is for certain we can't afford to re-equip our armed forces for the foreseeable future.'

'So you are saying a way has to be found to get at least our modern fighting vehicles out. Can you do it?' asked General Leach.

'We haven't really got a choice have we Boss, never mind the financial

side of things, morale will be non-existant if all the gear is just blown up
or handed over.'

'I see your point Paul' the General put on his thoughtful expression.
'Might I enquire as to how you plan to achieve this?'

'Find the line of least resistance I suppose' , replied Paul. 'There is
another thing to consider Boss', the Colonel continued.

'What might that be?'

'As you are very well aware Boss, I get to hear about a lot of things I
shouldn't really get to know about.'

'Such as? In this instance,' asked the General.

'Think back a week or so, the strange deployments of the Iranian forces.
We couldn't make any sense of it at all, could we?'

'From that comment I presume you now know why?'

'Well, Yes.' replied Paul, 'What I was just saying about the line of least
resistance. This idea required an incursion into Iran, following the only
good road out of Afghanistan down to a small but capable port in Parkistan
near the Iranian border. The problem being for about four hundred miles
this road is inside Iran. It would seem from intercepts our American cousins
had already thought of this possibility and some how the Iranians have
become aware of the plan'

'Good Lord!' exclaimed the General.

'I don't think he had much to do with it Boss', replied Paul. 'The plan
was thought up by the military, and until Suez was blocked, offered the best
chance of getting the bulk of NATO equipment out'

'So you are saying Suez was blocked to thwart this plan., presumeably
by Iranian backed terrorists.' suggested General Leach.

'That is the obvious conclusion Boss,' replied Paul. 'But, if you stop and
think about it, you might well come to a different conclusion. Would you
pick a fight with the yanks? At least a straight conventional head to head?'

'Well, no', replied General Leach, 'but then I'm not daft enough to try,
even if it was my stated intention to destroy them.

'Well, the Iranians know as well as you and I, with four carriers in the
area in addition to land based assets, by dawn on the first day they would
be lucky to have anything other than a kite to fly and nothing effective in
the way of ground forces. I think they were tipped off to deter the American
military from attempting this route. However who ever tipped them off has
no understanding at all of the middle eastern mind. It is my opinion those
forces were deployed so it would appear to an outsider they would attack

any NATO convoys attempting to use that route. In reality they are there to appear to their own people they are screening most of their country from the invading western hordes, and the reluctance of the NATO forces to engage will be portrayed as weakness on our part.'

General Leach interrupted, 'When in reality they have agreed to allow passage of the convoys, assuming of course this was what the Americans were planning.'

'That's not an assumption Boss, like I said, sometimes I see and hear things I'm not supposed to', replied Paul.

'I don't understand all this Paul, why would the Americans be planning such a risky move?'

'They are in exactly the same situation as we are, more so if anything, despite their assertions to the contrary they are more strapped for cash than we are. If they were forced to make a rapid and total pull out to save the massive costs they are incurring, how would you do it, if it were up to you?' Paul asked. 'You would try to get your expensive kit out, so you still had real muscle if you needed it .'

'Absolutely.' replied General Leach, 'You implied the Iranians were tipped off, but were, unofficially prepared to allow it to happen. I still can't follow your train of thought Paul.'

'Why tip them off? replied Paul . 'At best it would take two weeks for them to get their kit into a position to interfere with a withdrawl. Their airforce would be powerless against the American fighters. I know where the tip off came from Boss, think for a moment, who, in the States, would gain from an emergency air lift which left most of the hardware behind? The amount of fuel would be horrendous, and the cost of replacing the most important equipment would be greater than the total cost of all of our military assets. It would also, without a doubt ensure a change of administration.'

'You are saying it is the same people behind most of our problems, a sort of super cartel?' asked the worried General.

'I know exactly who they are boss, between them they control oil, military hardware, civilian aircraft production, health care even large scale food production and distribution, not to mention the majority of utilities in the states. The same thing is beginning to happen in Russia, both want to control Europe as well as their own patches. The question is what the hell can we do about it?'

'Can any thing be done?' asked General Leach.

'Let me put it this way Boss, come hell or high water I'm getting our lads home. I don't care who gets in our way, they will not stop us, I will deploy all our technology to achieve our objectives.'

'You'll have to be careful Paul, for once in your life you will have to get political consent. What had you in mind?' asked the General.

'Exactly what I was just telling you Boss, the overland route, including the incursion into Iran, then back through Suez.'

'But the canal is blocked Paul.'

'The idea is we un-block it!'

'How do you propose to do that!, the latest information I have is the canal zone is firmly in the control of militants. The new government in Egypt seem powerless to do anything about it.'

'I can't see any alternative Boss, it would take too long via 'The cape' route, the cost of shipping would bankrupt the country. It is over five thousand miles longer than using the Suez canal, nearly double the distance. We are bound to have casualties getting out, there is already a back log of wounded awaiting evacuation. Never mind the problems getting fuel, most of the R.A.Fs. transports are over due for servicing. The last I heard nearly half are grounded awaiting vital spares, if we pool resources we should be able to pull the wounded and sick out by air, as well as most of the non-combat troops and the ladies. I know they won't like it, tough, the pull out over land is not going to be a drive in the park, having females in uniform is so against the culture in that area it will only inflame things more.'

'When were you planning on starting all this Paul?'

'Tomorrow if possible Boss, yesterday would have been better, but like you said, we've got to get the go ahead from our political masters first.' replied the weary Colonel. 'Now, if you will excuse me Sir, I really must get some kip.'

'You go ahead M'boy, I'll see you tomorrow before I return to London.' replied the ageing General. 'Oh, before I forget, you've done a good job getting the new head of the joint chiefs on side, I was a bit worried you two wouldn't hit it off. You go and get some sleep, I have a feeling tomorrow is likely to be a busy day.'

'Good night Sir'.

The General took his time, savouring the brandy, noting Paul had left most of his own drink. 'Waste not, want not' he muttered to himself as he poured the remainder of Paul's unfinished drink into his own glass.

CHAPTER ELEVEN

In spite of being so tired, sleep refused to come, in the end Paul gave up trying to get comfortable and headed for his office, if he was awake, he might as well do something useful.

'Morning Boss, world war three started?' was the greeting he received from the guard on the gate.

'Not yet', replied Paul, 'give it until dinner time, the answer might be different.'

By the time the Admiral and General Leach called in on their way back to London, Paul and his staff had the outline of a workable plan, the senior officers thought it would be a good idea if Paul came with them, 'to sound out opinions' as the Admiral put it.

By lunch time the basic plan had been approved, 'in principle' as the Chancellor described it.

'I will need provable figures Colonel. I take it you are not intending this to be funded from the M.O.D budget.'

'Let's put it this way Sir,' Paul began his reply. 'I'm not too bothered where the money comes from, but we get those troops home come hell or high water. The only relevant cost will be measured in lives lost.'

The Secretary of State for Defence leant forward in his seat, 'I fail to understand why we can't use the same route as the Americans appear to be preparing Colonel.'

'I was unaware they were preparing anything specific Sir. I am of course aware of the increase in air traffic in and out of theatre, as I am aware of their announced 'draw down'. I also know they have chartered a lot of rolling stock to shift their heavy kit out over land, the destination for these trains is, I believe Frankfurt. In my opinion this is somewhat impractical, as it will take months, is fraught with risk from all manner of militant groups and not least by the state of the eastern European railways.

'I can't understand why we can't use the route around The Cape of Good Hope Colonel?' asked an official.

' We might have to yet,' replied Paul. 'But it will need ships and fuel we haven't got. If however you can find the ships east of Suez, and the fuel to run them without the world and his wife realising what we are up to, then I can't object to using that route.'

'It must be easier than fighting your way through the Canal Colonel'. added the Prime minister.

'In many ways it might well be Sir, but it will still require a major deployment into the Med. Sir. The air lift requires secure bases to stage through and as fuel dumps. As we cannot rely on the current bases in Turkey, effectively the northern route is no longer an option.

Those planes will have to come out via Pakistani air space to bases in the Oman then onto Cyprus, Malta, Gibraltar then home. Even using French airspace can't be guarenteed, with all the trouble they have right now, us over flying could make matters worse.'

'Do you really believe the French Government is going to fall Colonel?' asked the shocked Foreign Secretary.

'I'd say the question is when rather than if Sir. We have already seen most of the countries bordering The Med descend into anarchy or be taken over by militants. Frankly I don't see the French being any more successful than Italy, Greece or Spain at stopping the rot.'

'So why take the risk of forcing passage through the Canal?' asked a minister.

'Speed Sir, we'll need those forces here as soon as we can get them home, do not assume we are immune to similar attempts to destroy our way of life. What ever we do it is inevitable there will be fundamental changes, we really have to get our forces home, and quickly'.

Paul left the meeting totally exasperated, the advice of the military was, as had often been the case, ignored.

The bulk of the forces would follow the original plan, overland into a western port in Pakistan, but the route would be via the Khyber pass, not the route which encroached into Iran. They would load onto ships in the small port of Omara.

Sitting in his office the following morning, Paul tried to work out the practicalities of the so called plan for rapid withdrawl, drawn up by the civil servants.

Timothy Pilgrim

He had temporally abandoned his efforts to make sense of the figures supplied by M.O.D. civil servants on the fuel requirements and was watching the pictures from the first sortie from a reconnaissance Canberra since the lack of fuel supplies had grounded them weeks ago.

This one had refuelled in Cyprus and would be based in Kandahar for the time being, one way or another enough fuel had been acquired for about ten full length sorties with enough left to get it back to Cyprus.

The door opened to reveal not only Taff, who was expected, but General Leach and the Admiral, neither of whom where expected until that evening

'What's this?' Paul asked, 'A dawn raid on my coffee supplies?'

It was General Leach who replied, 'We met Taff at breakfast, so we cadged a lift. I was going to show the Admiral around, then we discovered you were already in, so here we are.'

'Might I enquire what you're looking at?' asked the Admiral, as he peered over Paul's shoulder.

'Real time images from one of our recon. Canberras Sir. He is on his way to Kandahar, it has been very illuminating so far.'

'Illuminating in what way ?' the new chief of staff asked.

'I don't suppose you know much about the Iranians deploying their forces to the eastern area a couple of weeks ago, but they are still sitting there, digging in, in the positions they deployed to. There is every indication those positions are medium term defensive deployments, no sign even of reconnaissance patrols being mounted.'

'Ignoring for the moment your grounds for spying on Iran, might I ask the significance of this lack of movement?'

'I'll explain in a bit Sir, the principle area of interest is now in range of the sensors on the 'blue bird'. Paul tapped some keys on the terminal on his desk. The new picture showed a winding road through spectacular, if barren scenery.

'The famous Khyber Pass, in HD,3D from about 80 miles away'. Paul announced. He tapped a few more keys and a large screen mounted on the wall came to life.

Together the men watched the unfolding panorama.

'I can see why you're not to keen on that route Colonel', observed the naval officer, 'Even to my untrained eye it has ambush writ large at every twist and turn.'

Then before their eyes there was a substantial flash, the shock wave clearly visible on the high tec screen. Before it became obscured by the growing dust cloud, an avalanche of rocks could be seen crushing the railway tracks and tumbling into the small river below.

Before they had time to comprehend exactly what had happened, there was a repeat performance a couple of miles further along the pass, this time at it's narrowest point. This explosion brought down nearly half a mile of cliff face, blocking the narrow gorge with over a hundred feet of rock debris.

'I guess someone doesn't want us to use that route anymore', observed Taff.

'I haven't seen any reports suggesting the Taliban had so much explosive available Colonel.' said the shocked Admiral.

'That's because they haven't', was Paul's reply.

'Then how....?' Taffs question tailed off as he too noticed the stream of figures on the bottom of the screen.

Paul prodded a button on his desk console, 'Is Archie from the under world in today?' he asked.

'I'll check Boss, hang on a tick,' the officers could hear the clicking of keys in the back ground, then the duty operator came back, 'he's actually in his lab now Boss.'

'Good, get him up to my office asap.'

'Will do boss' came the reply.

'Am I thinking the same as you Paul?' asked a concerned sounding Taff, 'You're thinking it was more of those mini nukes aren't you?'

'It has all the signs mate, the only reason we didn't lose the image is the extra screening and the range.'

Paul stabbed another button, 'Chris, was that a nuke?'

Almost immediately a voice distorted by a bit of static came back. 'Looks as though it could have been, we thought it was you checking our scans, it must be early morning on base, what happened, your missus kick you out for snoring?'

'It wasn't my fault you drew the short straw mate', replied Paul with a chuckle.

'You might want to extend your view about ten clicks north, there was another blast there, simultaneous with the ones you were watching, the pass is cut in three places. From what we can see any one of the sites would take weeks to clear and repair, by then the monsoons will have reached the Hindu Kush and that babbling little stream will be a raging torrent'.

'Give me some good news,' Paul almost pleaded.

'Radiation is surprisingly low.' replied the airman, 'definitely higher than it was, at the rate it is decaying it will be safe in an hour.'

There was a gentle knock on the door of Paul's office, 'Come', he called.

The visitor was indeed Archie, the young man seemed nervous in the presence of four senior officers, 'What can I help with Sir?' he asked.

'We've just had some explosions in a very inconvenient location, we think we know what they were, but I'd like your opinion,' he added 'please', almost as an after thought.

Paul re-ran the pictures high lighting the data stream. 'Well?' he asked.

'You think those explosions were more of the new nuclear canisters don't you Sir?' the young scientist sounded worried.

'Are they?' Paul asked.

'Most definitely Sir, and with the same unstable triggers as the previous explosion, I am absolutely certain of it.' was the reply.

'Any indication of what triggered them?' Taff asked more in hope than expectation.

Archie motioned towards Paul's terminal, 'May I?'

Paul struggled out of his seat, 'don't get too comfortable'.

General Leach guessed Paul was going to make the coffees, so noticing Paul's difficulties even moving he offered to be 'mum'.

'Thanks Boss, I tweaked my blasted back again, would you believe putting my socks on!'

'If I might say so Colonel, should you be at work?' asked the Admiral.

'Oh, it'll wear off Sir, it usually does. In case you hadn't noticed most of the old hands about here are crocked to a greater or lesser extent, it goes with the job I'm afraid.' replied Paul.

To reinforce the point, there was another knock on the door which announced the arrival of the wheelchair bound intelligence chief, Kenny.

'What brings you in at this early hour?' Paul asked.

Before he got an answer Archie let out a groan 'Oh no!, please not that!'

'Not what, might I ask?' was Paul's response.

'I know exactly what triggered those bombs boss, it is the remote explosives detector. The moment Steven, the systems operator, switched it on, the device exploded, it seems as though our detector set up a sympathetic resonance in the detonators.'

'The ones you told the Americans not to use?'

'Yes,' the young man replied.

'I might as well go back to bed then,' said Kenny. 'It seems as though you have already found out what I was going to tell you'.

'Which was?' asked Paul.

'Our friends at Langley have dispatched a team to Afghanistan to recover, and I quote, 'unauthorised ordinance' in the possession of N.G.Os operating on behalf of a security contractor.

Paul turned to the long haired youth, 'Archie, get your team together and try to come up with something we can use to detect explosives without detonating those bloody mini nukes.'

'It's not the nuclear part our sensors set off Boss, it is the explosive compression triggers we are setting off, just as the Americans side scan sonar's did in the straights of Hormuz', replied the young scientist.

'What ever, just figure out something which works without blowing everything up', replied Paul.

'I take it you want it today Boss?'

'Yesterday would have been better,' muttered Paul. 'Go on, get back to your toys Einstein.'

'If that's all Boss?' replied the young man.

'Go! If there is any thing you need, just ask, now get out of here!'

'I'll let you know as soon as we have anything boss', said the scientist as he left.

'Shut the bloody door!' Paul called after Archie.

The tousled head reappeared briefly, 'Sorry boss'.

'Was that wise Colonel?' asked the Admiral, 'discussing such things in front of civilians, young ones at that'.

'If you had any idea of what that slightly eccentric young man designs, even builds for us you wouldn't have asked Sir, what he and his even odder friends don't know about physics isn't worth knowing.' was Paul's reply.

'What do I do about this CIA intercept Paul?' asked Kenny.

'Verify it, and find out, anyway you have to, exactly how many there were, how they got there and who issued the order as well as who told them too. I want the meddling bastard behind all this totally stitched up. Our two guests might be able to shed some light on the supply route and who does the hiring.

Get Al to help you, somewhere there is an electronic file about it all, find it, copy it and give it to me, no one else, then if there is any comeback it will come on me not Taff or General Leach, clear?'

'Did I just hear you order one of your senior commanders to hack into computers Colonel?' asked the shocked Admiral.

'You didn't hear anything Sir, did you?' replied Paul.

'I'm not sure what you meant by that Colonel, I am quite certain you just issued an illegal order'.

'Before you get all upset Sir,' Paul interrupted, 'consider this, we are faced with what amounts to a modern day Dunkirk, granted the numbers are significantly less but the distance is much greater. Some money grabbing bastard is out to stop us, or at least make it as expensive as possible in terms of fuel and equipment loss. The same sod stands to gain out of our misfortune, never mind we're already strapped for cash, as is his own country, he, and his cronies don't care, all they want is more money and more power. Well, it ain't gonna happen if I can help it, in my book this lot are as dangerous as any insurgents, more so in many ways.'

'How do you know all this Colonel, and who are 'they'. asked the Admiral.

'They', are a consortium of mainly American so called businessmen, combined, their power is probably greater than their governments. In simple terms they manipulate events to drive trade their way, what ever it takes to get a contract which they can make millions out of. They don't care who gets hurt, as long as they get another shed load of money, it is simply greed gone mad. I know many of the players, what I don't know is who is pulling the strings, yet.' he added the yet with some feeling.

'And if you ever do find out?' asked the Chief of Staff.

'Not if Sir, when', replied Paul, 'then we shut him down'.

CHAPTER TWELVE

The following few days descended into total chaos, most of southern Europe was swept by what could only be described as anarchy. The politicians finally gave up any pretence of having any control, many fled the chaos admitting their dream of a federal states of Europe was just that, a dream. The Euro became worthless, almost overnight, triggering all manner of further problems, suddenly the developed world was bankrupt, seemingly incapable of finding any solution to the problems.

Britain somehow escaped the worst of the immediate trouble, the states bordering the Baltic also managed a degree of success at maintaining a sense of normality, how ever tenuous. It came as a total surprise when even Germany, so long the power house of Europe looked to the U.K. for leadership.

Parliament had been recalled from it's Easter recess and the decision was taken to hold an all party conference, including county and metropolitan borough representatives to try to find a workable solution to see out the crisis and avoid the fate of so much of Europe. The venue chosen was the N.E.C., with it's excellent transport links and vast capacity it was the logical choice.

The senior military commanders had travelled to Birmingham on the train with the Prime Minister and a handful of the inner cabinet to brief them on the plans to get NATO forces home from Afghanistan. It took several hours meeting in closed session for agreement to be reached and the military men left to go about their business.

As for the conference, emergency measures were agreed, after a fashion, but would reconvene in one months time, to assess how things were going. Measures were agreed to ensure everyone should at least have the basic needs to carry on some semblance of normal every day life.

Another meeting was arranged, this time for the leaders and top military commanders of the countries with significant forces in Afghanistan. It was probably one of the most secretive meetings of the modern era, and for good reason as one of the matters on the agenda was how to ensure there was no interference from the 'cartel' .

A concord was dispatched from the All Arms Unit's base to collect the Canadian and American delegations while a second speed bird took the European representatives. A giant tanker loaded with fuel had already left for the 'secret' meeting to refuel the concords for their return trips.

Lajes Field had played host to President Bush [jnr.] but never to as many V.I.Ps as this in one go. The Base commander, a Portuguese officer, berated his American counter part for not warning him of the arrivals. The first hint had been when an unidentified aircraft asked for permission to land, this caused some confusion as the only radar contacts in the immediate area were two local planes, neither of which qualified for the 'speed bird' call sign.

A mere two minutes from touch down the sophisticated radars finally detected the unexpected arrival as it lowered it's nose and under carriage.

An American captain was in charge of the control tower at the time and was scanning the lightening dawn sky with his binoculars. 'My god', he uttered, 'it's a concord!!'

The control tower team had just about recovered their wits when another call came over the radio, 'This is R.A.F flight 36 heavy requesting permission to land and instructions'.

This caused yet more consternation as this aircraft also seemed invisible to the radars, a situation made worse when the mystery plane emerged from the early morning haze to be revealed as a massive Tri-Star tanker.

By now the control tower team had been alerted to the impending arrival of a second Concord, which appeared right on cue and parked beside the tanker.

The general consensus around the now sealed air base was this meeting probably indicated the start of world war three!.

For reasons never satisfactorily explained it later emerged the only person on base prepared for the V.I.P. influx was the duty head chef! By some miracle he had breakfast ready for all the delegates when they trooped into his canteen, or as he put it, 'upgraded to a dining room for the occasion.'

Considering the gravity of the discussions the meeting was remarkably short, barely an hour and a half, even the Americans raised few objections to the plan once the alternatives had been discounted for various reasons.

Paul managed to have a quiet, private word with the President, during the conversation he outlined what had been happening with the 'cartel', and how they tried to manipulate events world wide for their personal gain. He confided to the President that he knew the Khyber pass had been blocked by three of the new high blast, low radiation canister devices, and how he knew. He also informed the President that the C.I.A director had personally ordered a team to the area to recover the devices when he became aware of them.

'I am horrified by what you have told me Colonel, not least by the way you found out, I can however understand why, but I don't think I'll ever understand the how'.

'Now, even more than before, I am sure you understand the need for secrecy Mr President. We are already getting the fuel and other supplies in place and are already moving troops to their supporting positions. We are taking great care over the deployments, the intention is, should anyone notice, that we intend to intervene in Syria and Asiatic Turkey.'

'When in reality you will be deploying to secure the northern sector of the Suez Canal.'

'Exactly, we can, if every thing goes to plan, do it.' replied the tired Colonel.

'And if things go wrong?' asked the worried President.

'Things will only go wrong Sir if the cartel find out what we're up to. Insurgents we can deal with, the Egyptians will help us, of that I am absolutely certain. It is in their interests for the Canal to be open as much as it is in ours.'

'The entire scenario is scary to a non-military man like me Colonel, but once they got over the shock my team seem to agree with you, this 'Plan B' seems to offer the best solution, and if it works will certainly be the cheapest. When do you intend to start the offensive in Afghanistan? '

'We already have, we now have nine of our reconnaissance planes operating in theatre, and both our AWACS supported by tankers. Ground liaison teams are guiding forces onto insurgents as well as detonating roadside bombs detected by our Canberras. NATO units have begun to leapfrog each other in a steady westwards movement and the first air force units have begun to leave.

West of Kandahar troops are securing the roads leading north as though a retreat into Uzbekistan is planned and British troops along with American

Timothy Pilgrim

Marines are working towards the Pakistan border, in particular the Khyber Pass. Which will take months to clear and rebuild the road, even for light traffic.'

'I just hope your deception works Colonel,' replied the worried President.

'Oh, it will work well enough Sir, as long as the Cartel don't find out what we're really up to. The C.I.A have agreed to 'lose' and shut down the satellites which cover the area, in return for us beaming them coverage of the bits we want them to see.'

'In the knowledge that what ever you send them will be seen by some segment of the 'cartel?' The President allowed a flicker of a smile, 'I like your style Colonel. You are aware I have ordered an F.B.I. investigation into what has been going on, the missile fired at Air Force One, the carnage in the straights of Hormuz etc?'

'Oh yes Sir, and I like the B.S. press releases about a couple of the incidents, we're actually working with one special team, who we are certain have no links with the 'cartel', any way, it's time we were going Sir, before someone starts to ask questions and twigs we're all here.'

Paul lifted his coffee cup, 'to plan B, it's too early in the morning even for me to reach for anything stronger.'

The building seemed to shake to it's very foundations as a heavy aircraft took off, this was the Tri-Star, destination Gibraltar from where it would support the build up of forces headed to the eastern Med.

The delegates said their farewells and boarded their aircraft for the flights home, the westbound plane leaving first, as it had an extra thousand or so miles to travel.

General Leach was sitting beside Paul as their plane climbed out of the now quiet Lajes Field air base, a pair of F16s circled further along the coast of Terciera island having rapidly given up any pretence of escorting their President.

'Why are you looking so sad Paul ', he asked, 'I thought it all went very well'.

'You are aware that the Azores are renowned for the biggest Blue Marlin in the world, and this is the height of the season?' Paul replied. 'You won't be able to see them from your seat Boss, but there are at least three big game boats down there, headed out to the fishing grounds, I would give my eye teeth to be on any one of them'.

'You haven't got any teeth, eye or otherwise Paul! I happen to know all of yours are false!' the General chuckled at his own reply.

'I'd still rather be down there Boss. Given the option, fishing, even for tiddlers, would win, the way I'm feeling just now'.

'Is all of this beginning to get to you m'boy?' asked the elderly General, sounding concerned.

'I wouldn't say it's beginning Boss', replied Paul, 'It is getting to me, big time! Terrorists I can handle, even rogue states led by nutters, I know how to cope with that. This is totally different, many of those involved are some of the most influential people from our most powerful ally, there are even indications a couple of them are Brits.! They certainly have people in places of power and influence within the government. Even if we can prove they have manipulated things to their own advantage what can be done?'

'I see your point Paul, I suppose fraud or embezzlement charges could be brought against them.'

'What then? You know as well as I do the 'old boy' network is as strong as ever, granted it is more discreet than in the past, but it still operates. What ever we do they'll walk away with bulging coffers and the blood of soldiers and probably civilians on their hands. As long as they have the money, they won't care, and they'll still try to help their mates make yet more, for a cut of course.'

'A bit cynical, even for you Paul. I'm not saying you're wrong though.' replied General Leach.

'What's that old saying Boss? Keep your friends close and your enemies closer?'

The Prime Minister joined the military men, 'I do hope you're not planning a military coup,' he remarked, 'may I?' gesturing to an empty adjacent seat.

'By all means Sir,' replied Paul.

'I must say Colonel, I was very impressed with the way you organised that meeting, very efficient, and productive. Clearly something is worrying you, might I enquire as to the cause of your concern?'

'I feel I should warn you Prime Minister you might not like his answer', offered General Leach.

The Prime Minister raised an eyebrow, 'Oh', was all he said.

Paul explained his concerns about what he called the 'cartel' and how they could, as he rather indelicately put it, 'screw up' the only practical way of getting N.A.T.O's. force out of Afghanistan more or less intact.

'So you are planning on countering this by conning the very civil servants who are tasked with organising the evacuation.'

'That's about the size of it Sir, if we get it right, then by the time they realise they have been tricked it will be too late. We've been doing some research of our own Sir, the biggest ships they have been chartering to bring home the heavy kit won't make it. I'm not prepared to tell you how we found this information but most of them will make it as far as Nigeria, then they will have to refuel.'

'Why should that be a problem Colonel, I am of course aware of the instability in the region, which is why we have maintained strict neutrality in what is essentially a tribal squabble for power.' replied the Prime Minister.

'It's a bit more than that Sir. But the relevant point is the 'cartel' have set up a local company there and it already has a virtual monopoly of available marine grade fuels.

The current Government are desperate to get their hands on modern heavy weapons to defeat what they call insurgents.

Here's the conundrum, do we support the current corrupt clique who seized power by force, or the so called rebels. The current lot are in the pocket of the cartel, the rebels, are in many respects the majority, how ever, among their supporters you can include Al Qaida.

I think the best thing is to stay out of it, right out of it, if we go the Cape route, one way or another at least one of the transports will end up in a harbour there and I know there are plans to nick the kit'

The Prime Minister expressed his concern, 'what are you saying Colonel? The implication of what you are saying is we have people here, in positions of power who are hand in glove with this 'cartel'.

'Exactly Sir.' was Paul's reply.

'Then surely this is a job for special branch, get them arrested and charged as is appropriate'.

'In an ideal world I'd agree with you Prime Minister,' replied General Leach. 'The problem with that is when some expensive barrister asks how the authorities became aware of all this, what are we supposed to say, I'm sorry but that is classified. We can hardly say we have been listening to their telephones or hacking their computers can we?'

'I'm horrified if that is the case,' replied the Prime minister.

'You understand our problem then Sir, We can't arrest them, or even overtly investigate them. The only thing we can do is wait, one will make a mistake, something which calls for an investigation. Then, before anything else is done get a search warrant and raid the appropriate office, seize what ever needs seizing before any thing can be done to 'lose' evidence'.

'In the meantime you have this evacuation to run.' The Prime Minister sounded depressed. 'How far advanced are your plans Colonel? You hinted earlier some elements of your plans are already under way'.

'Indeed they are Sir, in Afghanistan offensives are well under way, the objective being to give the appearance we are clearing the way for withdrawl according to plans leaked by the cartel.

They can't use C.I.A satellite intelligence, the only stuff on their screens come from us, with the directors agreement. He knows we only send the information we want the cartel to see. He is rattling their cage by sending a team to Afghanistan to search for what he described as 'unauthorised munitions' in the hands of N.G.O's. in other words those new mini nukes. We are waiting to find out how many more of them are loose.'

'I am aware of larger than usual numbers of T.A. troops being called up Colonel. It has been very discreet but not un-noticed.' The Prime Minister then asked what was the purpose of this considerable deployment.

'You are aware of the increasing tensions in Cyprus. The British have a leading role as peace keeping troops in that troubled Island, with this in mind we have increased our troop numbers. This increase also means the troops need a bigger base and more facilities, all of which need protection,' replied Paul.

'When in reality the troops there are to be used to secure the Suez Canal at short notice. Can they do it Colonel, won't you need regular army units as well?

'Most definitely Sir,' replied Paul. 'The air assault brigade is quietly preparing to deploy supposedly to Afghanistan, to relieve the marines who have had a rough time.

Elements of air assault are already in Cyprus, preparing to receive the rest of the brigade. The story being they are going to stage a pre deployment exercise.'

'I wish you well in your deception Colonel. It all seems very under hand, we will of course do what we can to support you, I suppose the major headache is financial?' said the Prime Minister, a note of resignation in his voice.

'It's got to work Sir. The Khyber pass is unusable, it would take months to reopen. The other 'preferred route' is out through the north via the unpronounceable 'stans to Baku, cross the Caspian by ferry to Azerbaijan on to Georgia. Then by ship home, the problem with this route is half the countries are almost at war with each other, put a tank on some of those ferries and it will most likely drop straight through! There is also the small problem which seems to have been overlooked in that the Dardenelles are to all intents and purposes closed to shipping.

The Canal, at the end of the day is the best option.'

The worried Prime Minister looked General Leach in the eye, to gauge the elder statesman of the military's reaction. 'Do you believe this somewhat unorthodox plan devised by the Colonel will work General?'

'I believe it is the plan which offers the best chance of getting our forces home with the fewest casualties Prime Minister. I am convinced it offers the highest chance of success at the lowest cost in terms of equipment losses, in financial terms and most importantly lives.'

Convinced of the Generals sincerity the Prime Minister relaxed back into his seat, 'Very well, you have my unqualified support gentlemen. You also have my word I will not tell anyone not privy to our meeting of what is actually happening, and then only by extra secure connections, with your approval Colonel.'

'Thank you Sir, if our fathers could fool Hitler, lets hope we can fool this lot!'

'The only thing which worriers me Colonel is this will be seen as running away from the Taliban.'

'I wouldn't worry too much on that score Sir. The offensive is going well, with any luck there won't be any organised Taliban left in Afghanistan. The blocking of the Khyber Pass is a double edged sword. We might not be able to use it, but neither can they, all the other passes capable of carrying supplies are watched by our special forces. Our supplies are still getting through, theirs aren't, we can move at will, they can't.

It will take about a month, all the time we will be getting every thing we need in position for a rapid pull out. In the mean time the draw down of non combat elements as well as dragging the ladies kicking and screaming out of theatre will continue, as will securing and stocking the bases we will need on the route home.'

'I just wish I was as confident about the upcoming re run of the conference in Birmingham in couple of weeks time,' the Prime Minister sighed. 'It is promising to be one of the most difficult events of my political career. Unlike you I have no real answers to the problems we are facing. The collapse of the Euro is a problem, although many member states deny it has collapsed, from our perspective it is already a fact.

Then there is all the trouble with the American economy, in this respect

I suspect there is common cause with your objectives, as it seems to me things are being manipulated politically for financial gain by a few powerful individuals.'

'There is no doubt you're right about that part Sir, it is the widespread civil unrest nearer to home that's worrying me. Most of Southern Europe seems to be descending into anarchy, next thing you'll have extremists of all shades taking power, not all will be friendly to us, quite what we can do about it I have no idea.' replied Paul. 'We'll be home soon Sir, I wish you well. It's times like this I'm glad I'm just a soldier.'

Once back in his office, having seen the Prime Minister and his party safely on their way Paul put his feet up and enjoyed a cup of coffee 'just so'. For once there was no seriously bad news. About the worst thing was a memo from a group of high powered civil servants at the M.O.D. counselling caution in any dealings with Turkmenistan as damage to their rail net work and ferry loading facilities could jeopardise natural gas supplies from the area.

Taff walked in just as Paul propelled the folder into the 'out' tray, his enquiring look got a simple response from Paul 'Read it'.

Having got himself a coffee without offering Paul a refill he settled in the chair opposite. His grunt was followed by, 'who needs the gas anyway, with all the hot air that lot generate we should be self sufficient in energy anyway.!

'Quite!' responded Paul.

'So how did everything go? asked the base commander. 'I'll bet the Yanks weren't too happy. No doubt they want to control every thing?'

'Quite the opposite Taff, they were glad things seem to be working. Doing things our way is isolating the bulk of the Taliban, it enables the Yanks to use their firepower without risking civilian casualties. This in turn means they are pulling units out with no lessening of the pressure on the insurgents. It is also enabling the engineer units to make a real difference improving roads, drainage, irrigation and power supplies. The pace of progress is almost breath taking, well ahead of schedule, the better the progress, the greater the co-operation, and the lower the demands on the combat troops. I know it's too soon to claim success but it's looking good so far.'

Taff passed a thin folder across the desk, 'this might dim your enthusiasm, it is from the Pakistani government. There are two things of concern,' Taff continued.

131

'It seems as though they are concerned about our push towards the frontier and point out that their engineers will have to repair the road through most of the Khyber Pass. It seems as though if our military do the repairs it will be viewed as aggression.

They also want us to modify our proposed route for the with-drawl to avoid the city of Quetta, to avoid stirring up the locals.'

Paul's reply surprised Taff, 'Oh good, perfect!!'

'You what?' asked the confused Welshman.

'Perfect,' Paul repeated. 'Get our engineers to repair and strengthen the road to as close to the border as time will allow. It's a pity there won't be time to get it all done, but it will add credence to the appearance that is our route out. Then get the authors of the reports and plans from Whitehall to negotiate safe passage through Quetta.'

'That will be a waste of time,' replied Taff.

'Totally,' was Paul's reply, 'but then we're not going that way so it doesn't matter and it will keep the Whitehall warriors busy for weeks. The entire exercise is pointless anyway as I've been doing some checking of my own. The port we are supposed to be using is unsuitable for the bigger ships and worse still the most powerful crane in the port can only lift thirty five tons on a good day. From this we can conclude the architects of this so called plan are either totally incompetent, saboteurs or an unholy hybrid of both.'

'That's not nice,' replied Taff.

'Yes it is,' replied Paul, 'It is bloody brilliant as it gives, or will give, our political master all the ammunition they need to fire the useless bastards, some more problems solved and another small fortune saved on the wages bill.'

'Yet you are planning on using them to help keep everyone in the dark as to what we're really doing. You devious old bugger!' chuckled Taff. 'I like it'.

'I don't suppose for one moment we'll be able to maintain the deception all the way, but the longer the better.'

A week or so later Taff was sitting in Paul's office, discussing the general position, every thing considered, things were looking remarkably good, 'makes a change' observed Paul.

The office door fairly flew open to reveal Kenny at full speed in his wheelchair! 'Come in Kenny', commented Paul.

'Look at this Paul!' Kenny stood up, ignoring the obvious pain as he leaned on Paul's desk to hand over a file.

'Calm down mate, before you do yourself an injury,' Paul said as he took the offered file. As he scanned the couple of pages he was very conscious of the varying expressions on the faces opposite, Taff curious, Kenny excited.

'Now that is what I call a problem,' observed Paul, 'and we know this how?'

Kenny now handed over another slim folder, a little thicker than the first, but not by much. 'And these are what?' Paul asked.

'Photographs taken by Seal Team six, when they killed Bin Laden. It has been confirmed by the new scanner on blue bird two.' replied Kenny.

'Have you taken something strange in your coffee Kenny, or is it just me being thick, do you know what he's rabbiting about Taff?'

'Nope!' was Taffs reply, 'Go on Ken, tell us before you blow a fuse.'

'There, right in front of your eyes!' Kenny almost shouted.

'What for fucks sake!' exclaimed Paul.

'There Paul!' Kenny's trembling finger indicating a pair of fire extinguishers standing in the hall way.

'So, he was afraid of a fire.'

'No.No!' was Kenny's irritated response, 'When did you see fire extinguishers wired up to a mobile phone, I know you're tired Paul but I thought you might have cottoned on to it a bit quicker, especially after the first folder.'

'Sorry mate, it never entered my mind, and you say there are another pair in the downstairs hall way.?'

'The scans confirm it'. replied a now calmer Kenny.

'I wonder why they didn't go off when the shooting started? asked Taff, 'it looks as though they are wired to detonate'.

'I think I can answer that too Taff', Kenny sounded pleased as he produced another photograph, or at least an enlargement of an item in one of the others. This was a picture of a mobile phone, which had clearly been dropped, the casing had flown open and the battery had popped out breaking the circuit.

'If you're right Kenny, how close was that!?'

'Too bloody close I'd say, ' Taff suggested.

'Of course, this leaves us with the problem of what to do about it?' said Kenny.

'Don't it just.' Paul muttered. 'Can you get Archie up here please Taff, I can never get him on the intercom, we need his knowledge of these devices.'

'If you wanted me to leave you and Kenny alone, you only had to ask, no need for excuses.' Taff levered himself out of his chair to go in search of the units scientific genius. 'I'll see you later ', as he headed to the door.

'What the hell are we supposed to do about this Kenny?' Paul asked, 'We can't leave them there, we can't tell the Pakistani authorities and we can't explode them where they are, it would kill thousands.'

'What would happen if we let the yanks know were their noisy toys were? suggested Kenny, 'they have got a team in the area tasked with recovering them.'

'Are you trying to increase my blood pressure Kenny, because you are certainly succeeding!' exclaimed the harressed commander. 'We need things as calm as we can for the withdrawl, we must come up with a way of getting a team in there unobserved. More to the point getting them, and the canisters out, without upsetting the locals. We need a lot more information on the area, and specifically the site if we are to mount any sort of operation. Then there is the problem of the dodgey triggers or detonators to consider, we'll have to wait for young Einestein on that. In the mean time can you get your team to gather as much information as possible about the immediate area please.'

'You'll have to get clearance for a trip like that Paul, things are far too touchy not to get clearance from our political masters.' said Kenny, 'even if every thing goes perfectly it will cause one hell of a fuss.'

'Not least from our American friends,' Paul said almost under his breath. 'I suppose our options will depend a lot on what Archie has to say, but obviously they can be moved for them to have got there in the first place. What ever he says, I'm going to have to see the P.M. about it, and he's back in Birmingham at this crisis conference, part two.'

'That sounds like fun,' chuckled Kenny.

'I doubt it will be fun, but it will have to be a face to face, and without the world and his wife knowing I'm even there, never mind why.' was Paul's worried reply.

Paul called the 'air' department, enquiring about the availability of a helicopter, he wasn't pleased by the reply of 'Sorry Boss, there's only the damaged Chinook we're repairing, it might be ready tomorrow with a little luck.'

The flight sergeants' reply hadn't really come as a surprise, his unit was as stretched as the rest of the armed forces, more so if anything, as they struggled with the logistics of the planned withdrawl.

After a pause the flight sergeant offered a solution. 'I've just had a thought Boss', he began, 'I've just remembered, the old communications Lynx is in the big barn at the 'farm'. We keep it there as General Leachs' emergency transport.'

'That will do nicely 'flight', thank you, I take it Paddy usually flies it?'

'He does Boss, I think he's at home right now.'

'Thanks 'flight' I'll sort it from here.'

Paul called 'the farm', and was put through to the veteran pilot.

'Paddy, I need a taxi, urgently, give General Leach my compliments and could he come with you please. Something rather urgent has come up, and we will have to go to see the P.M. about it. As soon as you like mate.'

'I don't know!' Paddy let out a sigh, 'can't a bloke have a day off about here?'

'Paddy!' Paul scolded.

'Already got my boots on Boss, see you A.S.A.P.'

As good as his word, Paddy was landing outside the H.Q. block in a bit less than half an hour, with a worried General Leach as a passenger. Met by a combat clad Paul he asked, 'where's the fire?'

'I'll brief you on the way Sir'. replied Paul as he jumped into the open door with an agility belying his age.

'Fine,' replied the even older General, 'after I've been to the toilet! Out of a warm lounge into a draughty lynx tends to shrink ones bladder!'

In the Generals absence Paul checked with Paddy that the was sufficient fuel for the round trip as he was unsure when Paddy had last fuelled the helicopter.

'I know I've been caught short before Boss', replied Paddy, 'but we'll be fine, even with a head wind both ways'.

Paul grinned, 'Only an Irishman could come up with an answer like that!'

CHAPTER THIRTEEN

The old, but speedy helicopter crossed the M6 over Corley bank, informed they would have to wait until a charter flight from Birmingham Airport had left, Paddy did a wide orbit to the east. The noise of the helicopter panicked a huge flock of Canadian geese on the lakes at nearby Packington. His orbit took them out to Atherstone, well to the east as the instructions told him to wait for at least 15 minutes, this was to allow a second chartered airliner to clear the area.

Paddy asked for permission to enter the airspace between flights to land at the N.E.C. but the controller was having none of it. So they waited, not, it has to be said patiently.

As soon as the second airliner appeared on Paddies radar scope he turned back towards his intended destination, without waiting for the air traffic controllers' clearance. As the helicopter crossed the M6-M42 interchange there was a colossal fireball ahead of them, a towering black billowing cloud climbed nearly a thousand feet into the clear blue sky, right over the N.E.C.

'What the fuck was that?' Paul asked, actually remembering the switch on the intercom head set he was wearing.

'I think the second charter jet just crashed, smack on top of the N.E.C.' came the incredulous reply.

'Get us in there Paddy, just make sure we're upwind of it!' Paul ordered.

'Consider it done Boss.'

The veteran pilot made it look easy, dodging the flood light towers and cables, he set the old Lynx down in a vacant patch of car park reserved for V.I.Ps yet to arrive.

The huge main exhibition building was devastated, even the bit not a roaring inferno was wrecked, most of the roof had collapsed, taking a bit of the outer wall with it.

The obvious conclusion was terrorists and hi-jacking, but there wouldn't have been time, thought Paul. He ran towards the nearest part of the building hoping he might be able to do something, though unsure exactly what that something might be. Sirens could be heard approaching but this wasn't going to be a five minute job.

To his utter amazement he could see people crawling from the rubble and tangle of girders, some were even staggering to their feet, trying to run from the carnage.

It was amazing how many emergency crews arrived in the next ten minutes, Paul talked to General Leach and reached a decision, if the Prime Minister, the deputy Prime Minister and Foreign Secretary had survived and were pronounced fit enough to withstand the flight, they would be transported to the units medical facility, deep beneath 'the farm'.

It was already becoming apparent the stage and podium areas held most survivors, the forward momentum of the doomed airliner had thrown the wreckage and fuel forwards, away from most of the V.I.Ps. Even so most of the survivors from this area were terribly injured.

Paul spoke to Paddy, 'If the General stays here to take charge of security and I go to the airport control tower to try to find out what the hell happened can you take four casualties to the farm, refuel and get back here ?'

'No problem Boss, I'll be able to take two medics as well,' replied Paddy.

The unconscious and burnt Home Secretary was the fourth casualty loaded onto the old Lynx.

Barely an hour later a huge Chinook helicopter landed among the floodlight towers of the car park. A team of mainly army medics ran out and reported to the doctors who had set up an emergency triage, the local medics were glad of the help. They were even more relieved that the giant helicopter could carry twenty stretchers and was equipped for casualty evacuation.

Paul arrived back just as the last stretcher was being secured, all of those on board were in a serious condition, but assessed strong enough to survive the hour long flight. Some of the medical team would stay to help, the rest would return on the Chinook to look after the casualties for the flight to 'the farm'.

Paul asked the senior medic remaining, 'how come I was told that chopper wouldn't be flying before tomorrow?

'Just between you and I boss, it shouldn't be flying now, none of the avionics are working. Even the radio and lights don't work, oh, and the tailgate only comes up half way. He'll make it back before dark, even get to the main base, but that will be it for today, he'd have time to get back here, but not back home, it's a one hit wonder I'm afraid.'

Paul's trip to the airport had solved one mystery, the fully laden Boeing 737 had hit a large flock of Canada geese, nose up in a full power climb the crew had been unaware of the hazard until the multiple impacts had knocked out their engines, at that speed and altitude there was absolutely nothing they could do. The aircraft simply pan-caked onto the huge conference hall and it's fuel blew up, there were few survivors, even in the front few rows of the auditorium. From ten rows back, there were none, and predictably none from the plane.

By the time Paddy landed his old faithful Lynx back at the farm after his second trip it was dark, he had the rest of the medical team along with Paul and General Leach on board and one casualty, the Admiral who was currently head of the defence staff. As well as his burns, 'flame grilled, but still rare' as he put it, he had a badly crushed shoulder and some broken ribs, he would be in the bed next to his son for sometime to come.

Such was the casualty list it effectively left the country without a government. The attempt to have a wide ranging and meaningful conference to sort out a course of action to put the country on track for a recovery, or at least to survive the crisis, had ended in the death of over two thousand people.

As Paul was heard to mutter, 'you'd think someone up there wants us to fail!' .

By the following morning the media, world wide were in a frenzy, in the absence of any meaningful information they could only speculate, even foreign governments were left guessing as to the true nature and scale of the disaster.

Paul was chairing a meeting of senior military staff. 'We absolutely must put out a statement gentlemen, if for no other reason than to quash the rumour mill.'

'What had you in mind?' enquired General Leach.

'A simple statement to the effect that leading government members, including the Prime Minister, are being treated for serious, but not life threatening injuries at a secure military base. We could add that there will be further statements as is appropriate,' replied Paul.

'What about the cause of the catastrophe?, asked an elderly former chief of the defence staff. 'Speculation is a suicide attacker was to blame.'

'I think we can safely say it was due entirely to a flock of Canada geese,' replied Paul. 'I saw what was left of the port engine. That was the unit which ended up on the railway tracks in the station, it snapped off on impact and wasn't affected by the fire. There were remains of what were clearly Canada geese stuck in the intake, it appears so many struck, their remains basically jammed the engine, I can confirm, first hand, it was a gory mess.'

'Tell me Colonel, are any government ministers up to making a statement,? Asked the senior R.A.F. officer.

'I wouldn't have thought so Sir, I'll ask the medics, but I agree, it would be helpful if one of them did so as soon as possible.' replied Paul.

'So who is running the country at the moment? It is my understanding that over seventy percent of M.Ps. were in the hall when disaster struck. As I believe were the majority of senior civil servants and many from the House of Lords, in particular ministers and Law Lords. As far as I can see the ship has lost not only it's captain but it's crew, clearly someone has to take the reigns. Someone has got to say this, I think it is going to have to be the military, at least until new elections can be arranged'. Some members were quite taken aback by the suggestion from the oldest of the generals present.

'I hate to say it,' Paul began, 'but he does have a point.. Excuse me gentlemen, I must answer this', as his communicator bleeped softly. 'You what?' the surprise obvious in his voice. 'Yes, yes, bring them in'.

'Well?' enquired General Leach, 'I'm intrigued as to who our guests might be'.

'You have got to be the luckiest man alive!' was Pauls' welcome to the young politician who was second only to the chancellor in the treasury. 'How on earth did you escape unscathed, never mind turning up here with a royal chauffer', acknowledging the tall man with him in flying gear.

'I wasn't actually there Colonel', replied the man, 'I should have been, but I got held up in London so badly I missed my train, then all trains were cancelled on the direct services to Birmingham. The technical problems turned out to be cable theft, so a car from the motor pool picked me up from the station, eventually, this then broke down in the middle of nowhere. This was after we had been stuck for two hours because of an accident, only to be diverted onto choked A roads on a diversion miles out of our way. We ended getting towed into a hotel, a holiday inn I believe. I was actually unaware of the disaster until I was woken up this morning! On arrival at what was left of the N.E.C. I was welcomed by a major, one of yours I believe Colonel. I was bundled onto a helicopter with the comment 'The boss will want to see you Sir', I shared the transport with two terribly injured men and their medics. I have no idea where I am, I was shocked to find out my pilot was a member of the royal family. Now I am totally confused as to what is going on and what you want me for.'

'First of all, I'm glad we have one senior cabinet member intact. We were about to discuss which of us would be temporally leading the country. What you hear in this room stays in this room, do you understand?'

'I understand about the secrecy, but not the subject of the secret.'

'Okay, General Leach and I were in a helicopter approaching Birmingham when air traffic put us in a holding pattern so we didn't disrupt flights in or out of the airport. I think it was our helicopter which spooked the geese which brought down the plane. We were en route to see the Prime Minister on a very serious and delicate matter.'

'Might I enquire as to the nature of this matter Colonel.'

'We were seeking permission to launch a raid into Pakistan'. replied Paul.

'In the current climate I would have thought it unlikely the P.M. would have agreed Colonel'.

'Well, in the event, I'm now going to ask you. There are four live nuclear devices in Bin Ladens' old compound. They shouldn't be there! If left it is likely they will detonate, Abbottabad will cease to exist.'

'My God!' exclaimed the shocked minister.

'I don't think yours or anyone else's can help in this case Sir. There's more to it, it is the origin of the devices. It would seem they belong to an American outfit who supply private security among other things. This company is part of a much larger conglomerate responsible for many of our current problems. It is vitally important we, not the Americans recover these devices. The C.I.A. have a team out there looking for these things with orders to recover them at all costs, or destroy them.

If we tell them, there are several possible out comes, none of them good. One, they recover them, probably starting another war. Two, they detonate them, certainly starting a war. Three, they actually retrieve them, only to 'lose' them to the people who are messing us about, the final alternative is they make a total horlicks of the operation, then your guess is as good as mine as to the consequences.

Equally I am of the opinion it would not be a good idea to inform the Pakistani authorities. Most are alright with us on security matters, some most definitely are not. Should we inform the powers that be of our intentions, there is no doubt in my mind these devices would end up in the wrong hands.'

'Am I to understand you want me to make the decision Colonel?' asked the shaken politician. 'Why does it have to be me?'

'Because old son you are the only elected member of the government still standing!'

'I can't take that sort of responsibility Colonel, I simply can't'.

' Very well,' replied Paul, 'can you do your boss's job for the next six months?'

'I think so, it is my area of expertise,' was the less than confident reply.

'Very well,' was Paul's response. 'As things stand I can see no alternative to a temporary military government. It looks as though you will be the only civilian member. I suggest it is lead by General Leach, he is well known and respected. The sooner the rest of you sort out the other positions the sooner we can see H.R.H.

I have far too much on my desk to want any part of it. The only requirement I have is the funding for getting the N.A.T.O. boys home, from where ever they may be. Afghanistan is top priority. Over seventy percent of the fuel and supplies are already in position and paid for, so it won't be as bad as you expect. You can also factor in that the Americans will pay their share on completion, so as to speak.

Our biggest problem isn't lack of cash or hostile forces, it's not even the block ships sunk in the Suez canal, it is this blasted cartel. We are doing everything we can to disguise the fact that our plans are already being put into action.

You are no doubt aware of the major operations going on at the moment, you will not be aware of the sophistication of some of our kit. The aim of the current sweeps is to either register or destroy every fire arm in the country. As this is done a data base is being assembled of all the registered arms, complete with a fired bullet and it's cartridge case. Over five thousand troops are involved in the registration process, it is actually ahead of schedule. Anything else discovered, R.P.Gs, machine guns, rifles greater than .762 calibre, explosives etc. are either handed over to the Afghan forces or destroyed.

At the same time forces are hunting down the Taliban and their allies with considerable vigour and success, again guided by technologies you will be unaware of.

As the forces sweep westwards along the border with Pakistan, a series of forts and strong points are being constructed, linked with solar powered sensors, even rats are being detected crossing the border. Each post has it's own access road from a supply route being constructed parallel to the border. We are giving the Afghans the means to look after themselves, what they do with it when we've gone is another matter.

While all this is going on we are already pulling out troops, the airlift is continuing as normal on the surface. Flights in carry lubrication oils, food and crack troops for the combat in the mountains. Flights out bring sick and wounded as well as non combat troops and ladies serving out there. They don't like it, but it is the way things have to be for reasons I won't go into right now.

What we are trying to achieve, apart from completing the mission is to make the cartel believe we are going to come out over the Khyber pass, which incidentally they have blocked, and the bulk of the heavy kit out via the northern route which will take an age and cost a fortune. It is of course pure coincidence much of the extra cost would be for equipment the cartel produces or services they provide.'

'How long will it be before you have the troops home Colonel? As you are well aware funds are very limited.'

'I don't know about home Sir, but they should all be on their ships and under way in about six weeks.'

'How can that be Colonel?' asked the young man. 'I happen to know about the explosions in the Khyber pass. The Pakistan authorities have been in touch asking for funding to the tune of ten million pounds before they will start work on opening up the route. They claim it will take at least ten months, and then only for light traffic, they also say our engineers must not work within five miles of the border.'

'I am aware of all that crap Sir. The Royal Engineers have been instructed to drive a road to within a foot of the border, capable of carrying loaded tank transporters, with room to pass safely. They are supported by most of the heavy armour we've got out there, as well as by two battalions of the best infantry we have available. The bulk of the insurgents should be trapped between this force and the units advancing from the east.'

'It all sounds very dangerous to me Colonel.'

'War tends to be Sir!' replied Paul. 'We must make it appear we are doing what they want us to do. The Pakistan authorities keep changing the route they will allow our convoys to use, the port they have designated is useless, although we haven't told them that, yet.

As for the Yanks and Canadians they appear to be pulling back and securing the route north out of Kandahar.'

'So how are you getting all your fuel Colonel? As far as I am aware there have been no requests for extra fuel.'

'What you don't know can't hurt you, let's just say it is for services rendered. I haven't got time to brief you in detail of our plans right now, but the important thing is to keep these bastards in the cartel thinking we are dancing to their tune.

If their plans work disengagement will cost us a fortune, delays will force us to abandon most of our equipment. This will be down to the fact we will have to use the Khyber pass when it is eventually opened. The cartel will of course supply the Pakistan authorities with the equipment they will need, then offer us the fuel, at hiked prices, sufficient only to extract our troops in light transports.

They are hiring ships east of Suez, which they will lease to us to bring our forces home via the cape route, necessitating refuelling, probably in Nigeria.

They have arranged a similar stitch up for the northern route, which they expect the Americans to use. What have I forgotten?' Paul paused for a moment. 'Ah yes, their ships have already been ordered to sail singly down the usual shipping lanes off the east African coast. Sitting ducks for those bloody pirates as the average size of these hired ships is only around eight thousand tons, fully laden. The reason given is if they were any larger they couldn't get into the designated port to pick us up!'

'How on earth can you know all this Colonel. It beggars belief, what could possibly be the motive,' asked the young politician.

'That's easy, greed, on an industrial scale. There are nine, possibly ten people orchestrating all this mayhem. One, and this is the individual not yet positively identified, seems to be an ex President. Personally I think there is someone else pulling his strings, my opinion is he is just an expendable pawn as far as the cartel are concerned. My aim is to cost them as much money as I possibly can, make them come after the unit, and me in particular, this is one fight we cannot lose.

They are counting on a couple of things, firstly we have no way of knowing what they are planning, although they are well aware we know about some of their activities. They also think because they have so much power they are untouchable, bringing them down would totally collapse any economies in the west which haven't imploded any way. The other thing they have over looked, and this answers in part an earlier question you asked, 'how can we know', the full title of this unit is the all arms strike and intelligence unit, in short we are spies!'

'Well young Daniel', General Leach began, 'now you know what we're up to, will you be able to handle being the only elected member of what will be in effect a military junta, at least for the next six months. It will take that long for most of the survivors to recover sufficiently to resume their offices, not to mention sort out new elections, remembering many of the candidates will have to be found to replace those killed.'

'I think you had better get Royal accent General, as the sooner we make a start, the sooner our service men will be home'. replied the still shocked young man.

'I agree,' Paul added, 'because if a ship load of nutters decided to cross from the near continent we have precious little with which to stop them. It is true we have troops in the U.K., but it's getting them to where they are needed in time and sufficient strength for them to do any good which will be the problem.

'I suppose you'll be taking the defence post Colonel?' asked the politician.

'No Sir,' Paul replied, 'I've got more than enough on my plate getting our troops home. That will only happen if I can keep the cartel wrong footed, because make no mistake if they can screw things up in regards to equipment or fuel then they will.

There doesn't seem to be any lengths they won't go to, as long as they can make more money. Well, they've upset me now, and if they think I'm going to let them rip off this country, then they have made a big mistake.

But first things first, are there any serious objections to mounting an operation to retrieve those nukes?'

'When will we be able to scrutinise your plans for the operation Colonel.' It was a recently promoted Major General who asked.

'When those engaged are safely back Sir,' replied Paul, making a mental note to be careful what he said in future when in the presence of the newest General.

CHAPTER FOURTEEN

'How's it going Boss?' enquired Kenny as he wheeled himself into Paul's office.

'For once there doesn't seem to have been any major snafus' overnight, which makes a change,' replied Paul. 'To what do I owe the pleasure of your company Kenny?'

'I thought I'd bring the latest intel reports up myself, that's all Paul, nothing sinister. In fact things are going really well, for once, at least from the military stand point.'

'Uh-oh, I don't think I'm going to like what comes next,' said Paul as he headed for the coffee.

'It's these yanks, they have offered British Areo space a huge interest free loan for some new co-operative project.'

'And you think they are trying to take control through the back door?' replied Paul. 'Anyway, what is this project, I haven't heard anything about such a venture.'

'Thanks Boss', said Kenny as Paul placed the steaming mug in easy reach of his disabled friend. 'That's the point Paul, it was supposed to have been set up by the previous government. The deal hinged on the yanks making the money available, at the time they declined. Then they said they would, but it would take a year or so to get such a vast sum together in the current climate and they would require the company it's self as security.'

'Surely no-one was daft enough to agree to that sort of condition?' retorted Paul.

'It would appear some-one did, there's all sorts of skulduggery going on, the loan is equivelent to about half of the companies stock market value, or it was. Some senator stood up and proposed British Aero Space products be banned in America, which caused the share price to crash. Now the value of the loan exceeds the value of the company. It is looking bad Paul, we depend on them for all manner of things from jet engines down.'

'Well,' Paul began, 'at least they've shown their hand, now we know how they intend to stop us.'

'You think that's what's behind it Paul?' asked Kenny, 'if so, how do we stop it?'

'Ask the top brass, they're running things, my suggestion would be nationalise it, without compensation, at least for now, simply seize the company as being vital to the defence of the realm.'

'Can we do that?' Kenny sounded worried.

'We can't, the government can, give all that stuff to General Leach, use the secure link, mark it 'priority one plus' that should get his attention. I've got all I can handle here right now Kenny.

Everything is either in position, or ready to move to get those bloody mini nukes.' Paul checked his watch, 'In eight hours time the herc will be taking off to drop the recovery team in. What worries me is there is no margin for error, never mind a piece of kit going U/S'.

'Just who is on that team Paul,' asked Kenny, 'as far as I am aware all our fit comat troops are deployed. I've seen the plan, dropping into what is little more than a tree lined gully, at night, is going to be one hairy undertaking.'

'I am well aware of the risks Kenny,' replied Paul. 'I think I've put together the strongest team possible, four from Hereford and four from here. One of the Hereford boys is currently with the 14th regiment and has the reputation of being the best field signaller in the army. I've nicked Helga's sergeant major, he handled Somalia well last year, and knows what he's doing around dangerous chemicals including nuclear material. I've put Martin as commander, he's about as good as it gets, nothing phases him, he always keeps a cool head no matter what's going on. My main concern is sending young Archie, I didn't really want to send him, but was left with little choice, we know the damned things are unstable and he is probably the best on earth to deal with that.'

'But he's a gremlin Paul!' exclaimed Kenny in disbelief.

'I am only too well aware of that Kenny,' replied Paul. 'What persuaded me was the fact he has, completely unbeknown to me, done somewhere in the region of two hundred free fall jumps, on the down side, none have been at night. He also has three Bisley medals, which I know isn't like doing it for real, but proves he is an accurate marksman. I just had to take the risk and send him, I'm not happy about it, but the risks of those things going off if mishandled are just too great..

The rest of the team are all old lags, been there, seen it, done it types. It's pissed off at least three section commanders, nicking their best men, but that's the way things are, they'll just have to live with it.'

'Can they work together, as a team, you know as well as anyone putting together a team is more than simply getting a few bodies together,' said Kenny, 'they might be the four best at what ever, but if they don't gel, then things can quickly go tits up'.

'Well, we've done all we can in the way of training in the short time available, including a couple of dry runs,' replied Paul. 'Without the drop, I'm not sure how useful it's been, but at least everyone is clear on what part they are expected to play.'

'That's something I suppose,' replied Kenny. 'What about egress, surely it's well out of range of a Lynx, with eight guys and the kit, plus the crew, it wouldn't get near to doing the round trip.'

Paul allowed himself a little chuckle. 'I'll admit to a bit of underhand stuff myself on that Kenny.' Paul refilled his coffee mug as he related the plan to his longtime friend. 'We have sort of borrowed a long range black hawk from the unit which operates with the Seals. Out side of these walls the only people who know are the squadron commander and the pilot, and they don't know where it is going or what the mission is. The official cover story is it has gone for repairs and to have some of it's kit up dated.'

'At least it will have the range to get the job done, they are good bits of kit from that squadron. I presume an A.W.A.C. will be screening them back into Afghan airspace?'

'That is the general idea mate,' replied Paul. 'The other possibility is fly them onto Fearless, if things get noisy, that might prove the safer option. We are keeping that possibility open, just in case. Fuel then comes into play, but it is do-able, as Fearless can come in quite close if she has to.'

'What have the Brass got to say about it?' asked Kenny.

'Not a lot,' was Pauls' vague reply, 'other than be careful.'

'You have told them, haven't you?' Kenny sounded worried.

'Sort of, there's a bit of a problem.' it was Paul's turn to sound worried.

'Like what, clearly there is something you're not happy about, other than the obvious.'

'Maybe it's me getting paranoid but I don't trust that new member of the General staff. I can't put my finger on anything, other than he is too nosey about the goings on here for my likeing. Check him out Kenny, I'm certain he was involved in all that fuss over our fuel trains a while back.'

'Well he was in the logistics department at the M.O.D. so I'd be surprised if he hadn't been involved,' replied the disabled soldier.

'Fair enough Kenny, but isn't or wasn't he a legal eagle? I'm sure I saw his name on one of those memos about breaking contracts, and I don't think it was designed to help us, check him out, full background, family ties the works please.'

'I suppose you want the report yesterday.' chuckled Kenny as he turned his wheelchair towards the door.

Paul was about to get up to open the door for his old friend when it unexpectedly open to reveal General Leach.

'Morning Boss, or should it be Prime Minister,' was Paul's welcome, 'I take it this is a raid on my coffee supplies?'

'Don't mind if I do,' replied the normally amiable senior officer, as he held the door open for the departing Kenny.

The two old friends settled into their chairs with steaming mugs at hand.

'These nukes Paul, how soon are you planning to go?'

'As soon as it's dark out there, I am aware of the urgency, but why ask Boss?'

'It's just our newest member is kicking off about all sorts of legal points, violation of Pakistans territory, even theft, he's come up with an amazing list of why we can't do it.' sighed General Leach.

'Frankly Boss, he worries me,' replied Paul, 'I don't know why, but I wish I hadn't said anything about the nukes or our intention to recover them in front of him.'

'Well, what's done is done Paul,' sighed the silver haired General, 'I take it you'd prefer it if the impression was created suggesting it will take a couple of days to get everything organised?'

'A week would be better Sir,' replied Paul, 'but I can't see anyone believing that.'

'I suppose not, it might prove impossible to retrieve them if word got out,' the General was obviously thinking of the consequences of failure. 'Have you any contingency plans, in the unlikely event of failure.'

'For a start, I'd say there is a very high chance of things going tits up Boss, and I'm fresh out of practical alternatives, any ideas?' Paul asked more in hope than expectation.

'Like you, I'm convinced it must be us who retrieves those devices, if for no other reason than it will give us valuable leverage on the cartel. There is a problem however, it would seem as though our new member of the General Staff is firmly of the opinion it is an American mess and therefore it should be the Americans who clear it up.' The General paused. 'It has to be said his views have found a degree of support. He is not your biggest fan Paul, he sees you as a loose cannon, and in his opinion you are likely to create more problems than you solve.'

'That's nice of him,' replied Paul, 'Any way where did he suddenly pop up from, I'd never heard of him until a couple of weeks ago, most unusual, I thought I knew all the army Brigadiers, how did I miss him?'

'I'll make a few enquiries Paul,' replied General Leach, 'the more I think about him, the less I like it. The situation being what it is calls for swift positive action, with a degree of care, not the pedantic approach Sir Selwyn is advocating'.

'What's his full name Boss?' Paul asked.

'Sir Selwyn de la Fontaine, for what it's worth, why do you ask?'

'I knew I'd seen that weasel face before,' exclaimed Paul. 'A few years back there was an almighty row, behind closed doors, over some dead terrorists. We were supposed to have captured them and handed them over for trial. The problem was they knew we were coming and things got a bit noisy, there had been a leak at the M.O.D.'

'Nothing new there then,' observed General Leach.

'Suspition fell on the legal department, in particular a section run by a young officer with dual nationality, who had transferred in from the American J.A.G corps.

If I remember right, he was educated at Eton or Harrow, had more degrees from Oxbridge than I've got combat troops. He went to the 'States to be with mummy after his dad had an affair with a maid or some such. Daddy pops his clogs and as the eldest son he returns to claim his inheritance. Damn it he was just promoted to major when all that fuss blew up, how the Sam Hill has a pratt like him got promoted at all, never mind so far so fast?'

'You know the answer to that one Paul, the degrees, the old boy net and the title of Baronette'.

'You're in nominal charge of everything Sir, can't you find a post for him which will keep him out of the way, at least until we've got our troops home?'

'Like what pray?' asked General Leach.

'I don't know do I Sir, Her Majesties inspector of public bogs, Officer in command of Tristan da Cuna' Paul suggested.

'I take your point though Paul, we'll see what can be done.' chuckled the General. 'I must be off, this is by far the biggest challenge of my career, frankly I could do without it. That flock of geese did more damage to this country than all the combined terrorist attacks have done in the past fifty years!'

'Good luck Boss, I've a feeling you're going to need it. I've got a lot on in the next twenty four hours myself. I'll keep you up dated.'

The General left, he would much rather have been here with this unorthodox unit he had helped create, than what lay ahead of him over the coming months. He had seen the state of the survivors, they were not going to recover quickly.

Paul spent a frustrating few hours dealing with reports on the readiness of the various units in preparation for the big pull out and on the logistics situation, in particular fuel. Things were actually going much better than expected, which made a pleasant change.

The operation to retrieve the nuclear devices was under way, even the Black Hawk had left it's forward base unnoticed amid a major ruck with a large party of Taliban trapped in a valley near the border. Both AWACs, known as 'The Ugly Sisters' were on station, one screening the Hercules with the retrieval team on board, the other ensuring no Pakistan radar picked up the Black Hawk.

He sat with the inevitable cigarette and, by now distinctly cool cup of coffee watching the progress of the Hercules live on the big plasma screen, a big part of him wishing he was there with his men. He was concentrating on the data stream beamed back from the Canberra flying on the very edge of the atmosphere above the target, on the look out for any potential unforeseen problems.

He almost spilt his half drunk mug of coffee when a phone rang on his desk such was the surprise. He had another surprise when the caller identified himself as the current C.I.A. director.

'I was going to say good morning Colonel, but I suppose it is afternoon where you are now.'

'It certainly is Sir', replied Paul.

'I thought you and I were friends Colonel,' said the American.

'That makes two of us Sir,' was Paul's response, he guessed what was coming next.

'I just got into my office and find a document, marked for my eyes only. The gist of it being you have found those missing nuclear devices and will be mounting an operation to retrieve them in the next few days. Is this correct? It also says you think they may be in Bin Ladens old compound.'

Paul took a deep breath, 'might I enquire as to the source of this document Sir?'

'I'll level with you, if you level with me, does that sound fair?'replied the American.

'Very fair Sir, the source?'

'From your own ministry of defence, I can't read the signature but it starts with what I think is an S then four or five squiggles, de le something or other, might be Fonban? ' the Director struggled with the name, 'My grand kids can write better than this signature'.

' Sir Selwyn de la Fontain?' suggested Paul.

'Could well be Paul, do you know this guy, is he reliable?'

'Not especially Sir, and yes I know him, he's a bloody military legal eagle, a glory hunter. As for what he's claiming, we might have found those missing devices, we do not know for certain yet, as soon as I know, I'll let you know, just as I promised.

If I had phoned you every time we thought we might have had a lead, then neither of us would have done anything other than answering the phone over the past couple of days. I will conceed however this one looks more promising, at best a definite maybe.'

The Director was sceptical, 'I know you better than you think Colonel, I'll guess you'll put an S.A.S. team in there to have a look in the next few days.'

'As you well know Sir,' Paul began, 'S.A.S. troopers are a scarce and precious commodity. You are also well aware for a mission such as you are suggesting to have any chance of suceeding you only discuss it when those involved are back in friendly territory.'

'Absolutely Colonel, I totally concur, and to stop you worrying my personal secretary took the message, I assure you no-one else is aware of it, much less it's contents, nor will they be until I hear from you.'

Paul thanked the American, lit another cigarette and tried to calm down before he contacted General Leach. His demeanor did not improve when he returned to watching the plasma screen, eight canopies were clearly visible, despite it being dark, drifting down towards the gulley. The call from the American making him doubly glad he had decided to send the team straight in and get them out, all in the space of one night, instead of in one night and out the next.

Flicking a couple of switches on his communications terminal he called Fearless to crack on full speed to a position just below the horizon and just outside the coastal radars opposite the point the Black Hawk should make it's exit.

On the ground, far in land the ground team went about their work, Paul watched and listened to the communications between the Canberra and the team. The lead pair were directed onto the sole guard, a quick blow laid him out and an injection ensured he would stay out cold for at least four hours.

Less than twenty minutes after hitting the ground Archie had removed the last detonator circuits from the unstable devices.

One of the troopers with him noticed Archie was obviously intent on leaving the unstable bits behind.

'We are supposed to take everything with us Archie.'

'I know, but the combination we have here is far too dangerous to move, the explosive component has deteriorated to such an extent I'm thanking my lucky stars I have steady hands, one minor bump and we would have been atomised.'

'Is there anyway you can make one of those things safe enough to take back as evidence?

'You mean the electronic bits?' asked Archie.

'As much as you can Archie, and as soon as you like,' replied the trooper.

'If you can hold the torch for me please, I can separate the explosives from every thing else in about five minutes, but please don't sneeze'.

'If that stuff is so unstable didn't we ought to destroy it in case kiddies find it?' asked the trooper assigned to guard the scientist.

'Good idea, except it would rather give the game away, and we haven't got any time pencils,' replied the leader of the team.

Archie came up with the answer, 'I can explode them remotely, long after we've gone if you like.'

'Just get the bits we need, then you can explain how once we're out of here,' was the sergeants reply.

As the team approached the selected extraction point they became aware of an approaching helicopter, the timing was absolutely perfect, in less than a minute it was lifting off, headed back to the doubtful safety of it's base. Once clear of the town and the garrison area the pilot turned to a new heading having received new orders via the AWAC towards the distant coast, it was going to be a long night. By reducing his speed he also greatly reduced the noise at the same time increasing his range so he could reach Fearless, with a bit to spare.

About twenty minutes after they had turned onto the new heading, Martin, the young Major nominally in overall command of the team, turned to Archie.

'What were you saying about detonating what we left behind?'

'It's quite easy Sir, any time in the next half an hour and all it will take is a quick call to the Canberra which has been guiding us, a flick of a switch, push the button and poof!, just as if it was an I.E.D.'

'How do you know all this stuff Archie?' asked a trooper.

'My team designs and often make the bits we design, we have to be certain they do exactly what the Boss wants', replied Archie.

'You mean your Boss sent a scientist on an operation like this? He turned to Martin, 'What is this Boss like Skipper, you were part of our lot 'till you got hurt a couple of years ago, I thought you were there to get fit again then you were coming back?'

'That was the idea, I'm far from a hundred per cent even now, honestly I'd get no where near to passing the selection course.'

'Yet your Boss put you in command of this operation? The trooper clearly wasn't impressed. 'It's a good job we didn't know that on the way in!'

'Out of idle curiosity what the hell is in these fire extinguishers that is so important?' asked the sergeant who had led the team into the villa.

'Didn't anyone tell you?' asked Martin.

'Not a bloody word skipper, we sort of assumed they were chemical weapons.'

'They are actually nuclear devices, very powerful ones. It was one, just like these which destroyed that American battle group a while back.'

'Holy shit! And we're sitting on four of them!' exclaimed a trooper, 'stop the bus, I want to get off!'

'Oh. They are quite safe now,' said Archie casually, 'you could drop them, kick them, probably shoot them, and nothing would happen.'

'I like the sound of the dropping option,' observed one trooper who had been quiet up to now. 'Is there any danger from radiation from these things, I would hate for any of my kids to have three legs or two heads.'

'You haven't got any kids', said one of his mates, 'you were only saying yesterday this operation meant you had to stand up that red head you'd been dating and she'd be off it happened again.'

The sergeant major from Helgas team held out his gyger counter so they could all see the reading, 'According to this there is less radiation coming of these things than you get from a day on the rocks down in Cornwall, so stop flapping lads, we're quite safe.'

'He should know what he's talking about ,' Martin added, 'he's from the M.O.Ds health and safety unit, or was, until he joined the All Arms Unit.'

'So your boss sent us as nurse maids for a health and safety bloke, a scientist and a half fit Rupert, if you'll pardon the expression skipper, I daren't ask what you do?' The question aimed at the other All Arms Unit soldier.

'Basically I'm a linguist, Pashtu, Arabic, Farsi, as well as several dialects.'

Again Martin chipped into the conversation, 'He could have added field medic , to a standard any trauma team would welcome him on their staff, he also runs escape and evasion courses and survival training, an incredible natural marksman and unarmed combat instuctor in several techniques. Did I forget any thing Eddy?'

'You are a weird bunch, but you've got a hell of a reputation.'

'Only the best,' replied Martin, 'that's why the Boss picked you individually, you're all the best at what you do.'

'So why don't I feel flattered sitting in the back of an American chopper with a nuke as a foot rest, on the way out from what has so far proved to be a milk run!' replied the unhappy trooper.

'Have you any idea how many Pakistan army troops there were within a couple of hundred yards of you tonight?' asked Martin.

'One, as far as I know, and he'll still be asleep.' said the sergeant from Hereford.

'Try just over a hundred and fifty, all armed and ready for a helicopter assualt on the villa, the one gap was down the gully. You got in and out unnoticed, that is a measure of how good you are.'

The men were shocked at Martins reply, 'and you know all this how skipper?' asked the veteran sergeant.

'On this, my lap top, pictures beamed down in real time from the Canberra overhead. Talking of which, do you want to do your thing with those explosives Archie? We should be safe enough by now, if things have gone to plan they'll be looking north, not west.'

After a brief conversation with the crew man on the old recon plane, and a quick check to ensure there was no-one close enough to risk serious injury the crew detonated the unstable explosives the team had left behind.

The team watched it on the screen on Martins lap top..

'Ouch,' said one of the men, 'that would have chafed a bit. I am trained with explosives, we all are, you're good, damned good son, I wouldn't have known where to start on those circuits, even if I had, I'd have sweated more than that explosive was leaking. You are one cool customer. How the hell do you learn such things?'

'Simple, I designed the original system which would detonate the nuclear part of it. I told the Americans not to use that specific trigger and why, but they chose to ignore it.'

'You designed these things?'

'Well, the bit that should make it work. But you know our American cousins, they have to do things their way,' replied Archie.

The signaller who had been concentrating on his radio suddenly announced I have contact with Fearless, she will be thirty miles off shore by the time we get there'.

'We're going all the way to the sea?' asked the sergeant, 'sounds dangerous, won't the Paki's radars pick us up?' he asked. 'They won't be very happy after the Yanks incursions.'

'We should be alright, there is an A.W.A.C. somewhere above us, he'll blot out any radars pointed our way,' was Martins casual reply.

The rest of the trip in the Black Hawk could best be described as tense, if boring, much of the last half an hour was spent flying over the apparently endless floods which had engulfed this hapless overcrowded land. The increasing sense of security was about to be rudely shattered , the coast was barely forty miles ahead when the pilots received a message which heralded trouble ahead.

The protective old A.W.A.C. high overhead had developed a problem, the outer port engine which on this aircraft generated most of the electrical power had developed an intermittent fault. If it lost power then it would lose the ability to screen the helicopter from radars, indeed the plane it's self would then be vulnerable. It couldn't have happened in a much worse place, this stretch of coast was heavily defended, being on the direct line between the major ports and a normally hostile Iran.

Under almost any other circumstances there would have been no question, the engine would have been shut down, the crew took the descision, the risk would have to be taken until the Black Hawk was clear of the coast.

The twelve crew on the A.W.A.C.well aware they risked their own lives protecting who ever was in the helicopter. 'The Boss' himself had stressed this mission must not fail, no matter what, so the troublesome engine was kept running, risking a fire. To help as far as they could, the crew shut off every system possible except the vital emmiters which blinded any radars pointing in their direction.

Time, which up until then had simply passed slowly now seemed to almost stop, it didn't seem possible for a minute to take so long to pass.

Those last few dangerous miles seemed to take for ever, well aware of the problem the Skipper of the Fearless rose to the occasion.

'Bugger orders number one! What are you waiting for? Full speed ahead. That way!' pointing towards the coast.

Within two minutes the old assault ship was travelling at a speed destroyer captains could only dream of, 'Just don't run aground!' he added as an after thought.

As soon as the helicopter was detected by the ships radar, which was immune to the emmitters the great ship slowed and turned, presenting her landing deck to the exhausted crew of the Black Hawk, which was quickly secured as Fearless dashed back to international waters. 'Mission completed' was flashed through to the units head quarters and everyone heaved a huge sigh of relief.

This relief was to prove short lived, the A.W.A.C. called in, the troublesome engine had been shut down and the internal automatic fire extinguishers had gone off. All seemed well, or at least manageable, they would head for the U.E.A and if nothing else went wrong should make Salahla safely.

No sooner had the signal been sent than the other engine on the port side began to lose power and was running hot. Try as they might no cause could be found for the problem.

The captain of the old modified Nimrod took a fateful decision, they would still head for a friendly base as planned, even with two engines out on the same side the plane would still fly.

The three on the flight deck would stay to try to save the aircraft, the other nine would bale out near Fearless. There would be no panic, a carefully controlled jump from about eight thousand feet, four in the first pass, five in the second.

That was the plan, the first four got away fine, close together, but not dangerously so, two rigid raiders were racing towards the swinging parachutes long befor they hit the sea. Even the Black Hawk was back in the air as back up having been unloaded and given a splash of fuel.

The great stricken plane made a wide circle to come in again for the rest of the cabin crew to bale out. At the furthest point on its turn the crew on the Fearless watched, in helpless horror as a missile streaked in from below their horizon to explode on contact with the A.W.A.C.

It's electronics shut down, the crew didn't even know they had been 'locked up' by a radar, much less shot at.

Fearless raced towards the crash site, leaving her rigid raiders to collect the four parachutists, all that marked the spot was blazing fuel and a few bits of wreckage.

The radar operator called in a report to the Skipper, a small warship of about a thousand tons was approaching from the north west at about twenty five knots, the direction the fatal missile had come from.

Far above the Canberra which had been keeping a watchful eye on things on the way out and had already turned for it's Afghan base now swung back to see if it could help. To the horror of the crew they detected the launch of two sea skimming missiles, aimed at Fearless.

The warning just gave Fearless time, computers hummed and the twenty millimetre 'Darlek' as well as the thirty millimetre 'Goal Keeper' multi barrelled cannons locked onto the deadly missiles and chopped them to pieces at about three hundred yards.

A voice came over the radio on the bridge, 'Blow that thing out of the water Skipper'.

Paul had been watching events with helpless fury.

'It's a U.S. Coast Guard cutter Boss', replied the Captain of the Fearless.

'I can see the same pictures you can Bob,' replied Paul, 'sink it'.

Paul called the Canberra, 'mark the missile launchers and her stern for Fearless's guns.'

' Bob,' he called the ship again, 'have you got any solid shot on board?'

'No, but we have got a dozen practice rounds, they'll make a bang and a lot of smoke, why?'

'Can you hit the launchers with them?'

'Probably, AAAhh!' exclaimed the Captain, 'I'm with you now, you want the crew to find out why they shot at us'.

'As far as I'm concerned they can be left for the sharks, but that won't tell us much. Someone told them to fire, and I want to know who and why.

Get as many as you can on board, lock 'em up and sink their bloody ship in as many pieces as you can.'

There was concern on the coast guard cutter, 'what ever that ship is Sir, it seems as though she shot down our missiles,' reported the worried radar operator. 'It is a lot bigger than it seemed to be, I'd estimate fifteen to eighteen thousand tons Sir.'

'Launch a full salvo of missiles,' commanded the 'civilian liason' officer on board to over see operations.

'I don't think that is a very good idea Sir', replied the skipper of the fast cutter. 'What ever ship it is, it clearly is not an Iranian gun boat, I'm also having doubts about that aircraft you ordered shot down.'

'I am giving you a direct order, destroy that ship!'

An operator shouted a warning, 'INCOMING!'

A couple of seconds later the main anti ship missile launchers where hit and everything was obscured by thick choking smoke.

'Hard a' starboard, full speed', the young officer in command ordered.

Even as the cutter turned a pair of four point five inch shells slammed into her stern, right on the water line. The effect was dramatic as the rudder slammed into one of the twin propellers, stopping it dead, seizing the bearings instantly.

The fire crews had reacted very quickly to the first hits on the launchers, the small fires being extinguished almost instantly, which was just as well as the water from the fire hoses reduced to a dribble then stopped completely following the second hits.

A reservist, nominally in charge of the radars entered the bridge, just as a grey shape framed by two huge white wings of spray surged over the horizon.

'I know that ship Skipper,' said the grey haired reservist. 'It's either Fearless or Intrepid. If that is what we fired at we are in a whole heap of shit!'

'I ordered you to sink her,' snapped the civilian. 'You have our latest missiles, use them!'

'We had, her first shots wrecked both launchers,' replied the Skipper. 'Master at arms, place our 'guest' under arrest in hand cuffs if you please. I'm guessing the Captain of that ship currently headed our way like a giant speed boat will want a word with out 'guest'. We might survive this yet.'

The old reservist spoke up again. 'Have you ever had any dealings with The All Arms Unit Sir?'

'I can't say I have petty officer,' replied the Skipper, 'I have heard of them, but that's about all.'

'It's a mainly British outfit skipper, I would not want to get on the wrong side of the old guy who runs it. You've seen what they can do, those were not lucky hits on us. Remember she was over twenty five miles away when she fired and she'll be along side in a few minutes. I'll bet their commander is sitting in his office back in England watching all of this as it happens, probably even listening to this.'

'And you know all of this how petty officer?' asked the Skipper.

'I was on the Kerasage last year when they launched a raid into Somalia, something to do with those chemical weapons. What I saw convinced me it is not a good idea to mess with these guys, they'll chew you up and spit you out.'

The civilian lay at the rear of the bridge, groaning as he came to. He had tried to resist the master chief, who was the ships policeman. The tough former marine had been an unarmed combat instructor before joining the U.S coast guard, he had simply parried the blow aimed at him and struck back with some force.

'I'm guessing our friends on the Fearless will be wanting a word with our guest Skipper.' suggested the former marine.

The young officer in charge of the engines appeared, 'We're taking on water Sir, we can't control the leaks and the emergency pumps can't cope, we've got about ten minutes before we sink Sir.'

'Very well, abandon ship, launch the life rafts. Send a message to JIOTFCOM tell them our co-ordinates and we are sinking.'

'The radio is dead Sir,' replied the signals officer, 'All channels are blocked, I can receive messages, but not transmit. I even tried a couple of mobile phones Sir, no out going signals are possible Sir.'

'I told you these guys are good Skipper', observed the reservist.

The cutter was beginning to settle by the stern as the pair of landing craft which emerged from the stern doors of Fearless came along side. With commendable disciplin the injured Americans were passed down to the Royal Marines manning the landing craft, it did not go un-noticed that they kept the crew of the sinking ship covered with their guns.

'Throw your weapons over board, in their holsters!' commanded the Royal Marine captain, to a man the Americans complied. In a matter of minutes they were back in the 'wet dock' inside Fearless, the stern doors closed and the dock emptied as if by magic. The captured skipper was escorted to the bridge. On arrival he could see his vessel, much further away than he imagined it would be, the stern awash and the bow beginning to rise. His heart sank as he heard the order 'Open fire'.

The twin four point five inch guns thundered into life, four shells from each gun in less than half a minute, his ship was obliterated and had vanished, only a patch of rubbish strewn foam marked the spot.

Bob, the skipper of Fearless walked over, 'Alright! Let's hear it!' he snapped at the American.

'Hear what Captian?' replied the American. 'I demand you take us to the nearest American ship, so our wounded can be treated properly.'

'Did you hear that Boss?' asked Bob.

'I did, came a voice from the speaker built into the consol at the front of the bridge. 'You have a simple choice, answer our questions, immediately and truthfully, your reservist petty officer was quite correct, we could hear your conversations on your bridge. I'm sorry six of your crew were injured, but you attacked Fearless with two harpoon missiles of the latest type. You also destroyed a priceless irreplaceable aircraft, worse still, it seems you killed most of the crew.

Now answer our questions or your ship will go down in the records as being lost with all hands. Do you understand?'

'Who are you?' asked the American skipper, 'I do hope that wasn't a threat.'

'I am the operational commander of The All Arms Unit, and it wasn't a threat, it was a statement of fact! You have just killed several good friends of mine, quite deliberately, and we are supposed to be allies.

Who issued the order to shoot down my AWAC, and more to the point why?'

'We shot at a hostile aircraft.' replied the American skipper.

'Bull shit.' snapped Paul. 'It was in enough trouble with electrical problems without you firing at it, what did you use, an SM3?'

'You seem well informed. If you must know, I was ordered to shoot it down,' it was dawning on the young coast guard commander how lucky he was to still be alive.

'We had a civilian liason officer aboard, it was made very clear when he joined the ship I was to obey his orders no matter what.'

'I take it he is the one in hand cuffs?' asked Paul. 'Might I enquire when the coast guard started taking orders from civilians on such matters? More to the point who and what is he?'

'We were not told his name, his orders came from the Senate committee with oversight on defence,' replied the now compliant American.

'Bob, look after the crew and throw that 'official' in the brigg. No contact with anyone. I'll meet you in cripples creek, get Kelly to pick me up in Abu Dhabi.

'Will do Boss'

'Any news on survivors from the AWAC?' asked Paul.

'The Black Hawk will be on board in a few minutes, we're just slowing down to pick up 'the raiders'. Give me five minutes Boss.'

'Will do, I'll call you back Bob.'

'What the hells gone wrong?' asked Taff as he walked into Paul's office.

'We've lost an AWAC', was the blunt reply from Paul.

'What? How for heavens sakes?' asked Taff, 'surely the Pakis didn't find it in the dark?'

'No mate, the yanks shot it down just after dawn. The plane had engine trouble and was circling Fearless so the crew could bale out a few at a time to make rescue easier. Some got out, four I think, then it got taken out by a missile fired from a coast guard cutter. I'm afraid it looks as though the other eight have had it.'

'That is terrible Paul, do we know who yet?' Taff asked.

'Not yet mate, Bob will let us know in a few minutes. It gets worse I'm afraid,' Paul continued, 'The cutter launched a couple of new harpoons at Fearless.'

'What !?' exclaimed the base commander.

'Don't worry, she knocked them down alright, they're in bits on the bottom of the Indian Ocean, along with the ship which launched them.'

'Fearless sunk a U.S Coast Guard cutter? Oh my gawd, there'll be a fuss about that! What are their casualties?' he asked Paul.

'As far as I know, there were a handful of wounded, about half a dozen, they are in the sick bay on Fearless. It seems as though they were on a special operation under the control of some civilian sent by congress. I'm off out there to find out what the hell is going on. And incidently the mission was a success, we have all four of the devices, everyone intact and we've temporally gained a Black Hawk on Fearless. All of which makes the loss of the AWAC the harder to take.'

'What were you going to take Paul,' asked Taff.

'I was thinking a speed bird, then we'd be able to bring the team back as well as the survivors of the AWAC, the bodies if they found any and the devices.'

Paul was about to call Bob, the skipper of the Fearless when Bob called him, Paul put it on speaker so Taff could hear as well.

Timothy Pilgrim

'Bad news I'm afraid Paul,' the captain began. 'As we feared, only four got out, we have five bodies, two of them Julie and Christine were still alive when they were picked up. Julie was still conscious, it seems the two girls were blown out of the door by the blast, but got caught by the fireball when the plane exploded. She said the flight deck crew were not wearing their chutes. It seems as though the plan was to try to make the U.E.A on just the two engines. Paul,' the captain hesitated, 'those girls died because their 'chutes melted as they came down, their burns were survivable according to the doc. I have some very shaken marines on board after those girls died in their arms. That bastard in the cooler has a lot to answer for. I never totally agreed with you about women on active service, but let's just say, this has made me reconsider my position.'

'Thanks for the update Bob,' replied Paul, 'send the full report as soon as you can please so we can notify the families, you know what the bush telegragh is like around here.'

'Will do Boss,' replied the distressed Skipper.

Paul shut down the link and turned to Taff, 'there are times when I really hate this job. How the hell do I tell Julie's hubby the mother of their two little girls won't be coming home?'

Taff was sure there was a tear in the corner of Pauls eye, the Colonel turned towards the window, gazing across the wide expanse of the old airfield

'Damn it Taff, Julies kids play with my grand daughter, I'm too old for this bloody job, what do I do Taff? At least three of the others have kiddies as well.'

'I'll tell you what you are going to do Colonel, I'm pulling rank, and you will do as you are told, for once.'

Taff leaned forward on Paul's desk, 'I'll deal with the families, that's my job. You have a plane waiting, get your kit and go get the bastard behind this, you know as well as I do it isn't that arsehole in the slammer on Fearless. Find out who he is, who sent him, who pays him. I want the head of the sod behind all of this and frankly I don't care how you do it.'

Paul merely grunted something which sounded like 'okay' and went into the little back room where he kept his kit and even slept sometimes. When he emerged he was in combats, carrying his kit bag and rifle, his webbing slung over his shoulder.

'I take it you'll be staying out there somewhere to supervise the evacuation,' Taff asked.

'Makes sense, there is a tempory head quarters being set up, it over looks the main logistics base just short of the Iranian border. I'll be there once we've sorted this other business out.'

Taff looked at his old friend, 'Any ideas?'

'What on, why the attacks on the AWAC and Fearless?' replied Paul, 'The only idea I can come up with is it was a last resort plan in case we got those nukes. Bloody desperate, but if the teams the Americans sent couldn't find them, then it makes some sort of sense. We are the last people the cartel would want to have them.'

'Wouldn't the attack imply they knew we'd got them?' asked Taff.

'May be, they probably knew it was us messing about, it would need to be something very serious for us to risk upsetting Pakistan. It's not a great leap to work the rest out, assuming you had an idea where the damned things might have been hidden'.

'Do you think that was the real reason for the raid which killed Bin Laden?'

'Buggered if I know Taff,' replied Paul, 'but I wouldn't have thought so. What I can't understand is how they got there in the first place. We'd been watching, and listening to everything in and around that compound for months. It's possible the lads watching when our planes were grounded missed something, but all the surveillence footage has been checked over and over. The whole thing stinks Taff, the timing, the death of most of seal team 6 so soon after the raid. I'm damned if I know what's going on. Every thing is coming unglued and all this lot seem to care about is grabbing as much money and power as possible. I suppose it could be as simple as that, and they see us as a threat.'

'You've got a plane to catch, go on, I'll look after the store.'

'Thank's Taff I don't think I could have handled facing the families.'

'Go on, have a safe trip, and good luck Paul.' In truth the stocky little Welshman wasn't looking forward to the job any more than Paul had been, but it had to be done.

'Keep me posted on the condition of our other guests, the sooner some of them are back at their desks the happier I'll be,' was Paul's parting shot as he left Taff refilling his coffee mug.

'You and me both boyo,' Taff muttered under his breath, 'You and me both!'

CHAPTER FIFTEEN

The flight turned out to be uneventful, hardly surprising as apart from a handful of technicians to help turn the concord round, ready for it's flight home there was a single flight attendant to keep Paul company. He took full advantage of the opportunity to catch up on some sleep.

As is often the way with such things, arrival was timed for just after dark, a pair of helicopters landed near the plane, parked in a remote spot on the airfield, as far away from prying eyes as possible. The cargo hold had a perculiar mix once loaded, four crates containing the miniture, but extremely powerful nuclear devices.

Archie may have assured everyone they were perfectly safe, somehow no-one seemed convinced, even when the young scientist pointed out he would be on the aircraft for the homeward flight there was still an air of unease.

The rest of the 'cargo' consisted of five body bags with labels identifying the occupants and another simply marked 'MISC', concealing to some extent the grizzly nature of it's contents. In reality these were a few pieces which could have been from any of the flight deck crew. It would be a D.N.A. job to identify any of the body parts.

Paul collared the scientist as he was about to board, 'I need to know everything about those damned devices Archie, where and how they were made, who by? I also need to know where they've been, get Kenny to help and the forensics lot, the real prize will be who signed the checks. Oh, and bloody well done defusing them.'

'Thank you boss,' replied the young man. 'I have a lot of the firing mechanisms in this bag boss, we'll probably learn more from these and the mobile phone than the devices themselves, we already know where they were made, there is only one lab. capable of making them.'

'Have a good trip home, and I hope you're right about everything being safe'.

As the ground crews were completing their checks a third helicopter arrived, this one turned out to be a Lynx which belonged to Fearless, even in the dim light Paul recognised the skipper, 'Hello Bob, I didn't expect to see you here.'

'I don't know if I've done the right thing, but I have brought our mystery man along.'

'No doubt you had your reasons Bob,' replied Paul, 'care to share them?'

'It's a bit difficult to explain really,' replied the skipper of the warship.

'Try me.' said Paul, sounding interested.

'Well the crew, my crew, that is, seem to have accepted the crew of the Coast Guard cutter we sank as being alright, just doing as they were told, nothing personal, and now can't do enough to atone. Of course, there isn't anything they can do in that respect. Our lot know enough to realise the radars on the cutter would have produced weird readings from both us and the AWAC, so they have been forgiven, so as to speak.'

'Fair enough,' replied Paul, 'but I presume they haven't felt the same towards our other guest.'

'Exactly, I genuinely believe his life is in danger, if he had remained on Fearless Boss,' said Bob.

'You mean to tell me some of our crew would have topped him?' asked Paul. 'I thought their discipline was better than that.'

'No, no, you misunderstand me Boss, it wasn't our lads, although one or two of the Marines on the rescue boats were praying for a reason. It was the Americans, the most popular suggestion was feeding him to the sharks.'

'Difficult to find a reason to argue with that Bob,' replied Paul, 'but I see your point. Bring the scum bag out here.'

Paul called the S.A.S. team on his communicator, 'Sorry to disturb you lads, but we've got another passenger, if you could come and get him please.'

The mystery man was dragged out of the Lynx by a pair of marine sergeants, as he approached Paul, he almost hissed, 'why don't you quit old man, you can't stop progress.'

To every ones surprise the man collapsed, being violently sick, Paul hadn't even blinked as he kicked the man, very hard, squarely in the crutch.

He turned to the nearest S.A.S. man. 'Keep him fully restrained for the trip home, hand him over to my provost staff, he is to be kept in solitary until I return. He is to have no contact with anyone, and an armed escort will accompany anyone taking him his food.

He might not look it right now, but he is one of the most dangerous men around.

I'd tighten those cuffs if I were you sergeant, and get some leg irons on him before he starts to recover.'

'I presume you know him Sir?' said the tough S.A.S. veteran.

'No need for the Sir,' replied Paul. ' He is Carol McNight, thrown out of every special forces unit in the U.S. Delta Force, Seals even the C.I.A. black ops, all branded him as an unstable whack job. He was directly responsible for the deaths of four lads from Hereford in Sierra Leone several years back, then three of our lot got hit on the retrieval mission, I was one of them! He vanished about three years ago when he killed three out of the four feds sent to arrest him for killing his section commander because he took the mickey out of his name.'

'Oops!' uttered the sergeant.

'It will be more than oops if he sees the faintest glimmer of a chance, someone did well to get those cuffs on him Bob'.

'Don't look at me Paul,' replied the Skipper of Fearless. 'It was the master at arms from the cutter, funnily enough he said not to take the cuffs off.'

One of the technicians approached the little group. 'Excuse me Boss, but the plane is ready to leave. The control tower indicated they would like us all out of here as soon as possible.'

'Right, lets get going then. Watch him sergeant!' was Paul's parting comment. 'Come on Bob, let's have a chat with those Americans then we can pack them off home.'

The three helicopters all headed off to their different destinations, the Black Hawk to a transport headed home to the States, for the crew it had certainly been an eventful tour of duty.

The Chinook left to meet a C17 detailed to take it back to the U.K. for a major refit and overhaul, both long over due. The crew looking forward to some leave, at last.

Paul and Bob sat in the back of the Lynx as it headed back to rejoin Fearless.

About thirty miles away on a rough dusty road a Humvee headed towards the remote old airfield.

'Go bloody easy will you!' pleaded the passenger, 'that's the second time in a mile you've nearly tipped us over.'

'That's the least of our worries, have you any idea what will happen to us if we miss that bloody plane.'

'I think we've already missed it,' said the man nursing a stinger launcher, as he pointed to a bright blue spot in the distance, 'that looks like an afterburner to me.'

'Oh shit!' muttered the driver, 'there is a certain senator going to be so pissed off with us.'

The pair sat there, the engine switched off now as they listened for the sound of the aero engines to reach them to confirm their prey had eluded them. The concord promptly obliged with it's distinctive double boom as it eased through the sound barrier.

'I guess senator O'Rourke will throw a major wobbler, that lot will trace those bloody nukes back to him, there'll be hell to pay. Know anywhere bomb proof?'

'We do!' came a very English voice from the darkness.

'Oh crap!' uttered the driver as the two Americans lamely lifted their hands.

Five minutes later the Chinook popped up over the ridge and collected the men and both vehicles.

'I like working with this lot,' commented one of the S.A.S. team who had appeared as if by magic. 'I wonder how they always know?'

Far, far above an old Canberra wheeled for home, 'they got'em boss, no fuss, we've got it on tape too, nice and clear. Some times I love this job.'

'Have a good trip home, thanks Freddie.' Paul spoke into what looked like his mobile phone.

He turned to Bob, 'that should upset the apple cart. Taff was right, the bastards had sent a team to have a crack at Concord. You know the crafty sod leaked the location of our little rendevous, just happened to get the time wrong and have a squad from Hereford waiting for them. I'm right proud of him Bob.'

'With one of the old Canberras keeping an eye on everything.' added the skipper of the Fearless.

'Well, it should make them think for a bit, it might buy us a bit of time. Let's get your passengers statements and get them on their way. Then we can get on with getting an army home.'

Paul spent an hour or so talking to the crew of the Fearless, many of the old hands he had known for years, although he rarely got to see them these days.

'Right Bob, lets go and see our American friends. Can we start with the Skipper?'

'We'll use my cabin if you like Paul,' offered the captain of the old assault ship.

'Sounds like a plan, I could use a coffee if there's one going.'

A few minutes later, sitting in a comfortable chair, mug of coffee in easy reach Paul was introduced to the Skipper of the destroyed coast guard cutter.

To say the greeting was frosty would be fairly accurate, 'I want some answers from you,' Paul began, 'and I'll warn you now any bull shit and it will be a bloody long time before you, or your crew will be free to go home. Your actions killed eight of my people, all friends of mine, if you try to tell me you were just obeying orders I will probably feed you to the local sharks! Just so we understand each other, this is no idle threat.'

'You won't do that Colonel.' replied the American.

'I wouldn't take bets on that. Right, who gave you the orders to shoot down my bloody AWAC?'

'I believe you already have him Colonel, we handed him over in handcuffs, we placed him in custody when he repeated the order to attack this ship after one of our crew positively identified it.'

'So who is he? Do you always take orders from civilians?' Paul asked.

'I told your captain here, I was never told his name.' said the American, 'I was simply told to obey his orders, no matter what.'

'Okay,' Paul took a deep breath, 'who told you to obey that bastards orders, I want a name!'

'He is a retired Admiral, currently honorary commodore of the south eastern command, his name is Admiral Bennett, he is a powerful man.'

'That's as may be, but he hasn't the power to give you, or any other serving officer orders, so why do it?'

'My flottila commander told me to do as I was told, and get on with it, not to argue.'

'And his name?' asked Paul, beginning to lose his patience.

' Vice Admiral Clough.'

'Do you know if he was told by anyone to order you to obey that civilian nutter?' Paul asked. 'If so who and when?'

'All I know Sir, is the civilian came aboard as we finished the loading before we left Aden . We had to wait for some extra missiles to be loaded and for the civilian to come aboard. As soon as he arrived Vice Admiral Clough called, just saying to "obey his orders." He made it very clear our mystery man had absolute authority, and his orders were to be obeyed at all cost.'

'I already know when you passed through the Suez canal, I also know when you took up your station off Aden on anti-pirate patrol. What I don't know is when you left and where the hell you have been hiding since?' Paul asked.

The American was beginning to relax a bit at last, 'We went into Aden to refuel two weeks ago, then headed to a position off the Iranian coast to wait for fresh orders. The civilian ordered the new missiles, the ones we had to wait in Aden for, to be loaded onto the launchers and we were to await instructions.'

'What were these new orders, when did you get them and where did they come from?' Paul asked.

'We were ordered to our new patrol line two days ago, the orders came from our flottila head quarters. We were told we were to watch out for Iranian gun runners who were supplying and supporting militant attacks on the Pakistan coastline, their objective being to disrupt NATO supplies.'

Paul turned to Bob, 'what's it to be Captain? he began. 'Do we believe him and let him go home, or is lieing and holding back? In which case the choice is the slammer or the sharks?'

'The only other thing I know Sir, is the last orders I received from our base did mention the fact we were to look out for Iranians, the intel was supposed to have come from the CIA.'

'Did it now?' Paul sounded interested. He pulled his communicator from his belt and used speed dial for the directors direct number.

After the usual pleasantries Paul came to the point. 'This stays between us for now , you are probably aware we lost an AWAC early the day before yesterday.'

'There was a rumour going round this morning Paul, so it is true. Might I ask what happened?'

'I hope you are sitting down Director,' said Paul, 'as this might come as a bit of a shock.'

'Go on.'

'It was shot down by a coast guard cutter, supposedly on orders from your organisation. Do me a favour please and just check, discreetly, if any such orders were sent to Admiral Bennett, or Vice Admiral Clough in Norfolk naval yard.'

'I will indeed, but I should tell you it appears we have lost touch with a coast guard cutter in the Indian ocean, one of the ships on the anti- pirate patrol. She hasn't been heard from for a couple of days? The current theory is she was run down by a bulk carrier off Aden during the night. There is no sign of her at all.'

'I wasn't going to tell you this just yet Sir, but she wasn't in the gulf of Aden, she was off shore from the Pakistan, Iranian border. Your cutter is now on the sea bed, not only did it shoot down one of my AWAC's they also fired anti ship missiles at Fearless! At that point I ordered Fearless to sink it!'

The Director was stunned by the brutal bluntness of Paul, with whom he had always got on well. 'Oh my god,' he muttered, 'what were the casualties?'

'Eight dead on the AWAC, seven wounded on the cutter, two have nasty burns and a few non lethal shrapnel holes, they'll live.'

'And the rest of the crew, were they all lost?' asked the American.

'If you mean the crew of the cutter, they didn't even get their feet wet,' replied Paul, 'the skipper is in front of me as we speak. He is adamant the orders came from Langley via Bennett. What he has told me, and this is supported by the crew, means the civilian on board who gave the order to fire, knew about our mission about the same time you and I spoke about it. Now, as I totally trust you director, the only explanation is someone else in your agency received a similar message to the one you got, and at about the same time.'

'You think this Sir Selwin character repeated that signal to someone else here.'

'Can you think of another explanation Director,' asked Paul. 'The pain in the arse at my end has dual nationality, and served with your JAG corps before coming over here to plague us. The other thing which might help you find your problem body is the civilian who was chucking his weight about was none other than Carol bloody McNight!'. The dislike, even hatred of the man clear in the tone of Paul's voice.

'Can't be Paul,' replied the Director. 'After we requested he leave the Agency he went to work for an NGO in Bagdad as a body guard, he was killed in an explosion which took out a party of engineers he, and some others were escorting.'

'I assure you director the bastard is very much alive, I knew him the second I laid eyes on him.' replied Paul.

'Do you know where he is now?' asked the shaken director.

'Oh yes, He and I are going to have a little chat when I get the chance. He was sent to stop us getting those bloody mini nukes, which is why a clapped out coast guard cutter was equipped with the latest advanced missiles. The question is who sent him, and how the sam hill did they, who ever they are, know we would find them rather than your team.'

'I hope they didn't know Paul. If we are lucky it will turn out they were just allowing for the possibility.'

Paul replied, 'I don't like the sound of either thank you. But on the plus side you can now stop looking for both the mini nukes and the AWOL coast guard cutter. I'll be in touch later Director and good luck finding your rotten egg.'

'Thanks for the up date Paul, I'll call you as soon as I have anything relevant to report.'

'Thank you Sir,' replied Paul, 'have a nice day'.

The captain of the now sunken coast guard cutter sat there, almost in a state of shock, 'you've got the director of the CIA on speed dial !?'

'I've got your President's mobile, the one he carries in his pocket, on there as well! So is there anything else you want to tell us, or change, bearing in mind I was listening to most of what was said on your bridge.' relied Paul. 'And before you ask, I have no idea how the system works, I only know it does.'

CHAPTER SIXTEEN

Taff walked into the head quarters block of the All Arms Unit , he had seen the concord land as he arrived at the main gate, how he hated the task which he knew was coming next. Mercifully it didn't happen often but eight bodies at once, well five and some bits, in this case made it harder to take. He and B.J. had personally told all the families face to face of the loss of their loved ones yesterday, as soon as they were certain of who had survived and who had perished. Today was likely to be a difficult day, to further complicate matters some how the media had got hold of the news that an AWAC had been lost, the assumption being it was an R.A.F. Boeing Sentry. Although the M.O.D. denied it the rumors persisted, Taffs first act of the day was to get G.C.H.Q. to watch out for any calls about the subject. He didn't have to wait long, he was stunned when the call came through, it was the source of the call which was the surprise. It was traced to the office of the suspect senator, it quoted an 'impeccable' source, an eye witness.

After some frantic checking, it turned out the man Paul had kicked so hard in the family jewels, had got off a radio phone message to his boss, gleefully confirming the destruction of the A.W.A.C. This was just before a signal from the Canberra fried every transmitter and mobile phone on board the cutter.

Taff went in search of Paul, he should have been back in his office by now. Claires response of 'I haven't seen him Sir,' in reply to Taffs query calmed his enthusiasum a bit. Taff pulled out his communicator and called Paul, but he only had it set to 'local net work' so he called B.J. who he knew had gone to meet the concord and it's passengers.

'He's not here Taff, he wasn't on the plane.'

'Then where the hell is he?' Taff demanded. 'mind you, he did say he might stay out there, something to do with the evacuation.'

'Last I heard he was going with Bob back to the Fearless, something about having a face to face chat with the Captain of that cutter.' replied B.J.

'I hope he doesn't do anything daft, like shoot him!' Taff sounded worried, as he knew just how upset Paul had been over the incident.

B.J's. reply allayed those fears a little. 'I don't think he'll do that Taff, although he did kick the civilian who gave the order to fire. In fact the guy is currently on his way to our medical unit under armed guard, the medic with the team reckons he'll need surgery.'

'Is it serious?' asked Taff.

'Lets put it this way, I don't think there is much chance of him ever sireing any offspring from here on.'

B.J. heard Taff mutter, 'Oh lord'.

'That's probably a good thing Taff, the thought of a flock of little Carol McNights' running around is not is not a pleasant prospect.'

Taff nearly choked on his reply. 'Not THE Carol McNight, he's dead!'

'Apparently not Taff, I'll grant you he didn't look very well, but he is definitely alive.'

'As soon as you've got things sorted out over there B.J. can you pop into my office please for a chat, and while I think of it get some security on those devices and Archie until they're safely back in the underworld.' the worried tone was back in Taffs voice again.

'Fair enough Taff.' replied B.J.

Back in his office Taff called Fearless, 'could you get Paul for me please Bob, I need a chat.'

'I'm sorry Sir, he left some time ago by helicopter. I presume to join up with a transport headed back to base with the S.A.S team who caught those two Americans you set up, the ones trying to shoot down concord as she left for home, he did say he was proud of you.'

'Nice of him,' replied Taff, 'Out of idle curiosity what are you doing just now Bob, apart from talking to me!'

'Headed to a map reference Paul gave me, at roughly three quarters of maximum speed to hand over the crew of the cutter we sank. Strange really, it seems to be about two hundred miles more or less south east of Diago Garcia. Nowhere near any air or shipping routes, nowhere near anywhere really.'

'Alright Bob, bon voyage.' Taff didn't wait for a reply before flicking a switch.

He called the units old Hercules droning homeward with the S.A.S. team and their two captives.He was pleased at the successful out come of their trap, but far from pleased at the discovery Paul was not on board.

Just then his door opened to reveal General Leach, followed by B.J.

'Is Paul around, I'd like a word,' said the amiable General, who was acting as a defacto Prime Minister until the real one recovered from his injuries sufficiently to resume his duties.

'We would all like a word with our errant comander,' replied Taff. 'No one has seen him since he left Fearless on a helicopter a couple of hours or so ago'.

'That is bloody inconvenient ,' observed General Leach, 'should we be worried?'

'Knowing him he's switched off his communicator to get a bit of kip, he is pretty knackered at the moment,' B.J suggested trying to be helpful.

'You have seen the news, I take it Taff? Said the General, 'All the speculation, it is causing mayhem behind the scenes. What do we do about it?'

Taff thought for a minute before replying to the Generals question. 'That is a bit of a trickey one Sir, I know what I'd like to do, but it's not very practical.'

'I don't understand Taff, please explain.'

'Here's my problem Sir.' Taff began. 'The information the media are putting out came from the Americans, to be precise that gobby senator we've been having trouble with, well at least from his office.'

'How pray did he know? The C.I.A. I suppose,' surmised General Leach.

'No Sir, he had a call from the man who ordered the crew of the cutter to fire the missiles. You do know it was Carol Mcnight don't you Sir'.

'But he's dead!' exclaimed General Leach, 'Killed in Bagdad, I remember thinking at least some good had come out of all the misery when I heard the news. You are sure it was him?'

'There is no doubt about it General', said B.J. 'I saw him get off the plane and onto a chopper to 'the farm' less than an hour ago.'

'He's here!?' General Leach was not easily shocked these days, but this shocked him. 'I presume Paul knows all this?'

'He knows about McNight, it was him kicked him in the nuts, so hard the medics say they'll have to operate. It is possible Paul is still unaware of the furore in the media, or who released it.' replied Taff. 'One other thing,'

Taff continued, 'while we've been talking I've had an email, on the secure link from the director of the C.I.A.'

'What has he got to say for himself about all of this?' asked General Leach.

' He says that he can't get in touch with Paul, but he, meaning Paul, was right, Sir Selwin had copied the message about the operation to retrieve those nukes, not to anyone in the C.I.A. but to a certain senators office. It seems as though someone in Washington then repeated it to a 'black ops' department at Langley. Two of that team have, as the director put it, gone off the grid, and are officially missing!'

'The two on the herc headed here?' asked B.J.

'Paul did say to expect extreme measures to stop us getting our hands on them, which is why I set the trap.' said Taff, 'To be honest I didn't expect it to work, I wonder what he's up to?'

'He hasn't shared any thing with either of you which might explain him vanishing?' asked General Leach.

Both shook their heads, 'not a hint Sir,' replied Taff.

'You think he's alright though?' asked the General. 'He's a devious sod, you don't think he has gone 'missing' on purpose do you?'

'Why would he do that Sir?' B.J. asked.

'I wasn't planning on staying more than a few minutes, but as I'm here, you couldn't get me a coffee could you B.J.' the General asked. 'I've been thinking about all this interference Taff, these sods know we're on to them, what more than any other single thing might push them over the edge and do something daft?'

'With the power they've got, not a lot Sir,' replied Taff. 'You're not suggesting they've got Paul are you?'

'Knowing our missing commander I would have thought that was highly unlikely Taff.' The General accepted the steaming mug from B.J., 'thank you. Now where was I? Ah yes, Paul's absence. He has a bit of a reputation for being, how can I put this, a bit of a loose cannon. He tends to take out anything which gets in his way. If you were one of these C.E.Os. manipulating events, or that rogue senator and you knew the commander of the one force which could really damage you had vanished, what would you think?'

'Oh bloody hell!' exclaimed Taff. 'You don't think he's gone after them do you?'

'He did take his old rifle with him Boss,' added B.J.

'Knowing him, although I wouldn't rule it out, but I think that is exactly what he wants everyone to think.' replied General Leach.

The three senior officers spent nearly an hour discussing the various problems, not the least of which was what to do about Sir Selwin de la Fontaine.

'Won't arresting or removing him tip our hand to the cartel Boss?' asked a worried Taff.

'It might, but what else can we do?' replied General Leach, 'It will be almost impossible to keep sensitive information away from him, and as is obvious he has friends in high places, his rapid promotion proof of his connections.'

'A thought occurs to me,' said B.J. 'If we let him 'accidently' over hear something about Paul's vanishing act, then carefully monitor all his communications, it just might help us prove our case against him, and the cartel to some extent.'

'You are suggesting using him to feed the cartel snippets of information we want them to know. You have been Paul's number two for too long!' observed General Leach. 'You are becoming almost as devious as he is.'

'Well, we all have a lot of work to do, any idea when you'll be in again Sir?' asked Taff.

General Leach thought for a moment, 'If I can have a room for the night, I'll be back about nine o'clock tonight, twenty one hundred if you prefer.'

'Until then Sir'.

'Nothing much happened for the next couple of days, apart from the deepening crisis in southern Europe. All efforts to locate Paul came to nothing, this was of course relayed to the cartel in the U.S.A. via Sir Selwin and the Senators office.

Then came the news that the C.E.O. of the largest defence contractor in the 'states had been killed in an explosion at his mansion on the Californian coast. The official cause was a faulty regulator valve on the gas bar-b-que he was using at the time, the conspiracy theorists began to wonder.

The following day the rogue senator complained of feeling 'unwell' and as medical help arrived dropped stone dead from a massive heart attack. The rumour mill began to get going, was this really coincidence?

General Leach was beginning to worry and went to see Taff, 'Please tell me it isn't Paul on a rampage.'

'If it is any use, we still don't know where he is or what he is doing Boss. Personally I think he is in Afghanistan, about twenty of the best special forces troops, from all manner of units also seem to be missing. The consensus is Paul has put together a group for something to do with the proposed withdrawl, quite what we haven't figured out as yet.

I've traced and spoken to the helicopter pilot who flew Paul ashore from Fearless. He says he dropped Paul off at a remote spot in the Oman, he was met by several men, who the pilot says looked like special forces. The thing is no one I know knows bugger all about any operations there.'

'Niether do I Taff,' confided General Leach. 'All I know is the American authorities are beginning to wonder if Paul is on a revenge mission.'

As the two old friends discussed the possibilities a news flash came up on Taffs computer screen.

'Oh shit', Taff muttered, 'this looks bad Boss.'

'Now what has gone wrong?' asked General Leach.

'Another of the top cartel members has died, the C.E.O. of the biggest security provider has been killed when his car left the road and crashed into a gully, he was headed to the Senators ranch to pay his respects.'

'Oh dear, this isn't looking good is it Taff?' General Leach was really worried. 'Do we know what caused the crash?'

'According to the local Sheriff there was a rock fall triggered by a small earth quake in the area shortly before the accident, it seems as though there were some loose stones and rocks in the road, just round a blind corner. The chauffeur driven limo hit a rock, skidded on the loose stuff and went over the edge killing all four occupants.'

'For all our sakes, find him Taff, and please let it be a long way from Southern California!'

One strange effect of these deaths was on the stock markets, especially Wall Street, things had been on the slide anyway, because of the economic situation. Suddenly the stocks of any company linked to the cartel collapsed in the most dramatic crash any dealer had ever seen. The rumours spread like a wild fire, were the bosses of these huge conglomerates being targeted?

Panic set in, yet other stocks steadied, only cartel linked shares continued to plunge, within an hour most were worthless and trading was suspended pending an enquiry. Something was wrong, what really sealed things was the sudden death of one of the most powerful oil men in Texas. He had, it seemed suffered a massive heart attack when playing golf with some business colleagues. It was well documented he had a history of heart troubles, and was fitted with a pace maker, it was very plausible that the news of him going from billionaire to bankrupt in an hour had proved too much.

On hearing this news General Leach actually went quite pale. 'It is him, isn't it Taff?'

'It is beginning to look that way Sir' admitted the stocky little Welshman. 'If another one goes then it will be certain someone is taking them out, I just hope it is the Americans 'cleaning house'. I happen to know they have a combined task force of assorted Feds investigating the entire scam.'

'Call in the heads of departments Taff, one of them must know something pertaining to Pauls' whereabouts. As for the sudden demise of not so nice Americans, I'm not certain if I should raise a glass and say good riddance or retire to somewhere inaccessible.'

Within five minutes most of the senior officers were gathered in Taffs office in response to General Leach's request. Once they were all seated General Leach faced them, leaning against the front of Taff's desk.

'As you must all be aware by now, your operational commander has gone missing,' he began. 'What was that Al?' certain he had heard the big electronics chief mutter something.

'I said he's not the only one Sir,' replied Al.

'Oh, do go on.' said the General, 'so who else has vanished?'

'One of the gremlins Sir, Giles, the communications genious, he is also the one who develops all the weird stuff, scanners, electronic cloaks and the likes. He supposedly went on leave last week, yet it seems as though he boarded the herc which took a party of S.A.S to a remote part of the Oman, the one you sent Taff to get those Yanks. I only found this out a few minutes ago, I knew he'd booked some leave earlier, but that's all.'

'And you think he might have joined up with Paul?' the General grunted. 'Why on earth would Paul want a gremlin with him?'

'I think he might have taken a proto type of a new computer with him, it makes our most powerful computer about as advanced as an abacus. The scarey thing is it fits in your pocket, it is the same size as a packet of super king cigarettes '

'Apart from the location is there any reason to suppose he was meeting Paul?' asked Taff.

'He did take a full carton of cigarettes with him, Paul's brand, and Giles doesn't smoke!' replied Al.

'So you could be right Taff,' General Leach heaved a small sigh of relief. 'He's doing it to panic the cartel, and is sitting on a hill top in Afghanistan directing units to their positions for the big bug out.'

'But why no contact with us?' asked Taff.

'Two things, one, if we knew we wouldn't be looking,' said Kenny. 'The other thing is he suspected someone was monitoring our traffic on our long range communicators, they may be not able to listen to what was being said, but enough to know exactly where the caller was, and probably who was talking.'

Just then Pete, walked in. Pete had been one of the original tanker pilots when the unit had first been formed, now he was in overall command of all things with wings. He addressed General Leach, 'sorry I'm late Sir. A slight problem has arisen.'

'Is it serious?'

'Damned if I know, to tell the truth. A box of new tricks arrived in Kandahar last week with instruction on how to fit it on 'eagle eye one', our oldest ex R.A.F. Canberra. It took off on a test flight and was followed by one of our high altitude victor tankers. Niether have been seen since!, I have no idea what they are up to. We had an enquiry from the yanks as they had detected some chatter between what they thought might have been two of our planes over the Kuril islands and wondered if it was any thing to worry about?'

'Call Giles'. said B.J. 'see if he answers, if he does then we can clear this up now.'

Taff pushed a few buttons on the consol on his desk.

Far away on a wild hill top a young man on the adventure of his life jumped as his communicator vibrated and buzzed quietly. 'I think we've been rumbled Giles, you'd better answer that', came a voice from a tent hidden in the rocks and scrub.

'Giles?' enquired the caller.

'Yes Sir,' replied the young man.

'Where are you?' asked Taff as casually as he could manage.

'I'm on holiday Sir.' came the non-commital reply.

'I know you're on holiday Giles, but where are you on holiday, clearly you're not at Butlins in Skegness!'

'I don't think I'd like it there Sir. Too noisey for me, all th…'

'Giles!' Taff interrupted the young man, 'I'm guessing Paul is with you, can you put him on please.'

Paul looked at the worried youngster, he nodded and held out his hand for the communicator, 'Took you long enough to figure it out Taff,' he said.

'What the bloody hell do you think you're playing at! Vanishing for the best part of a week! Explain!' Taff had almost shouted the comment.

'If you figured this bit out then I would have hoped after chatting to Kenny you would have twigged some bugger was tracking my signals. Don't worry they won't track this one, apparently it will seem as though it is coming from the moon.'

'You could have at least let us know you were alright!'

'If you had known, then it would only have been a matter of time before the cartel would have known where I was. The thought of that lot wondering what is going on, and not being able to find out, frankly I find it quite uplifting.'

'Half of them will never know now, they are dead! Heart attacks and freak, but plausible accidents, have killed four of them in three days.'

'Oh dear what a pity, how sad.' was Paul's reply, 'and you thought it was me!? I know I am a fairly good shot, but I'm guessing they were in the 'states, so they are a little bit out of range!.'

'Are you certain this link is totally secure Paul?' asked General Leach.

'As sure as I can be Sir,' replied Paul.

'Very well, what exactly are you doing?' asked the exasperated General.

'Trying to ensure the units arrive here in the right order to resupply for their trip to their embarkation port. It is also important to make sure the ships arrive in the correct order and at the appointed time. The idea being a unit arrives and goes straight onto their designated ship. It's a bit like playing several games of chess with several hundred pieces on some sides, all at the same time. It is an interesting test of the new toy Giles brought with him.'

'So everything is alright, no problems?'

'Not at the moment,' Paul replied to General Leach.

'By implication you are aware of an impending problem?' observed the General.

'You could say that Sir,' Paul paused to light a cigarette, 'apart from the predictable foul ups, it seems as though we have a substantial force of supposed Pakistani border guards headed our way. When they were asked to go home, they responded by firing on our patrol, their local head quarters say they are here to help. The only problem with that is they didn't say who they would be helping!'

'Be careful Paul, one wrong move and things could get difficult.'

Paul's reply was to the point, 'It's not exactly easy as it is boss, trying to get close on two hundred thousand troops out without anyone realising how you are doing it isn't the easiest task I've ever been given. Now we have the added complication of these border guards, they have already injured twenty five N.A.T.O. troops, none too seriously. Twice so far they have mined the road we are using, we cleared the first lot, some of it under fire. We asked them to pack it up, and they promptly replaced the mines we had removed!'

'I'll have a word Paul, just be careful.'

'I wish you would Sir,' replied Paul, 'because as from midnight our time the first units will start to arrive in this area and I'll be damned if this is all going to be happening overlooked by these bloody nutters. Basically they have ten hours to pull out and head back home, because from then onwards we will retaliate using lethal force.'

Before General Leach could reply he heard a shout 'INCOMING' in the back ground, followed by some loud explosions. Then Paul's voice 'Batteries, one, three and five, return fire, fire for effect.'

'Paul, are you alright?' the senior officer asked.

'At the moment Boss, we've lost two American rangers to a direct hit on their position. I've got to go, it looks as if they aren't going home yet.' All those listening heard a crack followed by 'Shit!' and a few more expletives, 'I'll call you back.'

The next half an hour was very noisey to say the least. The allied guns had quickly silenced the mortars being fired at three N.A.T.O. positions protecting the temporary logistics base in the valley. The ground troops were not so easily dealt with, the team in the position with Paul were all veteran special forces apart from Giles. Paul reckoned his tent was the safest spot for the young scientist, it was on the reverse slope, in between two large rocks and almost under an overhang.

'Get in there, on the floor, protect your kit Giles, move!'

Being old hands, the men in the forward position didn't panic, they were quickly into their pre selected firing positions. In their semi circle they not only protected their own flanks but could support the positions either side. They soon had to resort to taking snap shots at the attackers, such were the casualties they inflicted, the will to attack them soon faded and targets became scarce. Out of nearly two hundred border guards who had attacked less than fifty made it back out of range of the deadly fire of the defenders.

As a semblance of calm returned Paul called back to his base as promised.

'Sorry about that,' he began, 'things got a bit hectic there for a few minutes.'

'Are you alright?' asked a very worried General Leach.

'Pretty much, we lost those two rangers to a direct hit at the beginning, but apart from a few minor nicks the rest of us are near enough intact.'

'I know you Paul, define a few nicks and near enough alright please.'

'Honestly Sir, there is nothing a few band aids and a change of underwear won't put right,' was his reply to the Generals enquiry.

The General was far from convinced. 'Can you explain a couple of things Paul, like why all the subterfuge and what is so important you feel the need to keep even us in the dark, never mind raid special forces from all over for their best men?'

'We have with us possibly the most secret bit of electronic kit there has ever been, as this place isn't exactly the safest on earth I felt it necessary to put together the strongest team possible without attracting attention. Our team needed to be as small as possible, yet powerful enough to protect the kit.'

'What is this new technology Paul?'

'Switch your lap top on please Sir,' Paul asked.

The General opened his brief case, similar to the one Paul normally carried, almost instantly the screen lit up and there was a picture of a distinctly scruffy Colonel, even by his standards.

'You should see an icon flashing top left Sir, that is indicating your computer has received the complete plan for getting N.A.T.O. out of here. It will take you a couple of days to read it all, four or five more to take in the details. Please don't lose it!'

'When on earth did you have time to work all that out?' asked an amazed General.

'Most of it on the flight out here after I joined up with the rest of the team, and the rest since I've been here, and I didn't exactly do it my self Sir,' Paul confessed. 'It is this new box of tricks Giles brought out, I told it what we had, and what we wanted, and it did the rest, in a matter of minutes.'

'Remarkable, quite remarkable,' muttered General Leach.

'If you have been so bloody careful Paul, then how do you explain the attack just now?' asked Taff. 'It sounded pretty serious, I am also puzzled why you weren't warned by a Canberra?'

'We did know about the force of border guards, granted the mortars were a bit of a shock. As for the canberras, there is a patch on the live recon mosaic which is old footage. This was recorded some time ago, before we built the logistics depot, remember we beam all this stuff to the C.I.A. so the cartel get to see it. What they see is current footage indicating a three stage pull out, the air lift, the northern route and us out via the Kyhber pass when it is reopened. It would rather give the game away if they saw the construction of a huge fuel dump.'

'Fair enough, but it doesn't explain the attack, never mind the scale of it, how did they know you were there?' asked Taff.

'I don't think they did know I was here Taff'.

'No you idiot! Not you personally!' exclaimed Taff, 'Oh Lord!' groaned the Welshman. 'Will you be serious for one minute! As you very well know, I meant N.A.T.O. troops in general.'

'It is inevitable local tribesmen have seen something, even in this desolate place. Someone decided to try to discourage us from being here and called in a few favours, could have been the cartel, more likely a major drug smuggler.'

Pete, the officer in charge of the aircraft took his turn, 'I don't suppose you can throw any light on the vanishing act performed by eagle eye one and one of the old victor tankers could you?'

'I could, they are on a special deployment for an allied power, they should be back late tomorrow, or the day after.' replied Paul being deliberately vague.

'I suppose it is something to do with North Korea sabre rattling again.' Pete guessed.

'It is always a good idea to keep an eye on them Pete,' replied Paul, 'they are unpredictable at the best of times.'

'Alright,' sighed Pete, 'so you're not going to tell us'

'Would I lie to you?' Paul feinged a hurt tone.

'You didn't lie Paul, you just didn't tell us.' General Leach interjected. 'Any idea when we can expect you home?'

'If everything goes according to plan, lets say,' he paused, 'a couple of weeks?'

Just after the meeting broke up the link was closed down to enable the signallers and Giles to get every thing hooked up, a news flash came up on the terminal on Taffs desk. The base commander called General Leach back, just as the senior officer reached for the door handle.

'I think you should see this Sir.' Taff turned the screen so the General could see it.

The breaking news was being screened by C.N.N. it seemed as though an executive jet had crashed when taking off from L.A.X. and exploded on impact. They even had footage of the crash, filmed as it had happened, on board was the owner, reputed to be one of the richest men in the country, his stock holdings in a wide variety of companies, mainly in the defence sector were on a 'corporate' scale. Stock market rumours were rife he was about to attempt a take over of the British defence giant B.A.E.

'It bloody well is Paul behind these 'accidents' Taff. He was watching something out of shot while we were talking to him. He was looking beyond the camera, I'm certain I saw him push a button on that little console he had there. It is all to do with that 'detached' blue bird with the call sign 'eagle eye one'. We were talking a few weeks back and he said to me he would use all of this units technology to prevent the cartel interfering with getting N.A.T.O. troops and their equipment home. That is exactly what he is doing, he is taking out those who pull the strings, in the certain knowledge none of them will ever be brought to trial as judges would rule the evidence inadmissible.'

'It would explain a lot Sir,' said Taff, 'but if it is Paul, then how the hell is he taking out 'untouchable' V.I.Ps. half a world away? '

'Something to do with young Giles being with him possibly?' suggested General Leach. 'Another thought occurs to me Taff, ' he continued, if it is being done by 'eagle eye one', using some technology we know nothing about, where is it based? I know there is a tanker involved, but even then there is a limit to the range. I think he has done a deal with the American administration, and kept us in the dark in case it goes 'tits up' as our errant commander would put it.'

'I don't know wether to hope you are right or not, Sir,' replied Taff.

Things got very busy for Paul and his team trying to syncronise the movements of all the multitude of units on the move, apparently in random directions.

In the event everything went like clockwork, even the unexpected change of embarkation port worked well. The people most upset by the change were the Pakistani authorities who lost a fortune in port fees, at least they were when they found out. The first signs of activity in the little port of Jiwani, one of the designated ports for the exodus, was the arrival off the port of the three ships of the all arms unit.

A senior officer came ashore to co-ordinate things, the three warships had escorted two large cruise liners and a pair of substantial cargo ships modified to carry a lot of vehicles. The first group of units consisted of a mix of light infantry battalions and their support units, a handful of light tanks and mobile artillery. The balance made up of Engineers, R.E.M.E. Signals plus sundry cooks, medics and other assorted troops vital to the self sufficiency of the battle group.

Some how they all fitted on the commandeered liner and to the disbelief of the dockers all the vehicles fitted on the cargo ship. The following day was a repeat of the first, as another battle group bordered their ships. Again everything arrived in the right order and was loaded in an amazingly short time.

Half the population of the town turned out the following day, expecting a repeat, instead of a sleek cruise ship and a large modern freighter there were two large grey war ships with lop sided funnels and a flight deck, their stern doors open and landing craft shuttling to and fro from the beach. The troops being ferried onto these two strange vessels proudly wearing green berets, just off shore a sinister looking destroyer patrolled back and forth, watching over the operation.

As suddenly as they had appeared the ships were gone, the first batch of Pakistan 'officials' arrive just in time to see the three warships against the western horizon as darkness descended. They were furious about the lack of consultation on the part of the British, it seemed as though no more than the standard mooring fees had been paid to the company operating the little port. It also appeared the British had paid the dock workers wages for the week, plus a nice bonus, by local standards. The 'officials' had spent the time on the journey, made longer by having to skirt the floods, dreaming up extra charges which would have to be paid to them, in cash of course, before the ships would be allowed to load, a fee for each person and a percentage of the value of each vehicle loaded would be levied. No doubt there would be more charges before permission would be granted for the ships to sail.

This diversion was more successful than Paul could ever have hoped for, as long as British troops had been arriving at the port the Pakistan authorities didn't look for any of the alternatives. They were more interested in how the British had simply 'turned up', no one it seemed knew they were on their way. Now they had slipped away without being 'stitched up', the search concentrated on finding who had been paid to keep quiet, rather than for any more troops on the move.

By the time any one realised what was really going on the rear guard covering the engineer units repairing route 95 for the Iranians were less than forty miles from the embarkation port.

The last minute change caused many a raised eye brow as the main embarkation point was to be the Iranian port of Chabahar. It's big deep water terminal easily coped with even the huge American aircraft carrier pressed into service as a vehicle transport, due to be decommissioned she had been hastily modified below decks to allow an extra deck to be used for vehicle storage.

The vast military convoy took over a week to travel from the Afghan border, crossing near the Iranian city of Zahedan and following route 95 through Khash and Transhahar to the port, indeed when the first units were loading onto their ships, the rear guards were still arriving at the logistics base at Char Bojak.

It had taken just ten days from the first N.A.T.O. troops crossing into Iran until the last ship sailed from Chabahar.

Critics in Iran were calmed by the claim that 'the N.A.T.O. crusaders hadn't dared to attack the strong defences further west in the face of the republican guard units defensive manoeuvres.' Which is more or less what Paul had predicted they would claim. The port fees, all paid in cash would also boost the local economy.

The night after the last ship sailed a Hercules from the 'all arms unit' landed on a stretch of dusty road which had been the main route for the logistics base, this had now gone. The crew waited nervously with the tail ramp down, having already turned into the wind ready for a quick get away if needed. Less than a minute after the big plane had come to a halt four land rovers, two with small trailers appeared out of the dust and drove straight into the plane. All were quickly anchored down and seven minutes after the plane had touched down the wheels left the ground again. Within minutes most of the men who had boarded the Hercules were fast asleep!.

CHAPTER SEVENTEEN

An hour or so after the Hercules with the last of the Nato troops from Afghanistan had taken off General Leach and the young number two from the treasury, accompanied by the acting chief of the defense staff arrived at 'the farm'. This was the original base where the unit which was to become the All Arms Unit had been formed. Outwardly it still looked like a small, if prosperous, small holding, the driver had never been here before and had followed General Leach's instructions on the journey from London.

He was surprised when the General directed him to drive into the open door way of a large barn which held a couple of tractors and several items of machinery he presumed were for use about the farm. Surprise gave way to mild concern for the safety of his V.I.Ps. When the outer doors closed and another set opened in front of the armoured limo, now he was intrigued. This part of the barn contained several cars, all of which to his trained eye were pursuit cars and six land rovers, all looked like V8s and were fitted with mounts for machine guns. He was directed by the General down a ramp to what was clearly a lower level, a couple of soldiers appeared, indicated were he should park and escorted the driver to the canteen. Their greeting to the General, currently the most powerful man in the country, had been casual, more as one would greet a friend. It was the way the V.I.Ps. had simply been left in this strange subterranean car park which really surprised the driver.

The elderly officer led his two colleagues to the concealed lift, hidden beneath the stairs in one corner, once in he pressed the button marked 'H'.

There was no real indication of how far down the lift was taking them, but when the doors opened a brightly lit corridor stretched away in front of them. It seemed deserted for a few moments, a single soldier appeared from the little office near the lift and invited them to sign in.

'Thank you Sir' was all he said, then into a communicator, 'General Leach, plus two'.

'Received John. Out' came the reply.

Two minutes later they were in a ward, full of bandaged, mainly bed ridden bodies, survivors of the carnage at the N.E.C.

General Leach went straight to a bed with a heavily bandaged figure, propped up by pillows. 'Good evening Prime Minister, how are you feeling?'

'Good to see you General, and I can see you, which is good in it's self. I'm told by the medics that I am doing a lot better than it looks, I have little choice but believe them.' The man in the bandages shifted and vinced. 'How are you getting along with the military Danny?' he asked the sole civilian in the party.

'It is, how can I put this? It's different,' answering his own question. 'There is a lot of disquiet about the declaration of martial law, yet among the general public there seems to be a reluctant acceptance. Most of the objections are coming from those who see their perceived power curtailed. These vary from union chiefs to city bankers but they have all been told for the time being this is the way things will have to be.'

'I can just imagine,' the badly injured Prime Minister managed a little chuckle, but decided it hurt too much. 'Why don't you have a word with your Boss, he is the one doing an impression of the 'mummy' in the bed opposite.'

The young man left, followed by the senior Air Force officer who was acting chief of the defence staff who went in search of the injured Admiral who would normally hold the position.

General Leach now sat down next to the Prime Minister, 'At least I've got some good news Sir, all N.A.T.O. troops are out of Afghanistan and either on ships or already in Cyprus. I have no idea how he did it so quickly, but the entire force is out, along with everything which matters equipment wise.'

'That is excellent news General, what were the casualties?' asked the bandaged figure.

'As far as I know Sir, two American rangers were killed and about twenty assorted troops wounded, mostly minor injuries. These occurred when a rouge unit of Pakistani border guards attacked the outposts protecting the major staging area.' The General paused, 'the other bad news is Pauls' unit had an A.W.A.C shot down, killing eight of the crew. It has caused quite a furore as it was destroyed by an American coast guard cutter which was subsequently sunk by Fearless after it fired at her. I don't know how Paul achieved it, but he seems to have kept the majority of the Americans on side'

'I have to say that was unexpected General' said the shocked Prime Minister. 'Any news on those missing nuclear devices?' he asked.

The General shifted in his chair, 'We have them Sir, safe and sound out at the main base. It was at the end of that operation the A.W.A.C was lost.'

'I really would like a chat with our Colonel, where is he at the moment, General?

'To be perfectly honest Sir,' replied the General, 'I don't know, I know where he has been, and I know where he is intending to be tomorrow night. As to his current whereabouts? It is all to do with this cartel of mainly power mad Americans. It would seem as though they have been tracking Paul's movements. He seems to think he has come up with a way of stopping this, but understandably isn't taking any chances. In consequence he keeps vanishing, only to turn up unexpectedly a few days later.'

The Prime Minister was getting tired but insisted the General stayed a little longer.

'So what, if anything is happening, I was lead to believe the F.B.I. had been charged with curtailing the power of this cartel, as you call it.'

'Someone is, that's for sure, five of them, including the rogue senator are dead! Two with heart attacks and three in unusual, though perfectly plausible accidents.'

'Tell me it's not our Colonel!' said the Prime Minister.

The General shifted again in his chair. 'That was our first thought Sir, the thing is I was actually talking to him at the precise moment of one of the deaths. As he pointed out, if you are sitting on an Afghan hill top, California is a little bit out of range!'

'Yet you have your doubts General, I can hear it in your voice.'

'He was in Afghanistan for the entire period during which the deaths occurred, I can't see how it could have been him Sir,' replied General Leach.

'And yet?' said the Prime Minister.

'As you say Sir, and yet!' was the Generals reply. 'If it was anything to do with him I can't see any lawyer ever being able to prove it. The team he put together for the pull out contained several high ranking Americans,

Timothy Pilgrim

including the N.A.T.O. commander on the ground. They were all together during the critical period, he could have sent a team I suppose, but all his men can be accounted for. Someone will make a fuss for sure, but I can't see how they can link the demise of a handful of ruthless greedy bastards to the Colonel.'

'Well if he did have anything to do with it, let us just hope you are right about him being in Afghanistan.' replied the tired out Prime Minister. 'Thank you for the update General, please keep me informed of any developments.'

'I will Sir, and get well soon.'

As General Leach and his party emerged into the cool air of an early April evening in Norfolk, the senior officer allowed himself a few moments to remember the early days of the unit. It's original mission had been to quietly eliminate leading terrorists threatening the security of the U.K., the nagging thought persisted this is exactly what Paul was doing.

'How long have you known about this place Sir?' asked the politition. 'It's just that I can't ever remember seeing anything about it the accounts when we did a review of expenditure on military bases. Even the main base had only very scant records of expenditure, it is all very odd.'

'I can remember it being set up Danny, in fact it was at my instigation the original unit was formed. As I recall there were about twenty of the most effective killers we could find in the original unit, plus a selection of support troops, all the very best at their trades. Even the then Prime Minister visited, she was very impressed with the set up and the results. Things were so much simpler then.'

'There are no mentions of the unit until much more recently in the records General.' said the senior airman. 'Although I remember an attack on what was then a tanker base, which must be nearby, I was straight out of Cranwell, only been on base a few days. As I recall there was a big attack, unprecedented in those days, and it almost succeeded, when suddenly the best part of a squadron of what we supposed to have been S.A.S. turned up and virtually wiped out the terrorists. I've only just made the connection, those men came from here!'

'They did,' replied the elderly General. 'Sadly, there are very few of them left. Of the originals there are only about half a dozen, Paul and Taff, Al, the electronics chief and Kenny, head of intel. and B.J, Paul's number two. Brian in the stores and that is about all. There are still several who joined as the unit and it's role expanded, Pete, in charge of the air wing used

190

to be a tanker Captain on your original base. Many of the ground crews for the canberras used to be at the same base, there are a lot of links to your first posting Air Vice Marshall.'

'To have kept so much so secret for so long is remarkable,' said Danny.

'Personally I could live here,' sighed the General, 'the quiet, there is even a small trout stream, no wonder Paul settled here when he was discharged on medical grounds. Seems like a lifetime ago now.'

'This used to be Pauls home,? So that is why the cover held so well for so long.' commented the airman.

'I wonder where he is now,' General Leach mused. 'The invaision force should have left Cyprus by now to clear the canal zone of insurgents. At least the Egyptian army should be helping our lads. On paper it is overkill, tanks down the road on the west bank. Light forces on the eastern side. He has deployed almost everything we've got to ensure success, but then the thought of failure doesn't bear thinking about.

We'll meet in the conference centre tomorrow, out at the main base, shall we say 10am, if you can handle the notifications please for the cabinet and chiefs of staff. I'll go home tonight for the first time in weeks, it's only a ten minute walk through the woods. I'll see you in the morning.'

'You live here too?' asked the airman.

'When I manage to get home!' replied the General.

He took his time walking along the well trodden path from the security gate towards the senior officers quarters, the carpet of pine needles brought down by the combination of drought and breeze, soft under his shoes

Although he was looking forward to supper with his wife and a glass of wine his mind was racing, far away he knew British troops were about to go into action against a fanatical enemy, determined to prevent the troops getting home if they could. Failing that then a terrible price was to be extracted, maybe their zeal and enthusiasm would have waned had they any idea of the force they were about to be hit by. After supper he made his excuses to his long suffering wife, now dressed in casual clothes returned to the briefing room and called Paul for an up date, before returning to his home for some much needed sleep.

The assault had been carefully planned and was now being watched over by no less than four canberras, all beaming their data back to a container which had been mounted on top of the helicopter hanger near Kelly's stern. Paul took his seat in the tempory control room. Kelly, her guns at action stations silently slipped along in the wake of the two big old assault ships.

191

Both Fearless and Intrepid also had identical containers bolted on, the idea being any of the three All Arms Units ships could act as command ships. Paul had summed it up as 'belt and braces'.

Fearless snuck in close to Port Suez on the west bank of the entrance to the canal, Intrepid did the same off Port Tewfiq on the eastern shore.

The landing craft went in first with rigid raiders hanging back a little on the flanks, in the dark there was always the chance of their being mistaken for fishing boats or Somalia based pirates who often called to see their 'brothers of the revolution'.

Before the extremists realized what was happening the marines overwhelmed their primary defences, the remainder of the 'royals' raced ashore in more rigid raiders and the pair of hovercraft each ship carried. Any attempt to flee was blocked by the remainder of each marine assault group dropped in by helicopter.

As soon as the troops from Fearless had completed their landings, Paul transferred from Kelly to Fearless where he would be joined by the other force commanders in a unified command. The reason was simple, there was so much more room in the old assault ship compared with the destroyer.

By dawn the southern end of the canal and it's vital ports were secure and a troop ship was moored in the docks either side, her troops being reunited with their equipment as it was swung ashore from the freighters.

It was much the same at the northern end. Here the bulk of the marines had stormed ashore on the western side, securing Port Said with very little opposition. The two strong points built on artificial islands in the salt flats on the eastern shore were attacked buy a pair of harriers which swooped out of the night sky just as the marines were making their presence felt on the far bank. There were few survivors from the attack, before they worked out what was going on, the marines from two hover craft which had sped across the otherwise impassable salt flats were all over the insurgents like a rash.

Even as the ships closed on the port to unload, Hercules transports droned overhead to drop one para and their attached T/A units at pre selected positions along the east bank. As these turned back for Akrotiri a flight of C.17s lost hieght and dropped three para, again with their T/A support further south. By lunch time the east bank all the way to just north of the vital swing bridge at El Firdan was secure. The only remaining insurgents on the east bank, north of the bridge were dead ones.

It had been nearly ten a.m. local time, before the awesome challenger mark two tanks of the guards armoured regiment got going. As these terrible fighting machines approached the road block on the southern outskirts of the spawling suburbs of Port Said they came under fire from R.P.Gs. To the horror of the militants manning the position their missiles which had stopped the T65s of the Egyptian army hardly scratched the paint on these tanks. Even the 'Grad' fired at the leading tank had no visible effect on the armoured monster.

A single shot from the 120mm gun on the leading tank destroyed the road block and those manning it. The militants hiding in ambush positions either side of the road found themselves trapped between the tanks and their supporting infantry and troops sweeping in from behind their positions, guided by the all seeing sensors on the orbiting canberras.

With all the technology and fire power there was only ever going to be one outcome to any fire fight, yet in spite of all the advantages available to the mainly British forces, casualties were beginning to mount .

When General Leach called Paul for a sit-rep that afternoon, he was dismayed to hear at least thirty two British servicemen were dead and over one hundred wounded.

Paul's attempts to allay those fears achieved little.

'Sir,' Paul tried again, 'when you consider we have put close on twenty thousand troops ashore in the last twelve hours, and the resistance we have encountered, then as unpalatable as these losses are, they are well under best estimates. Add to that the fact twelve of the fatalities occurred when a small landing craft was hit and sunk by an R.P.G. then the men on the ground have been extraordinarily lucky.

The main cause for concern is the relatively slow progress along the highway on the west bank of the canal. Resistance has been significantly greater than anticipated, and this has slowed the advance. The spearhead should have reached Ismalia by now, infact they are still just over ten miles north of this vital target and under considerable fire. They are compelled to wait for the main force to catch up, before they can mount an attack on the insurgents holding the bridge at El Firdan. .

The Egyptian army are pushing towards the town of Ismalia from the west, but are taking a hammering, inspite of support from the air.

On the plus side the forces in the south are doing well and are already in Shandur, at the southern end of the Little Bitter Lake. Casualties in the southern force are three dead, two of them killed by a suicide bomber and one by a sniper. Of the eighteen wounded only four required hospital treatment, the remainder have been patched up and have stayed with their units.'

'So things are going reasonably well, inspite of the job being harder than anticipated?' the General was trying to sound optimistic.

Paul's reply would quell that optimism, 'not really Sir, we are held up by the sunken ammunition ship, the damned thing has broken it's back. We can't pass it as it is slap bang in the middle of the channel between Port Suez and Tewfiq. I am not going to let our ground forces get out of the range of our guns, as it is only our three ships can support them, nothing else has the range.

Going back to this block ship, we can't refloat her as originally planned, because of her design we can't seal either half, even if we could separate the two halves. We can't do any welding as half of the stuff on board has become unstable, the entire cargo has been booby trapped just to make life interesting. If we backed off and blew it up we would wipe out the ports on either side.'

'So what options are there Paul?' asked the concerned General.

'One of our engineers has come up with what I thought was a daft idea, but I am informed by those around me it might work. At the moment we have divers fixing heavy cables around the ship either side of the break, the idea being they use just enough lift from floatation balloons to straighten it up. The next stage is to fix steel beams across the break to take the strain. Quite how they intend to drill the holes without exploding the cargo I have no idea, again those who know assure me it can be done. The holes will then be plated over, you have seen the plans for the double plates bolted together and the sealant. If we can get her to float then we can tow her out of the way, into deep water and explode her cargo without flattening any thing.Best guess is two days, working around the clock.'

'Will it work?'

'I have no idea Sir, but I have learned to trust specialists when it's something I know nothing about, at least when it's their lives on the line if they are wrong.'

'Well, m'boy,' replied the General, 'it's good to know I taught you something.'

'At least we have a potential solution to this problem. The ships from the northern force can't get into the canal to support the main advance, there is another block ship at a place called El Ballah. The problem there is it is still in range of the insurgents at El Firdan, they keep dropping shells into the canal and the explosions would do serious harm to any divers, two of them have been seriously injured already. The revised plan is to try to take out their strongest positions from the air. It's risky, as they have stingers and there are civilians nearby.'

'Let me know how it goes Paul,' replied General Leach, 'Bye the way, the C.O. of two para isn't very happy with you, it seems he and his men are sitting in Cyprus beside their aircraft, waiting for the order to go.'

'As they are the strongest of the para battalions at the moment, I'm holding them in reserve. They are if you like, my fire brigade, even with all our recons working we are still getting a few surprises. I'm throwing almost every thing we have got at this, I don't want to disembark any troops I don't have to as this will screw things up badly time wise. I haven't got many cards to play in this deadly game so I'm keeping my ace, two para, until I have to use it. And if Sandy contacts you again, tell him from me to shut up! Radio silence means just that, if that blasted cartel finds out he's there then we will lose that element of surprise.'

The General replied, 'I can put your mind at rest, on one thing at least. Sandy sent me a letter delivered by hand, with the crew of a supply flight. Are you still worried about 'the cartel', I'd have thought those we know about would be kept busy going to the funerals of the members who have died recently.'

'Don't underestimate the damage that lot can do Sir,' replied Paul, 'I've said it before, those power mad, money grabbing bastards are more dangerous than any gang of A.K wielding nutters. Some people call me a control freak, well I have got news for them, I'm not even a novice compared with 'the cartel', they won't be happy until everyone depends on their corporations for everything we need to live. Well, as long as I'm breathing it ain't gonna happen Boss, as you once told me, 'what ever it takes!'

'Well, good luck with your problems Paul, I must go and get some sleep. I hope it is alright with you, I'm using the conference center at the farm as my office for now, and the big room out at the main base for cabinet meetings. It gives me secure communications and rapid access to the P.M who is doing really well. He can't get about yet, but is alert and taking an interest, I'm finding it very helpful to be able to seek his advice. Call me if there is anything to report, otherwise we'll talk later this evening.'

'Bye boss'.

After a brief check round the unit commanders on the ground Paul headed for his bunk, it had been a long night, and morning.

Granted the day hadn't gone perfectly so far, what with the extra block ship in the north and the discovery the ammunition carrier across the southern entrance had broken her back, things had been slowed down somewhat.

Against these set backs the forces on the eastern bank had done well, although the much more powerful thrust down the canal road on the west side had encountered some problems, which they had overcome up until now.

What ever else they did, the swing bridge at El Firdan had to be taken intact so they could open it to allow the ships to pass. The tactic being tried tonight was to use scimitar light tanks with their deadly accurate thirty millimeter cannons to 'snipe' the insurgent spotters and gun men out of their positions on and around the bridge. Using shoot and scoot tactics it was hoped they could avoid the fire from heavy anti tank guns near the bridge.

CHAPTER EIGHTEEN

It was about three in the morning when reports started to filter in, some Egyptian army units were on the move. One or two forward British units had even come under fire, indeed they had suffered casualties, at the time credited to friendly fire.

To avoid escalating things the duty controllers ordered some advanced patrols back to their main units. After a couple of hours had passed, the attacks, far from declining were escalating, something had gone badly wrong, the first clue came when the Commanding Officer of one Egyptian regiment turned up at a British check point and asked for asylum! He had been ordered to attack the British unit he had been working with to out flank one group of insurgents, he had refused to comply and incurred the wrath of a General from the governing council.

In the confusion two columns of tanks were approaching the vital bridge which the scimitars were firing at, trying to snipe the defenders with their accurate cannons, with, it has to be said, considerable success.

Suddenly the western most scimitar disintegrated when it was hit by a high velocity tank shell, two others suffered minor damage from very near misses. The quick thinking young captain in command of the group ordered an immediate rapid retreat. The attacking T72s may have been armed with a massive 125mm gun but against fast moving targets at night at any range above about five hundred yards it would require a little luck to get a direct hit. The young commander of the scimitars positioned his light tank hull down behind a sand dune and stayed just long enough to count the tanks in the column which had attacked his unit, there were thirty eight of the armoured monsters headed towards the area of the vital swing bridge.

As the command group were digesting this turn of events a Canberra began transmitting images to them of another armoured force approaching from the east, out of the Sinai desert. This force was also led by about thirty of the formidable T72s.

The voice of the systems operator on the Canberra came over the speakers.

'Sorry we're a bit late, had a bit of a technical hitch which took out our sensor pack, all fixed now, I'd watch that lot of tanks if I were you, they are looking a bit aggressive.'

'Thank you eagle eye three, better late than never', replied the officer in charge of the command group as Paul slept.

As the controllers tried to make sense of what was going on, one of the operators, a sergeant, suggested waking 'The Boss'.

'Why on earth would we want to do that sergeant?' asked the senior officer.

'Those tanks are all refuelling and topping up on ammunition Sir, supply trucks are crossing the bridge, there is no sign of resistance, yet there are still plenty of insurgents on and around the bridge,' replied the experienced N.C.O.

'So, you would expect them to refuel after a long drive.' was the reply.

'True Sir. But if they are already on their objective, there is no urgency to refuel. At least not until they have cooled down a bit, they are doing it with the engines running, that is dangerous, and is purely a battle tactic. I think they are going to attack our lot and drive north as far as they can before dawn.'

'Why on earth would they do that sergeant?' asked the officer in charge.

'Because they have been ordered to Sir. You did see the report of some Egyptian officers asking for assylum, because they had refused to obey orders to attack our forces Sir?'

'I did, but that is just a excuse to avoid having to fight the insurgents sergeant, they came from units which had been hit quite hard,' was the officers reply.

One of the other operators turned to the Major. 'Sir,' he began, 'I think the sergeant could have a point, over the past few minutes there have been twenty or so more similar requests. One Egyptian army unit has made a mass request to be taken prisoner by one para'.

'Get the Boss, but on your head be it if this is just another cock up.' said the Major, conceding the point.

'The west bank spearhead is coming under heavy tank fire Sir,' came from another operator.

'Tell them to pull back out of range until we can work out what the hell is going on,' commanded the now worried Major. 'While you are at it, tell them to get as many fully fuelled, fully loaded Challengers as far forward as they can, but to stay out of range of those T72s for now. This could yet be a horrible mistake.'

Half an hour later eight challengers were growling forward, through the British advanced positions. Clearly the Egyptians had seen them and they opened fire. To the relief of everyone the incoming shells dropped short. A couple of the British tanks pulled off the side of the road, now four of them could return fire, as the third salvo from the T72s exploded a hundred or so yards ahead of the Challengers all of those in the control room heard Paul say 'shoot!'

On the screens showing the images from the canberras, those watching saw four of the T72s explode as the shells penetrated their heavy armour as though it had been tinfoil. More tanks exploded on the east bank as the second group of four Challengers opened fire as the Egyptians' tanks appeared over the high bank to try to bring their guns to bear.

Both formations of T72s tried to hide behind a smoke screen, this was no more help than the darkness had been. They may have had slightly larger caliber guns than their opponents, not to mention numerical advantage but both were useless against the Challengers. The few shots which did reach the British tanks bounced off the new Dorchester armour as if they were tennis balls. Few of the T72s from either formation managed to escape the carnage and return to their regimental areas.

When Paul asked the tank commander for a report he was shocked to hear all but two of the challengers had taken hits, but, he assured Paul, all except the lead tank, were, to all practical purposes fully functional. The lead tank had taken a bit of a pounding, hit several times by shells from the T72s, yet, apart from a track every thing still worked. In other words it could fight, it just couldn't move, but not to worry the R.E.M.E. were on their way.

Brief skirmishes were breaking out all over the canal zone, generally these were half hearted affairs and the Egyptians showed little of the spirit they had been showing against the militants.

Paul called Taff, 'What the hell is going on?' he asked.

'I was going to call you and ask the same question, you're on the spot, you tell me!' was Taffs' reply.

'The only thing I can think of it is a new tactic to tie up all our forces guarding prisoners! This is bloody daft! Try to find out why the change of orders from helping us, to doing all they can to stop us. They are totally out gunned and a lot are refusing to obey their orders, some units are still fighting beside our lads. As far as I can make out the orders to switch came from a couple of old generals on the governing council. Check signals intel, see if they picked anything up which might help work out what's going on please.'

Taff sounded as confused as Paul, 'alright mate, I'll get back to you as soon as I have anything.'

Paul got back to the commander of the forward battle group nearest the bridge.

'Get your tanks refuelled and rearmed, there are ten more Challengers on the way, they should be with you in half an hour. I don't care how you do it, take that bridge, just don't wreck it we must be able to open it to get the ships past. When you've secured the swing bridge push on with everything you can get your hands on and take the road bridge over the sweet water canal. I'll get the guards battle group to back you up.'

'Will do Sir' , came the willing reply

Two hours latter the battle groups struck, Harriers from the American marines took out the anti aircraft defences and any radars operating. This cleared the way for Apache attack helicopters to run amoke, all organised resistance had been swept aside in barely an hour. The mainly British troops were kept busy until lunch time winkling out odd insurgent snipers, but that was about it.

As things seemed to have calmed down, Paul announced he was going to try to catch up on lost sleep, again!. Work on removing the newest block ship to the north had gone well and the frieghter was almost ready to tow away. The work on the gas tanker just north of the swing bridge was going well, most of the holes were now plugged and it was hoped all would be ready to refloat it the following morning.

Even the ammunition ship in the southern entrance wasn't causing any more problems, work on holding the two halves together was actually ahead of schedule and was 'looking good,' as the engineer in charge had put it.

Just as Paul was about to leave the hot control room, as the container bolted to the hangar roof on Fearless was grandly called, a call came in from the C.O. of one para. A group of Egyptian vehicles had approached one of his patrols under the white flag. Most of the occupants were officers, survivors of the tank attack on the British forces north of the swing bridge.

They had a present for the British Colonel who had negotiated the deal to pass the huge allied convoy through the canal.

They were sorry about the attack, and promised to help clear the canal zone of insurgents as originally agreed. To the utter astonishment of the paratroopers the delegation handed over a badly beaten up General, who they claimed had ordered the attack. A colonel willingly stayed with the paras until transport for the prisoner could be arranged.

It seemed as though the General and two of his colleagues had been paid a great deal of money to reverse their orders. The Egyptians were blaming the Iranians but Paul, on hearing this, had his doubts.

This quickly became the main topic of conversation in the ward room on Fearless, the General in charge of all the American forces involved was quick to say, 'I wanted to nuke them when the battle group was destroyed. We've got three carriers fit to launch a strike. I could have a hundred and fifty hornets in the air in an hour, we should teach those S.O.B.s a lesson.'

'I don't think they even knew about it Sir,' replied Paul. 'I'm as sure as I can be about that. You won't know this Sir, but the Iranians were the target of that nuke, not the attackers.'

'What?' exclaimed the American, 'How come no one told me!?'

'Need to know, I believe is your expression for it Sir,' replied Paul. 'I'm letting you know now so you can judge things over the next few days more accurately. You know about our A.W.A.C. being shot down, and the subsequent loss of a coastguard cutter?'

'Of course I know Colonel, what have all these things to do with each other?'

'One of our units recovered four other nuclear devices, the same as the one which detonated in the straights of Hormuz. Our A.W.A.C. was part of that mission, your cutter was the source of the missiles which shot it down. This ship then sank your cutter when the cutter launched anti ship missiles at Fearless. The point of all this was to prevent us recovering those devices. The same people are behind all this crap making it as hard as possible for us to clear, and ultimately use the canal to get home. I'll explain it in more detail later, but I can assure you, for once, as much as I detest the regime, it wasn't the Iranians. In fact, without their reluctant co-operation we wouldn't be out of Afghanistan yet.'

'If the people behind our problems aren't the Iranians then who the hell are they? asked the American General. 'How the hell am I supposed to be able to protect my country and my troops from an unidentified threat?'

'This isn't the place to discuss this Sir, but I promise to bring you up to speed as soon as I get a chance. Take it from me Sir it is not pleasant, and if it proves impossible to deal with the situation quietly, with minimum fuss, then there is no telling how things will turn out.'

'I don't like the sound of that Colonel,' replied the American, sounding genuinely worried.

Before Paul could reply, his communicator buzzed, it was the commander of the battle group on the hotley contested swing bridge, Paul listened to the message on an earphone, the American watched with increasing concern as Pauls expression darkened visibly. 'So when the hell did this happen?' he snapped.

The reply only increased the Colonels' rage, 'Get your engineers and R.E.M.E. lads and start cutting, call base and ask for what ever you need, add expidite and my name.'

'Thank you Colonel' replied the C.O. of the battle group.

The American commander gave Paul an enquiring look.

'Just what we don't need! It appears the bastards have welded the bridge in position. Both ends as well as the gap in the middle, and just to make life interesting they have welded up the massive bearings as well!' Paul slumped back into his seat. 'Oh for fucks sake,' he cursed. 'We can't just blow it up, the debris would rip the bottoms out of half of our ships. It would take ages to clear all the steel from the canal. The Brigadier in command there reckons some Egyptians have told him the welding was started three weeks ago, which is before we started to pull out!

Put your fingers in your ears please Sir, I'm calling my base and I don't think you'll like the answer to the question I'm going to ask.'

Paul pushed a couple of buttons, 'Taff, get intell to check payments to these bloody Generals who have been screwing things up, it seems as though someone has paid them a lot of money, I need to know who and when,' then after a pause, 'whatever it takes'.

'You know who is behind all of this don't you Colonel? So why don't you stop them?' asked the American General.

'If only it were as simple as launching an air strike, or sending in a special forces hit squad, believe me I would do just that Sir.' replied Paul. 'Come on Sir, let's go out on deck, and I'll give you an outline of what we are up against, subject to your assurance you will tell no-one anything of about what I tell you.'

'Very well Colonel, you have my word.'

Paul had spent nearly half an hour briefing the American Commander when his communicator bleeped urgently, it was Taff.

'Well. It looks as though you were right Boyo,' the little Welshman sounded quite cheerful. 'The going rate to turn a General seems to be about five million dollars.'

'Split between three of them, what's that?' Paul paused, 'about one point six mil each, I'd have expected more.'

'No you twit!' replied Taff, 'five million each, and there were four, not three of them who got paid at the same time. We are still working on identifying the fourth individual, but we don't think he is military.' Taff paused for a moment, then continued .'I'll let you know how the trace goes, but I think we can guess were it will lead us, any bets he's already dead?' Then, almost as an after thought, 'You were wrong about the timing, it was ten weeks ago when the money was transferred into their accounts.'

'Oh, crap!' muttered Paul, 'Keep digging, although I don't want to think about what you are likely to dig up.'

'Did I just hear right?' asked the American General, 'because if I did, it means Americans are paying for something which will probably kill American troops.'

'I'd say that was a fairly accurate assessment Sir,' replied Paul. 'Although, and this is just a personal opinion, I think the real objective is more about costing equipment than lives, dead servicemen are colateral damage as far as the cartel are concerned. Lose as much heavy equipment as possible, use as much fuel as possible, identify 'new threats' which will entail massive rearmament. All that new kit just to replace the losses will be expensive. Guess who makes all the money?'

'I'm beginning to understand you Colonel, I also understand why you are keeping this a mainly British operation. But am I right in thinking this latest problem with the swing bridge could cause a costly delay?'

'I has already been costly Sir, the unexpected attack by previously helpful Egyptian units, apart from the damage and casualties, has broken the frail bond of trust which existed.' Paul got up from where he had been sitting with his feet over the side of the deck.

'Have you any idea when we might be able to get through the canal Colonel? It is just keeping men crammed on these ships, going nowhere is bad for moral, some of my commanders are suggesting going around the Cape route,' said the American. 'They may have a point Colonel.'

'They might at that Sir,' replied Paul. 'I happen to know there are two very large tankers, full to the brim with navy grade fuel, just sitting there, waiting for a convoy of thirsty ships to turn up 'bringing our boys home'. They left Galveston about a month ago, there isn't a drop of that Texas oil which is any good for the boilers on most of the cargo ships, which will of course run out of fuel, they'll make Nigeria, put in for fuel and probably get seized. By the time the diplomats sort it out, most of their cargos will have vanished. We have thwarted that idea to a great extent by using the old carrier, due for decommissioning when she gets home, to carry a lot of the expensive kit, as she is nuclear powered.'

'If what you've said is true, then that was a smarter move than it seemed at the time,' the General said. 'I like the way you think Colonel.' he added.

'I've had a rather outrageous idea,' Paul suddenly seemed revitalised.

'Dare I ask?' said the American.

'How would it be if a task group suddenly sailed off heading down the East coast of Africa?'

'Okay,' said the General, 'I'll bite, what have you come up with Colonel?'

'Just suppose the Marine element of your forces got fed up waiting and apparently headed off home, taking the long route back 'states side. Knowing now how the cartel get most of their general information, I think we can make them take their eye off the ball for nearly a week. At the same time prevent your marines getting bored and kick the shit out of the militant Somali rebels Al…. what ever they call themselves this week. With just a little bit of luck we should be able to free a load of hostages, not to mention several very expensive ships.'

'Such a raid would take a lot of planning Colonel,' replied the American. 'I would also need approval at the highest level.'

'Alright.' Paul thought for a moment, 'If I send Intrepid south to act as command ship, with a special forces detachment on board, we can use them to rescue any hostages we locate. The plans can be drawn up en-route, Intrepid will get there at least a day before your task force. I can have a flight of canberras on station, with a base in easy range in about eight hours.

We can use this time to acquire targets, that way your marines will know what they are up against and where they will find their targets. Intrepid has her own team of operators, the same as here on Fearless, it will be easy to liase with the U.N. forces already there. The same with the Kenyan forces and the Somali government troops, schedule the operation to last 24 or at the most 36 hours, then haul arse back here to take up your convoy positions. It should work out about right, by the time you've got down there and back, hopefully the canal should be clear about then.'

'What about clearance Colonel,' asked the American, 'I can't order our troops onto foreign soil, it will take weeks to get clearance, if it's given. The wheels of the pentagon tend to turn rather slowly these days.'

'But you agree in principle to such an operation, given that you are aware of the capabilities of our canberras to locate targets and supply real time information to troops on the ground?' Paul asked innocently.

'Given our present situation, then it makes a lot of sense, if we could go tonight. But that isn't likely, unfortunately,' sighed the General, he seemed quite disappointed.

'I have to confess Sir, I have been less than honest with you,' said Paul.

'Like how,' the American seemed more curious than angry.

'Well, there was always a real chance of a significant delay in opening the canal for our convoy, so contingency plans were drawn up some time ago for this operation. As soon as it is dark, the Keresarge and Iwo-Jima, with their support ships will head south and join up with the Regan battle group which is acting as a sort of rear guard off Aden. Intrepid is actually waiting for you Sir, as you are the designated commander for the operation. Regard it as pay back for Mogadishu.'

'I don't know what to say Colonel,' responded the senior officer. 'Your last comment inferred you are aware of my involvement in that operation. We do still need authorisation however, without it we simply can not do it.'

Paul produced his communicator and pushed a few buttons, then handed it to the still surprised General, all Paul said as he stopped leaning on the ships guard rail was, 'Your commander in chief', then walked away, out of ear shot.

By the time the big U.S. marines assault carriers and their support group whieghed anchor and headed south, Intrepid was clear of the last of the waiting ships and working up to about two thirds of her maximum speed. The big old ship made an impressive sight, throwing up a huge bow wave as she sped for the open ocean at a rate of knots no destroyer could achieve.

High over head a Canberra headed south as part of the flight detached to cover the upcoming raid, the crew ran a systems check with Intrepid, among other things they beamed down a live image in Hi-definition of the old ship travelling at speed. The General was in the control centre at the time with the Captain, and was mightily impressed.

'Tell me Captain, just how do you guys do it, ' he asked. 'As a young newly promoted Captain I was seconded to your 40 commando unit for three months. I spent half of that time on this very ship! Her maximum speed was barely twenty knots, she rolled like a pig and I spent most of the trip as sick as a dog. It is travelling at twice the speed and is steady as a rock.'

'I can't tell you how the propulsion works Sir,' replied the skipper. 'Think of it the same as the evolution of air travel, from balloons to propellers, jets and the development of rockets, in ships you had oars, sail, propellers now this. As for the stability, well that is simply down to advances in hull design.'

Back on Fearless Paul was catching up on sleep, at last, there were no major problems, in fact things were going remarkably well. The second Egyptian General to take his bribe had been caught and handed over to the local authorities, the last one was still at large and was thought to have escaped into the desert, possibly into Ethiopia, may be headed for Somalia. The other recipient of a five million pay off was a militant cleric now with ample time to question the wisdom of his actions as he was in an Egyptian jail. The authorities were delighted, as they had been longing for an excuse to remove their number one trouble maker. They had the proof as well, the fact it was American money only strengthened the case, at the same time totally undermining his support.

As far as the block ships were concerned, the northern most freighter was afloat, and the consensus was she could be repaired, the tow had already started and was making a steady two knots towards Port Said.

In the south the munitions carrier was being gently raised, her main deck now just above water as work continued to strengthen her broken hull, sufficiently to tow her out into the open sea.

The general opinion was the canal would be open in about a week, the big swing bridge was the main problem. As a stop gap measure, until ships carrying engineers could get to the bridge, helicopters were ferrying mostly American engineers up from the south. These were to assist in getting the structure working again. The insurgents had done a lot of damage to the bearings and the massive hydraulics which moved the thousands of tons of metal. There simply wasn't a quick fix, but , they were making progress.

The other problem turned out to be mines and improvised explosives planted in the canal, not as many as had been feared, it was true, but they still had to be located and dealt with, not an easy task. The specialised mine sweepers of the royal navy were proving ideal platforms for finding them, divers would then go in and plant a charge to destroy the hazard. This was slow and painstaking, not to mention 'bloody dangerous', as one diver put it after discovering a booby trap on a mine he had been tasked with neutralising.

The other problem was all of the minesweepers were at the northern end of the canal, true, they could get past the block ships, and did, but until the all important swing bridge was working again, that was as far as they could get.

The really annoying thing was the last two had passed through the canal only days before it was closed, on their way home after a long deployment in the Persian Gulf. Their task there had been long and tedious in the heat, checking for stray mines left over from the various conflicts. They had only found four in the past year, and none for the past seven months, now it was one or two an hour!

To help out in this task a pair of powerful Sea Stallion helicopters from one of the American carriers spent a couple of fruitless days towing their acoustic sledges back an forth on the bitter lakes.

It too was a tedious task, the crews doubtful of the need for a third day, as was their squadron commander, and he said so to his superior and on up the chain of command.

Paul's reaction shook the Americans, unused to his direct approach. He called the squadron commander directly, and after the briefest of introductions asked, 'Are you absolutely certain there are no mines in the Bitter Lakes shipping lanes or holding areas?'

'It doesn't seem as though there are any Colonel,' was the unbowed reply.

'Very well, so I can send a signal to all ships in the convoy that you THINK,' he emphasised the word, 'that the channel is clear, and are prepared to sit on the fore deck of the leading ship when we move into the area. Does that seem fair?'

'When you put it like that Colonel, maybe I should have thought about it before shooting my mouth off.' he paused. 'I guess an apology is in order Colonel.

'Accepted, there have been enough, 'I'm sorry to have to inform you', messages as it is. It is up to us to ensure there are no more, there will be, it is the nature of our trade, so let's make sure there are no more avoidable ones. Alright?'

'Alright Sir.' was the clear reply.

CHAPTER NINETEEN

'Right!' said Paul, stretching as he stood up from his swivel chair in the sweaty 'control room', on Fearless, 'does anyone know a reason why I can't try to catch up on some sleep?'

The task force sent south to help the U.N. and Kenyan troops subdue the groups of al-Shabaab militants on the southern Somali border were well on their way. Intrepid had raced off ahead with her detachments of special forces to rescue any hostages located by the Canberra's already on station. All seemed well on this front.

The canal was being cleared without any new problems cropping up, in fact with the help of American engineers things at the bridge were going better than expected.

All was well with the Egyptians, a remarkable camaraderie existed between troops who had been fighting each other only of couple of days before.

The final convoy from Cyprus had discharged all the remaining troops assigned to the operation. Most were already in their positions, effectively sealing the canal area from further interference from remaining militants. These were now being pursued by the Egyptian army, each major unit had a small British liaison team attached , these relayed information from the orbiting Canberra's.

At home, all seemed remarkably calm, this was generally attributed to the skills of General Leach making a nightly appearance on television, giving as much information as he could to viewers questions. Any he couldn't answer he always explained why, or if he genuinely didn't know, promised to find out, and usually did! In short, the vast majority of the population came to trust him.

With everything looking good, Paul finally began to catch up on some sleep, the next couple of days were quiet, at least along the canal. There were a couple of minor incidents, both of which resulted in the capture of a hand full of militants without injury to the allied troops involved.

The mainly American force sent south to deal with al-Shabaab were also successful, they had lost four dead and about twenty wounded, but had cleared a large area of insurgents. This area extended nearly a hundred miles in land and between forty and sixty miles from the Kenyan border. The biggest success was in destroying so much of the insurgents arms and ammunition, four huge dumps were destroyed as well as many smaller ones.

They left the area firmly under the control of U.N. and African Union troops, about half of the Marines had already re-embarked. The special forces operating from Intrepid had rescued more than seventy hostages and taken control of fourteen out of fifteen ships being held by the pirates. All had now either continued their journey's or in one case was joining the war ships to pass through the canal with the convoy as soon as it was opened.

The merchant ship they left behind was too badly damaged to do anything with, and was left, firmly aground, although it's crew were among those freed.

A week to the day after the first marines had stormed ashore on Egyptian soil, the first ships entered the Bitter lakes. The block ships, although yet to be removed, had been re-floated and made near enough water tight, the ships nominated to tow them away were being prepared.

Kelly had led two frigates, one American, the other Canadian gingerly along the channel, all had their sonar set to hopefully detect mines. Surprisingly they were into the Great Bitter Lake before anything to worry about was detected, this turned out to be a second world war German two hundred and fifty kilo bomb. The explosion was, as one eye witness put it, 'larger than expected, but very satisfying.'

It wasn't until the 'ad-hoc' group of would be mine hunters, operating with the two marine helicopters ahead of them, reached the northern exit of the great bitter lake they began to find mines.

Another quiet day passed, the decision was taken as soon as the block ships were removed ships of the convoy would start to move into the Bitter Lakes. The ammunition carrier was due to begin her tow around dawn, the following day, this would be the single greatest danger removed.

Paul was heard to comment, 'I wouldn't want that job' referring to the crews of the three ships which would be towing the 'floating bomb.'

In the event it took three days of delicate manoeuvring to get the stricken vessel to the selected spot. It proved difficult to get all the local fishermen to move out of the danger area, however all went well, if an hour later than planned. One sailor who witnessed the explosion summed it up as 'apocalyptic'. It certainly was a spectacular sight sending a cloud thousands of feet into the air, it was several minutes before the rain of falling scrap ceased. The fishing boats raced into the area and were soon scooping out the masses of dead and stunned fish floating over a wide area, some of the smaller boats were dangerously overloaded.

'At least someone has benefited in the short term,' the captain of an American destroyer commented.

The other block ship south of the bridge was towed out of the channel, into the Bitter Lakes, where more permanent repairs could be carried out. The general opinion was it was worth repairing her, and if all went well this tanker could complete her journey to Euro-port, Rotterdam as part of the convoy which would head to Britain.

Work on the problem bridge was slow, but was making progress, a couple more days and the engineers would try to open it, they sounded optimistic.

Paul turned in early, content things were going alright, the first ships were already moving into the Bitter Lakes, a steady orderly procession headed north.

About two a.m. local time, things changed. The alarm on Paul's communicator woke him with a start from his fitful sleep.

'What the hell do you mean up at this time of night Taff?' he asked.

'We've a bit of a problem Paul.' replied Taff. 'In fact it's more of a full blown disaster.'

'Like what?' Paul was worried, Taff wouldn't have called for a minor incident.

'It appears we have a new government, all government buildings in and around Whitehall, including the Houses of Parliament have been seized, along with most of the national media. According to 'auntie beeb' we are now the 'Islamic Republic of Britain' and subject to Islamic Shariah law. A number of lists of people to arrest and execute have been issued, apart from the Royals, you and General Leach are names which crop up frequently.'

'Bloody hell!' muttered Paul. 'How did this happen Taff?'

'Horribly easily mate, four truck ferries docked near the Dartford crossing, the trucks simply drove straight into central London. Any one who got in their way were simply swept aside. The latest I heard nearly a thousand are dead already. We got lucky in a way, we had just enough time to alert troops in the capital and have been able to contain them for now in White Hall and Parliament square. We are trying to reinforce the cordon. There are too many other incidents to tell you about now but this is bad Paul, really bad, we simply haven't got the troops available, you've got them all!'

'I know Taff,' replied Paul, 'and I can't start thinning them down for several days, if we have the slightest gap in our defences these bloody militants will be through like a rat up a drain pipe. I've got ships packed with troops which would be sitting ducks, and I can't put troops ashore from the transports without screwing everything up. It would take a couple of weeks to sort it all out again. We simply haven't got the fuel, or money to do it.

I'll be with you by dawn, with two para. Sort out a drop zone, St. James Park if we can get there before it gets light seems a possible.'

'You crafty bugger,' retorted Taff, 'did you know something like this might happen?'

' No I didn't, not on this scale that's for sure. I expected something, but not this, hang on while I tie my boots, I need both hands for that.'

Ten minutes after Taffs call had woken Paul, a Lynx helicopter lifted off from the flight deck on Fearless headed for the airfield at Port Said were a speedy Lear Jet waited to take him to Cyprus, to join up with two para.

During the fifteen minute trip in the Lynx Paul made several calls, the first was to the American Marine General who had commanded the force which had headed south and , as he delicately put it , 'given al-Shabaab a right arse kicking'.

This task force was still nearly two days away, at least at an economic speed for the oil fired ships. Paul was of course aware the General had transferred to the American marine assault ship Iwo-Jima, this was fair enough as the operation was complete and the task force was headed back to await passage through the Suez Canal. The quarters were much more comfortable and the few wounded the American marines had were in the sick bay of the big ship.

Paul's request to speak to the General was initially refused by the duty signaller, 'I'm sorry Colonel, the General is asleep.'

'Then bloody well wake him up! I'm hardly making a social call at this ungodly hour! Get him please,' then after a pause, 'now would be good!'

'Problems boss?' asked the pilot.

Timothy Pilgrim

Paul looked at the pilot and shook his head, 'I'm sorry, he's asleep! I should hope he was at this time of day! Yanks! You've got to love 'em'.

While he waited he called Sandy, the C.O. of two para. 'Get moving Sandy, all the kit your men need will be their weapons and ammo, a light snack and a drink. You should be dropping just before dawn. Load your four 'Hercs' with gunned up land rovers, full tanks and plenty of ammo, three men per vehicle, the Hercs will be landing to discharge. I want you airborne in thirty minutes. Leave one C17 with your reserve company, they will wait until I arrive to join them, if you could provide me with a 'chute, I'd appreciate it.'

'Any chance of letting me know where we're going?' asked the para's C.O .

'London, central London. It seems as though we've been invaded in our absence. This is not going to be easy mate. I'm on my way to join you, but I've got a lot to do, so get cracking. You will receive a more detailed briefing when you're in the air. I want you on the all arms unit's C17 please, it will make communications easier and more secure.'

'Right Paul, we're moving, see you in London for breakfast.'

'I hope so'. replied Paul.

A new voice came from the communicator, it was the American General.

'What does a man have to do around here to get a proper nights sleep Colonel?' he asked.

'Ah, sorry to disturb you Sir,' replied Paul, 'but I thought it was only fair to let you know you are about to assume overall command in this area. With this in mind, it is my opinion, it would be a good idea to transfer to Intrepid, as soon as possible. You will at least have all the information immediately available to you.'

'Very decent of you to let me know, Paul, if you don't mind me calling you Paul,' the man replied.

'cause I don't mind General, I've been trying to get you to do that since we met,' was the reply from Paul.

'Might I ask why?'

'It seems as though Britain has been invaded General, well London has. I don't know many details yet but it seems there has been an armed insurgency, and to put it bluntly the nutters are running the mad house!.' replied Paul.

'I don't really understand Colonel,' said the American.

'It seems as though all the institutions of national government along with

212

most of the media have been taken over by several ship loads of terrorist fanatics of some kind. I've dispatched 2 para from Cyprus to help eradicate the problem. I am on my way to join them.'

'Leaving me to carry the can for any thing else which goes wrong out here,' chuckled the American.

'Without a doubt some thing will go tits up some where General,' said Paul.

'Like a mutiny of all the British troops you've got ashore, they are just going to love having an American Marine giving the orders.'

'The easy way to deal with that General is not to give them any!' replied Paul, 'other than, carry on as planned, and to get in touch with you if they need anything. Make it clear, you are there to help, not tell them how to do their jobs. They all know exactly what they have to do, let them get on with it, it's all I do, and I have to say, it works. If it ain't broke, don't fix it. You'll have all you need on Intrepid Sir. Good luck, I have got to go. I'll be in touch as soon as I get the chance, but if you hit a snag, don't hesitate to call me. Bye Sir, we're just about to land.'

The American looked at the hand set as the link clicked clicked off, 'And goodbye to you too Colonel,' then as an after thought, 'have a nice trip.'

An aide approached, 'Your helicopter will be ready in ten minutes General, but it will take us at least half an hour to get everything ready to go Sir.'

'That's easily fixed,' said the tough old marine. 'Get my side arm, webbing, lap top and a kitbag with small kit, shirts, socks and boxers, you stay here with everything else. On the double! These people don't hang about, even for Generals!'

CHAPTER TWENTY

Although a couple of hundred miles apart, and in vastly different aircraft, Paul and the General took off at almost the same moment. Paul's flight, although much faster, was also much longer in both time and distance, the speedy Lear Jet headed for Cyprus to link up with the last of the transports which would carry the tough men of 2 para into battle on the streets of London.

As ever, Paul took advantage of the relative quiet to catch a bit of sleep, more like a fitful doze, in between calls from Taff, Sandy, the c.o. of two para. The American General called to let Paul know he was safely on board Intrepid, and heading back to her position in the main fleet, very fast!

General Leach called him for an update on his progress, and with the sad news another senior politician terribly injured in the disaster at the N.E.C. had died. A young fit man would have most likely have succumbed to such injuries, in his late seventies, with a heart condition it was surprising he had lasted so long. All the other casualties being treated in the medical facility deep beneath the All Arms Units headquarters were doing very well. General Leach was hopeful that the Prime Minister would be well enough to make a short television statement at the weekend. It was still possible to over ride the B.B.C. television signals for a short time.

Paul's comment of, 'All I can say is I hope he looks a hell of a lot better than when I last saw him Boss, they'll have to screen it after the watershed!'

'Paul!' scolded the General.

'So apart from an unknown number of nutters running around with A.K.47s, things are doing alright?' Paul asked innocently.

'You know damned well things are anything but alright.' said General

Leach. 'If unconfirmed reports are correct then we could be in real trouble, it seems as though those four ferries returned to the continent and are now headed back with another load.'

'That's easily dealt with Sir, sink the bloody things!' retorted Paul.

'What with pray.' asked General Leach.

'There is a base just up the road from the farm with about fifty tornadoes, surely to blazes they can put four up with a couple of thousand pounders' a piece,' suggested Paul.

'The current 'government' for the lack of a better term, have banned all flying, military or civilian Paul. They have monitors stationed on several camps already to ensure the orders of the 'great leader' are obeyed.'

'For fucks sake boss!' exclaimed Paul, 'the mobile phone number of every C.O. in the country is on our terminal, get Taff to help you. Issue the orders, if those 'monitors' don't surrender, instantly, bloody well shoot them!'

'They have threatened civilian casualties if we act against them, it is a real problem Paul.'

'Are you alright Sir, it's just that you don't sound like the General Leach I know and have come to respect?' asked Paul, sounding concerned.

'I am not as strong as I used to be Paul, what with everything else, it is difficult, but you are right of course. I'll get those orders issued immediately. I'll get those tornadoes moving first. Stay I touch.'

'I will Sir', replied Paul

As soon as Taff had finished briefing the American General, Paul called his old friend, 'Hi Taff, I've just been talking to his nibs, is he alright?'

'Tired, like the rest of us, and a bit unsure quite how to handle the situation. The troops in London are holding the ring, just. There are incidents all over the country, some really nasty, frankly, until we get at least half a dozen canberras back and at least six battalions, ideally eight back then we'll struggle.' Taff too sounded over-whelmed thought Paul.

'What about those tornados?' Paul asked.

'They are loading them as we speak. The C.O. says he can put up five, with fuel to reach the French coast and get back safely. The plan is a single two thousand pound pave way on each attack plane, the other will mark the targets. The snowdrops shot all except one 'monitor' when they tried to stop the planes being fuelled up.'

In the event there was nearly a disaster, a small fisheries protection vessel, her captain unable to contact anyone, tried to intervene. Aware of the fact several ferries had landed heavily armed insurgents, and conscious more were likely to be on their way, he determined his crew would check as many ships as possible in an effort to prevent any more reaching a British port. Spotting the four ferries approaching in line astern he placed his little ship across their path and ordered them to stop, so they could be boarded and checked.

He had his crew mount two machine guns to support the single twenty millimeter cannon, the only fixed armament on the five hundred ton coastal patrol craft. When the ferries showed no sign of slowing down, never mind stopping, the young officer ordered a short burst across the bows of the leading ship.

The result was as devastating as it was unexpected, a shower of R.P.Gs. rained down on the little ship, while many missed because of the range, enough hit to knock out her main gun. The missiles also killed nearly half the crew, only quick thinking by some of the surviving crew in tackling the fires which had started and a rapid retreat out of range prevented the ship being lost.

Finally someone answered their radio calls and these were used to guide the tornadoes directly to the area, it also confirmed the occupants of the ferries were very definitely hostile.

The crew managed to get the cannon working again, sufficient to hit the leading ship with a few rounds, these did little damage, although they did inflict a few casualties. There was however a much greater effect, how ever accidental, this futile gesture provided the perfect distraction for the tornadoes attack.

Quite who was the more surprised is hard to say, the young sailors when their target blew up after being hit by about a dozen twenty millimeter shells, or the insurgents who survived the blast . These found themselves in a very cold English Channel when the two halves of their ship did an impression of a pair of submarines doing a syncronised dive.

Five minutes and three more explosions later the little naval vessel was alone on the sea, which was littered with wreckage, oil and bodies. There were a few survivors, which, being sailors they tried to rescue. Their first attempt was almost another disaster as the intended subject for rescue threw a grenade as the crew threw a rope, luckily the man in the sea totally misjudged the distance and the grenade exploded in the sea. It caused several casualties, but they were all silver and about eight inches long, the surviving young herrings regrouped and headed for safety.

The next survivor they attempted to rescue pointed his A.K. 47 at the little ship but was shot dead by an alert leading regulator.

The general consensus on board was rapidly becoming ,'leave the bastards'. It soon became apparent they had worries of their own as the damage was greater than the had thought. In the event only six insurgents were pulled from the cold water before the little warship headed for the safety of the nearest port before the rising water in her hull sent her to the bottom as well.

The gallant little ship just, and only just made it to Gravesend, minutes after her lines were secured the water reached her engine, which promptly stopped in a cloud of steam.

CHAPTER TWENTY-ONE

Paul feigned surprise when he boarded the waiting C17 to find it was full of reservists, the majority ex regular soldiers. Some one started singing 'why are we waiting', followed by a rendition of 'why was he born so beautiful, why was he born at all, he's no bloody use to anyone,' etc.

'Nice to feel wanted', Paul remarked, as a grey haired captain saluted and actually said, 'welcome aboard Sir.'

Paul returned a rather casual salute, 'Sorry you have had to wait so long, but I was on Fearless off Port Suez when this problem arose, I got here as quickly as I could.'

The captain thought for a moment, 'Isn't that at the southern end of the canal? You didn't waste any time getting here Sir'.

The rear ramp was closing fast and the engines which had been idling now began to run up to taxiing power. The powerful transport made light work of a company of paras and their signals detachment as it climbed easily to it's cruising altitude and settled on a direct course for London.

It was a sign of the times that four American F15s settled into escort positions for what, a matter of a few short weeks ago would have been a flight through friendly skies.

Paul settled into a rather basic seat next to the captain who had greeted him, 'I had expected to find a Major in command of your happy band Captain,' he began.

'The C.O. went with head quarters company Sir,' replied the Captain, 'he said it was so he could brief us when we arrived.'

'Did he now,' Paul wasn't convinced this was a good idea, and it showed. 'That is a little bit inconvenient Captain,' Paul replied, 'as we have a different objective. I actually told your missing Major I would brief you all on the flight. I'm surprised Sandy, your C.O., allowed him to switch planes.'

'In fairness to the Colonel Sir, I don't think he was aware of Major Dalrymples' change of plan,' replied the Captain.

'I thought Sandy ran a tighter unit than that!' exclaimed Paul. 'Are you telling me your Major simply upped sticks at the last minute without telling your C.O? simply leaving you in charge Captain.'

'Yes Sir,' the paratroop Captain sounded unsure of himself.

'Very well, loose those pips and find a crown, I'll make sure they are permanent, you sort out the other promotions to fill the gaps, It's your company now so it's up to you Major!' Paul turned to address the soldiers, 'my apologies gentlemen for the sudden change in your command on the eve of battle, but that is how things must be.

The task ahead is not going to be easy, anything but. It was no accident I selected this company for this vital task. The objective is straight forward enough, the eviction of a considerable force of insurgents from the B.B.C. television centre The objective may be straight forward, achieving it will not be so.

Platoon commanders, split your platoons into four man teams, as far as possible keep each of the teams of equal strength, nominate a leader for each team on ability rather than rank. Odd bodies will be in a headquarters section with the Major, signals detachment and myself. I also want a point section of your best scouts to lead the formation from the drop zone on a school playing field to our objective. We will have the assistance of a Canberra overhead and in contact with us, this will warn of any ambushes, stray patrols and the likes.' He paused, taking a drink from his flask. 'Get your sections sorted, section leaders, draw your stun grenades from the Q.M at the front of the plane. Then I suggest getting a bit of sleep, trust me, you are likely to need it! Good luck gentlemen, carry on Major.'

The flight proved to be boring, if one overlooked the turbulence created the air currents over the Alps.

The drop went fine, even though it took two passes over the playing field for all the troops to get out. Paul was one of the last to go, after hitting the ground fairly hard he remembered why he hated low level static line parachute drops!

'Are you alright Sir?' asked the newly promoted Major.

'I'm getting too bloody old for such daft stunts,' replied Paul, having got his breath back. 'I knew there was a reason I never felt the urge to be a 'para'!'

Within about ten minutes of the first man landing the company was moving out towards their objective. Acutely aware of the difficulties in assaulting a large heavily defended building at night, never mind in day light, the conversation between Paul and the company commander explored the alternatives, finally coming up with a workable solution, they hoped.

The insurgents had seen the parachutes, and guessed the reason, unaware they were being watched from far above they set what they thought was a perfect ambush.

As the insurgents settled into their ambush positions and waited, and waited, to their consternation firing broke out behind them, from the sounds of things snipers had opened fire on the B.B.C. building and their friends were returning fire.

Aware of the ambush, the paratroop company had halted a few hundred yards away, a sniper team of eight men had been sent to bring the building under fire, and a further two platoons sent to cover the route back to the B.B.C., hopefully to ambush the insurgents sent to attack the company as it advanced.

Sure enough, after about five minutes of gun fire the ambush team of insurgents began to run back to help their colleagues, who were taking casualties from the snipers. As they ran around a corner the waiting paratroopers eased off their safety catches and waited until it seemed all of the insurgents were in their field of fire. In short it was a massacre, almost all were dead before they were aware of a problem, such was the volume of fire which struck them from a direction they assumed was safe.

'That's altered the odds a bit,' commented the new company commander, as he detailed a section to find and take care of any prisoners.

Paul called him over, 'lets thicken up the sniper screen Major, we should be able to thin them out a bit more before we try to move in.'

It didn't take long to have eight men covering every side of the building, all of them had infra red capable sights on their rifles, this helped them to see into any room facing them. This proved very effective, to the extent targets soon became scarce.

'What do you think Colonel?' asked the company commander, 'should we thin the screen to add momentum to the attack on the main entrance?'

'Personally I'd be inclined to leave them Major. There is very little wind, why don't we lay a smoke screen across the front of the building and send two platoons forward, as far as that low wall. There are enough of us with M203 grenade launchers to lay a good screen, then blow in the doors with H.E. grenades.

My guess is any defenders will shoot blindly into the smoke, but we will still be able to pick them off with our infra red sights.'

'Which do you think it is our best bet Colonel, send the assault teams forward to the wall as soon as the screen looks thick enough, or wait until we've picked off as many as possible?' replied the Major.

'It's your call,' said Paul, 'I'd favour waiting, some of them must have infra red sights, they could do a lot of damage to thirty odd soldiers charging across fifty yards of bare car park.'

'Let's get a smoke screen laid lads,' commanded the major. A couple of minutes later the front of the building was obscured by thick acrid white smoke. This provoked intense fire from the defenders, the manic clatter of numerous A.K.47s interspersed with single cracks from the snipers as they picked off targets as quickly as they could.

Paul was lying prone with his old armalite, a high explosive grenade ready in the launcher beneath the barrel. With the bipod legs down on his rifle, he was using his hi-tec sight to pick off odd insurgents, as soon as the defensive fire slackened he carefully selected the grenade launcher and fired at the main doors which obliged by disintegrating under the impact of the high explosive grenade.

This provoked another blast of defensive fire into the smoke and further targets for the snipers. Shouts from within to hold their fire, obviously confirmed some of the insurgents did indeed have infra red sights, as Paul had surmised.

At a prearranged signal the smoke screen was thickened up. As soon as the smoke began to billow there were more thumps of grenade launchers, Paul and five others put high explosives through open ground floor windows, and another through the now wrecked doorway.

As soon as these exploded the assault teams took off from the shelter of the low car park wall to begin the dangerous job of clearing the building. First priority was to clear the front of the building, at least the lower floors, the snipers would be able to cover the upper floors above the thickest of the smoke.

The majority of the remaining paratroopers now charged towards the big building, in their squads of four. Paul had just picked off a gunman who had appeared at an upper floor window, when the sergeant leading the section which had been next to him suddenly collapsed without a sound, dead before he hit the floor.

Quite why he grabbed the mans M.P.5 and his belt with magazines and stun grenades he was never able to explain, but in a matter of seconds he was half way across the car park, urging the three remaining members of the team forward into the chaos.

He had left his rifle with a signal man with instructions to take care of it.

Once inside he turned to one of the squad, a thirty year old corporal who had served nine years with the battalion as a regular, 'you're in charge corp, where do we go?'

'Are you sure Sir?' asked the soldier, 'I mean, you're a colonel Sir?'

'I'm very sure corp., you know what your team was tasked with, I don't! but I do know how to use this,' he tapped the Heckler, 'and as well as anyone. Lead on.' Then as an afterthought, 'oh, call me Paul, there's no point in advertising the fact I'm an officer.'

'If you say so Paul, let's go, our target is the main studio which seems to be broadcasting in spite of the noise'.

Back at the main base of 'The All Arms Unit' Taff sat in his office talking to General Leach and several section leaders. The main topic had been the slow reaction of many military bases to deal with the teams of insurgents sent to ensure compliance with the directives of 'The Supreme Leader'.

'The 'Crack pot' is supposed to be making a broadcast to the nation at the moment' said General Leach, 'If your stomachs are up to it, why don't we see what he looks like and hear what he has to say?'

'It might prove interesting,' replied B.J. 'I've been hearing snippets which suggest at least one company from two para were sent to shut him up. The objective being to hand things back to 'Aunty Beeb'. I'm not sure of the timing, but attacking in daylight will be messy, there are thought to be about a hundred and fifty insurgents in the place.'

'They won't be easy to shift, even for a company of para's.' said Taff.

'How are things going with the withdrawl?' asked General Leach. 'We must not forget the bigger picture, I know Paul was planning to airlift as many troops as he could into Stansted, I am of course aware two para were dropped into central London. This has stabilised the perimeter around White Hall and Parliament.'

'Bloody hell!' exclaimed B.J. who had been half watching the television,

'It's Abu no hands, Paul will go nuts when he finds out! We've thrown him out of the country at least three times over the years and into jail! Yet he keeps turning up!'

'Talking of Paul and turning up,' General Leach began, 'does anyone know where he is? The last I heard he had handed over command to the American who had been in charge in Afghanistan. I think he was headed to Cyprus, presumably to link up with the Paras, I know he's not with Sandy, the C.O. because I spoke to him an hour ago.'

There was suddenly a lot of noise from the television, a crash as a door fell in followed by a couple of gunshots from A.K. 47s and the bang of stun grenades.

The civilian camera operator fell, but the camera on it's mounting kept running.

A pair of Hecklers purred their song of death as out of shot gunmen died before they regained their senses from the effects of the 'flash bangs' .

Every one watching saw what happened next, a grey haired, decidedly scruffy soldier laid down his sub machine gun to help the disorientated camera man.

Suddenly the 'Supreme Leader' shouted something in Arabic, things happened so fast the three paratroopers never had time to react. Paul fell backwards, kicking the camera man away from him, four shots rang out, the first two from an A.K.47. The second pair of shots from the Smith and Weston .357 magnum revolver in the hand of the still rolling soldier.

The effect of two rounds hitting close together in the centre of the 'Supreme Leaders' forehead was devastating, bits of bone and gore pebble dashed the back drop behind him. Most of the mess was around two holes in the canvas screen slightly larger than the two in the mans forehead.

Paul got to his feet, 'I'm getting too bloody old for this'. He turned to the camera man, 'sorry about that, are you alright?'

'Confused, and I'll have a bruise! Otherwise fine thanks,' the shaken man replied.

'Well we know where Paul is,' said General Leach.

'Did he get hit?' that old bastard had him cold, how the hell did Paul know he'd got a gun. There wasn't time from the shout to the shots to react.' asked B.J.

The stunned paratroop corporal asked the same question.

'I'm not superhuman corp' replied Paul, 'I heard his claw click on the

223

metal of the trigger guard and guessed the rest'. Paul poked a finger through a hole in his combat smock, 'that was close, the next would have hit, I wonder why he only fired two?'

Having retrieved his Heckler, he walked over to the dead man and removed A.K. from the claw hand.

'Now that was lucky!' showing the assault rifle to the soldiers, 'In all my years, that is only the second time I've know one of these jam, it really must be my lucky day!'

'You do know all this is going out live?' the cameraman asked, having just about regained his equilibrium.

'My apologies to any member of the public who witnessed that, it's not like the movies I'm afraid.' Paul addressed the camera. 'The B.B.C. will be off the air for a little while until we can hand it back to the rightful crew.'

At his signal, the cameraman switched the camera off. 'I know where the rest of the staff are Sir,' said the still shaken man. 'I can lead you to them if you like.'

'As soon as we get the all clear, I think that would be an excellent idea.' replied Paul.

'I've seen you here before Sir, you are the commander of The All Arms Unit.'

'For my sins, yes. With that pain in the arse out of the way,' Paul indicated the dead insurgent leader, still sitting in the chair with his head back as if snoring, 'I might even be allowed to retire.'

A double detonation, close by, followed by the sound of a pair of Hecklers, quickly refocused the soldiers attention. Calls began to come in as the various sections called in that their bit was clear.

A few minutes later the camera man lead several soldiers to a padlocked door.

'This is where the kept us locked up Sir, I've been in there twice, they came to get me when they wanted to broadcast. I don't know where the key is Sir.'

'We won't need a key,' said one of the soldiers, 'the hinges are on the outside, just unscrew them.'

'Bloody daft, what's the point of a lock if the hinges are exposed! Really secure!' observed Paul.

As the door was prised open the stench hit them, over fifty people in a cellar for three days without toilets. It rather defied description.

The welcome the troops got when the staff realised they were free was almost as overwhelming as the stench from the cellar. Of course there was always one! And of all people to have a go at, he picked on Paul!

'You took your bloody time!' he snapped. 'What took you so bloody long, any one would think you had to come half way round the world to sort out a hand full of thugs'.

'We did have to come a few thousand miles, granted nowhere near from the other side of the world but it was a long journey.' replied Paul struggling with his temper.

'Just because that gung-ho cretin they put in charge of getting our troops home from Afghanistan left this country undefended, taking all those troops was an idiot decision.'

Paul stepped back and lit a cigarette, knowing full well it was not really allowed.

'Put that out at once!' demanded the angry man.

'Bollocks', was Paul's reply, 'It's typical, a camera man who has only seen me once recognised me, in spite of being groggy from a stun grenade.'

'And a kick in the ribs Sir'. the cameraman interrupted.

'And a kick in the ribs' Paul added with a grin, 'yet you obviously haven't twigged. You have interviewed me twice, and been on the same panel in a chat show, just about sums you up! It did not go unnoticed that you pushed at least two ladies out of the way to get out of that hell hole in front of them. Keep this up and I'm likely to throw you back in there and replace the screws on the hinges.'

'Don't talk to me like that!' retorted the self important man. 'I demand to speak to who ever is in charge!'

'I guess that would be me then', replied Paul.

A Captain approached Paul, 'There you are Sir, the Major was worried when you weren't in the studio, good Lord, where did all these people come from, and that smell!'

'Give the major my regards captain, I'm fine thank you. Oh! And could you take this piece of detritus with you, take him outside and hose him down before sending him on his way. If I see him again today I am likely to shoot him!'

'Will do, Sir' replied the Captain. 'Come on Mr. Smelly, this way'.

People were still being helped out of the putrid cellar, which had been their prison for the past three days. As more soldiers arrived the rate of rescue speeded up, and very soon the freed staff were escorted to wash rooms to get cleaned up.

Two sections were detailed to the canteen to get tea, coffee and something for the released hostages to eat. It turned out one of the soldiers was a dab hand at making omelettes.

Paul called the base on a borrowed mobile phone, 'Just checking in Taff, I'll be headed into central London shortly. 'We lost eight dead and twenty three, no. twenty four wounded, clearing the rats out of the Beeb.'

'Are you alright,' asked Taff, 'we had the television on when you came busting into the studio. What the hell did you think you were doing?'

'I've asked myself the same question several times in the past few hours,' replied Paul.

'Let me guess what the answer was,' said Taff, 'your job!'.

'Yeah, well needs must', Paul muttered.

'Silly old fool! Just be bloody careful will you!' exclaimed Taff. 'Do you know how many insurgents there were in the building.'

'Not for sure, but we have accounted for one hundred and thirty two, six of them are prisoners, all except one injured. We have also released just over seventy B.B.C. employees. I think they'll all be okay after a bath and a decent meal, although one might not be if he has another go at me.'

'Oh dear, not a certain senior correspondent?'

'The same,' replied Paul. 'What really pissed me of was he didn't recognise me, even after we'd had a row. He was chucking his weight about, pushing ladies out of his way, then complained we'd taken too long to release him. What really got up my nose was him saying we shouldn't have sent so many troops to the med to get the NATO force out, I was sorely tempted to chuck him back in the cellar and leave him there!'

'Calm down,' said Taff, 'Those lads you've got with you did well sorting that particular problem so quickly. I would have expected more casualties in a day light attack, it is a great result Paul.'

'Not if you happen to be one of the lads who didn't make it,' replied Paul. 'We also found a lot of bodies of employees, maybe a hundred or so. From the condition I'd say they'd been dead a couple of days.

'What are your plans Paul?'

'I intend getting into central London as quickly as I can, other than the fact it is bad, it is difficult to get a handle on what is needed to finish it quickly. I'll borrow some wheels from the B.B.C. If I take the three lads who where with me on the rat removal here, I should be alright.'

'You be bloody careful Paul,' implored Taff, 'little gangs of insurgents are turning up all over the place. You will be interested to know the first flights have arrived at Stansted, and at least one battalion of the Rifles are on their way to inner London.

Some how another train load of fuel has got through, but we have been warned it is likely to be our last for some time, so we'll be okay for recon flights for a bit at least.'

'Thanks for the updates Taff, I'll call you from White Hall.'

CHAPTER TWENTY-TWO

The trip into central London was largely uneventful in the commandeered Range Rover. The four soldiers encountered one road block of a sort, but this turned out to be a local gang, and at the sight of armed soldiers, they fled.

Once in the general area the men could hear the constant crackle of small arms fire, interspersed with the louder thumps and bangs of heavier weapons and grenades.

The first soldiers they came across, turned out to be all that was left of company of guards, many of them had only recently finished basic training. They should have been training for ceremonial duties, instead they had taken the brunt of the initial attack. Of the twenty or so men only three appeared uninjured, a heavily bandaged colour sergeant seemed to be in charge.

Spotting the faded Colonels pips and a crown on Pauls' epaulettes, he approached the new arrivals.

'Please excuse the lack of a salute Sir,' he began, 'I'm afraid I can't lift my arm at the moment.'

'I wouldn't worry about it colour sergeant, by the looks of things you have more serious worries than saluting the likes of me.' replied Paul. 'It looks as though your lads have taken a beating, yet you're still manning a road block.'

'You should see the other guy Sir, we may have lost a hell of a lot of good men, but they lost a lot more, and we stopped them breaking out of Horse Guards Parade. We are watching the backs of 'A' company from 2 para at the moment Sir.'

'Apart from the obvious sleep, what do you need Colour Sergeant?'

Paul asked, seriously concerned at the battered state of the mostly young soldiers.

'Ammunition, food, some hot drinks and a medic' if you can find any of them Sir, I would be very grateful Sir.'

'I'll do what I can, I'm not promising any results, but I will try Colour Sergeant. I don't suppose you know where I can find the C.O. of 2 para do you?' Paul asked.

'I think he is setting up a new H.Q. in a container near the Admiralty Arch. If he's not there then try Trafalgar Square, a logistics area is being set up there. I believe the area around the M.O.D. has been cleared, but I think that is the source of the big column of smoke.'

'I suppose there's no chance of getting through Parliament Square and White Hall?' Paul asked, knowing the reply.

'I wouldn't recommend trying Sir, we tried shifting them with our armoured vehicles, scimitars and various A.P.Cs. They knocked out all of them Sir. You can see the smoke. They can't get out, and we can't get any further without some heavy kit to shift their strong points Sir.'

'Thanks for the insight Colour Sergeant, I'll have to go round the houses to find Sandy, I'll get you what help I can, good luck, and well done to your lads for stopping these buggers.' Paul saluted the bedraggled soldiers, he felt that was the least they deserved.

Half an hour later he arrived at the container, almost under the Admiralty Arch, just as a battle stained Sandy emerged from the smoke drifting out of White Hall.

The two friends greeted each other, before being promoted and offered command of 2 para, Sandy had served a six month detachment with The All Arms Unit.

Bloody hell,' exclaimed Paul, 'it looks more like a scene from Lebanon than London!'

'Hi Paul, you got here in the end then?' replied Sandy, 'any chance of having my other company back?'

'Not really mate, they are guarding the B.B.C. and helping get it back on air. I thought that was a tough fight, but it was a walk in the park compared to this!'

Sandy sat down, and accepted the offered cigarette, 'It is a bit of a mess. We have gone about as far as we can until we get some support. I think we may have tried to do a bit too much, but at least we've tidied up the perimeter, so it is easier to keep them bottled up. There's hundreds of the buggers, I can't understand how so many got in with so much fire power.'

As the two men sat in the sun discussing the situation, a heavy army truck pulled up, towing a mobile control centre, mounted on the truck was a communications unit and a large generator to power everything. Two other trucks were full of bits and pieces, such as aerials, cables and all manner of other useful paraphernalia, not the least of which was a tea wagon!

A bus load of engineers and technicians completed the convoy. Within half an hour everything was up and running, with the screens linked to the orbiting Canberra's sensors and cameras, it was possible to get a clearer picture of the carnage along White Hall.

There were dead soldiers lying in the road, cut down by machine guns, but it was the wreckage of the armoured vehicles which was hardest to take. One armoured personnel carrier had been ripped apart by missiles, it was still burning, it's infantry section could clearly be seen, charred mummies, still in their seats.

'What the hell are they hitting them with Sandy?' Paul asked.

'A new version of the R.P.G. mainly, they also seem to have something like a 'Grad' which they can aim. At least you can see what we're up against Paul.' Sandy pointed out a couple of strong points, 'those two positions are what's stopping us. We have hit them with our light mortars several times, to no visible effect, cannon fire from the light armour, before they got destroyed didn't shift them either. Any ideas?'

' What about an Apache, stick a couple of 'hellfires' into them,' suggested Paul.

'Wattisham sent the only serviceable one they had to help when we attacked the M.O.D. main building, it was shot down by heavy machine gun fire and a stinger, it is what set the building on fire when it crashed,' was the depressing reply from the paratroopers commander.

'Then I guess the only option is tanks,' replied Paul. 'That's if we can find any which work, the only ones I can think of remotely handy are the training tanks at the R.E.M.E base at Bordon. I'll get Taff to sort it out. I just hope they have the fuel to get them here.'

It was nearly an hour later when Taff called back with the news that three Challenger tanks had been loaded onto transporters and were headed to London.

Their fuel tanks were only half full as the rest had been needed to fuel the trucks, all three of which belonged to civilian contractors. The other problem was there were only practice shells at Bordon and these wouldn't fire! He was however working on it! On the assumption it was high explosive shells which were required.

The other worry, expressed by the instructors who would be crewing the tanks was the guns hadn't been 'proof tested', so technically should not be fired!

Paul reply was, 'great!' So all we have got are three clapped out training tanks which are not supposed to fire shells we haven't got! Surely there's some tank ammunition at Bovington?'

'All they have are a couple of dozen 'sabot' rounds, that's it!' replied Taff. 'Worse still there doesn't seem to be any propellant charges anywhere. The other little gem which will please you is central ordinance won't release any grenades without the correct paperwork from the M.O.D.'

'Give them the choice, they supply the grenades or they get shot! Don't mess about arguing with a bloody jobs worth, soldiers are dieing for the lack of those grenades, if they won't give them to us, take them! By force if need be!' replied Paul.

'That is exactly what I have told them, we'll see if the stuff is ready when the trucks arrive to pick it up'. Taff chuckled, 'I have even got General Leach's signature on the paper work. The other thing on the list are 120mm artillery shells, they are the right calibre for the tanks, an artillery captain claims we can separate the projectile from the shell case, then make our own bag charges from the propellant. He says they will only be half the velocity of the real thing and will smoke a lot when fired, but he assures me it will work.'

'As long as he doesn't expect me to help him!' exclaimed Paul, 'sounds bloody dangerous to me, but if it works, then we have to try it I suppose.'

'I'll speak to you later Paul, give Sandy my regards,' said Taff, 'and you'll be pleased to know the B.B.C is just back on air'.

'Before you go Taff, how are things going in the canal?' asked Paul.

'They are working on the last of the block ships, best guess is sometime tomorrow before they can refloat it. The really good news is the engineers managed to get the big swing bridge open just enough for the mine sweepers to pass, they have closed it again to work on the bearings. There have been some skirmishes with insurgents, it seems as though quite a lot have holed up in Ismalia. The air lift will have to be suspended after two more cycles due to lack of fuel. The Russians have donated a tanker carrying over 20,000tons of jet fuel if we can get it out of the black sea. The other ships which are stuck there are the convoy carrying an American armoured engineer regiment and a couple of companies of Rangers.'

'Thanks for the update Taff, I'll give you a shout about tea time.'

Paul turned to Sandy, 'What a fuck up, everything we need exists, but we can't get it! What the hell!'

A convoy of London transport double decker buses pulled into Trafalgar square loaded to capacity with men from 'The Rifles' Their C.O. marched smartly up to Paul and Sandy and 'reported for duty'.

'Welcome to the mad house Colonel, we are glad you're here. There are a couple of NAAFI wagons over there, get your men off the buses and dispersed around the square, there are odd mortar bombs being lobbed in this direction.

If you could get two bus loads of your men to go to the north end of Chelsea bridge they'll find a rather battered group of guardsmen. Get your men to take a spare boiler for the hot water, supplies of tea and coffee and plenty of sugar. About 40 bacon butties and chocolate. Draw three boxes of ammo for the S.A. 80s and three full belts for a 7.62 G.P.M.G from the ammo trucks over there,' pointing at a group of green lorries with armoured containers mounted on their trailers. 'And a couple of medics with bandages and stitching kit. Tell your guys to take their food and drinks with them. Those guardsmen have had a rough time and no real rest for three days.'

Ten minutes later one of the oddest relief convoys in British military history headed off to find the battered unit, lead by a London taxi carrying the captain in charge of the detachment and their sergeant major.

An engineer from the All Arms Unit wandered casually up to Paul and the little group of Officers gathered near a tea wagon, 'scuse me boss, the control room is up and running'.

'Thanks' Joe, we'll be over in a bit, now we should be able to see exactly what we're up against.' Paul replied.

'Watch yourself crossing the end of White Hall boss,' the veteran engineer advised, 'as well as stray rounds, it seems as though they have two, maybe three snipers with a clear view.' The soldier looked at Sandy, the C.O. of 2 para. 'Some of your lads are trying to pin them down, but there are so many firing points it is proving difficult to work out which ones are the snipers.'

Things got so bad the decision was taken to pull the forward troops back, at least into the last building which had been cleared.

'The lads aren't too pleased with you Paul,' said Sandy, 'paratroopers don't like pulling back.'

'I know Sandy, but then I don't like dead soldiers, especially when the deaths are avoidable. If they keep their heads down, and just hold their positions, we can have another go at getting into the next blocks when the tanks arrive. The tanks should be able to wipe out those strong points easily with their main guns, then between us and the tanks we should be able to keep the insurgents away from the windows long enough for the clearance squads to get in.'

'When should those tanks arrive Paul?' asked the para's C.O.

'Let's see if we can find them, the roads are pretty empty, they'll be coming up from Bordon, so I suppose they'll use the M3.'

It took longer than Paul expected to find them of the video beamed down from the orbiting Canberra. 'What the bloody hell!?' he exclaimed.

'What's up Paul?' asked Sandy.

'Damned if I know, hang on, we'll soon find out' Paul tapped a few keys on his lap top which was now linked to the main computer in the control centre, he and Sandy watched the screen as the Captain in charge of the convoy fished his mobile phone out of his pocket.

'Holdsworth, who is this please?'

'What the bloody hell do think you are doing Captain, this is not the time for a soddin' NAAFI break. Get those bloody trucks moving. NOW'

'It is not that simple Sir,' as the captain noticed Pauls I.D. come up on his phone.

'What's not simple, the order was straight forward enough, load up and get you arses into Trafalgar Square as fast as the trucks can go.'

'We have several problems Sir, We are not allowed to refuel at these services, the management of the company which owns the place have banned any military vehicles from having fuel. The police pulled us in on instructions from the ministry of transport vehicle inspectors who have issued prohibition notices on the three transporters and the ammunition carrier.'

'Put the senior cop on please Captain.' said Paul, taking a deep breath, trying to calm down.

'Inspector Thorn, Hampshire traffic division ,' came the voice on the phone.

'Inspector Thorn,' Paul began, 'I take it you are aware of the situation in inner London?'

'I am aware of some localised terrorist activity'. replied the police officer.

'Well, this localised terrorist activity, as you called it, has cost the lives of over three hundred soldiers and well over a thousand civilians. We need those tanks to shift the bastards. Have a look at the screen on the lap top the ministry pillock next to you is using, I'll patch through the live picture of what White Hall looks like at the moment, ready?'

They all heard the ministry man say, 'what the heck?' as his form vanished from his screen, to be replaced by the battle torn scene which was White Hall, Paul zoomed in on the still smouldering remains of the armoured personnel carrier, complete with the charred bodies.

' Now do you understand why we need those tanks?'

'I do indeed,' replied the police inspector, 'but it is up to the man from the ministry.'

'Stop right there inspector,' Paul interrupted, 'If he won't release those trucks I am going to order them to get moving, if ANYTHING or anyone gets in their way their orders will be keep going. If they need fuel, and it is my understanding they do, then I am authorising them to fill their tanks and to shoot anyone trying to stop them. Be very clear, I have that power. I also have the power to order you to arrest anyone who impedes their progress, that includes the ministry idiot and the staff of the petrol station, and who ever told them to refuse to serve the military. In particular those who issued the no fuel order. The choice is yours Inspector'.

'So it was all true about a new government being declared by the insurgents, we thought it was all a load of rubbish being spread around by some extremists to make the temporary military government look bad.'

'I find that hard to believe Inspector, see to it those trucks are filled up and on their way as quickly as possible, a great many lives depend on their prompt arrival. If you could pass me back to the Captain please.'

As the Inspector handed the phone back Paul heard the policeman ask, 'Who the hell was that?'

Paul also heard the reply, 'He is the C.O. of the All Arms Unit.'

'Well, who ever he is, if the man from the ministry says those trucks can't move. Then that's it. They stay put until the prohibition is lifted. No arguments.' said the police officer

'I heard all that,' said Paul, 'put your phone on speaker please Captain, so I don't have to keep repeating myself.' Pauls' patience was rapidly evaporating. 'Consider these as orders, Captain Holdsworth, get the drivers back into their trucks, then take two armed soldiers into the fuel kiosk to ensure the diesel pumps are not switched off. Inform the staff that the bill will be paid over the telephone as soon as those vehicles, including the tanks are all topped up. This is not a request, make it clear, we must have the name, and contact details of the idiot who issued them that order. If it is the manager and he is on site, bring him with you, as I will want a word!'

'Understood Colonel.' replied the officer.

'Now, inspector Cleuseau,' Paul began.

'It's Thorn actually,' the man sounded quite miffed.

'As this is a matter of national security, the pen pushing pillock, or rather button pushing burke beside you has absolutely NO authority to interfere with the progress of those trucks in any way what so ever. The drivers orders are to deliver their loads no matter what, this includes physically shoving any vehicles aside which are parked in the way to impede that progress. Do you understand?'

'I heard what you said Colonel, but I'm not sure you can do that.' replied the Inspector.'

'I am very sure I have these powers. Now, why don't you go with the Captain and ensure the staff comply with the request for fuel and pass on the information about the origin of that order. As for the man from the ministry, suggest he buggers off and tries to find something useful to do, like sign on the dole! As the ministry of transport building is still in the hands of the insurgents he, and his colleagues will not be getting paid for the foreseeable future. As it is, his name will go to the bottom of the pile for wages and the top of the pile of those facing redundancy. Now please do everything in your power to get those trucks fuelled up and moving, taco graph hours do not apply neither do speed limits! Just get them rolling!'

'Very well Colonel,' replied the police inspector, 'with a couple of provisos, firstly I actually witness the payment for the fuel.'

'I was going to ask you to do that anyway,' replied Paul, 'and the other condition?'

'Inform my head quarters you over ruled me on assisting the ministry inspectors.'

'I will be delighted to do that as well inspector, if that is what it takes to get those trucks moving.' was Paul's heart felt reply.

Shortly after the convoy resumed it's journey, another problem came to light, the Captain was checking the preferred route into London, what he found made Paul's blood pressure rise once more.

'Yes Captain Holdsworth' said Paul, answering the call in the control centre.

'We have another problem Sir,' the officer replied.

'Oh gawd,' Paul muttered, 'what's up now?'

'We won't be able to use the M3 inside the M25, the road works, the low loaders will ground, in several places, even if we could reach Kew bridge the link to the M4/A4 is also dug up and only light vehicles can get through. We can't use the M4 either as the Hammersmith flyover it shut for repairs so we can't use it. If we tried to get under it then we'd bring all the scaffolding crashing down!'

'Oh bloody marvellous,' sighed Paul, 'I suppose that means the M40/A40,' he thought for a minute. 'Shit, there are still some insurgents around the Park Royal area, and I've got nothing to send to deal with them yet. There is the possibility I might be able to get a couple of sections of paras to at least get their attention to help you get past them. I take it your turret machine guns are operational?'

'They are, but we may have to wait until we are through the underpass under the gyratory system before we can mount them. I believe there are new height restrictions, something about repair work. Of course! we can at least take the big trucks up the slip road and back down onto the A40.' the Captain sounded less worried now he had a possible solution.

'Do what you have to do Captain, keep your guns manned, regard anywhere inside the M25 as bandit country. Good luck and see you as soon as possible.'

As Paul had warned, a group of insurgents tried to stop the thundering trucks near Park Royal. Forewarned of the danger the drivers were going as fast as the trucks could manage, with an all up weight of nearly 100 tons this was just over 50 miles an hour. How ever travelling at this speed with extra strong steel bumpers and solid front tyres, a barricade consisting of a pair of hi-lacked cars didn't stand a chance when hit square on in the gap between the cars.

There may have been thirty gunmen on the road block, but the heavy turret machine gun of the tank on the leading truck firing long accurate bursts meant a high risk to anyone trying to aim an R.P.G. at the lead truck. Just as the first doubts crept into the insurgents mind that these truck were not going to stop they became aware of another problem. There might have been only eight paratroops, but the amount of accurate fire they poured into the road block was devastating. It might not have been very sporting, attacking without warning from the rear quarter, but sport wasn't a major consideration.

The impact of the first truck on the road block was the final straw, the few uninjured insurgents thought about running, some tried to surrender, that didn't quite work out either as the big solid Peugeot estate car was hurled into the air by the force of truck striking it. Unfortunately it landed squarely on one small group trying to surrender to the section of paratroops.

Three gunmen fleeing the other way were struck by the rolling people carrier, which had formed the other half of the barricade. At least six, it was hard to be sure, were struck by the speeding convoy, some where no doubt dead from gunshots before being all but obliterated.

The only visible signs of the encounter as far as the convoy was concerned were a couple of minor dents in the tough steel wings of the leading truck, a broken head light bulb, although the glass was still intact behind it's protective grill.

True there were a couple of bullet holes in the cab, but that was about it. The most obvious signs of the encounter were on and around the wheels.

One of the paratroopers was heard to say, 'I'm bloody glad I haven't got to wash that shit off.' as they waved the convoy past.

The sergeant in charge soon tempered the relief by informing his squad they might not have to wash the trucks down, but they would have to clear up the road, and not just the weapons and ammunition strewn around.

In the event it proved harder than anticipated to get the tanks into Trafalgar Square, a vast number of traffic bollards and keep left signs fell victim to the over hanging tank tracks. Twice the leading low loader grounded on projecting raised curbs. The first time it happened the powerful truck simply dragged the curb out where it had snagged on the reinforced trailer.

The second time it was immediately obvious this wouldn't be an option and everything had to back up for nearly a mile to take an alternative route. Negotiating this route wasn't without it's hazards and more than a few bollards were crushed by the trailers. Eventually the convoy arrived, and under the unblinking gaze of Nelson the great battle tanks were unloaded and prepared for a task for which they were not designed, urban warfare, the 'tanky's' nightmare.

Paul had made the hazardous trip from the control centre to Trafalgar Square once more to have a word with the tank crews, as he stood talking to the captain in charge of the detachment, a R.E.M.E. staff sergeant approached the two officers.

'Excuse me Sir, if I could have a moment?' he was a little unsure, he knew the Captain but Paul only by reputation. 'Could you give my men half an hour before you launch the attack Sir?' he asked.

'If you have a good enough reason Staff,' replied Paul.

'I'd like to weld missile grills onto at least the lead tank Sir,' replied the Staff sergeant. 'I know Challengers can take hits from R.P.Gs., but that lead tank is going to get hammered and the grills will take the sting out of most of the hits. I've got the men and equipment standing by Sir.'

'Then, get on with it staff, if you have the equipment put at least partial guards on the other two. Damned good idea Staff.'

'Thank you Sir,' the man replied as he ran towards his crew signalling start up the engine on their old Stalwart amphibian.

It turned out this was a T.A. crew who had been overlooked when putting together the force sent to secure the Suez canal, the stated reason was their kit was too old.

Paul and the captain watched as the crew made it look easy, using the 'hi-ab' hydraulic crane to swing out the heavy armoured grills from the cargo bay on the Stalwart and place them precisely against the tank hull, so the welders could fix them securely.

'They are good captain, damned good,' remarked Paul , as the second grill was placed perfectly next to the first. Twenty minutes later the R.E.M.E. lads were almost finished, having run out of their home made grills. The welders were just completing the last of the reinforcing welds to increase the durability of their work.

Paul turned to the captain. 'Give me twenty minutes to check on every ones positions, remember use the lead tank to take out the strong points and the turret machine guns on the other two to cover the lead tank. We'll give covering fire with every thing we've got in the way of machine guns and light support weapons as well as the sniper teams. If it works, there are four clearing teams ready to assault the next occupied buildings on either side.

We'll see how far we can go, but do not pass the cenotaph, we simply haven't got the man power to take a bigger bite. Good luck' he added as he left the captain to brief his crews.

In the event, everything worked perfectly, the forty or so R.P.Gs. fired at the lead tank hardly scorched the paint work. On the other side of the equation, the twelve modified rounds fired out of the main cannon of the armoured giant totally destroyed the eight strong points constructed out of sand bags and sheets of armour.

The first six had been easy, single shots resulted in total destruction, not only of the emplacements but of those manning them. The two near the Parliament Square end of the debris strewn road were built much stronger and moments after the first hits there was still fire coming from both positions. As strong as the fortifications were, they were no match for flat trajectory shells from the tank guns, even with their reduced velocity. The total of five layers of sand bags, two layers of 15mm sheet armour and concrete sections of barricade might have given the illusion of security, but it was only an illusion.

As soon as the newly liberated buildings were secure Paul withdrew most of the combat troops and pulled back the tanks, leaving just the well protected lead tank sitting in the middle of the road, level with the limit of advance through the buildings on either side.

This wasn't exactly popular with the adrenalin fuelled troops but Paul was adamant. Food, re-equip where needed and a bit of rest, sleep if possible before the next push.

In the face of obvious disapproval Paul called all commanders, down to platoon level together, he sat down on an empty ammunition box and motioned them to sit as well.

'I hear what you are saying, and I understand your reasoning in wanting to go further. We have just lost four killed and six, may be seven more injured. Think what would happen if we continued, there is no point in attacking until our resources in man power and ammunition are exhausted.

Just so you are aware of what the situation is, we have used 60% of our small arms ammunition and 80% of our stun grenades. There are four truck loads on their way, but it will be at least eight hours before they arrive. The first plane carrying another infantry battalion has just landed at Stansted. It will be a couple of hours before they are all down. Then they have to get here, the lads from the 'rifles' can tell you how long that took. So get some rest!

I have no intention of letting the insurgents rest, the number of troops tasked with sniping has been doubled. Their orders are one round at anything which moves. Now we have a solid cordon, and the extra buildings we have cleared mean can cover most of the area occupied by the insurgents, if one of them moves, there is a real risk of being shot.

Go back to your men and explain to them why I ordered the pause. I believe there is a truck load of sleeping bags over near the main first aid tent. Also there is no truth in the rumour started by some wag, that the first aid tent is next to the food tent to deal with the predicted out break of food poisoning!

One last thing, disperse your platoons around the edge of the square please, and in the grounds of the M.O.D building, as there is still a risk of renewed mortar attacks. That will be all gentlemen, thank you. Dismissed.'

Sandy, the C.O. of 2 para came over to Paul. 'You handled that well Boss. It even made sense to my gang of hot heads.'

'I must have got it right if they say so' replied Paul, 'I wanted a word with you anyway Sandy.'

'Oh 'eck what have I done now,' replied the para commander.

'Twit,' chuckled Paul. 'I wanted to ask you about Major Dalrymple, you don't happen to know where he is do you?'

Sandy looked puzzled, 'I sort of assumed he must be in charge over at the B.B.C., from the tone and tenure of your question, clearly he isn't there.'

'It seems as though he took it upon himself to come on an earlier flight, leaving his men behind to await my arrival.'

'That's news to me Paul, frankly I have no idea where he is, he only joined the reserve company about six months ago. To be honest I'd never met the guy until we arrived in Cyprus, and I didn't see much of him there.' replied Sandy, sounding a bit worried.

'I thought the reserve company were all veterans and long service T/A, do any of your company commanders know him?

Sandy, the C.O. replied with a shrug, 'That's the funny thing, as far as I can tell no-one knew him, his own company hadn't heard of him until he was appointed in command by the M.O.D. Thinking about it, I've never seen his service record, the adjutant might be able to shed some light on it, but he is getting emergency treatment at the moment for a nasty gun shot wound.'

'Great!' replied Paul, 'why am I getting a bad feeling about this?'

'What are you thinking Paul,' asked Sandy, 'All I know is he was appointed by the M.O.D. and he has what I would call a 'mid Atlantic' accent.'

'Oh, crap!' exclaimed Paul, 'not another one, there is one on the General staff who's loyalties are, how can I put this, dubious to say the least. Is your battalion office still manned?'

'It had better be,' replied Sandy

Paul passed him his own communications device. 'Call them up and get them to either fax or email those personnel records, the email address and fax number are both on the screen..'

As soon as Sandy had made the call, stressing the urgency, Paul called his H.Q. and asked them to find the mans mobile and both track and monitor it.

Suddenly among the sounds of rifle fire and exploding rocket grenades there was the unmistakeable sound of the mighty 120mm cannon of the Challenger firing, followed quickly by the even louder bang of the shell exploding. A minute or so later there were several quite long bursts of machine gun fire which could only have been the point five inch heavy machine gun in the turret of the tank.

The two senior officers decided to investigate.

The two old friends worked their way forward, dodging from cover to cover with practiced ease, well aware of the spent rounds whizzing by and the odd whining sounds made by the ricochets from incoming A.K, rounds.

'What are we doing Sandy?' Paul asked as something heavier chipped a lump out of the masonry above his head.

'Trying to find out what's going on?' was the reply, barely audible as the point five machine gun on the tank ahead of them burst into life again.

The main gun fired again, producing the predicted cloud of smoke.

'What the hell is he firing at?' asked Sandy 'I can't see a bloody thing.'

'We can soon find out,' said Paul, grabbing his communicator from his belt. He called the Captain from Bordon who was in command of the tanks.

'Sorry about all the noise Sir,' the Captain apologised, 'we kept getting hit by R.P.Gs. All the bangs were giving us a headache, we could see the firing point, so we took it out. I do hope that was alright Sir?'

'Of course it was alright, but what's all the racket with the M.G.?' asked Paul.

'The position was in the corner of the outer security barrier of The Houses of Parliament, our first round blew a decent gap in it. Through this gap we could see all along the inside of the wall facing the square, there were hundreds of them so we decided to thin them out a bit. It also revealed the strong point which has, or I should say had, been hitting our troops across the square, that was the second round we fired. I do hope I did the right thing Sir'.

'I'll get the other two tanks back here, see if your collective machine guns can thin out these bloody snipers, but if you spot another strong point, hit it!'

'Will do Sir.'

Paul and Sandy made their way back to the command centre.

'Any danger of getting a decent cup of coffee around here?' Paul asked.

A trooper answered, without looking to see who had asked, 'the N.A.A.F.I wagon, it's only 50p a cup.'

'Here's a quid,' replied Paul, producing a pound coin, 'The Colonel takes his black with one sugar, mine is strong and sweet, the opposite to me, not too much milk! If you don't mind.'

'Sorry Sir, I didn't realise it was you,' replied the embarrassed soldier.

'What's next Paul?' asked Sandy.

'For the moment, simply keep the pressure on using the tanks and snipers, thin them out as much as we can. When the next battalion arrive and the ammunition gets here we'll see if we can clear White Hall, at least as far as the Cenotaph. If things go well we might have it cleared by tomorrow evening. I'm not going to lose more men than we have to, so we only take what we can.

There are six more tanks on the way from Bovington, they have their real crews, by all accounts they even have a tanker full of fuel with them, which is amazing. They don't however, have any high explosive shells, which is also amazing, no-one seems to know if there are any, never mind where they might be. Some one is, or has been playing silly bastards again.' Paul took his polystyrene cup from the trooper as he returned from his mission, thanking him as he took the steaming brew.

'Frankly Sandy,' he continued, 'I'm more worried about the supply problems than I am about these crack pots. What really worries me is we have at least two officers, the new member of the General staff, and your missing bloody Major, who have very questionable loyalties. I'm concerned there may be more, in fact there must be more to have caused the problems we have.

I can't believe they want these nutters to succeed, so it must be to do with this bloody cartel, but why foul things up when they know everyone is broke.'

'Except them?' suggested Sandy.

'As you say, except them, although the stock market regulators seem to have screwed some of them for now. I'm thinking of leaving you in command here for a bit while I nip back to our base to see if I can identify, and hopefully solve some of our problems.'

'Oh thanks a bunch Paul' replied the Para troop commander.

'Regard it as a vote of confidence, just keep nibbling away around the edges for now. When you hit a spot, hit it hard, with enough force to ensure success. Isolate a building, pick off as many as you can before the clearing squads go in. Keep them guessing where you will hit next. That tank blowing a hole in the wall is a bonus, it has effectively cut their forces in half, use that to our advantage. I'd concentrate on this side of White Hall and around Parliament Square. They can't reinforce these positions without heavy losses, or offer much support, all we need is patience, more troops and more ammunition, both the latter are on the way. Have you got the patience?' Paul asked.

'I think so, punch hard, then keep pecking away, to keep them off balance until the next punch is ready,' Sandy actually sounded pleased about it.

'There should soon be a refitted Canberra on station, then you will be able to see into any building so you will know what you are up against before you commit to an assault. It can even detonate any booby traps totally remotely. Use the technology to save your guys lives Sandy, we are going to lose men any way, but let's keep the casualties as low as possible.' It was obvious the sight of dead soldiers was getting to Paul, maybe more than would have been expected.

'Fair enough Boss, I'll take good care of our troops.' replied Sandy.

It was a nervous journey home for the commander of The All Arms Unit, there was little traffic, mostly it consisted of groups of trucks, travelling together for at least the feeling of mutual support. He also noted, with a smile, speed limits seemed to be ignored by the truckers, the occasional police road blocks were making no attempt to stop the speeding trucks, simply waving them past.

'Common sense taking over?' he mused, too much to hope for!

A single car however was a different matter, every one pulled him in, reaction varied from, 'have a safe trip Sir' to, 'get out of the car' and even having guns pointed at him. Generally, the further away from the capital he got, the less stressed the police seemed to get. Even the motor way cops who pulled him over were more interested in how things were going, once they were convinced of his identity.

He didn't really begin to relax until he was almost in sight of the base.

CHAPTER TWENTY-THREE

'Nice of you to drop in', was the greeting he received back at his base.

'Never mind the welcome home,' Paul answered Taff, 'we have one hell of a problem mate.'

'You don't say,' replied Taff, 'I can't say I'd noticed! Any thing in particular bring you back, or are you just home sick?'

'Daft bugger,' chuckled Paul. 'This goes way beyond these lunatics with guns, I'd say they are the least of our problems. It's all this interference with supplies, I saw the message about the grenades, or the lack thereof, I'm also aware of the supply problems for the starter cartridges for the Canberra's engines. We all know about the fuel supply foul ups, now it seems we can't even get ammunition! This is getting stupid Taff, in addition to all this it seems as though it's not just Sir bloody Selwyn we can't trust. The commander of 2para's reserve company has gone awol, a major Dalrymple' it seems as though he was appointed by the M.O.D. not long ago, no-one I can find knows where the hell he came from. Their battalion office wasn't a lot of help, they are still waiting for his service record to come through. I'll bet they aren't the only rotten eggs.'

'So what do we do about it?' asked Taff, 'we already agreed we use Sir Selwyn to feed the information we wanted the cartel to know, are you saying he's no longer useful in that role?'

'Personally, I'd just shoot the bastard, but we first need to know who appointed him, and bloody Dalrymple. It had to be someone high up in the M.O.D., there can't be many of the top ones left, what with the Birmingham disaster then the M.O.D. main building being taken over, then destroyed. Sandy doesn't think anyone got out. My information is about ten of the top civil servants were not in the Exhibition centre when the plane hit, two of them, we know were killed by the insurgents. We'll have to find the rest and check them out.' Paul sounded exasperated, 'as if we haven't got enough problems'.

'I'll get Kenny in here,' said Taff, 'I have the impression he was thinking along the same lines as you.'

'Call an 'O' group in my office, in twenty minutes,' with that Paul spun on his heel and headed for his own office, leaving Taff staring at the slowly closing door.

'Yes Sir, right away sir', he muttered under his breath, as he began to call the department heads to attend the meeting.

As soon as he had made himself a coffee, Paul made a couple of calls. He had hardly finished the second when Al, the head of electronics entered the office, in response to Paul saying in a loud voice, 'come in Al'.

'Okay, I'll play,' said the big man, 'how'd you know it was me? A new camera I suppose'.

'Nope! You are the only one who knocks these days!' replied Paul. 'Any way, that was a bit swift, I said twenty minutes, and that was five minutes ago.'

'What was?' asked a mystified Al.

'You're not here for the meeting then?'

'What meeting would that be?' Al was still puzzled.

'The one I just called, never mind, you're here now.' said Paul. 'You obviously wanted something else, so…….'

'I only came in to check the connections on what ever it was the gremlins buried in the floor of your office. A couple of techs joined up all the wires, cables and fibre optics, they weren't sure they'd got it right, and asked me to check.' He moved round the end of the desk. 'So where is it?' he asked.

'I suppose it's that,' replied Paul, pointing at a single cable with a braided wire protective sheathing, which emerged from a standard looking flap in the floor.

Al lifted the flap and shone his torch into the small void, all he could see was a very normal looking cable connector.

'So, Oh great wise one, I presume all is well?' asked Paul.

'If I knew what it was, I could tell you,' replied a perplexed Al, 'What the hell is it hooked up to? The computer cables are all in ducts, and there aren't any ducts down there, just concrete.'

'You know our gremlins have developed a new computer of sorts. Well, what's buried down there has more power than our main frame,

Cheltenham's, White Halls, Langley's and a dozen more like them put together, the biggest difference is you can carry this one, in a decent pocket!.'

'Bloody hell, that's what you had in Afghanistan to plan the pull out.' said Al.

'Not quite, that was a prototype, it's in the mobile H.Q. under the Admiralty Arch, hooked up to the system to help Sandy.

This one I'm told is twice as powerful, quite what the implications of that are,' Paul paused, 'I'm not quite sure.'

'What's on it?' asked Al, 'I suppose you'll be down loading everything from our mainframe on to it .'

'Nope, already done,' replied Paul.

Al looked shocked, 'How? When? It would take hours to do that, even if you could get in! Damn it it's not even hooked up to the web.'

'I know, but by all accounts it took less than thirty seconds to get in and copy every file, less for Langley. As I understand it the thing has copied every file there is to be copied, sorted it all and filed it all, no duplicates, although it made a note of every computer which had any given file.'

'Oh bloody hell, how the devil does it do that? What happens if someone tries to hack into it?'

'First of all you've got to know it exists, if you try to gain unauthorised access it will fry the enquiring equipment, so I'm told. Try to physically nick it and it will self destruct. I haven't got the faintest idea of even the principle it works on, not even it's power source. There's no where to fit a spanner so I'm lost.'

'It's this thing which has upgraded the scanners on the Canberras, isn't it?'

'And a lot more besides mate,' replied Paul, 'You don't know the half of it, and I hope you never do,' he added with feeling.

'What happens when it's memory is full?' asked Al.

'I asked exactly the same question, and was told it is unlikely that will ever happen in our life times.' replied Paul. 'Remember when we first started, how we watched false colour images being beamed back live from our reconnaissance planes, able to zoom in on what we wanted? Damn it most mobile phones can do that now. This stuff however mustn't ever get out, I can listen to any phone conversation I want to, read any email, nothing is safe anymore. It is one scary tool to have at ones finger tips, it is also a frightening responsibility.'

'Rather you than me mate,' replied Al with feeling.

'On the plus side, it means we should know by dinner time just who is screwing with our supplies.' said Paul.

'It can do that? asked Al. 'How the hell can it do that, it would have to check thousands of records and phone calls.'

Paul opened up his brief case, the lid of which contained his lap top, he pulled out a jack plug on a self winding cord and plugged it into a port on his desk top computer terminal. 'Let's see, shall we'.

He typed in 'cancellation of stun grenades' and search.

He had hardly released the key when the information began to appear on the screen and copies of relevant emails began to be printed out. There were lists of phone calls on the subject, who made them, and to whom, duration and even which of the calls had been recorded. Queries of a similar nature about tank ammunition, small arms ammunition, even the debacle over fuel, all produced itemised printouts with names, dates and times.

Al was gob smacked, he really jumped when his communicator buzzed to denote he had a call.

'Where are you Al?' Taff asked, 'there's a meeting in Paul's office in ten minutes.'

'I'm already there Taff, I should bring your valium if I were you, see you soon.' the big electronics chief replied.

'It's all very well having this information, the question is what the hell do we do about it?' muttered Paul. 'We can hardly go around topping the lot, we'll have to find a way of separating the willing from those coerced into passing stuff on.

We'll run some financial checks on the originators of these 'economy measures'.

'Any bets on where that will lead?' said Al.

'No,' replied Paul.

Just then Pete, the head of 'the air wing' arrived for the meeting, 'nicking my bloody planes again Paul?'

'Not really nicking them Pete, just borrowing them for a week or so to help a friendly power.'

'Of course, it is just coincidence it is our oldest Canberra which has a modified electronics pack, which no-one understands, damn it our service techs don't even know what it is supposed to do!'

Paul stood up and headed for the kettle, 'let's just keep it that way Pete.'

Taff and most of the others appeared, 'you haven't lost your sense of timing Paul, can I have an extra sugar please,' asked the stocky little Welshman.

Just as Paul took his seat a phone rang on the desk, all he said in reply was, 'they'll be leaving shortly Director.'

Al handed out folders he had prepared for each head of department, these contained copies of the list of those interfering with military supplies.

'Bloody hell Paul!' Taff exclaimed, 'this is dynamite , where, or rather how the devil did you get all this from?'

'More to the point, what are we going to do about it, from what I can see it would take forensic accountants several life times to unravel all this.' B.J. sighed, 'are we stuffed on this Boss?'

'Probably,' Paul replied, 'at least as far as anything even near to being legal goes.

The problem is this lot control the media, there's not a national daily in the country which would run that story, they wouldn't be allowed to.'

'What about the B.B.C.? they owe the military, big time,' suggested Taff.

'You would have thought so, but the official line is it was all our fault anyway, allowing the insurgents access in the first place,' was Paul's reply.

'So what do we do about it, is there anything we can do about it?'

'Do about what Kenny?' asked General Leach as he entered the office.

'This Sir,' said Taff, passing the General his copy of the folder. 'Although I would suggest sitting down before you read it Sir.'

B.J. ambled over to the kettle and made the General a coffee.

'Good Lord above,' muttered the elderly General. 'I'm not even going to ask where you got all this Paul. It certainly shows who has the real power today, and who is manipulating things to their own ends. The question is how the devil can we use it to at least enforce a degree of stability.'

'Well at least we know who is calling the shots Boss,' replied Paul. 'I'll grant you it came as a bit of a shock, I knew he had links to the cartel, but tenuous links at best. I think you and I should go and see the Prime Minister, I take it he is up to having a chat?'

'To what end Paul? You do know he is a close personal friend, I believe they even went to Eton together. Is there anything you can show the P.M. in the way of hard proof that the 'Honourable Lord' is far from honourable,' The General who was acting Prime Minister asked.

'I've got a couple of teams tracing a few possible links, we may have something in an hour or so. What we need is something which traces directly back to him, I'm off to the farm in an hour or so. In the mean time there are a couple of decisions to be made, in that respect I'm glad you're here Sir,' Paul addressed General Leach.

'Sounds like a bit of buck passing coming up,' was the observation from the senior officer.

'Not quite Sir,' replied Paul. 'In view of the current catastrophic supply situation, I've taken a decision which has, or could have serious implications. Give Sandy and the men with him a couple more days and he should have the insurgents bottled up in The Houses or Parliament. It might take until the week end but it is the likely end game, as far as the big gang are concerned.

That is where the problem lies, by then Sandy and his men will be out of ammunition or nearly so, and definitely out of stun grenades, not that these would work in most of the building, put simply, the rooms are too big for them to be effective. Even if we can get a Hercules into City air port with a load of ammunition from Cyprus, it will not solve the fundamental problem, we can expect about fifty per cent fatalities among the attacking troops, this is totally unacceptable. As far as we can tell there are no civilian hostages, so this is not a factor.'

'Good Lord!' exclaimed General Leach, 'You are not proposing bombing The Houses of Parliament!'

'The thought had crossed my mind Sir,' replied Paul, 'but I discounted it you will be delighted to hear.'

'Thank heavens for small mercies,' muttered the old soldier. 'So what nefarious scheme have you come up with which will cause trouble?'

'Remember what we have in our deepest ammunition bunker from all the shenanigans of eighteen months back?' Paul asked.

'No!' said General Leach, 'absolutely not! I have heard you come up with some outrageous things in my time, but this.' his voice tailed off.

'Give me one good reason why not Sir?' replied Paul. 'We'll be out of ammo, have only exhausted troops, and nowhere nearly enough of them, our stun grenades wouldn't work, even if we had any. Levelling the place isn't really an option, ergo; gas the bastards. I am informed that it is still as viable as ever, less than two per cent degradation, we have Di-oxin free supplies. One whiff of it and that's it, lights out in seconds, they are dead, our troops alive and the stuff has degraded in a couple of hours. We can clear up the following day, job done, building more or less intact.'

'You can't Paul, it's against all rules and conventions,' said General Leach.

'Like this lot have signed up to any rules! They have murdered virtually everyone they have come across, we've already taken heavy losses. If anyone has an alternative, I'm listening.' was Paul's uncompromising reply. 'And just for the record, last time I had contact with Sandy, a lot of our troops are already out of ammunition and are using A.Ks. taken off dead insurgents.'

General leach asked, 'How are you planning to get the gas into the building Paul?'

'A squad from our mob, full N.B.C. suits, get up to the low boundary wall using tanks as cover, their smoke mortars can lay a thick screen in a matter of seconds, smoke canisters are something we actually have! There is a team working in the bottom bunker as we speak filling 40mm grenades for our launchers with the stuff.'

'You are going to send men in and use the grenade launchers on your rifles!?'

'Unless anyone has a better idea. The amounts then can be the minimum required, delivered with precision. Works for me,' said Paul almost casually.

'Might I enquire who you had in mind to lead this suicidal attack?'

'You know darned well I will lead it Sir,' replied Paul, 'So why ask, you know there is no way I would ask anyone else to do anything I'm not prepared to do myself. I don't happen to think it is suicidal, in spite of what you lot think I haven't got a death wish. I just want to retire and spend my days cursing my inability to catch the 'big one', by that I mean a fish not a bloody terrorist. Frankly, I'm sick of all the killing, but what has to be, has to be.' He drained his cup of nearly cold coffee.

'Right, now you're all up to speed on White Hall, exactly what do we do about all this?' he indicated the pile of printouts on the activities of the cartel, 'In particular the thoroughly dishonourable Lord .'

CHAPTER TWENTY FOUR

As the General and Paul were preparing to leave for 'The Farm' , Helga appeared in the office door, she seemed a little unsure in the presence of General Leach.

'Oh, I'm sorry Sir,' she began, 'I didn't mean to interrupt.'

'That's quite alright my dear,' replied the amiable General, 'come in'.

'I think I might have found what you wanted Boss,' she addressed Paul. 'It's just as you said, everything through third parties and holding companies. Knowing the critical nature of the ammunition supply we decided to look a bit closer. Lord Johnny, as he likes to be known, was on the defence procurement committee when the decision was taken to award the contract to an Indian company for all small arms ammunition. We checked out who owned the company, there didn't seem to be a link until we discovered a company registered in the Cayman Islands had the contract to transport all export orders of ammunition they manufactured.

It is all very convoluted Boss, but one way or another he gets a cut of all the shipping profits, indirectly owns the site, so he gets the rent, a percentage of the profits of all products as he owns the company which supplies the brass alloy. He has a controlling interest in the insurance company which deals with the in transit insurance, as well as the local bank which financed the factory.

He is linked to the company which chartered the ships to transport the ammunition. Now how daft is this, they ship it to the U.K., then back out to Afghanistan! Three ship loads have been lost. Two to Somali pirates and one had it's cargo seized by authorities in west Africa when the ship was refuelling, his insurance company have not paid out as they claim it was the British governments fault for inadequately protecting the ships against

251

known risks, in every case the ships and crews were released unharmed.

The money trail was interesting as it all ends up in an offshore account of yet another paper company and eventually through an investment brokerage into the family trust fund. Guess who the land lord of the brokerage company is? There's loads more, but it could take weeks to sort it all out as the crafty begger hasn't got his name on anything, his wife has.

If you asked me, I'd say it was her insurance policy, as Lord Johnny seems to have a fancy woman, he appears to be quite worried about her, keeps leaving messages on her answer service. We haven't traced her yet, she is American, a Carol McNight.'

Paul shot out of his chair and planted a huge kiss on Helga's cheek, 'Helga, I love you and if I wasn't married already..!'

The tall blonde looked totally stunned, not to say confused, she looked at General Leach, 'What did I say?' she beseeched.

'She is a he Helga,' said the General.

'So he's gay? That's not a crime these days'.

'No, no Helga,' said Paul, 'McNight is one of the most dangerous, evil bastards on this earth, he is a total psycho, and is the cartels ultimate Mr. Fixit , he'd torture his own mother for the fun of it! Have you found any payments to McNight?'

'About two million over the past eighteen months, it's usually out of the trust fund via yet another company based in the Cayman islands. There are at least six with the same address. The other thing is, although many of the transactions are through, or on behalf of the British government, it's only been the last six months he's paid any tax, and then not much! In fact, I've paid more! And that has pissed me off!' Helga suddenly blushed a little, 'Sorry Sir.' she said sheepishly.

'Don't apologise dear girl, I like that, don't get mad, get even attitude. Splendid work, absolutely splendid. Well m'boy,' he said turning to Paul, 'we'd better get going, there's your ammunition Paul.' The General sounded quite relieved they at last had something provable.

Arriving at the farm the two senior officers went straight to the medical centre, the duty doctor directed them to the common room further along the corridor. To Paul's delight over half of the cabinet were up and about, although far from well, all were at least on the road to recovery.

The P.M. actually stood up to greet the visitors, not out of deference, simply because he could, 'Good to see you Gentlemen,' as he extended his now shakeable hand in greeting.

'You might not be so pleased to see us when you see what the Colonel has turned up Sir.' replied General Leach, 'I recommend you sit down first Sir, you have the report Paul?'

Paul handed over the thin folder to the P.M. There was an awkward silence for a few moments as the P.M. scanned the pages. His expression varying between disbelief and anger, 'Surely this is some horrible mistake Colonel,' the shaken man began. 'I've known Johnny since we were teenagers, these connections are tenuous to say the least, and the suggestions of an extramarital affair are absolutely scandalous, you won't find a more dedicated husband and father anywhere. This is outrageous, he is one of the pillars of our society, the very suggestion he has 'a bit on the side' to whom he pays substantial sums of money will be certain to provoke legal action.'

'One little point you missed Sir, Carol McNight is a he, and a nasty he at that. He was the man giving the orders when our AWAC was shot down.' said Paul.

'You seem remarkably sure of yourself Colonel,' the Prime Minister obviously still intent on protecting his friend, 'how do you know this McNight is the same McNight as the one you claim is responsible for the loss of your plane? Where is your proof?'

'There is no doubt Sir, the bank account numbers dear Johnny pays the money into, are the same as the account which exclusively pays McNight. They are all numbered accounts, but there is no doubt.'

'And McNight,' the Prime Minister, 'has of course vanished I suppose?'

'As far as his employers and friends, if he has any, are concerned, he has, as you put it vanished.'

'You say that as though you know where he is Colonel,' replied the Prime Minister.

'I know exactly where he is, five floors below us, along with the two who 'lost' the nuke which destroyed the U.S. task force. We also have the two sent by the cartel to shoot down our concord which brought the nukes we retrieved from Bin Ladens compound, the bodies we recovered from our AWAC and McNight back to our base. I can also prove Johnny paid the fuel bill for the plane which flew the team into the Oman to shoot down our plane.'

'How could they have known where you were Colonel, I know how you operate, I'm puzzled' said the Prime Minister, 'So how?'

'We set a trap, we just happened to get the timing wrong in the information we let slip.' replied Paul.

'Go on, clearly there is more, who did you let it 'slip' to?' the P.M. asked.

'You're not going to like this either Sir,' Paul began, 'I'm afraid he's another of 'the old boy net work', Sir Selwyn de la Fontaine. Your titled twerp of a school mate, in his committee days at the M.O.D. suggested a rapid promotion for another of your school mates, and you gave your personal approval, letting it be known you thought he would be the man to sort out the parlous supply situation, when in reality he was a large part of the problem.'

'You got one thing wrong Colonel,' said the greatly saddened Prime Minister, 'I might have gone to the same school as Sir Selwyn but he wasn't exactly a friend. In fact I didn't like him very much, he was an arrogant individual, but he got things done, then with a double first in Law and Economics, somehow he seemed a natural choice. What with Johnny Dolby's recommendation along with the chaos we inherited, I have to say I rather took things at face value.'

'Have you any idea how big this 'cartel' is Sir? We've been digging around for weeks, months even. It all began over fuel for our planes, we were under the misapprehension it was a purely American venture, we kept stumbling onto tenuous connections to companies with strong British links. I was as shocked as you were when Lord Johnny Dolby emerged as head honcho, but there is little, in fact ,no doubt now this is the case.

I have one piece of the puzzle which doesn't fit anywhere how ever. This is a Major Dalrymple, appointed by the M.O.D. as a company commander to 2para.

He left his men in Cyprus to get back to the U.K. ahead of them, so he could brief them when they arrived, the thing is, he didn't tell the C.O., who incidentally has barely met him. The other thing is he has also vanished, no one has seen him since he jumped over St. James Park.'

'Not Claude Dalrymple?' uttered the Prime Minister, 'He is Selwyn's younger half brother, their father had a well publicised affair, which resulted in a divorce and young Claude. Claude is very friendly with the Royals, he spends a lot of time with them.'

Paul yanked his communicator from his belt, he called Martin, who on his return from the raid which retrieved the mini nukes had been dispatched to Sandringham to command the Royal protection detail.

'Hello Boss, I wasn't expecting to hear from you, how can I help?'

'You haven't seen a major Dalrymple from two para there have you?' Paul asked.

'I have actually, he signed in a couple of days ago, said he was a personal body guard for one of the young princes. Every one seemed glad to see him, it appears he is an old friend, and highly regarded.'

'Take two of your best men and nick him, desertion, conspiracy, conduct unbecoming etc. I don't care if he is sitting down for 'tiffin', cuff him and send the off duty section back here, to the farm with him. There is a room on level eight waiting for him, and put those cuffs on tight!'

'This sounds serious Boss,' replied Martin.

'Are you still there major?' Paul snapped.

'Okay, it's serious, I'm gone Boss'.

'One very small fish netted General,' said Paul calming down, 'am I right in thinking Sir soddin' Selwyn is here at the moment Sir.'

'Yes' replied General Leach, 'shall we?' gesturing towards the door.

'Excuse us for a moment Prime Minister, we have a rat to catch, I am actually going to enjoy slapping the cuffs on this arrogant bugger. I haven't forgotten our first meeting yet!'

It turned out remarkably easy to put the cuffs on Sir Selwyn, he seemed to go into shock for those vital few seconds. Having got his breath back, 'I'll have you know the Prime minister is a personal friend!' he wailed.

'I hate to be the bearer of bad news old son, but it seems as though he doesn't like you much more than I do!' replied Paul.

Having delivered the crooked General to the Provo's, Paul and General Leach headed for the next, and lowest level beneath the farm. The guards were surprised to see the two senior officers, 'We're here to see McNight,' said Paul by way of introduction.

'You'll have to sign in Sir,' the senior provost officer said to General Leach, 'and you to Sir, you will have to leave your side arm here Sir.'

Paul reluctantly complied, 'I never realised the depth of security you had down here Paul', said General Leach as they were admitted through the third locked metal door to the area of the cells.

Paul was a little alarmed at the nervous state of the guards who accompanied them to McNights cell.

'I advise caution Sir,' said the senior man, 'he is classed as extremely dangerous.'

'I am well aware of that thank you staff.' replied Paul.

The welcome the two senior officers wasn't quite what they expected, but then with McNight, who could predict any thing.

'You are in so much shit Colonel,' he began, 'I'm going to piss on your grave!'

Timothy Pilgrim

'Interesting,' replied Paul, 'As I'm not dead, and you're the one in chains.'

Paul, knowing full well the only way he had a chance of getting this hard man to say anything which might be useful, was to wind him up so much he would lose his temper. This in it's self wasn't without risk. Young and fit, Paul would have been a match, now?

Pretending to take his eye of the American for a moment, he hoped he had guessed right as to what McNight would try. Paul said to General Leach, 'It is a funny thing Sir but I expected him to have a higher pitched voice than he has, what with losing a nut, and that name! You know our analysts thought they were looking for a girl!'

Luckily Paul had guessed right, as McNight launched himself at the grey haired soldier Paul was just, and only just quick enough to duck out of the way of manacled wrist aimed at his temple.

Off balance now Mcnight had no chance and found himself pinned to his bunk with the chain from the wrist manacles tightly across his throat, one arm locked behind him and the other held by the metal cuff, tight against his head.

The General, although not really approving of Paul's methods put his arm out to stop the guards intervening. The American laughed, 'not bad old man,' and tried to break the vice like grip, but that didn't work either.

Paul released his grip and stood back, 'Sit down, and listen and answer my questions.'

'What's in it for me?' replied McNight.

'That's better,' said Paul, 'What can I offer in return? In truth, not a lot, a choice of state to extradite you to, I suppose that depends on your preferred method of execution, hung, fried or the needle or do the marines still use a firing squad? '

'You'd do that for me,' replied McNight in a sarcastic tone, 'It will never happen, there are lawyers who would get me out before my bunk was warm!'

'I wonder who would pay them?' asked Paul, 'Not Senator O'Rourke, he's dead, so is Robert Kelly and at least three of the others, they suddenly became very accident prone, or the stress got too much for their old tickers to take. Pity really, I missed all the fun, sitting on the top of a mountain in Afghanistan.

There is another mate of yours, just along the corridor, in fact there are two of them, Sir Selwyn can't help you and Dalrymple can't threaten the Royals to get you released. As for the not very honourable Sir Johnny no mates, he will be in the next cell by dark. Oh, but living down here you won't know whether it is day or night.'

'I don't believe you,' replied McNight, 'You couldn't have got him here,' then a significant pause. 'He's got too many friends in high places, they would never allow it. You really haven't got any idea what you are up against, have you?' sneered McNight.

'Then you enlighten me,' replied Paul, 'As far as I can work out, you are little more than a delivery boy for the cartel, I'm sure it was you who chucked that mini nuke off the stern of the freighter in the straights of Hormuz. The target was the Iranians nuclear plant just up the coast. I know the plan was to instigate a war with Iran, which would have had all manner of implications. What I cannot understand is why? None of the countries who would have been involved could have afforded such a conflict, my simplistic little brain can't work out what benefit there is in bankrupting the western world. The almost certain outcome is a rash of dictatorships, or as we are seeing across southern Europe a state of near anarchy, which in turn will spawn chaos and will only be stabilized by dictators.

Is that 'the big plan'? or have I missed something?'

'You can't be so naïve Colonel, it's all about money, and the power it brings. You haven't got any money, and therefore no power. The 'cartel' as you call it, know how to use money to command what happens, you are pathetic if you think you can stop them. Wise up! You could name your price, as a consultant to them on hostage rescue, you could be paid more for a couple of hours of advice than you will otherwise see in your life time.'

'Well, I didn't expect a job offer, that's for sure. So who do I apply to for this consultancy post?' asked Paul.

'A word from me will help your application a lot,' replied McNight.

Paul looked at General Leach, 'If we stay here much longer I'll either throw up or hit him!' Turning back to McNight, 'keep this up and you'll be looking at a new career as a 'lady boy' in the back streets of Bangkok, the operation courtesy of our medics. I'll remind you, you are the one in a cell and apart from us, no-one knows where you are. Your paymasters are no doubt aware we have you, but even they won't know how to get you out of here.' Turning to his boss again, 'come on Sir, we have better things to do than waste our time talking to this loser.'

'Apart from establishing your 'alpha male' dominance what did all that achieve?' asked a slightly perplexed General Leach, 'he certainly didn't give much away.'

'Actually Boss, I think he gave a great deal away,' Paul sounded almost pleased.

'Oh? Like what, all that about you offering your services, and not being able to find Sir Johnny Dolby, or at least it not being possible for him to be here in the immediate future'

'If we can't find him, and even if we had, we couldn't fetch him here, what does that tell us Boss?'

'You are thinking someone else has got him,' the General smiled, 'makes sense, and when you put it with your reputation on hostage rescue, being able to name your price also makes a lot of sense.'

The two officers returned to the Prime Minister, just in time to hear him being roundly ticked off by a pretty little Q.A. nurse for not wearing his tinted glasses to protect his damaged eyes from the glare of the lights.

Paul chuckled, 'who's been a naughty boy then'.

'That woman!' replied the chastened politician, 'she could nag for Britain! The thing is she is always right, and does it in a way which makes you feel bad at having,' he paused, 'not done the right thing!'

'Sounds like officer material to me Boss,' Paul said to General Leach.

'Sounds like a chip off the old block to me,' replied the General, 'just like her mother.'

'And you know this how Sir?'

'I'm 'great uncle Brian', she is so like my sister in law, it is scary' , General Leach shuddered a little at the thought.

'Oho yes, very becoming Prime Minister,' Paul chuckled as the nurse returned with the variable tinted glasses. After planting them carefully in position, the nurse flounced off , 'only take them off when the night light regime is in operation', was her parting shot.

The P.M. made a helpless gesture, 'How did the rat catching trip go?' he asked.

'Fairly well Prime Minister, a recently promoted Major General down stairs talking to the head of our Provost staff and a missing Major isn't missing anymore, on his way here.' replied Paul.

'It sounds like the night of the long knives.' suggested the P.M.

'We had a little chat with Carol McNight,' said General Leach.

The Prime Minister almost interrupted the General, 'He's the American who ordered the crew of the American Coast Guard cutter to fire on your forces Colonel.'

'That's the one Sir, I didn't think he gave anything away, but Paul thinks differently,' the General gestured to Paul.

'It maybe nothing Sir,' Paul began, 'but something he said could explain why we can't find any trace of Sir Johnny rotten Dolby. What was it he said?' Paul paused for a moment. 'I hinted Sir Johnny would soon be in lockup with McNight. It was his initial reaction which gave it away, he knew Dolby is, or at least was, somewhere we couldn't get him. Now with our technology if he made a call, sent an email, anything electronic we'd know in seconds exactly where it originated from. For someone who spent half his life telling people on the other side of the world what to do, to suddenly go off the grid, totally off the grid, can, to my mind mean only one of two things. The first is he is in prison, not a normal nick, as his legal eagles would be flapping around to get him released. I don't even believe the C.I.A. have him in one of their 'secret' sites, as word would have leaked out. Which leaves us with the possibility he has been kidnapped, it's the when and where we don't know, or the who. From what McNight said who ever has got him, and I think McNight knows, or at least has a good idea, he is being held by someone very nasty indeed. Why else would he in effect offer me a job with the 'cartel', naming my price and the reference to my alleged abilities in hostage rescue?'

'He did what?' exclaimed the shocked Prime Minister.

'In front of General Leach Sir,' replied Paul. 'There is one other possibility,' Paul continued, 'he could already be dead, but that doesn't really tie in with what McNight said.'

'Could he simply have been winding you up Colonel.' asked the politician.

'Possibly, but I don't think so.' replied Paul.

'I've heard of your legendary gut Colonel'.

'As you say Sir, my gut!' replied Paul.

'What are you going to do about it Colonel', asked the Prime Minister.

'I'm going to try to ruin him, first of all via Her Majesties Revenue and Customs, over the years he has fiddled millions of pounds. I have a team putting together accounts of his actual income, when they have sorted out his accounts the figures will turn up on the relevant computer, as if by magic. All provable with exact evidence of where the money came from, bank account numbers, where it comes from and where it goes.

The other line of attack will be on his creditors, through his shell corporations he has borrowed billions, there are countries in trouble who have borrowed less. As far as we can tell there are no arrears, how ever, if a bank, or major creditor gets spooked and start to worry then things can go pear shaped in the blink of an eye, or push of a button. If we can spook a couple who are shaky themselves, it will spread like wild fire. If his empire does collapse, then if he is hostage somewhere the chance of a ransom goes out the door, odds are who ever has him will top him, or simply kick him out, either way he's stuffed.

On the other hand, if he is simply hiding, he'll have to do something to try to stop it, and we'll be watching and waiting.'

'Do you think it will work General?' asked the Prime Minister.

'In the absence of any better ideas, I think it is worth a try, especially the tax angle.'

'Well, he may have been a friend, but I must wish you well. How are things going in London? It is a major concern.'

'To us as well Sir,' replied General Leach, 'We are being reasonably successful so far, but there is a serious problem looming. We think we may have enough troops to clear everything except the Houses of Parliament. Even with a small aircraft load of ammunition brought in from Cyprus we will be out of small arms ammunition by the time we have cleared White Hall. This is allowing for the fact many troops are already using captured weapons and ammunition. We are almost out of stun grenades, there simply aren't anymore to be had.'

'So you are saying there will be no way to clear the Parliament buildings of these insurgents General.' the Prime Minister sounded depressed.

'Even if we could fly substantial numbers of troops home Sir, which we can't, it wouldn't help as they don't have the right equipment, stun grenades and hecklers.' replied Paul.

'So, have you got a plan to clear the Houses of Parliament, without doing substantial damage?' asked the Prime Minister.

'Oh yes, he has a plan Prime Minister,' was General Leaches reply, 'He', indicating Paul, 'will end up being called a war criminal, if any one finds out exactly what he's planning.'

'It is the only way I can see to remove the bastards Sir, short of levelling the place or losing most of the troops engaged.

We have stocks of the gas which wiped out god knows how many people in London a while back, this is from the missiles we captured. The plan is to use the forty millimetre grenade launchers on our assault rifles charged with this gas. We will use the Challenger Tanks as cover for about a dozen of us, in full protective gear to fill the entire building with gas, they'll be dead in minutes. If anyone has a better idea, I'm open to suggestions. The gas we are using will have no dioxin in it, so no harmful residue. As unpleasant as it is, I can't see another way. No damage, and hopefully no more casualties among our troops who have taken a hammering.'

The Prime Minister was shocked and said he needed time to think about it, in the mean time he wanted an up date on the operation to get the Nato troops home.

'As soon as my units three ships are clear of the canal, they along with a couple of old navy destroyers, due for decommissioning and some of the other warships with significant guns are going to try to get a convoy out of the Black Sea. The Russians of all people have donated 20,000 tons of jet fuel to the 'cause'. With Canberras overhead aiming the guns, we think we have a good chance of getting in, and out again with the ships carrying the American rangers and an armoured Engineer Regiment as well as the tanker.

The Turkish government forces hold all of the north shore and about half of the southern shore. The Syrian and Iranian backed insurgents hold some vital headlands on two choke points. We do at least have ample ammunition for the 4.5 inch guns as well as the twenty and thirty millimetre multi barrel cannons.

As for the main convoy, hopefully the first ships should exit the canal tomorrow, and all of the nato troops should arrive off Cyprus over the week end.'

'So what are your immediate plans,' the Prime minister asked Paul.

'Top priority, get White Hall and Parliament cleared out by any means at our disposal, and get you lot back to work! I dare say you'll have to rule by decree until there can be new elections. It is one hell of an opportunity for a new start Sir.

My priorities; clear out these bloody insurgents, get our troops and gear home then take out this power mad cartel. After that, then quietly retire, so I can take my grandkids fishing, look after my garden and eat breakfast with my missus.'

'Then I can return the sentiments, in wishing you well in your endeavours Colonel.' replied the Prime Minister.

'I'll leave you gentlemen to discus things above my pay grade, there are a few things I have to do. I'll be returning to London tomorrow,' said Paul as he headed for the door.

CHAPTER TWENTY-FIVE

Paul returned to London with a small but heavily protected convoy, consisting of four of the units armoured Land Rovers and a modified, armoured seven and a half ton truck. Happily the journey was incident free, leaving the M11/A406 at Redbridge police at first tried to stop them at a check point, then decided to escort them into the city with flashing lights and sirens.

Paul called the lead escort car up on the radio, pleading for the sirens to be switched off, and the lights, but to no avail. Eventually he pulled his vehicles over near the city end on the Mile End Road. The journey had set his back off again, so he wasn't in the best of humour as he approached the leading police car.

'I asked you nicely officer, now I am telling you. Switch those fuckin' blues and twos off, NOW!'

'You can't talk to me like that soldier,' retorted the officious inspector.

'Yes I can, and these faded pips and a crown mean I am a Colonel,' replied Paul, indicating his epaulettes. 'Now, thank you for the escort, we can manage from here. I don't want your sirens and disco display alerting those nutters to the fact that something is happening. If they know something is arriving in Trafalgar Square then they tend to say 'hello' with a mortar barrage. Mortar bombs are not only noisy, they are bloody dangerous. So, if you don't mind, we'd like to creep in un-noticed.'

'You are transporting live ammunition Colonel, our guide lines are you need an escort to keep the public a safe distance from your vehicles.' replied the head cop.

'When were these guide lines issued?' Paul asked.

'Several years ago, but they have always proved effective.'

Paul sighed at the reply, 'Things have changed somewhat of late Inspector, now for the last time, go back to your check point.'

'I absolutely insist on escorting you, according to the laid down procedures, to your destination,' the inspector was adamant.

'Very well, you leave me no choice, you'd better call A.T.S. Try to follow us and I will shoot your tyres out. I will not have you putting soldiers lives at risk, for the sake of some ancient guide line. Do you understand!' Paul's temper was very near breaking point.

The sergeant from the second car back came walking up, obviously aware of 'the atmosphere' between the two men.

'What seems to be the problem Sir?' he asked politely.

Paul explained, patiently about alerting the insurgents to arrivals, and the likely consequences.

'Sounds reasonable to me Sir,' replied the traffic sergeant, 'As you say Sir they are guide lines for ordinary times, not hard and fast rules.'

'You'll do as you are ordered sergeant', snapped the Inspector.

'Yes Sir, I will, I'll take my men back to where we are supposed to be, on the road block. As we are from a different force, I feel under no obligation to obey your commands in this instance. Good day Sir, and I wish you and your men good luck Colonel.'

'I hope you have a quiet day Sergeant,' replied Paul as he returned to his Land Rover. 'If you attempt to follow us Inspector, I have ordered my men to shoot your tyres out, trust me, they will, if I don't do it myself! Good day!'

The two Essex traffic cars had already turned round and were headed outward bound, back to 'their patch'. The 'jobs worth' Inspector merely sat fuming as even his own driver expressed doubts about finding out if the soldier would carry out his threat, 'you can see his point Sir'. said the driver.

The convoy swept into the logistics area, and moved to the side of the Square nearest White Hall. There was the crackle of small arms fire from the direction of the Parliament buildings, acrid smoke still drifted around in the breeze, much of it from the smouldering remains of the main Ministry of Defence building, it was clear things had moved on since Paul had been gone.

Leaving his men to get themselves a cuppa, he headed to the mobile control centre next to the Admiralty Arch in search of Sandy, the C.O. of 2 para.

The two men greeted each other, Paul then asked how things were going.

'We have taken several more casualties Paul,' Sandy began, 'including another twenty eight dead, twenty of them my lads. On the plus side we are just in the process of clearing the last of them out of the Treasury annex. You can follow things on these screens Paul. Your new scanners are remarkable bits of kit, they have saved many lives. As you can see there are only about six of them left.'

'You certainly haven't been wasting any time Sandy,' replied Paul. 'Would your casualties have been lighter if you had taken more time?' he asked.

'In my judgement, no,' Sandy replied. 'It is only my opinion, but I think fatigue would have become a serious factor had we taken our time. There is also the ammunition situation to consider Paul.'

Paul lit a cigarette, 'fair enough, why don't you and I get ourselves a cuppa and find a quiet corner so I can tell you what I've got in mind the clear 'The House' of these insurgents.'

'I hope it is a good plan Paul,' said Sandy, 'We might have nearly enough men to do it, if we had anything left to fight with.'

'Do we know how many are holed up in the Parliament buildings?' Paul asked.

'As near as we can tell, about two hundred and ten, and they have heavily sand bagged positions covering every entrance, at least, that is what your scanners are showing us.'

'Alright, lets get some print outs of the scans, I need somewhere quiet where I can sit down with my team,' said Paul. 'We need to work out exactly where we want to place the grenades.

We've got a couple of tiny drones with us, if we could get someone to lob a smoke grenade in, then we can see how the smoke travels through the building, it could make the difference between success and failure'.

For the next couple of hours the team who were to launch the deadly gas grenades watched the drifting smoke on the monitors relaying what the drones were seeing. Eventually the insurgents not only spotted the little machines but destroyed them, however by they had done their job.

Each man of the eleven strong squad Paul had selected knew exactly were he was to fire from, and exactly which window was his target to place the gas grenades in the desired spot. There was to be no escape for those inside once the attack started.

'Right gentlemen, all clear on what you have to do?' Paul asked.

'Yes Boss,' was the synchronised reply.

'Get suited up then, lets get this over and done with.' Paul called Sandy, 'Give them a last chance to surrender, if they aren't out with their hands in the air within the next fifteen minutes they will all die in the following fifteen!'

'Fair enough Paul,' replied the tough Para troop commander. 'I won't pretend I'm happy about it, but I can't see any alternative. The tanks will be ready when you arrive, the crews have all been briefed and know exactly what they have to do.'

'Thanks' Sandy,' replied Paul

Twenty minutes later four armoured leviathans trundled along the front of the Houses of Parliament, firing their smoke mortars as they progressed. Three men clad in their black protective suits with respirators walked along on the protected side of the armoured giants, as the smoke thickened the amount of incoming fire increased. Bullets pinged of the armoured hulls, there were the loud bangs from the anti tank missiles which exploded without damaging the tanks on the extra grills welded on for the purpose.

As they reached their designated positions the tanks stopped, now almost hidden by the billowing smoke. The great turrets swung round, it seemed as though they were about to open fire with the big guns, instead the smoke mortars on the other side of their turrets launched another salvo of smoke grenades.

Paul was watching carefully from behind the second tank. Already sweating in the heavy protective suit he first called Sandy, 'is every one out of the smoke? He asked.

'Yes Boss, every one is clear, and know not to go anywhere near it. Although they don't know why' was the reply.

'I hope they are, we are about to take our positions,' Then after a brief pause, to change frequencies he called his squad. 'Just remember, keep your heads down, Go!.'

The number of near misses indicated the insurgents must have had some fairly sophisticated gear, much of the incoming fire was no doubt random. It was obvious the smoke wasn't as much help as Paul had hoped. Suppressing fire from the turret mounted machine guns on the tanks, coupled with that of the army snipers, soon reduced the defensive fire from the insurgents.

'Fire when ready,' Paul commanded. The distinctive thuds of grenades being launched could be heard all along the line of black clad soldiers. Just as Paul went to reload for his second shot, there was an enormous bang, just behind him, for a moment he couldn't breath. It took a moment or two to realise his breathing gear had been hit by shrapnel from the missile which had struck the tank behind him. Clearly the tank and it's crew were fine as the turret machine gun continued to fire into the smoke using the sophisticated sights.

Paul was far from alright, apart from the difficulty breathing he noticed a large gash on the right forearm of his N.B.C. suit, worse, there was a substantial amount of blood around the gash, strangely, it didn't hurt, 'yet' he thought.

To the horror of the trooper to Paul's left, he ripped off his helmet which had the breathing mask fixed to it, then casually launched the rest of his grenades into the main entrance and the windows above, which had been his targets.

Paul grabbed his discarded helmet to use the radio, 'stay put, there is an APC coming to pick us up. Everyone, sound off.'

He soon became aware the soldier to his right had not called in, as quickly as the bulky suit would allow he crossed the gateway, throwing himself down beside the prone figure. Paul feared his old friend Ronny had been hit by debris from the same explosion which had hit him, but there was no obvious injury, there was the fleeting fear a grenade might have leaked. He shook Ronny, 'Where are you hit mate?' he asked but received no reply.

Paul tried to roll his friend over into the cover of the pillar, then he saw why Ronny wasn't answering, a small hole in the centre of his helmet was the only sign of what must have been an armour piercing bullet. One of the longest serving members of the unit was dead.

A quick check revealed there were two unfired grenades, conscious of the danger Paul sent both deep into the main entrance hall, safer in there than here he thought.

The heavily armoured personnel carrier was making it's way along the line, picking up the squad as it rumbled along. By the time it reached Paul the troopers to either side, ignoring their orders to stay put, were with Paul.

'Take Ronny with you, and my suit, I'm going to the control centre,' he said.

'It might be a good idea to get that arm seen to first boss, that looks nasty.'

'Fair enough, drop me off at the first aid post just into White Hall, then get yourselves back home and keep out of sight!'

It took the medics nearly a quarter of an hour to clean, stitch and dress the wound, much of the time waiting for local anaesthetics to take effect.

Paul noted how his nagging to hurry up had absolutely no effect on the medics. The only response he got was, 'If I am going to patch you up Sir, then I'm going to do it properly, so you will have to be patient. This is the first time for a week there hasn't been any gunfire, so I think it is unlikely we will suddenly be inundated with casualties, now hold still please.'

Paul cadged a lift with the commander of the regiment from 'The Rifles' who had been airlifted into Stansted, and ferried into London on a fleet of buses.

'I take it this operation is over Colonel?' the officer asked.

'Apart from the clearing up' replied Paul. 'For reasons I will not go into, initial clean up will be confined to White Hall, north of the cenotaph and in other roads up to, but not into Parliament Square, that area will be strictly off limits for two days, with no exceptions. This no-go area may change if the wind changes.'

By the time he arrived at the mobile command post near the Admiralty Arch, the blood had soaked through the bandage and a thin trickle had reached his wrist, his arm was beginning to stiffen and for the first time it was beginning to hurt.

'Are you alright?' asked Sandy, sounding genuinely concerned for his old boss.

'I've felt better, but have had worse,' replied Paul.

'I was watching on the relay Paul, if one of your men had done what you did, they would have got the bollocking of a life time, what the hell did you think you were doing?' scolded the Para C.O.

'Calm down Sandy, the same blast which got my arm, took out my re-breather, I couldn't breath, the cut in my suit would have let any contamination in anyway, so I ripped the mask off.' replied Paul, 'I know you're right, but sometimes you just have to take a risk.'

'I know you lost Ronnie, was that the same blast?' asked Sandy.

'A bloody sniper got him, the only saving grace was it must have been as instant as it ever gets. It is a hell of a blow, six years with the paras, twelve with Hereford and nearly ten with us, he was one hell of a soldier.' Paul leaned back in the afternoon sun, lighting another cigarette. He was aware of a group of mainly men in suits approaching the command post, when he looked he recognised most of them.

'Oh Lord,' he muttered , 'we don't need this now.' Paul said to Sandy.

Sandy stood up and walked towards the party of suits, spreading his arms in a gesture which clearly meant no further.

'I'm sorry gentlemen, you cannot go any further. This area is yet to be cleared of ordinance and is strictly off limits to civilians', Sandy tried to get them to go away, but the civilians were having none of it.

Three of the party were senior opposition politicians, and were well known, they and some of their lesser known, but more left wing colleagues had flatly refused to attend the ill fated conference. With them was an individual few would have recognised, as one of the most senior civil servants at the M.O.D., he had been in the honours list of the out going Prime Minister after the last election and given a life peerage.

Paul also knew he was the man behind the dodgy appointments. This was confirmed when the man demanded to speak to Major Dalrymple.

'And why would you need to speak to him Sir?' Paul asked , 'You are standing in front of his C.O. ask him,' Paul suggested.

'I haven't got anyone by that name in my command Sir,' replied Sandy having caught on quickly to what Paul was doing.

'Surely you must know your own company commanders, what kind of unit do you run Colonel,' sneered the man in the pinstripe suit.

It was Paul who replied, 'A bloody good one as it happens.'

'Some would disagree Colonel,' then spotting soldiers throwing bags into the back of a truck, 'If I'm not mistaken those men are collecting spent cases, I trust they will be shipped back to the suppliers, as per contract.'

'Yep,' replied Paul, 'straight up the M1 then the M6 to the Royal Ordinance Factory.'

'Our contract specifies all available cases are returned to the factory in India Colonel.' replied the man.

'Is that why you wanted to see Dalrymple?' asked Paul.

'Not that it is anything to do with you, but yes, it is vital we uphold our contracts.'

'Well, I guess I have some bad news for you, that, with a lot of other contracts you drew up and signed have been torn up. More bad news is you are under arrest for corruption, that is taking a massive back-hander for fitting it all up.

Before you start shouting the odds, I can prove payments of over half a million quid which you have trousered from Sir rotten Johnny Dolby, so contracts went to his companies.' Paul called over two passing soldiers, 'Get a set of hand cuffs from one of the cops over at the tea wagon, slap them on this piece of detritus and find somewhere secure to keep him until there is transport headed to my base.'

The former Prime Minister stepped forwards, 'I think you may have overstepped your authority Colonel, you can't go around arresting people simply because you don't agree with them, or because you don't like them.'

'As unfortunate as it is true,' replied Paul, 'but then the last time I checked, being an idiot wasn't a crime.'

'I demand you allow us access to our offices Colonel, we must be allowed in,' demanded a grey haired man in a shabby grey suit.

'The area is not safe as yet, if I allowed any of you access and you triggered a booby trap, I would be in serious trouble. So as much as I would like to allow you in, the answer is NO. Best guess is it will take at least another week to clear the area, so sod off and let these brave men get on with their very dangerous job.'

At the precise moment Paul finished speaking there was a loud bang, from somewhere round the corner, followed by the sound of glass hitting the pavement and shortly after a billowing cloud of dust.

Paul went to grab his communicator with his right hand, but it refused to work, 'Ow Shit! That hurt!' he cursed. Having retrieved his communicator with his left hand and punched some buttons 'What the hell was that?' he asked.

'Sorry about that Boss, our friends left us a little present in the drains, it was too unstable to make safe, even if we could have got at it. The bad news is there are at least six more like it.'

'Oh great, try not to destroy too much, but no risks, we have had too many casualties already, take care, out'. Paul replied.

Another smaller bang, further away signalled the destruction of some R.P.Gs which had been fired but failed to explode. They had been collected by soldiers and gingerly placed in a sandbagged position on the edge of Parliament Square, directly opposite to the main gates of Parliament .

The next few days would be punctuated by such detonations.

'Very well, Colonel,' the ex Prime Minister said, 'We will return in a few days, and you will grant us access. In the mean time I want to see the prisoners, to ensure they are being well treated.'

'What prisoners?' asked Paul, 'As far as I know there are only about half a dozen and they are all injured and in a top security facility, to which you will not have access. I presume you were talking about the insurgents rather than crooks like the one you brought with you, and there is no way, you or anyone else will have access to them until we have sorted out the extent of their fiddles, and that could take some time!'

'Surely there must be more than six insurgents taken prisoner Colonel, my information is there were several hundred of them,' said one of the politicians.

Paul grunted , 'Frankly, I don't give a shit about them, it's the couple hundred or so dead soldiers and their families I'm concerned about. I haven't got the exact number yet, add to those the number with life threatening or debilitating injuries, then losses have been serious.'

The politician was clearly not impressed, 'If it transpires you issued a 'shoot to kill' order Colonel, there could be serious consequences.'

'Then give me the benefit of your advice, on just how the hell you deal with suicide bombers and fanatics. There is no choice, many of them had body armour, so you have no options other than a head shot.' Paul retorted sharply.

'You negotiate Colonel, you don't kill them all! You talk to them and reach an agreement.'

'Tell the families of the dead soldiers that! Bloody old fool ! At least twenty of our fatalities have been medics trying to help wounded insurgents, only to find out too late they are suicide bombers. The other little problem with your thinking, is how do you deal with a man walking towards you with his hands up?'

'You search him, then you take him prisoner of course,' replied the politician.

'What if they have a couple of claymore mines strapped to their chest?' asked the tired soldier. 'There have been at least five such incidents that I know of.' Paul turned to the politicians, 'you might also be interested to know, some of the claymore mines we have recovered, unexploded, were originally made for the British Army. Add to that the fact the bulk of their ammunition was made by the same company contracted to manufacture our army's ammunition. Now, call me a cynic, but I'll take a bet the orders for this lots bullets are one of the main reasons for delays in manufacturing ours.'

'Surely things can't be as bad as you are indicating Colonel,' said the former Prime Minister.

'Oh there is a long list,' Paul winced as he tried to push himself up with his injured arm. 'We have had to resort to buying fuel from filling stations,

The Undefended Land

we've even been told the parent companies have told the operatives not to supply the armed forces. Have you any idea of the cost of filling a tank at the pumps?

There's no ammunition for the main guns on the tanks, we had to adapt artillery shells!. Most of the troops engaged ran out of ammunition for their own weapons, and we totally ran out of stun grenades. Now it is no good blaming the current lot as the contracts for supplying, or rather allowing the companies involved not to supply these rather vital commodities, were set up and signed by your lot! The current crew had at last started to try to do something about it, but bloody lawyers kept blocking things, then there was the disaster at the N.E.C.'

'If things were so bad, then why dispatch nearly everything we have to the Suez Canal zone? As I understand things, there is very little American involvement, yet over three quarters of the troops on the ships are American.' asked the senior man.

'If the operation had been an American one, then I hate to say it, then it would have been a blood bath. It is their philosophy at fault, they have no concept of minimum force. It seems a contradiction, I know, but to use minimum force you need overwhelming power to make it work. The power has to be visibly available, but you only use just enough to achieve your objective, avoiding collateral, that is, civilian casualties. It's all about hearts and minds and being sneaky. It had to be us leading things, and it really needed more than we actually had. Still, it seems as though a lot of the convoy are clear of the canal, and last I heard things were going well after the early problems.'

'Thank you for the updates Colonel. I presume the fighting here is over, as I haven't heard any shots since we arrived, I really would like to see what damage has been done to the historic buildings.' the former Prime Minister was becoming quite insistent about being allowed into the area which had been occupied.

Paul called a Para troop sergeant over, 'Do me a favour Sarge, grab half a dozen of your guys and escort this lot up to what is left of the M.O.D. building then into the medical centre in Trafalgar Square. They do not, under any circumstances go into White Hall.'

'Will do Sir.'

'I had hoped you would accompany us Colonel,' said the senior politician.

'I am rather busy, ignoring the fact I really ought to get this arm seen to.

271

Timothy Pilgrim

The field medics did a good job as far as they could, but this is a job for the docs, as soon as they clear the back log of more serious injuries. Now you go with the sergeant here, and do not, under any circumstances try to go into White Hall, go only where he takes you.'

CHAPTER TWENTY-SIX

The following weeks were chaotic to say the least, but eventually a degree of 'normality' returned. The operation to extricate the ships from the Black sea turned out to be much easier than expected, the insurgents on two strategic headlands had no answer to the combination of the canberras overhead, spotting their positions and the long range guns of the warships, aimed by the reconnaissance aircraft. The bombardment enabled the Turkish army to clear these positions before the ships returned. The safe and timely arrival of the Russian tanker enabled the air lift to get under way, initially taking T/A troops home as well as casualties. The situation eased further when a huge tanker turned up from Galverston, with a split cargo of the various marine fuels and a further load of jet fuel.

Paul heaved a sigh of relife as he formally handed command of the evacuation to a team headed by the Nato General and his staff. The plan was simple enough, there would be three convoys, each with one of the massive American battle carriers. In addition there would be a Canberra overhead until the convoy cleared the Mediterrainean, the perceived threat being small suicide craft packed with explosives. In the event only the first convoy was attacked, none got even close, and all the vast array of ships sailed past Gibralter unscathed.

As more troops became available security was increased, the last of the insurgents were quickly hunted down, a degree of peace returned to Britain.

Such politicians who were still alive resumed their jobs, and set about the task of trying to rebuild the instruments of government.

General Leach felt as though a great weight had been lifted off his shoulders as he relinquished his unwanted powers to the now recovering Prime Minister. The veteran commander walked slowly through the forest track towards his quarter, savouring the feeling, about half way he felt a bit strange, and sat down at the base of a large pine. The sound of the breeze sighing through the tree tops was very relaxing, he listened intently to a bird which had struck up singing in a nearby thicket, the nightingale, absent last year was back!

The bird was still singing when retired R.S.M. Howard, universally known as 'Frankie' who was admin officer at 'The Farm' came along, headed home. He didn't notice General Leach in the dim lighting until he almost tripped over him, it came as a shock to find the revered General was dead.

There was a shock in the United States as well, at about the same time as General Leach slipped peacefully away, the leading figure to stand against the incumbent President in the race to the Whitehouse was addressing an out door rally.

He was critisising every thing the current administration had done and rubbishing every thing it was planning when he suddenly collapsed. Even his vast wealth couldn't help him, any more than the medics could, as fast as they were, he was dead before he hit the floor. It seemed as though he had suffered a massive stroke, try as they might the experts could find no real reason for it, or any sign of foul play.

During the previous couple of weeks five 'captains of industry' across the country had died suddenly as well as at least three bankers and two leading stock market figures. The 'Cartel' had ceased to exist, only Sir Jonathon Dolby remained unaccounted for among the major players, of him, there was no trace.

The mood among the senior officers of the all arms unit as they gathered in Paul's office on returning from the funeral of General Leach was sombre to say the least.

It seemed to have affected Paul worse than most, he raised his glass, 'To General Leach, rest in peace my old friend and mentor. I'll miss you, we all will.'

'Are you alright Paul?' asked Taff.

'I suppose so mate, it's bad enough losing a friend doing our job, So why does this hurt even more?'

'At least he died peacefully Paul, in a spot he loved, I'd often come across him sitting there on my way home. You must have noticed, even the slightest breeze used to 'sing' some how in that big old pine. He'd spend hours there some evenings watching the wild life.'

'True enough Taff, but we have work to do, he'd be wanting us to get on with things,' replied Paul.

Peter, for years number two to their respected O.C formally took command of all anti terrorist and security forces.

'We face trying times gentlemen', he began his speech, 'there are calls for enquiries into the actions of the security forces in clearing the insurgency, as well as into how the insurgents were able to enter the country in the first place. Yet more enquiries into the operation to get our forces home, specifically why the country was left undefended. For what it is worth you have the support of the remains of our government, but certain opposition groups are baying for blood. Things are likely to get nasty, unfortunately I haven't got the clout our late lamented General Leach had, but you have my full and unqualified support, and I will do what I can.

Is there any progress in the quest to find Dolby? Peter asked. 'I think his arrest and trial are vital to conclude this sorry saga.'

It was Paul who answered, 'not a bloody sniff of him Boss, none of his bank accounts have been used, no credit cards, phones or computers. The rat has totally vanished, I wouldn't have thought it possible, we have looked every where we can think of. I think Mcnight has a good idea of what might have happened to him, but there is no chance of getting him to talk, I've tried to con him into believing we've got Dolby, but he just laughs. The current theory is Dolby is dead and McNight had a hand in it, but I don't really believe it. I think someones got him, McNight knows who, and we don't'.

'On the subject of Mr. McNight,' said Peter. 'It would appear our American friends want him, the formal extradition request is expected tomorrow.'

'Oh great!' exclaimed Paul, 'more hassle from the legal eagles, damn it Peter they cost the tax payers more than the defense budget!'

'Well, I'd say the application is likely to be approved,' replied the newly promoted Major General. 'Oh, I almost forgot,' Peter continued, 'the C.I..A. want their four operatives back.'

'That's strange,' observed Paul.

'How so?' asked Peter.

'Well, the director hasn't said any thing about them, he knows we've got them, of course.' said Paul. 'Some one check out who the request came from, I'll check with the director. He's been saying for weeks, there must have been more than just that bent Senator playing silly buggers with the agency. This might give us a clue where to look, as there are very few people even know we've got them.'

'You will be handing them over though?' asked Peter.

'That rather depends on who is behind the request Boss, it could prove handy in the future, having four guys on the 'inside' who owe us'.

Taff nodded his agreement.

'You are nasty, devious individuals,' replied Peter, 'I do however see your point.

But what about McNight? I take it you'll hand him over quietly if the extradition order is granted.'

'Personally, I think he should stand trial here for murdering eight of our personel on the AWAC .' said Taff, most of the others muttered their approval.

'So when the question is asked in court, what was it doing there, what do you tell them?' asked Peter.

'Anti pirate patrol?' suggested Paul.

'You would lie in court! I'm horrified Paul,' was Peter's shocked response.

'Well we can hardly say it was covering a raid into Pakistan to recover four nuclear devices which had been miss-appropriated can we?' Paul replied.

'That's another thing, the American corporation which built them, want them back,' said Peter 'But with General Leach dying along with everything else, it had totally slipped my mind.'

'It must be catching,' said Paul.

'What must?' Peter asked, sounding a little confused.

'Amnesia Boss,' replied Paul, 'I can't remember us having any nukes, can you Taff?'

'You'll have to return them Paul, just as you'll have to hand over McNight and those four operatives,' said Peter.

'I think we should just issue a flat denial, say we haven't got McNight or the other four, and know nothing about the nukes.'

'You're forgetting the entire crew of the coast guard cutter know McNight was handed over to us Paul.'

'That's true, I hadn't exactly forgotten, it sort of slipped my mind, Boss, but he is the only lead we've got to the whereabouts of Johnny bloody Dolby!

'Is he?' asked Peter, 'what makes you so certain he knows, Paul?'

'McNight is absolutely certain we can't possibly have Dolby, this implies he knows where he is, or what has happened to him. If he had been kidnapped, then there would have been a ramsom demand, and we would have heard about it. Like wise if he was being held by a foreign power, we would know. It therefore follows the bastard is hiding, and I have to admit he's doing it rather well.'

'Or he's dead!'

'Or, as you say boss, he's dead' replied Paul. 'You won't know this Boss but in a round about way, McNight offered me a job, based on my supposed hostage rescue skills. He did it in front of General Leach too, if I recall it was as a consultant in such matters, and he was talking serious money.'

'You refused of course,' replied Peter.

'Of course, but with hindsight, had I accepted we might have had Dolby by now, or at least some idea about his status.' Paul replied with all the innocence he could muster. 'There is another point Boss, as far as I am aware the only American we have told about all this is the Director of the C.I.A., I am certain he hasn't told anyone else we have the nukes or for that matter four of his operatives. We've still got a leak!'

'I'm surprised there is anyone to leak it to after all the sudden deaths of key members of the cartel. I, along with a lot of other people are convinced none were accidents, or natural deaths. Can you throw any light on this rather delicate problem, lets face it, if anyone knows what happened, it has to be you!' Peter sounded unhappy. 'I know how ruthless you can be protecting not just your staff, but your country. Personally I'm sure you know what happened, though quite how you were involved defeats me, I know where you were at the times of these extraordinary sequences of deaths. I also know who was with you at the exact times, collectively you couldn't have more bullet proof alibis.'

'Then what is the problem Boss?' Paul asked, 'why, if the world and his wife knows I was thousands of miles away at the time even bother to ask! Who is asking anyway Boss?'

'It is quite a worring list actually Paul, replied Peter. 'None of them exactly your friends, The international court of human rights, even the war crimes commision are asking questions, the latest to call for an enquiry is the U.S. supreme court, in fact there is a request for you to give evidence to at least three senate committees as well.'

'Hang on a minute,' Paul actually looked worried, 'It will drive me over the edge listening to the haverings of all that lot and legal eagles for the next five years! I can't answer most of the questions they are bound to ask, not without giving away state secrets.

The U.N. security council asked, on behalf of N.A.T.O. for me to get all manner of armed forces back to their homelands. There were, as you well know a lot more than just those in Afgahnistan to get home.

As far as dealing with the armed invasion of the U.K. was concerned, and make no mistake, that is exactly what it was, then I have no-one to answer to other than our own government and population. I am not going to be party to answering questions from a load of self important Muppets, only after as much money as they can con out of this country.'

'You might have to Paul, if the international court in the Hague call you, you will have to go.' replied Peter. 'Things have changed, every thing is in a state of flux, some sort of stability, with a set of rules is going to have to be imposed, the end no longer justifies the means Paul.'

'I take it you were referring to the way we cleared the Houses of Parliament,' Paul replied. 'You, more than anyone knew the situation Peter, what was I supposed to do?'

'Not use poison gas!' replied Peter.

'That didn't answer my question Boss,' replied Paul, 'I asked what I should have done. My orders were clear, get them out quickly, without destroying the place!. Damn it you were party to that order Peter. We didn't have enough fit troops to storm the place, most of those we did have were using captured weapons and captured ammunition as we had used all of our own. We had no stun grenades, not that they would have been effective in most of the structure. So, given the situation what the hell was I supposed to have done? Even if more troops had been available they would have been massacred, it was a job for special forces. Overall most units are already below fifty percent of their theoretical strength, I didn't have any choice, there simply wasn't a practical alternative. Prove to me there was another way, or a single innocent civilian was killed in that attack and I'll hold my hands up and resign, right now. You and I have always got on brilliantly over the years Peter, what's changed?'

'Apart from everything?' replied Peter. 'You have changed, you have become totally ruthless Paul. I think far too ruthless for todays world, the day will come when we have to work with the new governments in Europe. Power has shifted, you must look beyond the people who are taking over, look at who have the real power. We are going to have to find a way to exist with them Paul.'

'What the hell are you suggesting Peter?' asked a dismayed Paul. 'You have been my friend for more years than I care to even try to remember. I cannot believe what I'm hearing, are you suggesting we simply agree to the demands of the nutters who have siezed power in the southern half of Europe. Have you been 'got at' in some way, your family are safe, so how? Something has happened, you're not the Peter I've known for years, or do you know something I don't?' Paul stopped, mid rant as if he had suddenly had a 'ureka' moment. He turned to the assembled officers, 'beat it you lot, and not a word about any thing you think you might have heard in here, clear!? Taff, B.J. stay here please.'

Peter looked quite crestfallen, almost like the horse with a broken leg waiting for the vet.

When the door shut Paul turned to Peter, 'your family are safe, aren't they? It's just I remember you saying something about they were on holiday. It was when we were panicking about finding those bloody nukes, and it didn't really register at the time. Who's got them Peter?'

The senior officer was shocked by the bluntness of Pauls question, 'That is the problem Paul, I don't really know, any more than I know where they are.'

'You must have some idea Peter,' replied Paul. 'If only from what they are asking for, presumeably in return for your family at some point in the future. There has to be some way for you to communicate with them and vice-versa. You are going to have to trust us Peter, it is the only chance your family have got.'

'You have no idea', the senior officer began, 'it is anything but a simple kidnap for ransom.'

'I had actually figured that much out Peter. I'm going to bring Kenny back in here, you will tell him everything, and I mean everything about what has happened, miss nothing out. Kenny will run the operation to locate your family. B.J. will have oversight on the whole project. If we can, we'll keep the entire thing under wraps, even if we are successful. If you level with us, I'm confident we'll get them back once we've found them.'

'I wish I shared your optimism Paul', replied the crest fallen officer.

Paul prodded a button on the console mounted on his desk, 'Kenny, my office please.'

In the couple of minutes it took the wheelchair bound Kenny to make the return trip to Pauls office, Taff, using the new computer had already established Peters wife and family had not left the country, at least by any conventional means. So powerful was the new technology it had taken barely a minute to do what would have taken a team of operators several days to have checked.

'Well Peter, it doesn't appear they have left the country, they certainly weren't on the flight to Miami they were booked on.'

'I sort of already knew that Paul, what I don't know is why they missed the flight.' replied the senior officer.

'What's up?' asked Kenny as he came in.

Over the next hour or so every detail was gone over. 'I suppose one place to start is finding your other halfs car,' suggested Kenny.

Paul typed in the details and the date it was last seen, in seconds sightings by traffic cameras began to come on the screen, along with co-ordinates from the gps unit built into the car. These updates stopped in rural Buckinghamshire, efforts to track her mobile phone stopped in the same area.

'Well at least we know where what whatever happened, happened,' sighed Peter.

'A bit of an odd route to Heathrow,' observed Paul.

'Not really Paul,' replied Peter, 'Elseph hated driving on motorways, so she would always plan a route as near as she could without actually using them.'

Paul brought up a map of the area, but it didn't help much, the ariel photograph off the internet did though. It was Taff who noticed, 'That lay-by,' he pointed to it, 'I think you'll find it coincides with the co-ordinates where the gps was deactivated.'

'Pity we didn't know all this a month ago Peter, why the hell didn't you tell us?'

'Obviously there is someone in a position who would know if I had tried to involve you, someone with links to the cartel.' said Peter. 'There has to be.'

'If there is, then that person has to be in this room!' exclaimed Paul, 'the only other person who had the sort of access you're talking about was General Leach! No mate, if there is another mole here then it is at a low level. Now this new thing in the floor is up and working it will have bye passed the two most likely sections, the switchboard and the archives.

You know as well as I do. In a case like this nothing would have been commited to paper. It therefore follows we have a weak link in our signals security.'

'You have been saying as much for the past couple of months Paul,' said B.J. 'If my memory serves correctly then that was the very reason you introduced the new communication system routed through this new super computer thingy.'

'And a few days later Peter's missus and sprogs go missing.' Taff added. 'Are you thinking the same Paul? Taff asked. 'I'm not sure when you started using this new communications gear, I'm guessing it was before the rest of us knew about it. If I've got the chronology right, then you used the old gear to plan the raid to get the nukes, and the new stuff to launch it, and have used it ever since.'

'Near enough Taff, which accounts for the desperate measures the cartel resorted to in their attempts to thwart us. They were desperate for intel and assumed Peter would be in the 'loop', when in fact he was otherwise engaged most of the time.'

'So we know the where, the when and probably the why. Let's see if we can follow the car, check the cameras again using only the description of the car for the hour following the last confirmed sighting,' B.J. sounded hopeful.

'Put those cameras up on a map Paul,' suggested Taff. 'There!' he exclaimed, 'See, there's a gap in the ring, the camera covering the link road to the M40 wasn't working, I wonder why? he asked. Check the cameras both ways on the motorway.'

Paul typed in the time span they were interested in and the computer did the rest. Sure enough an identical car to the big B.M.W. Peter's wife drove was caught speeding by a camera north bound. Just as it was going out of shot it's left hand indicator began to flash. A quick check on the number plate came back as being a similar B.M.W., same colour, same series, slightly different model, Elsephs' distinctive flaming red hair could be seen in the front passenger seat.

Try as they might, even with all the electronic wizardry they had, there were no more sightings. 'Nice try Paul', observed Peter, 'we're screwed'.

'Maybe not,' said Paul cautiously. 'Kenny, use the spare terminal over there,' pointing at the other desk in the office.

'Looking for what Paul?' he asked.

'The details of every 'beamer' of that model and colour, including addresses. Taff, can you check the service records of traffic cams along all roads in the area around the time we're interested in?'

'You're thinking the relevant ones were disabled somehow at the time, very good!' .What are you going to do? asked Taff.

'Make the coffees of course!' replied Paul.

Before Paul had chance to finish making the coffees Taff had confirmed a traffic camera near Banbury had been sprayed on it's lenses and had been out of action for two days before they were cleaned.

'No surprise there then.' observed Paul as he passed the steaming mugs around.

'You've figured it out already haven't you?' Taff said, ' come on, what have we all missed?'

'I don't think you've missed anything as such,' Paul replied, 'It's just that I have remembered who that 'beamer' belonged to, or at least the one they borrowed the plates off .'

Kenny suddenly said 'oops!' then turning away from the computer to face the others, 'I know too, Sir Selwyn's wife!'

'She brought him to a meeting in it, a couple of weeks before we lifted him. Get a Canberra over that mansion and the surrounding area, I want to know how many blades of grass there are on the croquet lawn! B.J. with me!' Paul headed for the door, leaving his coffee untouched.

'Paul!' Taff shouted, 'wait here! I know what you're thinking, you were going to see Fontain and beat it out of him if you had to. Stay here and calm down we already have a recon in the area doing some calibration tests for Upper Heyford. We'll have all the data in twenty minutes at the most.'

'He's bloody lucky we're not at the farm,' muttered Paul. 'See if you can find any links between Selwyns' family and Peter's wife or any of our known moles, kids at the same school, anything, there has to be a link somewhere.'

The data stream from the orbiting Canberra began to come in, it didn't take long to spot the car in the garage, clearly enough to identify as a B.M.W. The only one registered to the address was standing on the gravel in front of the big old hall.

This was followed up by a room by room scan of the rambling old house, even the cellars were probed, to no avail, the only people in the house were the disgraced senior officers wife, the two staff and an unidentified man.

Switching on 'big ears' the scanner which could listen in to conversation didn't help much as there was little conversation!

'He's another bloody yank,' Paul said under his breath, he took a drink from the coffee he had been prepared to leave and sat back in his chair, gazing out of the window across the airfield.

'I've just had a horrible thought,' he announced.

'Like what?' asked Taff.

'I think Selwyn, as much as I detest the man,' he paused. 'What if they've got his family too?'

Kenny suddenly joined in again, 'I think I have just found one link Paul. It wasn't what we were looking for, but in his days with the J.A.G corps he was the officer given the job of prosecuting McNight.'

'This is getting complicated,' Paul observed. 'And it's not finding Peters family.' He turned to Kenny, 'I've just realised something, Selwyn has a Roller, with a chauffer, it's not there. Find it!'

'Yes Sir!' replied Kenny.

'Sorry mate, I didn't mean it to sound like that.' Paul apologised. 'Haven't the family got a place in Mayfair?'

'They have and guess what we have over the capital, Blue bird two, complete with it's full array of sensors. They are using it for a final detailed sweep over Whitehall, Parliament and the area in general to make certain there is nothing left over from the fracas.'

It only took a couple of minutes to scan the entire building, there was a car in the large garage, almost certainly the 'Roller', the only sign of any humans was what appeared to be a body sprawled on the floor beside the car. The rest of the multi million pound mansion was empty, Paul called the leader of the squad still in London, giving them the address and ordering two of them to 'get over there and wait for the police'.

It transpired the body was that of the family chaufer, shot at close range with a nine millimeter, probably a machine pistol like an ouzie. The presence of five part eaten meals on the table in the grand dining room served only to deepen the mystery.

A team had also been sent to the mansion in Oxfordshire, again with local police, B.J.had spotted a patch of freshly disturbed soil in vegetable garden, he was careful avoid saying anything in front of Peter, 'just in case'.

It turned out to be Peter's wife, stabbed at least twice and her throat cut, then buried in a shallow grave, best guess before forensic tests was she had been killed shortly after being abducted.

Paul broke the news, stressing the identification hadn't been confirmed, but from the clothes and the flaming red hair and the contents of the handbag, there wasn't much doubt it was Elseph.

'She would have fought to protect the kids,' Peter was near to tears. 'Who are these bastards Paul?' he asked.

The 'cartels' enforcers, from what I know, the only major player left is Dolby, sure there are the nasty minions still on the loose. Your family were taken before most of the major players died from what ever cause, and just after they lost the ability to track and partly eaves drop on my communications, I've still got to figure out how they managed that! We will find your kiddies Peter.'

'I suppose it hurts more because I left it so late starting a family.' It was obvious the man was near to breaking point.

'I don't think age has much to do with it Peter, there's nothing I or anyone else can say to make things easier mate.' Paul turned to Taff, 'can you take Peter over to the officers mess and sort him out a room for a bit, it might be an idea for the medics to give him a check over.'

'Will do .'

Paul sat back in his chair, a fresh cup of coffee in easy reach, searching for a way to find the other leak he knew must exist. He pushed a button on his console and called Giles, one of the 'gremlins' who inhabited what everyone called 'the underworld'. As usual he had trouble contacting any of these brilliant but excentric young men, after prodding the relevant button for the third time a voice timidly answered 'Yes'.

'Giles, can you come to my office please, now would be good' replied Paul.

'How did you know it was me Boss?' asked Giles.

'I called your communicator! My office, now, please'.

Eventually 'the gremlin' appeared in Pauls office, by then Paul was making another cup of coffee. 'Take a seat Giles, you and I have got to have little chat. If I recall correctly you only drink bottled water, right?'

'That's right Boss ,' replied the young boffin.

Paul opened the little fridge and took out a bottle, 'catch' as he gently lobbed the bottle to Giles. 'Right ,' he said resuming his seat, reaching down to open a draw in his desk he produced his communicator which he had thought was being monitored. 'I need you to explain in simple terms how anyone, outside this unit could earwig to my conversations using this communicator?'

'That's easy Boss, they couldn't, unless they had a similar unit, there isn't anything else capable of even detecting a transmission from those communicators, never mind decode the signal.'

'Why not?' asked Paul, not expecting an answer he would understand.

'Because those communicators operate on such a narrow wave band,' the young man paused. 'Think of it in terms of a rope Boss, the most precise radio in the world would have a signal thicker than the thickest rope used to tie up an American aircraft carrier. The signal from one of our units, such as that one is,' he paused again, thinking of an analogy, 'think of the thinnest spider web, it would take a hundred strands from the communicator spun together to make the finest spider web. Without the pre programmed computer in there you could never set your reciever with sufficient precision to even detect the signal, never mind track or listen to it.'

'Thank you Giles,' replied Paul, I think I actually understood that. What I can't understand is how, inspite of what you said, someone was doing exactly that, monitoring and certainly tracking the signal from this very unit.'

'Impossible Boss, G.C.H.Q can't even detect those signals, never mind decode them. When you send a message, even five minutes worth it is all digitally encoded and compressed into a few milliseconds of actual transmission.'

'Could anyone else have made one, and you don't know about it?' Paul asked.

'Only if they had our liquid micro computer technology, no other system could cope Boss.' replied Giles.

'Well, here's the problem,' Paul began, 'someone was listening to at least part of my transmissions, sufficient to have a good idea what I was talking about. On top of that they could get a fairly accurate fix on where I was. Now, you are certain it takes one of these sets to communicate with another, equally you are certain no-one else has the technology to make anything remotely like it. I happen to know none of the sets are missing, I have accounted for every set which was made here by you and your mates, so what have I missed? You see my dilemma?'

'I do indeed Boss, Oh Lord!' the young man suddenly looked worried.

'What?' demanded Paul.

'I doubt you'll remember Boss,' Giles began, 'I was a few weeks late taking up my post here, I was recovering from menagitis I contracted at University. I designed and built two prototypes while I was still house bound. When I took up my post here I got a flat in town, I assumed the two prototypes were still in my room at my parents house. I remember Uncle Johnny being very interested in them.'

'Johnny? Not Johnny Dolby!' exclaimed Paul, 'he's your bloody Uncle!?'

'He's not my real Uncle Boss, his mother and my grandmother were cousins or something similar, it's just they live near Mum and Dad and stayed in touch.'

'You don't happen to know where he is at the moment do you?' Paul asked more in hope than expectation.

'Well, he was at home over the week end, he and his family were going to fly to the states tomorrow, if his private jet is ready by then. A firm at Cambridge airport had been extending it's range or something and found something wrong it would take a while to fix.'

'You said he was at home? Yet his house is empty, I've got a team there at the moment?' said Paul thinking he had slipped the net again.

'No Boss, he's staying at our home, the electricity is off at his house, the transformer was struck Friday night in the storm, he has several of his family with him, there are eighteen of them all together, I had to sleep on the setee with the cats, it's the main reason I came back early, too much noise.

The raid launched at three o'clock the next morning was more successful than Paul had dared hope, both of Peter's youngsters were rescued along with Sir Selwyns wife and family, all four of the body guards were killed. One of them was using the very machine pistol which had killed Selwyns chauffer, forensics had confirmed this by lunch time.

Dolby, and his wife were thrown into cells, deep below the farm, 'couldn't you have shot them trying to escape or something Martin?' Paul asked as the pair were locked in their new accomodation.

'I never got the chance Boss, sorry,' replied the young major.

CHAPTER TWENTY-SEVEN

The rest of the week seemed to consist of endless meetings with all manner of legal eagles, as Peter predicted the Americans wanted McNight. The high court moved with amazing speed in agreeing to the request, initially refusing leave to appeal and agreeing McNight should continue in custody of the 'All Arms Unit'.

Quite how this was overturned remained something of a mystery, as was the order to transport him to Bell Marsh high security wing. It was emphasised over and over how dangerous this man was, the warnings it seems went unheaded, the private contractors van transporting him to court for the appeal against extradition stopped at some traffic lights. The two men in the cab became aware the rear door was open and on investigating found the two guards in the back lying on the floor, one dead, the other unconscious, of McNight there was no sign.

Predictably Paul went ballistic, there was all the usual buck passing. The security company claimed the security forces hadn't warned them the man was dangerous. This was publically proven wrong with the release, by the All arms unit of tapes of the conversations on the subject. Then it was 'the cuts' to blame, when this didn't succeed it was 'the courts' fault for not allowing video link, finally the lawyers got the blame for insisting McNight had the right to appear in person in court.

The next blow was the order to produce Dolby and his wife. To the disbelief of all involved the judge ordered his immediate release on minimal bail. He couldn't abscond, the judge reasoned, as all his bank accounts had been seized, this too, was in the judges opinion 'probably unlawful'.

Five hours later a private executive jet passed directly beneath a Canberra headed to the Carribean to help with the war against the drug runners. The crew of the fast Jet Stream were totally unaware of the presence of the old plane far, far above them. Johnny Dolby was dead long before the private jets' wheels touched the tarmac on Ajes Field in the Azores, the cause was a massive heart attack .

Paul was having a drink with Peter in the officers mess when the news broke of Dolby's death. 'Oh dear, how sad'. Paul was heard to say.

It was remarkable how quickly it was on the television, less than five minutes after the call from the American F.B.I. team in the Azores, the news reader was handed a piece of paper. The presenter stated he was fleeing from the U.K.as his lawyers claimed he wouldn't get a fair trial here. It seemed as though he had suffered a massive heart attack brought on by the stress of being hounded by the security forces.

'What a load of old bollocks,' muttered Paul.

Peter replied, 'I have no idea how you did it, but thanks Paul'.

'I have no idea what you mean Peter, it appears to have happened while you and I were dining. I will concede how ever this Scotch has markedly improved with the news.' replied the tired Colonel.

The following morning Paul called Giles, the brilliant young scientist to his office again. The young man was quite fearful after his previous visit, there was a shoe box on Pauls desk.

'These are yours I believe,' said Paul as he handed the box over to the young man. 'Please be careful in the future where you leave your hi-tec toys laying about, there's no telling who might pick them up, and we wouldn't want them getting into the wrong hands now, would we?'

'Thank you Boss, these might be prototypes, but they mean a lot to me,' replied Giles, somewhat sheepishly.

'Okay son, and thank you for the help in getting those hostages free from Dolby and his crew, but for you, he would have got away, and those kiddies would in all probability be dead.

Just after dark a blacked out van arrived on the base, having come from the 'farm' it drove out to a Hercules which had just arrived from nearby Milldenhall. Paul walked up the lowered loading ramp carrying a brief case with security locks, he handed it to a Colonel in charge of the squad on the plane.

'If you could give this to your Director personally Colonel I would apprieciate it, the contents are for his eyes only, I have copies. I should add these four men have co-operated fully with our enquiries, and although no saints, they have, to a great extent been used. In that respect they are victims rather than criminals, they were led to believe they were acting in the interests of their country. All the evidence is in the case, so take care of it please Colonel.'

'I will indeed Sir replied the American, I was led to believe two of these jokers were responsible for the destruction of the battle group entering the gulf.'

'To a point that is true, but they were unwittingly responsible. The real target was the Iranians, or at least one of their nuclear sites. Had the operation gone as planned then they would in all probability been vapourised themselves. It appears they hadn't been made aware of the power of the device they were supposed to have planted. They along with so many others are just pawns, expendable as far as those behind all this mess were concerned. I regard the presence of your men more as protectors than gaolers. Take care of them Colonel, they will be a great help to your boss in sorting all this out. Please give him my regards and have a safe flight.'

'I will pass on your message Sir, and thank you,' replied the American.

Paul headed for his office, 'another worry gone', was his main thought.

He decided to talk things over with Taff who was due back at any moment.

Although there was some argument about Major Dalrypmle as to whether it should be a civilian or military court which dealt with him, all the judges agreed he would stay where he was until the question of juristiction was settled. The only people unhappy were the defence lawyers, they were totally denied physical access, although they could talk on the phone more or less when they wanted to. The big problem was Lord Selwyn, it seemed obvious at first glance he had been co-erced , but Paul wasn't so sure now he had chance to reflect on matters.

Given his situation it would have been expected he would have been at least relieved his family were freed, even happy. The reality was he was threatening to have the unit totally disbanded and Paul, in particular, charged with recklessly endangering his family. It was perfectly true two of the guards had been shot dead in front of his children, but as they both were holding automatics, pointed at the children there really hadn't been any choice.

Try as he might Paul couldn't make any sense of the mans attitude, not the least sign of even a thank you! He kept citeing the fact that Peter's wife had been murdered by the kidnappers. Paul pointed out she had been murdered well before anyone was aware there was a problem, the units record was second to none in hostage rescue. Yet the man seemed full of hate towards the unit, according to Lord Selwyn, to give him his correct title, everything they had done, had been done wrong!

Paul and Taff spent most of the afternoon talking over the problem, the only conclusion they reached was something was still very wrong with the senior officer.

'It's times like this I really miss General Leach,' Paul confided in his old friend.

'It would be unfair to rope Peter into it.' Paul continued, 'but the Admiral is just about fit enough to be discharged, he is after all still the chief of the General Staff, see what his opinion is.'

'Fair enough Paul,' replied Taff, 'I know you and Selwyn don't exactly hit it off, but I agree with you, he has got to go, and quietly.'

'When you think about it Mate, he has been responsible for all manner of foul ups affecting this units operations, right back to the original fuel supply problems, that was over a year ago. It is almost as though he wants this country defenceless.'

'Ironically he might yet see just that Paul. The meeting I attended earlier today was discussing a massive round of cuts for all the armed forces, and I mean massive cuts.'

'Well as long as they cut all the dead wood, especially civilian administrators then I reckon they could save about a third of the budget,' observed Paul.

'I think it will be a lot more than that Paul, with all that is happening the country will be broke in a few months, not as broke as most, but there simply isn't any money. The best assessment was around about seventy five percent of our forces will have to go. Most of what is left will be a dedicated anti-terrorist and counter insurgency force. The overspend on new equipment over the past decade has been so great if nothing was spent for the next five years on new kit, the money saved wouldn't cover half the overspend.'

'Have they looked at Europe! As well as a north-south divide, Russia is growling again. Put against the situation across the channel our problems of soddin' Selwyn and the fact the mad man McNight is loose seem inconsequential,' Paul sounded depressed by Taffs gloomy forecast.

'How are things going in the search for McNight?' asked Taff.

'Not the slightest sign of him, all we know is he nicked a change of clothes within minutes of escape, since then, nothing.'

There was a knock on the door, it turned out to be Peter, 'do you mind if I intrude?'

'Of course not, come in Boss, you don't have to ask, grab a drink and pull up a pew.' was Paul's welcome.

'I won't thank you, I'm glad I've caught you together.' he paused, 'it is only fair I tell you two first. I've reached a decision, I'm retiring. It will save a lot of embaressment, should the events of the past few months come under scrutiny, as they surely must.'

'That is a bloody shame Boss, so soon after losing General Leach too, but I understand. Better to retire than have some faceless unaccountable burke push you into resigning with all the sniping and back stabbing. I just wish Lord Selwyn would do the right thing, he is proving a regular pain in the arse!'

'Then I can make it my final task in the military removing him for you. During their time as hostages my two youngsters became friends with his two. It would seem appearances can be deceptive, I believe his family were there by choice, both he and his wife are in it up to their necks.

Have a word with her Paul, she is an arrogant greedy cow to use the vernacular, she'll let something slip, I'm sure. I'll go and see Sir Selwyn and let him know his wife is going to be arrested on conspiracy to defraud or something similar, see how he reacts. We'll lose his phone, so the legal eagles don't get wind of the con trick. One, maybe even both will slip up for sure.' Peter sounded quite pleased with his plan.

'I'm not so sure it will work Boss,' replied Paul. 'We might have destroyed a lot of the evil empire he was part of, but we haven't got near to getting anything major on him. Sure we can prove the kick backs and back handers he has received, but on past performances some smart arsed lawyer will get it ruled out as evidence. As for the rest, he'll claim coercion, saying his family were held hostage to force him to comply.'

'What about his wife?' asked Peter. 'On paper she is richer than the Queen!'

'Being rich, even obscenely so, isn't a crime as such, how they got that way might well be, but prove it. They will claim it was shrewd investments, although the deals were dodgey, I can't see how we can prove they were illegal. The fact that the share price has collapsed for these companies recently is being investigated by the authorities on Wall Street. They know something is wrong but can't find a reason for the collapse, it would be good if this remained the case. Ultimately, we can prove nothing other than incompetence.'

'It's not like you to give up Paul', commented Peter.

'I'm not giving up Boss, he has got to go, and he will, hopefully without all the benefits which would normally apply. It is what he does after he's kicked out which bothers me, he has a vast capacity to create mischief.

There is another problem looming with him and his missus as well, he has dual nationality, and she is a Yank. Voices are being raised in the Senate insisting we release them. I can't work out why he was allowed to keep his dual nationality, I didn't think it was allowed for officers from outside the Commonwealth to hold The Queens commission, but what do I know about such things?'

'There are ways Paul, but in this instance I think we can use it to get shot of him, moves are already afoot to strip him of his title, but as it is hereditary the process is complicated.'

'Glad it's not me got to sort it out,' replied Paul, 'The damage that bastard has caused! All in the name of greed.' He paused, 'I have no idea what the answer to all this is, even is there an answer.'

The answer came in the form of a high court order for the release of the disgraced officer and his spouse, which arrived a few days later. The wife was released, the General wasn't, the army high command claimed him, and ordered a courts martial. The military judges solved most of the problems by stripping him of his rank, sentencing him to a spell in Colchester military prison followed by a dishonourable discharge.

Paul actually was quite complimentary to the military legal eagles, they kept it simple, the charges were conduct unbecoming and disrepute, the defence lawyers might have been expensive and may have protested very long and often loud, but to no avail!

He turned to Peter, who was on the point of retiring, 'shall we go to Stansted and wave them off?'

'Paul!' scolded Peter, 'we are well rid of Mr. and Mrs. De la Fontain, I do hope there isn't a Canberra on a trans Atlantic flight just now'.

'I don't know what you mean Boss,' Paul replied innocently, 'but no, there isn't, to stop you worrying'.

'Exactly how does it work Paul, what ever 'it' might be?' asked Peter.

'How did you know Peter?'

'I didn't know,' replied the General, 'I still don't, it's just that every time there has been, what shall we call it? a convenient death the old 'eagle eye one' has either been in the area or no-one knows were it was. Don't worry, I haven't mentioned this to anyone, although Pete, your 'air commander' did raise the matter, I think he suspects it is something to do with that particular aircraft. It has got a little black box none of his techs know what it does.'

'Let's keep it that way, shall we Boss.' replied Paul.

'Fair enough, I don't think I want to know, I'll enjoy my retirement in blissful ignorance thank you.'

Paul allowed himself a little chuckle, 'Let's hope your 'retirement' is more successful than my attempts have been. Since this unit has been up and running I've tried at least four times! It's like having another wife! 'Oh, Paul, can you just....' Next thing you know there's another full blown disaster to sort out, well the one which is looming large is well beyond me, and I'm powerless against it.'

'Are you planning to retire as well?' asked Peter.

'If I can, but I won't go until we've got McNight, if there is one loose end I can't leave, he's it!' Paul replied with some feeling. 'The cheeky bastard sent a letter to me here last week, basically promising to remove my family jewels, but without the aid of anaesthetics!'

'Nice of him,' replied Peter, 'I presume you are taking it seriously?'

'What do you think Boss? This is Carol bloody McNight we're talking about, he's killed tougher men than I.'

'What are you going to do about it Paul?' asked Peter. 'Have you any clues as to where he is?'

'Not a bloody trace, he's damned good at hiding, I'll give the bastard his due.'

'I take it you have a plan Paul? You can't just carry on as if the threat doesn't exist.'

'It is simple really Peter, if we can't find him, I'll have to make it so he can get at me, then just hope I'm better than he is. I've had the best of our two previous encounters, but then the odds were heavily stacked in my favour, him being in handcuffs helped.'

'You are mad Paul,' replied the General, 'you know what he's capable of.'

'If mountain won't come to, etc, I'll just have to make sure I'm ready for him won't I? ' replied Paul. 'As long as I see him coming, then I'll have the advantage I'm a better shot than he is, by a considerable margin, at least with a hand gun, that is his weakness, that and over confidence.'

'You're mad!'

'I'll go mad if I stay around here any longer Boss, I'm taking a weeks leave. I'm planning to go up to the croft at the weekend. The missus is staying in our quarters, the wives have some 'do' on during the week, so I'll have a week pottering in the garden or fishing if the weather is good enough. I need a break, badly.! I'm really looking forward to it Boss,' said Paul sounding tired.

'Fair enough, just watch yourself.'

'Yes mother,' chuckled Paul.

Early Saturday morning Paul left the farm in his beloved old Jaguar and headed north. He didn't go straight to the croft, but headed to Livingstone, just to the west of Edinbourgh. He was going to see one of the old hands, who was no longer in good health, but was still pleased to see his old boss. For ease Paul dossed down on the setee for the night, after breakfast he again took to the road. He decided to take the scenic route, well, why not, he was on holiday, just before he reached Dundee he turned west on the road which would take him to Crainlaric, a little way north of Loch Lomond . He continued on towards Oban, compared to the busy roads he was used to, the traffic was light and the powerful old motor made short work of the miles, soon he was passing the end of the mighty loch Awe. Turning off the main road he headed into the hills on the final leg of his journey. He called into the little village shop cum post office and had a chat with the post master, who was a retired soldier. They chatted for a bit over a cup of coffee, the entire village seemed to know he was coming up to his beloved croft.

Marie, the house keeper went in once a week, even when no-one was there.

She had gone to the croft on the shore of the Loch early this very morning to make certain all was well, Paul called in at her house on his way to his home, just to say thank you for keeping all in order.

Soon he had his feet up in the afternoon sun on the sheltered patio at the rear of the building, he was struck by the silence, not a man made sound to be heard. He knew that most of the village would turn up, 'just passing, thought I'd call in to see if you needed anything.'

It was young Craig, from the only farm at the end of the road past the croft who was first to call. He combined the jobs of deer warden, game keeper and water baliff for several miles along the wild western shore.

Paul was certain he detected a furtve glance at the bottle of malt on the table, he reached underneath the table for a glass he had put on the ledge, just for such an eventuality. He thanked Paul for the generous measure in the glass, then relayed some disturbing news. It seemed as though there was someone living up in the hills, who ever was living in the woods was good at staying hidden. There were very few signs, but to someone like Craig who had spent his life in these remote hills, it would be almost impossible to totally escape notice.

Craig thought who ever it was had been around for about two weeks, a stolen car had been found abandoned, apparently out of fuel, miles from any where about fifteen miles away. The police and mountain rescue team had searched for a week but there was no trace of anyone, and air sea rescue helicopter had spent several hours scanning the surrounding area, but nothing. It was all a bit strange Craig thought. 'Well, I must get on, thank you for the drink, you take care Sir. I take it you'll be fishing out on the Loch. If you want a ferox trout Ken says he's seen some in the shallows about a mile down the loch, feeding on all the fry collected there.

'I'll give it a try tomorrow , thanks for the tip Craig.'

Paul decided on an early start, so he had turned in by ten o'clock, having checked all the sensors around the Croft were switched on and working, no point in taking chances.

His last thoughts before sleep came were for Taff, he wondered how his old friend would cope now he was 'The Boss', as Peters retirement was effective as from midnight Friday.

Monday lunch time, Taff sitting in his office at the main base was seriously considering retiring, the past few weeks had been very hard, may be it was time for someone younger to take over. He had just about made his mind up to talk it over with Paul on his return, when the phone rang, interrupting his thoughts, he didn't recognise the voice, in it's self unusual, as this was his private number which few people knew. It proved to be the postmaster from Inverian, a veteran of the 'regiment' universally know as 'Snowy', he sounded quite choked with emotion.

It transpired Ken McBride, the local charter boat fisherman had been out on the Loch and had come across Paul's boat, barely afloat. He had towed it back into shallow water, there was no sign of Paul. Snowy suggested it might be a good idea if a team was sent to check things out, as Marie, the house keeper hadn't seen Paul today. It also appeared there were several holes in the boat, Snowy guessed from a fifty calibre sniper rifle, including one which had smashed the engine, as an former sniper himself he should know.

'And there is no sign of Paul?' asked Taff.

Timothy Pilgrim

'His fishing rods are on board, and his life jacket, even his flask and sandwiches are there, but no sign of him Sir, and Marie says his laptop computer has gone, but his car is still there.'

'Thanks Snowy, I'll get a team moving straight away. Bye the way, how did you get this number?' Taff asked.

'Marie gave me it a few minutes ago, Paul left it for her, in case of an emergency, I'd to call this one Sir.'

'Thanks' Snowy.' Taff had a nasty sinking feeling, the bullet holes in Paul's boat were as bad as things could get, short of a body.

Three and a half hours later the peace of the Loch was shattered as a Lynx helicopter landed near the converted croft Paul called home.

As a search by the local police had found nothing, about the only good news was there wasn't a trace of blood in the boat, it was possible any there might have been could have washed away in it's sinking condition.

B.J, leading the team, searched further afield, more aware of the range of a modern fifty calibre rifle, just before dark they found a body among some rocks over looking the Loch, beside the dead gunman were eight empty cartridges from the very latest Sniper rifle which was still in the dead mans hands. The body was that of Carol Mcnight, in the centre of his forehead , almost touching each other, were two neat holes.

THE END

Lightning Source UK Ltd.
Milton Keynes UK
UKOW03f1817120813

215259UK00010B/824/P